Praise for Barbara Cleverly's
Joe Sandilands Series

'A well-plotted novel . . . The atmosphere of the dying days of the Raj is colourfully captured.'
Susanna Yager, *Sunday Telegraph*

'Spectacular and dashing. Spellbinding.'
New York Times Book Review

'Smashing . . . marvellously evoked.'   *Chicago Tribune*

'A historical mystery that has just about everything: a fresh, beautifully realized exotic setting; a strong, confident protagonist; a poignant love story; and an exquisitely complex plot.'   *Denver Post*

'Evocative narrative, sensitive characterizations, artful dialogue, and masterly plotting.'   *Library Journal*

Also by Barbara Cleverly

The Last Kashmiri Rose
Ragtime in Simla
The Damascened Blade
The Palace Tiger
The Bee's Kiss
Tug of War
Folly du Jour

THE TOMB OF ZEUS

Barbara Cleverly

Constable • London

Constable & Robinson Ltd
3 The Lanchesters
162 Fulham Palace Road
London W6 9ER
www.constablerobinson.com

First published in the USA 2007 by Bantam Dell
A Division of Random House, Inc
New York

This edition published by Constable,
an imprint of Constable & Robinson Ltd 2008

A copy of the British Library Cataloguing in Publication
Data is available from the British Library

ISBN: 978-1-84529-696-4

Printed and bound in the EU

1 3 5 7 9 10 8 6 4 2

PEFC
PEFC/16-33-111
CATG-PEFC-052
www.pefc.org

For Sophia and Stella Panayiotopoulos-Cleverly

Prologue

The big gates were in sight and were standing open. I peered round the corner of the street, huddled at my mother's side, clutching a fold of her robe as I'd been told. I felt the sudden surge in her anxiety. We'd been terrified enough by the savage noise on all sides, but the unaccountable silence was even more paralysing. The drums had stopped banging; the muezzin's triumphant cries had ceased; the roaring of men, the screams and pistol shots had all mysteriously come to a climax and ended abruptly on the stroke of noon. Only the crackle from burning houses broke the stillness.

We had only a few yards to go when we turned into the tree-lined avenue. In the grand houses fronting it, I knew, the rich lived – the officials and the merchants. Time for boldness now, no more scurrying along in the shadows. I could see the Khania gate clearly, a pack of Janissaries manning it, a further platoon, riflemen, in position along the battlements, and beyond, drawing my gaze with the lure of a mirage, the gleam of silvery slopes covered with olive trees. I imagined I could smell the thyme on the hot hillside and make out a mule track zigzagging its way up to a village. To safety.

It was the dead donkey and its dead rider that unnerved me. I put my slippered foot into a pool of blood and offal, and I squealed. I'd seen worse sights that morning and stayed silent, but the stickiness of the clotting blood, the swarm of gathering flies, and the not knowing whether it was the man's or the animal's blood staining the hem of my dress made me cry out.

7

My thin wail of surprise and horror was instantly picked up. Two Turkish soldiers burst through the open door of one of the grand houses, stuffing gold chains and necklaces into their pockets. They stood before us, blocking our way. They were not local men, I thought. Rough men with pockmarked faces. Some of the freshly imported reserves from Istanbul. Albanian, most probably.

One took his dagger from between his teeth to ask my mother in crude Turkish, 'Where's your man? And where do you think you're going?'

My mother replied, eyes downcast even though they were obscured by her veil. 'Sir, my daughter and I are on our way to the baths.'

The men hooted in derision. 'Well, that's Turkish ladies for you! A bloody riot on, but they won't miss their weekly bath!'

'Twice weekly, if you please!' said my mother with some spirit and they laughed again.

'But you haven't told us – where's your man?'

'My man is lying dead. In the Greek quarter.' Mother gestured back the way we had come, releasing a trace of musky perfume from her sleeve. 'Last week. He was a tax inspector. The giaours – curse all Greeks – slit his throat. The Pasha himself came to tell me. I've searched every day for his remains. And now I must wash the filth of the unbelievers off my body.'

I'd never heard my mother lie before and suddenly here were eight lies, one after the other, and all told with absolute conviction. I have never been more proud of her. I shuddered and mewled pitifully in support and swished my bloodstained hem about.

'Well, you have no luck today. Baths not open for business.'

'Stokers not manning the furnaces,' said the second slyly.

The first gave a full-throated guffaw, as though his companion had made a joke. 'Not manning exactly . . . fuelling, perhaps! We chucked them in!'

My mother's hand tightened on mine. But her voice betrayed no alarm as she replied: 'A good use for them. I expect they burn well – all that oil they consume.'

8

They roared with laughter. 'Take my advice, mistress: Go back home by the shortest route and put up the barricades. This is going to get worse.'

She thanked the pair meekly for their advice and, instantly forgetting us, the two men turned back to their pillaging. As we hesitated, preparing to make our run, we saw the gates slowly begin to close and heard the clang as they came together. The Khania gate had never been closed at noon before. We and thousands like us were trapped in a city of red-eyed madmen wielding scimitars, daggers, and rifles. Men who would eviscerate a donkey whose owner was not of their religion wouldn't hesitate to slaughter a small girl and her mother.

We reached our cousins' house intact by walking with unconcern back along through the alleyways. No scurrying or slinking! With her basket over her arm, my mother appeared to be off to market, an everyday sight, unalarming, attracting no attention.

It took a threat to knock the door down noisily before anyone would come to let us in. We didn't know these city cousins well – had stayed with them only while we attended my great-grandfather's funeral. It pleased us no more than it pleased them to be stranded in their house in the Greek quarter while death and destruction swirled on all sides. It was my father who finally heard us and opened their door. He hugged us, glad to see us back again but devastated by the failure of our attempt to escape the city.

'It's worse than we had supposed,' my mother reported. 'You should never have sent us to try! There is no safety. The streets are full of crazy soldiers, pillaging and killing. Muslim – Christian – it no longer matters. All are dying. No one is in command. We must sit it out. If the worst comes to the worst, and the enemy comes through the door, you must kill us both. We have seen what they can do.'

I looked at my father's fierce face and the sinewy brown hands that were never still and never far from the silver hilt of the dagger in his belt. His ancient rifle was propped against the door frame, loaded and ready. My father was not a man to sit *anything out. Now that he had his wife and ten-year-old child at his heels to defend, he would not consider simply getting away. He would turn and fight. And all I longed for at that moment was to throw off my constricting skirts, seize a pistol, and take my place at his elbow.*

Two more days passed and we survived. My father made occasional forays into the street, mostly at night and prompted, it seemed to me, by mysterious raps on the door. He would return, panting, wild-eyed, and wipe his blade on the rag my mother handed him. Our water butt was running low and we were down to the last crumbs of barley bread. We could smell fire; we heard shots and shouting. Once my father called for silence while he listened through the door he'd opened a crack.

'Father, what do you hear?'

'Bugles. Commands in a foreign tongue.'

He was not smiling. Not relieved. Not yet. He stayed on watch.

An hour later there was a banging on the door and someone shouted my father's name. One of his cousins stood on the threshold, blood-spattered, breathless, not seeking entry.

'Come! Now! We need your help,' he urged my father. 'They've arrested Suleiman. Your uncle Suleiman. They'll execute him if someone doesn't speak for him. You're a Man of Law – come and do your bit! You speak Greek, Turkish, Italian . . . you'll make them understand somehow. Leave your weapons behind, man! They'll shoot you dead as soon as look at you if you present yourself bristling like a palikare!'

'A moment!' My father took his knife from his belt and gave it to me, then handed me his ancient pistol. 'These were your grandfather's. If it comes to it – trust the knife before the gun. Don't be taken alive,' he said, resting his hand on my head. He kissed my mother and left with his cousin.

I never saw my father again.

I know my mother saw him once more, but she has never spoken of it to me.

Chapter One

'Miss Talbot! Wait!'

Laetitia Talbot staggered on. She didn't glance back to discover who was calling her name. An abrupt turn of the head would have aggravated the seasickness that racked her; would have made her lose her balance on the slippery deck – might even have provoked a further stomach-wrenching attack of the unproductive retching that had tormented her for a good six hours.

There filtered, through her discomfort, the puzzling thought that she knew no one on the ferry. The only man on the boat who was aware of her existence was the Greek captain and he was unlikely to be chasing after a passenger, fully occupied as he was at the controls in this unexpected squall. She corrected herself: *mad March gale.* She corrected herself again: *fully blown Greek storm*, stirred up personally by Poseidon with his disgusting seaweed-dripping trident. So who would be calling out her name with such confidence? Perhaps she'd failed to notice an acquaintance in her circuits of the deck? She winced at the thought of holding up her end of the conversation that might ensue if she turned around: '. . . Three summers ago . . . at Binkie's coming-out do . . . surely you remember? You've been in Athens? But why? What on earth can you have been doing there, Letty?'

'Laetitia Talbot?' The English voice came again. Less peremptory. More uncertain. But closer.

Letty sighed and stood still, grasping the metal strut of a lifeboat housing and waited for her pursuer to draw level. A moment later a hand grasped her firmly by her free arm and tucked it under his own. This would have been an unforgivably intimate gesture under normal circumstances, and Letty would have shrugged it off with a sharp comment, but normality, she'd discovered, was suspended on ferryboats. She found she was glad of the unexpected support, and the touch of the rough Scottish tweed jacket was reassuring.

The stranger held out the book she'd carried up on deck with her that morning in a futile attempt at distraction from the horrors of the sea-crossing to Crete.

'You dropped this in a puddle,' he said, eyes narrowed against the wind, white teeth gleaming in a friendly grin. Good Lord! The man appeared to be relishing the storm. His wet hair was plastered to his skull and seawater dripped from his nose, chin, and eyebrows, but no adverse weather conditions, Letty decided, could detract from the nobility of this young man's jutting features.

She focused woozily on her battered copy of *Persuasion*.

'I do apologize,' she managed to reply politely through gritted teeth, 'but I don't believe I know you?'

'You're quite right. We've never met,' he admitted cheerfully.

'Then how . . .?'

'I opened your book and read the name on the front page. So – unless you've stolen this, you are the Laetitia Talbot who received it as a prize in the . . . what did it say? . . .' He flicked the volume open and read in a magisterial tone: '*Good Conduct Award – Most Improved Pupil*, at the Cambridge Academy for Girls in 1919. "Improved", eh? One is bound to speculate as to the less-than-perfect state of affairs that preceded the improvement. So, Miss Talbot, you must forgive me for saying – I feel I know who you are!'

He pressed on before she could protest: 'A Sprightly Girl but a Romantic who has matured sufficiently to become an ardent reader of the divine Jane's ripest work – I'm judging by the general dog-eared condition of the book. A volume now rendered quite unreadable by Cretan sea-water. I'm hoping you'll reject it with a gesture and say I may keep it. I've never actually read *Persuasion*, and I hear such good things ...'

Amused by the teasing formality and enchanted by the striking good looks, Letty smiled for the first time in a very long day. 'You may keep it ... Mr ... er ... Look – shall we consider ourselves introduced by the agency of the prescient Miss Austen?'

'Splendid! I think she'd be amused. And that's the way I shall tell it if anyone asks. My name's Charles St George Russell. My father is Theodore Russell. At present resident in Herakleion.'

He enjoyed her surprise at his announcement and the recognition of his name. 'Yes, Laetitia, *that* Russell. And I'm guessing you are the Miss Talbot who is to be our guest at the Villa Europa ... if we ever make it into port ...'

'Gosh! How do you do? You'll have to excuse my trembling – I've never met a saint before.'

'Friends just call me George,' he answered easily. 'I was born on the twenty-third of April so – naturally – named after the patron saint of Cretan shepherds. But we weren't expecting you until next week, Miss Talbot, surely? Do I have that wrong? Look here – I'm about to have a most spectacular motorcar unloaded. It's had quite a journey from Paris via Marseilles and Athens, and when we arrive I shall have to spend a good hour or so shouting at crane operators while they swing her on to the dock in a net. You're welcome to wait for me while I do this and, assuming I can start her, I'll be delighted to run you up to the villa in splendour and state.'

He considered her bedraggled state for a moment, then: 'Look here – common sense and courtesy urge me to recommend you turn down my harebrained suggestion and allow me to put you in a taxi. The city does now boast a taxi.'

Letty quickly weighed her options. 'I'd be delighted to accept your offer of a lift. In fact, I'll stand by with a screwdriver while you get your motorcar started. I've quite a useful pair of hands,' she said, extending them for inspection, wet and shaking with cold. 'Oh, dear! Not impressive! I couldn't do up my shoelaces with these! The weather was so clear in Athens – hot, sunny, calm . . . I couldn't wait to get to Crete! I telegraphed your father with my change of plans and took the first ferry of the sailing season. I think even careful old Jason might have thought it safe to venture forth in the last week of March, with or without his Argonauts. And, quite obviously, *you* didn't mind risking the wrath of Poseidon, Mr Russell . . . George.'

'Nothing is ever predictable in this part of the world, you'll find. I take it this is the first time you've ventured out on to the Aegean, Laetitia? Yes? Well, the first thing you must know is that those coloured postcards you buy in Athens are quite misleading. It's not always an improbably blue sky over a calm, turquoise, mermaid-infested sea. . . .'

She had noticed George Russell earlier. Several times from embarkation onwards her gaze had been drawn to him. A good head taller than herself, he had – remarkably – the same colouring as her own: light complexion darkened by a Mediterranean sun, grey eyes, and fair hair worn rather long. Earlier she had even toyed with the idea of standing close to him at the rail in the distant hope that someone would take them for brother and sister, and a laughing introduction might well have ensued. A friendship could have blossomed under the Greek sun, gazing out over the wine-dark sea, she had thought whimsically.

She had not, for once, followed her impulses, however, contenting herself instead with admiring him from a distance, embarrassed to meet his eye, edging around him with the odd sideways glance she might have cast at the statue of the naked sea god she'd covertly admired in the Athens museum. And now, thanks to a discarded book, here she was, arm in arm and chatting comfortably with this heroic figure. She wished she could have cut a better dash herself. In her get-up, consisting of dripping canvas motoring coat thrown on over shirt and trousers, she surely presented a far from glamorous image. She was conscious of her squelching tennis shoes and, crowning all, the damp fastenings of her brother's old leather flying helmet dangling with inelegant insouciance, dripping water down her neck.

George Russell must have caught her thought or perhaps a betraying twitch of her hand towards the helmet. 'It's very becoming!' he assured her. 'I took you for a Sylkie – shining round head and enormous eyes . . . you look quite like a wet seal.'

'But it was the bristly moustache that really impressed you?'

They laughed together and she allowed him to draw her forward to the prow of the boat. There he braced himself, nose to the wind, looking out eagerly towards the island as they cut their way through the still turbulent waves.

'Ah! The wind's gone about . . . we won't have a problem getting into port,' he said. 'And here you are, Laetitia – your home for the next season.'

Letty stared, speechless, struck dumb by the wild beauty of the scene, wishing she could paint. It would take a Turner, she decided, to record on canvas the unearthly quality of the slanting light piercing through the storm clouds now fleeing, ragged, before the wind; to choose just the colours to conjure up the intermingling of sea, sky, and spray: Tyrian purple, jade, steel grey, and flashing silver. In the far distance, beyond the huddle of the Venetian harbour, adding the element of earth to the kaleidoscope, sprawled a range of mountains, their summits, still snow-covered, catching the sun and lighting up white as swans' wings.

They gazed on in companionable silence, not even attempting by an exclamation to comment on the lavish display. When Laetitia found her voice, she was mortified to hear the flat, Baedeker tone of her comment: 'We're much closer than I had expected,' she said. 'I can make out Herakleion clearly now.'

'Herakleion? Ah, yes. Forgive me. I always think of it by its old name. Candia.'

Laetitia felt herself corrected and, in a strange way, excluded from his communion with the old seaport. 'You'll find the town very foreign,' he went on. 'By that I mean – very un-Greek. It carries the stamp of centuries of conquerors – Venetian ... Turkish ... There's the fortress guarding the harbour entrance. The ferry must go a little farther beyond the harbour – it's too small to take larger vessels. And those high arched structures just beyond the inner docks, do you see them? ... The Venetian arsenal. The boatyards.'

She looked and admired the cluster of white, red-roofed houses crammed in picturesque disorder within the fortifications. But her eye was drawn beyond, caught by a shape looming between the town and a farther, higher mountain range. 'George – tell me – what is that hill – mountain? – the one with the extraordinary shape over there?' She pointed.

'Ah! That's Mount Juktas. The mountain sacred to the king of the gods, to Zeus. He was born here on Crete, you know. In a cave on Mount Dicte. I must take you to call on him. Can you ride a donkey?'

Letty smiled to hear him speak so familiarly about the deity who was clearly on his calling list, a valued acquaintance.

'Now keep your eyes fixed on old Juktas,' he continued. 'I want you to turn your head slightly sideways, Laetitia ... No, like this ...' He put a gentle hand under her chin. 'Look again at the shape of the mountain and tell me what you see. Here comes the sun, on cue! It's beautifully backlit! You must see it!'

Letty gasped. 'Yes, I do! I can see a silhouette. The outline of a man ... or is he a god? Look – he's lying down ... his head's over there.' She laughed in delight. 'He has a jutting beard ... like an Achaean warrior!'

16

George Russell smiled and nodded. 'And, of course, as you've guessed – that's Zeus himself. Laid out on a marble slab, perhaps? Dead, at any rate. It's said his tomb lies somewhere at the foot of the mountain.'

'His tomb? George, what are you saying? Zeus is an immortal god and the gods don't die!'

'If they can be born, they can surely die?' He shivered and put up the collar of his jacket. 'It's a beautiful but blood-soaked soil you're about to step on to, Laetitia Talbot. On Crete, even the gods may die.'

Chapter Two

The light was beginning to fail and oil lamps were being lit in the houses as they threaded their way, headlights blazing, horn honking, scattering alarmed men and beasts off the road before them.

'They haven't seen a Bugatti two-seater sports-tourer before, I'd guess,' Letty shouted over the motor's roar. 'Not sure I have myself, I now confess. Certainly never ridden in one.'

'Really? But you seemed to know your way about the engine!'

'I think they're all pretty much alike. Carburettors all seem to flood in the same way. I say, the next bit looks rather narrow . . . are you sure about this?'

'I know these alleyways to the inch. Built with enough room for two laden mules to pass each other. I chose the smallest, toughest car I could find. We should scrape through. Curses! That wasn't there last time! Excuse me a moment.'

Leaving the car idling, George Russell climbed out and in fluent Greek apologized to the wizened lady whose display of oranges he had knocked over, gathering them back up into a pile and passing her a coin or two. He paused to exchange news with her, said something that made her roll about in a fit of giggling, then dallied longer to pay court to her ginger cat when it came to twine about his ankles. Through her impatience to be off, Letty noticed that the woman, clothed from head to foot in black, smiled at him as though he'd done her a great kindness, and when Letty turned her head as they started up again, it was to see her, still beaming, making a blessing sign after George's retreating back.

'Here you are, Laetitia,' he said, tossing a large orange on to her lap. 'Your first! The orange and lemon harvest has just started.'

'I've never seen one with its leaves on, freshly tugged from the tree!' she exclaimed, delighted with the simple gift. She dug her fingernails into the rough skin and inhaled the scented oils that burst from it. 'Delicious! I shall have it for breakfast.'

'Breakfast! I don't know what you've become accustomed to in Athens but don't expect the typical British spread, will you? My father takes quite a pride in living a Cretan life. He keeps a Cretan cook, too. Breakfasts tend to be a bit sketchy at the Villa Europa. It'll be homemade yogurt, delicious bread, fruit, of course, and I can promise that the coffee will be good. That's one habit Father won't give up easily. Only a few more yards to go. It's the rather grand house on the corner.'

They had entered a wider street lined with spacious houses of Venetian architecture, their regularity relieved here and there by small plazas and triangles of greenery. 'An avenue, no less!' Letty read off the sign: '*Odhos Avgoustou ikosi pende*. Did I get that right? That's the Twenty-fifth of August Street, isn't it? Oh, dear! I get a bad feeling about a street named with a date. It usually spells calamity for someone.'

'You're not mistaken. And, indeed, there was bloodshed. The full name of the street is 'The Martyrs of the Twenty-fifth of August.' In this case it was a bit of a disaster all round, I'm afraid, and the martyrs were a mixed bunch. But it was a disaster which was to prove rather crucial for *me*! Thirty years ago or thereabouts the native Cretans – Christians – were pushing (with the help of the Great Powers) to throw off the Turkish yoke. The Turks outnumbered the Cretans here in the city by nine to one, so it was a sadly one-sided affair. On the date in question, a

19

detachment of British soldiers was escorting Cretan officials along this street to the harbour. They were ambushed by a Turkish mob. A frightful riot ensued in which hundreds of Cretans died along with seventeen British soldiers and – the unfortunate British consul.'

'Oh, no! I hardly like to ask what happened next.'

'You hardly need to!' He smiled. 'What do the British always do when someone gives them a bloody nose? They sent in a gunboat! Well, actually, it was more in the nature of a small fleet. The first thing they did was capture the ringleaders of the uprising, and they hung a symbolic seventeen of them. Then they cleared the land of Turkish troops before you could say knife! And that was the beginning of the end of two hundred and thirty years of Turkish rule in Crete. And the beginning – though he didn't at that time know it – of an important stage in the life of one of the young British naval officers aboard that gunboat. This is where the story becomes significant for *me*.

'The officer's name was Theodore Russell. My father. After the turmoil had subsided, he took some leave on the island and fell in love with it. He was also to fall in love with the daughter of a German archaeologist working here.'

'Ah! Your mother?' said Letty, sensing a romance.

'Yes, indeed. My mother's family was well established in the Middle East – archaeological aristocracy, you might say! I do believe my mother was born in a trench with a silver trowel in her mouth! Anyway, the upshot was – Father decided that this girl and this world were for him. And as soon as he could, he married his Ilse. Engaged though she was by that time to someone quite other. He's a very determined man, my father, you'll see! Not a man to allow the inconvenience of an established fiancé to get in his way!'

'How romantic!' Letty said. 'I look forward to meeting your mother.'

'Not possible, I'm afraid.' George's voice lost its warmth. 'She's dead. She returned to Germany to visit her family in

1914 and never came back. She was quite insouciant about the political climate of the time – "But the Germans and the British are cousins, my love," I remember her saying to me. "It will never amount to war. Never!" My father had concerns, and rightly so, as it turned out. She died in Europe. Not in the fighting – a river ferry overturned and she was drowned. Father was devastated. So was I. I was twelve years old. I remember her well.'

'You have her looks?' Letty asked quietly.

'Yes. You'll see my father is dark – he's often taken for a native Cretan, which pleases the old rogue no end!' After a pause he went on: 'But never think you're about to land in an eagle's nest of nothing but male brigands – you'll be welcomed by my stepmother. Phoebe.' He gave Letty a speculative glance, then decided, 'You'll get on well. She's not much older than you. A lively lass! Has to be to cope with my father! She makes him very happy. Oh, I should prepare you for the other residents,' he added, slowing the car for a file of donkeys. 'There are three others. All chaps. The two youngest ones are archaeology students attached to the British School in Athens. The odd oldest one is an architect.'

'An architect? What on earth would an architect be doing here on Crete?'

'They're very much in demand! Every excavation hopes to acquire one! Arthur Evans set the style. Digging's not just about the holes in the ground, you'll find. *Reconstruction* – that's the thing! With two or three floors often supported by pillars, flights of stairs, and miles of corridors to make sense of in these ancient palaces, you need an architect's eye to inform you. And there are palaces popping up everywhere, it would seem! 'The island of a hundred cities,' as Homer called it, is proving to be exactly that! There are digging teams of many nationalities at work here, all vying with each other to reveal the next Knossos to the world. So if you have an architect with a neat drawing hand who'll help you to get into print before your competitors, you have a decided advantage.

'And the one my father has in tow at the moment is top-hole. These fellows can draw sketches from the evidence the spade turns up to show you what the palace would have looked like in its heyday, and then they can even supervise the rebuilding. They tell me it's essential for preservation, too. I'm no archaeologist, but I've seen their anguished faces when the gypsum thrones and wooden piers they've dug out and exposed to the elements with such gay abandon rot and dissolve in the foul wet weather we get in the winter.' He gave a smile at once indulgent and dismissive. 'Steel struts shipped out from Sheffield and modern ferroconcrete robustly take the place of the crumbling Minoan originals. And what a stroke of luck it is – you will agree, I'm sure, when you've seen Knossos – that the ancient architect whom King Minos employed should prove to be so in tune with the taste of his confrères thirty centuries in the future! I hope you're fond of oxblood?'

'Oxblood?'

'The colour. Dark reddish-brown, much favoured by the restorers of palaces out here.'

There was something in his tone she could not quite seize. It was amused, certainly, but the amusement was a light veil for disparagement, she thought. Letty repressed a smile. Most of the young men she knew affected this attitude of unconcern. It was tedious and, faced with languid masculine world-weariness, Letty's response was always brisk. 'If there's evidence of authenticity – and the slightest smear of ancient paint on a pillar will convince me – then I shall approve and love it,' she said crisply.

George grinned and pulled up in front of an imposing Venetian façade. The three-storied house was graced by wrought-iron balconies at the long windows and a double flight of marble steps led to a door flanked by carved stone panels. Letty peered upwards, impressed.

'The carvings are of lions like the ones in St Marks,' he said, following her gaze. 'Well, Laetitia – what are you thinking?'

'I'm thinking this is no *villa*,' she answered. 'It's beautiful ... a knockout ... but what it is is an elegant *town* house. Where does all this "villa" nonsense come from?'

He seemed entertained by her comment. 'Of course, you're right – the house does have a grander and more authentic Italian name. But everyone in Crete knows that my father has always seen himself as a rival to Sir Arthur Evans and a challenger for the old boy's position of master of the Cretan archaeological world. With old Arthur long established on the island as genial host to the wandering cosmopolitan high society at the house he built for himself in the country overlooking his site at Knossos ...'

'The Villa *Ariadne*? Ah! I begin to understand!'

'... inevitably, when my father set himself up here, some joker – come to think of it, it might even have been Pa! – referred to it as "the Villa Europa".'

'Europa being Ariadne's granny!'

'Thereby mischievously establishing a precedence. And making Sir Arthur look like a parvenu villa-builder from Wimbledon. Well – the name stuck. The Villa Europa perfectly summed up my father's piratical style ... Are you ready for this?'

He gave a brisk hoot on the Bugatti's horn, but the great door was already being flung open. A slender, fair-haired woman wearing a floating ankle-length gown ran down the stairs to greet them. Calling and cooing excitedly, she kissed George on both cheeks, then turned at once to open the door for Letty, not waiting for an introduction. The bones of the hand she offered were as light as a kitten's. Letty hardly dared to return the pressure.

'Oh, how wonderful! Our two birds in one Bugatti! I'm Phoebe, George's stepmother. Did he remember to tell you he had one, Laetitia? Oh, good! He sometimes forgets and people are left standing about wondering quite who I am.' Her voice was warm and throaty; the words spilled out excitedly. 'We're delighted you made the connection with each other on the ferry. How sensible! We would have wired to suggest George escort you but there wasn't time to telegraph before your boat sailed. George – what have you done about Laetitia's baggage? I don't see it!'

'It's on a mule somewhere between here and the harbour. Well, two mules. There was rather a lot. No room in this car for anything but people.'

Phoebe looked with concern at Letty's wet clothes and noted that she had no luggage with her, apart from a leather satchel thrown over her shoulder. She began to scan the avenue with some urgency. 'Oh, there it is! I think I see it on its way. Something bulky's just come round the corner. Thank goodness for that! I'll send someone up to help you unpack. Come in, you poor thing – you look quite exhausted! I'll have a cup of tea brought to your room. Ah, Laetitia, here's my husband. Theo! They've arrived, darling! Together!'

Theodore Russell, at last. Letty was looking forward to meeting him, though slightly nervous about the prospect. An ex-navy man turned diplomat, he had been the éminence grise behind two Prime Ministers. In his middle years he had become an amateur archaeologist of renown and was generally held by his compatriots to be the rising authority on Cretan life and history. Sir Arthur Evans was now approaching eighty years of age and loosening his ties with the island that had made him the foremost archaeologist of the twentieth century. Already, the world was looking to Theodore Russell to fill the gap, scientific and social, that the absence of the grand old man would leave.

And here he was, descending the last few stairs into the hallway, already in his dinner jacket and presenting a reassuringly conventional figure. He was dark and stocky, with an austere appearance relieved solely by a heavy silver ring of antique design that he wore on the hand he now extended to Letty. Rough, she noted with approval, and warm. Theodore Russell's beard was black, beginning to brindle with grey, and neatly trimmed in what she took to be a naval style. Being a tall girl, Laetitia was accustomed to finding herself on eye level with many men, and she was amused, but not surprised, to detect an automatic straightening of the spine and raising of the chin in the man now greeting her. The pressure of his handshake increased. He murmured polite enquiries but she was aware that his eyes were skittering past her, seeking out his son, who'd followed a pace or two behind.

Letty moved quickly aside, enjoying the sight of two men embracing with easy freedom. Theodore was a good deal shorter than George; in fact, you would never have taken them for father and son, would not even have placed them in the same tribe, Letty thought, but there was no mistaking the pleasure the pair had in seeing each other again after George's six months' absence.

'Come up with me, Laetitia, and I'll get you settled in,' said Phoebe. 'Student quarters? Is that really what you were expecting? Certainly not! I wouldn't hear of it. You are to have a guest room here in the villa kept for you for the season, or as long as you choose to stay. I have little enough female company – I intend to have you close by. We do keep rooms for students in the wing across the courtyard and we have three gentlemen with us at present. You'll meet them at dinner.

'Well – here you are! I've put you in a room overlooking the avenue. If you open the shutters and lean out you can see the Morosini Fountain to your left, and to the right, the sea and harbour. The plumbing's not bad. Not up to Minoan standards, perhaps!' Her grin was spontaneous and involving. 'But it's adequate. The bathroom's right next door. The bed's pretty but a bit hard. You'll get used to it.'

Letty looked about her. The high-ceilinged room was sparely but elegantly furnished with matching dark wood pieces of French workmanship. The highlight of the white room, drawing and fixing the attention, was a screen of dark red lacquer with an abstract design of black and silver slashing its way across the three leaves. The effect was as pleasing as anything she'd sampled in Paris and she said so. An artless remark, but it seemed to give great pleasure. Phoebe's large blue eyes, lighting up with joy, transformed her pale features, and suddenly Letty realized she was looking at a woman with all the ethereal beauty of Lillian Gish. She'd seen *La Bohème* before leaving London and had sniffed and sobbed along with every other woman in the cinema's audience (and not a few of the men) as John Gilbert held his Mimi in his arms, attempting, by the intensity of his feelings, to keep her alive.

'Ah! Paris!' A gusty sigh of nostalgia. 'You see – I've attempted to bring a little of the style back with me, Laetitia. I'm English – from London – but my parents have lived in France for the last ten years. My father was a diplomat – that's how I met Theodore. Sadly, Father died last December and I travelled to Paris for his funeral. A local couple were returning home for Christmas, luckily, and I was able to go most of the way with them. The Stoddarts are such fun – you must meet them! Theo was too busy with his book to come with me, but he was able to spare me for a month. Rather pleased to have me out of the way for a bit, I suspect! And I made the most of my time in Paris! It wasn't all doom and gloom! The shops! I spent such lots of Theo's money having fabrics and china shipped out to us.'

Phoebe smoothed down the white silk counterpane and moved a bronze figure half an inch along a table with a smile and a showman's gesture.

Her interest so deliberately invited, Letty looked more closely. 'Oh, I see! How clever of you to find it!' she said. 'This is Europa herself, isn't it? Riding her bull.' She ran a finger over the proud naked figure reclining almost negligently the length of the bronze bull's back, her flowing hair tangling around its horns.

Phoebe laughed. 'I simply had to have it! Theo thought it a little bold for the drawing room so I keep it here in the spare room. To scandalize or titillate our guests.'

'Bold? Beyond bold!' Letty found herself responding to the mischief in Phoebe's voice. 'It's downright indecent! And, what's more . . .' She picked up the gleaming object, admiring its balance and flowing lines. '. . . it's subversive!'

'What can you mean?' Phoebe asked with mock innocence. She raised eyebrows that had been plucked out of existence and pencilled in with more than a touch of Hollywood style.

'Well, according to the legend, this is supposed to be a scene of abduction and rape – yes?'

'It is! You know the story: A young princess is discovered walking, all unsuspecting, along the shore of her homeland in Asia Minor when, prinking out of the surf, there comes a darling, docile little white bull with gilded hooves and breath scented with roses. Well, could anyone resist?' Phoebe purred.

'Europa evidently can't! She climbs on to the bull's back and it swims away with her. And naughty Zeus – for it was he! – in disguise! – makes off with her to his lair on his own island – Crete! And here he has his wicked way with her . . .'

Phoebe burst into a peal of laughter. 'My own story exactly! And very saucy! The princess Europa seems to have plumbed depths of sexual perversion no modern girl would have the imagination, let alone the courage, to explore. And her unfortunate female descendants inherited her taste for the outré. But the story may have deeper significance – Theo says it's a traditional way of preserving a historical truth. It accounts for the assimilation of a race from Asia Minor into ancient Cretan society. Or perhaps establishes the precedence of a male god over the mother goddess. Theo's got a bee in his bonnet about that, I warn you. He seems quite prepared to stake his career on proving his theory right.'

'Well, it would certainly mark out a distinction between him and his illustrious predecessor,' said Letty thoughtfully.

'I keep telling him,' Phoebe confided cheerfully, 'Theo – you're going the wrong way about this. You shouldn't *first* have your theory and *then* dig up the evidence to prove it. Dig somewhere interesting and then listen to what the evidence is telling you – whether it suits you or not. But a

27

wife is the last person he would listen to. Well, *this* wife! I imagine he might have listened to his first wife, who really did know what she was talking about – you know – dirt-under-the-fingernails sort of knowledge. *I* have to feed him *my* theories through his architect. William, at least, seems to be able to get my husband's attention. Lord! Poor Letty! With all this petty politicking you'll begin to think you've fetched up at the court of the Sun King! Villa Europa's not *quite* as bad as that. Though rather male-dominated, you'll find.'

They both peered again at the figurine, seeing clearly why it had been banished to the spare room.

'I do wonder a bit about this artist's message,' said Letty thoughtfully. 'I'm not at all sure that that's what this particular Europa is telling me. Who is the seduced here and who the seducer? This is a powerful little bull, with all his bits and pieces proudly on display, but if you allow your eye to wander, you can see his front feet are about to step into a snare. And the languorous Europa is smiling. She *knows*. She's well aware that her tumbling locks are spilling down over the bull's eyes, blinding him to traps, and that his horns are caught up in the golden net of her hair. Watch out, Zeus! You've taken aboard more than you can handle!'

She replaced the statue on the table. 'Spirited and lovely! A fresh and modern vision.'

'So glad you like it! It was a great indulgence!'

'Worth every franc!' said Letty stoutly. 'Whatever it cost. *I've* never regretted spending more than I should.' She scrabbled in the satchel she had kept slung over her shoulder. 'Thinking of frivolities – I brought you something. *Harper's Bazaar* – wonderful Erté designs – and the latest *Vogue*. The spring millinery number.' At that moment Letty caught sight of herself in the dressing-table mirror and fought back a squeak of horror. 'Gracious! I look like the victim of a Viking raid!'

Phoebe eagerly accepted the magazines with murmured words of thanks and added: 'I can't deny you look as though you've been gone over with a rake. But I'd have said, more poetically, the victim of the Sea God ... toyed with for a moment and thrown back into the surf. And what does my stepson think he's about, involving a lady with his awful little toy?' She pointed accusingly to a smudge of engine grease across Letty's forehead. 'I see George has been *initiating* you into its inner mysteries. He really has a very sketchy idea of what is appropriate to sex, age, class, or even *species*, you'll discover. He treats everyone the same. It can be jolly awkward – but it can be funny and it can be touching. Anyway – I apologize for him. Though – if he thought about it at all – George would consider my remarks condescending and presumptuous. He's a boy who will make his own impression!'

'Oh, he already has,' said Letty and the two women laughed together in easy friendship.

Hearing a clunking on the stairs, Phoebe moved to open the door for two manservants carrying up Letty's baggage. 'Your things! That's a relief! You're a tall girl, Laetitia – I wouldn't have felt confident in offering you one of my cocktail dresses to wear. We don't stand on great ceremony here, you'll discover, but Theo likes to make a splash on the first evening at least. Tonight's meal will be quite formal, but the rest of the time it's come-as-you-are when the gong sounds, and the food is catch-as-catch-can. Have you brought a little dinner dress? Good. Oh, and I'd advise – do as I do! I put on a good pair of thick stockings and something warm to slip around the shoulders. This stone house can be as cold as the tomb these spring evenings.'

Phoebe hesitated, perhaps wondering whether to speak further, decided against it, and then began to slip away with an invitation to come down in an hour's time for an aperitif before supper. 'You'll find everyone gathered in the drawing room on the first floor or, as Theo insists on calling it: the *piano nobile*.' She excused his pretension with an indulgent smile. 'Well, he's a stickler for tradition and it *was* the Venetians who built this echoing old mausoleum, after all ... I'm just thankful they had the sense to leave out the canal under the window.' In the doorway she turned and said again, 'So glad you're here, Laetitia!'

Letty eyed with disfavour the chalky white mound of animal tissue folded in tightly curling waves and sitting in the middle of her plate. It looked like nothing so much as her aunt Dotty's permanent wave, she thought, and for a dizzying moment she was unsure whether she would burst out into giggles or noisy retching. This culinary delicacy was surrounded by a moat of reddish-brown fluid, flecked with something vegetable that might have been mushrooms and onions. Her stomach clenched in a familiar pain. It seemed her body had retained a memory of the recent affliction at sea and was inconveniently sending her a warning.

She'd been looking forward to her supper. She'd bathed and dressed in a little green silk frock from her trunk, a new pair of stockings, and a pearl necklace. With the example of Phoebe's artfully coloured face in mind, Letty thought it would very probably be acceptable to liven up her own washed-out pallor with a dab of rouge on her cheekbones and a touch of the warm coral lipstick she'd brought with her to impress or astonish Athenian society. Hearing the gong sound, she'd flung a soft green and blue fringed Kashmiri wrap over one shoulder and hurried down to the *piano nobile*. Gratifyingly, George and Theodore had stared when she'd entered the drawing room where they stood sipping dry sherry.

'Good Lord! The girl's a beauty!' George had exclaimed, stepping forward to welcome her. 'I had no idea I was smuggling a sea nymph into the house.'

'I think I shall have to greet you all over again, Laetitia. I had mistaken you for George's motoring engineer,' said his father. 'Sherry, my dear? Ah, here come your fellow diggers. Boys, both. And a year or two behind you in experience, but capable – very capable. Dick! Stewart! Come! Let me introduce you to Laetitia Talbot. This is the young lady you're to escort around the museum tomorrow. Help her to get a feeling for the culture and understand the exhibits before she goes off to add to their number herself.'

He paused and cocked a speculative eyebrow. 'Laetitia will tell you she was up at Cambridge and she's a protégée and student of Professor Merriman – yes, another one of those. We are indeed favoured! Can it be that my old friend Andrew is becoming a little overprolific with his generous references? We shall have to wait and see! Laetitia would have us know she's worked in Egypt and France so, my boys, she's well ahead of you both in experience.' He smiled indulgently at Dick and Stewart. 'But this is to be her first opportunity of *directing* a dig. In Crete. A good career move.' After the slightest hesitation, he added: 'I take it a *career* is what the young lady has in mind? An excellent choice of site, if so. Well away from any main-stream excavations. And, of course, wherever you stick your spade in this rich earth, you turn up something notable. With a skilled team to back her, this young lady can hardly go wrong, I'd say.'

Letty decided to hoard this statement, delivered with deceptive bonhomie, for closer inspection at her leisure.

Dick Collingwood was the first to hurry forward with words of welcome. Studious-looking with an abundance of floppy dark hair, a slight stammer, and the earnest manner and aristocratic accent of Old Oxford, he was very like dozens of young men she'd worked with in London and Egypt. 'Do call me Dickie,' he told her, and went on to establish that one of his cousins had roomed at college with one of hers before the war ... If she was one of the Cambridgeshire Talbots, that is ...

She thought she'd do well to reserve judgement on the second student, Stewart McGill. He held back, polite but cool, sifting every syllable she uttered, silently taking in every aspect of her appearance. She was entertained to see that the dark Scotsman, by his stance and his gestures, by the way he went to take up a position at Theodore's side, by the very cut of his hair, was emulating his employer. The prize pupil.

'No architect?' she enquired, looking beyond them for the third man George and Phoebe had mentioned.

'Not yet. He's been working at Knossos all day with the students from the Ariadne. We had some rain earlier ... I expect he's taken shelter and stayed on to finish,' Dick replied. 'That would be like him. Meticulous, you know.'

'"Meticulous" doesn't begin to describe him,' said Stewart dryly. 'I do believe he'd ignore the last trumpet call to Judgement if he'd an elevation to finish drawing. "Sorry, God, old man – busy, don't you know – you'll just have to wait,"' he drawled. 'That's rather his style. Lofty, wouldn't you agree? Typically English.'

Stewart's Scottish scorn was too outrageous to be taken seriously, but Letty found she couldn't encourage him in his prejudice and her warm smile faded. Her sympathies would always be with a man who would not hesitate to make God wait on Art. She was curious to meet this toff so disapproved of by the puritanical Scotsman.

'And, you know, God *would* wait, gentleman that he is. And he'd be jolly pleased to peer over the architect's shoulder. *This* architect's shoulder!' Phoebe had dashed into the drawing room like a bird released from a cage, a flash of blue silk and peacock-feathered headband, immediately involved in the conversation. She tweaked Stewart's ear playfully as she passed, raising, Letty was intrigued to notice, a flush on his granite cheek. 'So sorry I'm down late! You must all blame Laetitia! She brought me the latest magazines and, after one glance inside, I just *had* to redraw my eyebrows! Devastated to find I was six months behind the fashion! Did I get it right, Letty?' She put on a model girl's vampish smile.

'Very Greta Garbo!' Letty approved. 'Perfect!'

Dick was instantly at Phoebe's elbow offering her a drink. 'Your tonic water, Phoebe,' he said, controlling his stammer.

She took an unhurried sip. 'And you remembered the ice! Bless you, Dickie!'

32

Letty caught Theodore's sardonic smile and looked away quickly. It occurred to her that she'd be doubly intrigued to make the acquaintance of the architect who seemed to have won Phoebe's warm approval in the face of so much courtly competition.

And they'd settled down to table. After an old-fashioned grace in English pronounced by Theodore, they'd embarked on one of the oddest meals she had ever experienced. No attempt had been made to order the seating according to sex, though with two women, four men, and one absentee to juggle with, Letty would not have liked to be given the task. The grouping that had developed reminded her of the result of the clumsy and haphazard dash for places at a supper in the school refectory.

She and Phoebe occupied one long side of the table. Ranged opposite them were George and the two students. Theo sat at the head and a place setting had been left free at the foot, awaiting the late arrival. Not so much to do him honour as to allow him access, causing the least disturbance to the other diners when at last the architect appeared, Letty supposed.

The stomach pain came again as the scent of the dish wafted up to her nostrils. She caught a furtive glance between Theo and the three younger men, noticed the slightest evidence of over-brightness in their covering chatter, and, though she was at first unwilling to allow unworthy suspicions to take root in her mind, awareness broke through. A test! Could it be? Was she undergoing an ordeal by offal? They continued to talk amongst themselves, avoiding her eye, delaying making a start on the dish steaming gently before them, and Letty found she could stretch her disbelief no further. But how to react?

As always when confronted by perplexing social situations, she tried to imagine what her admired aunt Joan would have done. She remembered a nursery tea-party and a small girl offering a plate of highly decorated cakes. Joan had selected, and then eaten, the plainest one. When asked with more than normal curiosity by the child if she'd enjoyed it, her aunt had politely replied that indeed she had. 'Did you really? That was the bun I licked the icing off before you came' was the interested reply. And Joan's reaction was a wide, warm smile and a gracious 'Delicious, Letty dear. Quite delicious.'

Laetitia fixed a similar smile. She selected her cutlery. She speared the unappetizing lump with her fork and began a transverse incision with her knife.

Phoebe was the first to break ranks. After a defiant glance at her husband, her hand stole out and closed over Letty's knife hand. 'My dear, unless you really *do* have a fondness for lamb's brain – which is what this is – please do not proceed. We have a Cretan cook, you see, and I can't work out a word he says. He affects not to understand me when I'm settling the week's menus, although I do try.'

'You have only to take my persistently offered advice, Phoebe,' said Theodore, smiling blandly, 'if you *sincerely* wish to communicate with the staff. Miss Talbot, I am assured, is quite the linguist – I'm confident she would support me when I say – yet again – if you would only do as Ilse did ... my first wife, Ilse,' he added for Letty's benefit, 'and spend more time in the marketplace and the kitchen and less in the boutique and the boudoir, you would acquire a working knowledge of the language. The Mrs Russell of the day would then be able to convey her wishes and preferences to the cook.'

'A skill which *Mr* Russell has evidently acquired?' suggested Letty quietly, distressed by Phoebe's sudden stillness, the droop of her fair head. She bent to retrieve Phoebe's wrap, a length of fine blue angora, which had slid, unnoticed, to the floor, and tucked it gently back around her slim shoulders.

Theodore's head swung in her direction, eyebrows raised in mild surprise, questioning her gesture. Letty was dismayed to see that he was interpreting her instinctive attempt to offer comfort as a challenge to him and a declaration of support for his wife.

34

It was George who broke the tension with a burst of laughter: 'So you can jolly well come off it, Pa!' he said. 'Laetitia's seen through you! She's guessed who proposed this menu item! You can be such an embarrassment, you old funster! What you are witnessing, Letty, is a demonstration of an adolescent condition prolonged into middle age – a practical jokery of a kind . . . a predilection for buffoonery. Perhaps Herr Freud has identified the condition and dignified it with a medical label? Now what can we suggest? . . . Ludomania?'

His tone was light, playful, regretful even, but his harsh words made Letty cringe. She had little sympathy for their target, having conceived a disturbing suspicion of Theodore Russell, but surely this was an unnecessarily public insult, one delivered by the very last person she might have expected to aim a hurtful comment? Even in her bohemian world, sons showed due respect to their fathers. She could only interpret the outburst as a falsely jovial rap on the knuckles for his unkindness to Phoebe.

'Oh, don't worry!' George went on, apparently unconscious of the general unease. 'You'll not be encountering itching powder or an exploding cigar – nothing so unsophisticated – this is just Pa's way of testing the mettle of his guests. Unfortunately, the reactions of his victims do usually throw up revealing evidence. And – with the results of his experiments justifying his unconventional research – he persists.'

Letty had encountered bad behaviour at the nursery tea table – had been responsible herself for much of it. The baiting of newcomers in the school dining hall was a tradition everyone had to weather, but she would never have expected to encounter such rank bad manners at a civilized dinner party. She considered her options. She could react in the predictable way: she could hurry from the room in distress, leaving four men shaking their heads and murmuring with insincere concern of the susceptibilities of the fairer sex, thereby sacrificing forever her opportunity to establish herself in this masculine world. Or she could face them out.

'Throwing up evidence? Why, George – that is precisely what I had in mind,' she murmured. 'Well, well! We all have our own ways of getting the measure of strangers . . . salt in the sugar-shaker, spiders in the bath . . . The Greek bandit Procrustes did it all too literally by inviting benighted guests to recline on an over-long bed and then racking their limbs until they fitted. What's a dish of *cervelles d'agneau en matelote* by way of welcome in comparison with that? I have to think I've got off lightly.'

She leaned across the table towards Theodore and spoke in teasing reprimand: 'You'll have to do better, Mr Russell!'

Theodore nodded in acknowledgement of her thrust, and put down his knife and fork in a playful gesture of surrender. George threw him a triumphant look.

'You should have seen what he served up for the Italian ambassador last week!' Dick interposed, taken in by Letty's show of good humour and vaguely sensing with relief that the game was over. 'Bull's . . . er . . . *parts*! Steaming in a pond of white sauce.'

Letty stared. Phoebe tutted and shushed.

Theo, unabashed, motioned to a manservant to remove the offending dish.

'Actually, I thought it was rather good,' offered Dick hastily. 'If you didn't look.'

'If this is how you suffer, I think you all deserve a treat,' Letty said sweetly. 'One of my pieces of luggage is a hamper from Fortnum's. A present for you, Phoebe, from my father.'

'A hamper!' The cry went round the table.

'What's in it?'

'Foie gras?' Phoebe said dreamily. '*Do* say you've brought some foie gras!'

'A tinned haggis?' Stewart hardly dared hope.

'Black cherries in syrup?' Dick murmured. 'Or raspberries in a jar – that wouldn't be bad.'

'Brown Windsor soup!' said Theodore. 'There has to be Brown Windsor. Although beef consommé might just be acceptable.'

'I can't swear to any of those, though I can declare – Cooper's Oxford thick cut marmalade and two packets of Bath Oliver biscuits – oh, and a bottle of gin – I put those in myself.'

'Good Lord! I stumble into a chapter from *Wind in the Willows*,' said an amused baritone from the doorway. 'The picnic scene, perhaps? Don't tell me! You're all off down the river in a rowing boat tomorrow?'

They turned with a mixture of relief and pleasure to greet him. The newcomer – the architect? – unlike the other men, had not changed into a dinner jacket. He had obviously washed and shaved; a waft of Imperial Leather soap announced him and there was a fresh cut on his jaw. But the khaki cotton jacket thrown on over a white shirt, tieless and open at the neck, and the cord trousers were clear indication that he'd arrived anticipating the usual working supper. A handsome tanned face emphasized the blue of his eyes; his thick iron grey hair was neatly brushed back.

Theo rose to his feet to greet him.

'At last!' Phoebe whispered to Letty when her husband's back was turned. 'Enter the Water Rat! Now we'll all appreciate a firm hand on the tiller of this pleasure boat.'

'But we weren't expecting Miss Talbot for another week, were we? Theo, what *is* going on?' the newcomer demanded.

The very question Laetitia would have asked herself if she had been able to master her astonishment. But she could only sit rigidly in her seat, speechless and still.

'An early Easter present! Miss Laetitia Talbot, complete with hamper!' announced Theodore. 'Now – I ask myself – ought I to fear the English, bearing gifts? She took an early boat. Laetitia, may I introduce –'

'Please don't trouble,' snapped Letty. 'Mr Gunning and I have met before.'

Chapter Three

'Your father is well, I trust, Miss Talbot?' William Gunning
enquired politely. And, looking around and addressing the
room at large: 'I was last year briefly in the employ of Sir
Richard.'

'He's well, Mr Gunning, and if he'd known I was to have
the pleasure of seeing you here, he would have sent his
fond greetings, as would my friend Esmé, who has often
enquired about you since last we met,' she mumbled,
hardly aware of what she was saying.

Letty had spent many hours fantasizing about such a
moment and here it was: The treacherous, hateful Gunning
had fallen right into her lap. The gutless deserter, the man
unable to *recognize* a treasure when it stood before him,
offering itself – well, offering *herself* – was here at her
mercy. Her elegant satin T-strap was – so to speak – across
his neck. After all this time. How long had it been? She
didn't need to calculate. Eight and a half months since she
last saw him. And the anger still glowed.

Thrown together by circumstance not choice, they had
grown very close in France the previous summer. She'd
fancied herself in love with him. No self-deceiver, she
corrected herself: She'd fallen for him like a ton of bricks.
Letty blushed with shame to remember that she'd even, on
their return to England, driven him, not home to
Cambridge but to Fitzroy Gardens, to the privacy of the
family property in London. There she planned to make, as
he had disparagingly called it in the old soldier's term, 'the
ultimate sacrifice.' But her plan had blown up in her face

when they were greeted, on the doorstep of what she had calculated would be an unoccupied house, by her father and Professor Sir Andrew Merriman, her mentor. Unexpectedly down to enjoy the summer exhibitions. Unwittingly turning the night of passion she'd anticipated into a jolly junket.

Gunning had sailed easily into the situation. He'd showed not the slightest discomfort, while she had turned truculent. More of her father's friends had arrived, and Letty had retired to bed early and spent uncomfortable hours listening to the male guffaws and exclamations and calls for more bottles from below. In the morning Gunning was gone.

Without a word. Without a note. He'd vanished from her life as abruptly as he'd entered it. Relieved to have been handed a way out of a situation that was unwelcome to him? A situation that she had grossly misjudged? Or had he simply slunk away into the night after a warning-off by her father? She'd thought she would never know. But here he was again. And still up to his old deceptions, apparently. *Architect*, indeed! With one sentence she could destroy him before this company who, in their ignorance, appeared very much to admire him. Silently, she savoured a few killing phrases:

'Architect, you say? But surely when last we met you were a down-and-out on the streets of Cambridge – a man I plucked from the clutches of the Cambridge Constabulary and rescued from the House of Correction for two and six-pence, like the most miserable stray dog? And before that – remind us – you were an army chaplain? Wounded, bemedalled, quite the hero! Recommended for valour and honesty by your old friend the Bishop of Huntingdon, no less. I wonder what you'll be next year? Do tell, Mr Gunning! What an exciting life – lives! – you lead! And what eminent person have you lured into vouching for you in your present guise? I would have to guess – someone of the stature of Sir Edwin Lutyens.'

She took a deep breath and controlled her unruly

thoughts. She met his amused gaze, and the prepared speech dissolved on her lips.

The comic opera performance provoked by the master of Villa Europa had faded to a meaningless distraction the moment it had been challenged by Gunning's presence. But how was it possible that a man so devious and unpredictable could appear without warning in front of her and be at once the steady point to which her faulty compass needle unwaveringly turned? Grudgingly, she recognized that, whatever the man's sins, she would not give him away to Theodore Russell, for whom she was conceiving a much greater scorn. She glanced at her host – so confident, so manipulative – and decided to have her revenge for the lamb's brain and the distress his bad manners had caused them all. She saw her way through to making both of these men squirm a little.

'My father often speaks of you; Mr Gunning. He'll be thrilled when I tell him of this chance meeting,' she said brightly, getting to her feet. She crossed the room and reached up on tiptoe to peck at his cheeks in the Continental fashion. She might as well have been kissing a statue for all the response he made, she thought. Her tone became a few degrees warmer. 'I'm sure my father would congratulate you, Mr Russell, on having secured the services of such a brilliant man. I know we all set great store by Mr Gunning. And Sir Edwin – oh, come now, William, don't blush! – praised *extravagantly* his plans for the new faux-Gothic wing to our manor house near Cambridge. Those plans are merely *shelved*, William, awaiting your return. Father will use no other architect to see the scheme through to fruition. Ah! I begin to see the connexion! It was Sir Edwin who recommended you to Mr Russell. And you defected to pastures new and warmer climes. Curse you!'

Phoebe and the younger men were staring at Gunning with evident astonishment.

It was Theodore who threw a conversational lifeline. 'Lutyens? Why, no . . . William was referred to me by your

40

mentor, Andrew Merriman ... Did you not know this, Laetitia? Joint protégés of the great man – I'd have thought you'd have compared notes. How odd! I'm sorry to have deprived your father of his architect ... quite unwitting! Forgive me! It was last summer. Digging season well over and I was losing a struggle to draw up the year's finds, trench profiles, drawings speculative as to original elevations – you know the sort of thing – I've got a book coming out next year which I'm hoping will rival Arthur Evans's and, in a defeated mood –'

'Not something Pa suffers from ordinarily, you understand,' interrupted George. 'But in this case it was a godsend.'

'. . . I telegraphed Merriman in London begging his help. Andrew knows everyone. He replied saying he had the very man right there at his side – an accurate draughtsman with knowledge and experience of archaeology *and* an architect by profession. A gentleman scholar, with a deep appreciation of classical and preclassical culture.'

William Gunning stared straight ahead with a grim face, listening to this account of his talents. He might have been hearing the delivery of a death sentence.

'And William came out to us at once, before the weather closed in. He won't tell you himself, so I must say it for him – he's been spectacularly successful. He's learned modern Greek and – as you see – puts in hours of overtime in the field,' George informed Letty.

'My book, I have decided,' announced Theodore, '– and I haven't told him this yet – is to be dedicated to William. The last little flourish. All is ready now for the publisher; the text and the illustrations are complete. William's drawings and his photographs are a vital part of the lavish production we envisage. As well as historical accuracy, they have that arresting quality the modern reader seeks out. A fresh style, very much his own. We're planning many pages in *colour*, Laetitia. Every drawing room table in the land will display one!'

41

'I'll place my order at Hatchards directly,' said Letty. 'How thrilling! Whatever next, William? An exhibition of your sketches at Burlington House?'

'Not quite ready for that,' he growled. 'Though the Royal Society has proposed a lecture engagement. I'll send you an invitation when they've hired the hall.'

'Come and sit down, man!' said Theodore. 'Dimitri is about to send in the fish course. We're to have red mullet, I understand, then there's a stew of some kind, which will be helped on its way by a bottle of the excellent red wine of Arkhanais, just south of here. Oh, and to accompany the French cheeses I've had sent out, I've opened a bottle of the Clos de Vougeot. A particular favourite of George's. So good to have him home again, sure you'll agree.'

Gunning and George felt released at last to greet each other. The expected handshake was reinforced, Letty was intrigued to note, by warm smiles, a swift backslapping, and murmured compliments.

'I've asked for a dish of *horta* from the hills,' Theodore rambled on expansively. 'Wonderful stuff in the spring! Highly recommended for the liver. Just what you need, Laetitia . . . Laetitia is feeling a little liverish,' he confided to Gunning. 'And for dessert – well, it doesn't feature in Cretan cuisine so when we have guests I clear the chaps out of the kitchen and make my own. Tonight, as the oranges and lemons are with us again, I'm going to impress you all with my Boodles Fool.'

The meal was exceptional and in normal circumstances Letty's healthy appetite would have done justice to it but, after a token taste of each dish, her will to eat deserted her. Conversation flowed around the table, occasionally foundering on the reefs of silence stretching between herself and Gunning.

George talked entertainingly of the six months he had just spent driving and walking around Europe. The young man puzzled her. She had assumed, from the delight he showed in owning his splendid new automobile, that he was the spoiled son of a rich man, but when she had trailed before him remarks alluding to the more frivolous aspects of life in France and Italy he appeared nonplussed. No casino gaming table, no racecourse, no gilded box at the music hall had had the benefit of the sight of that remarkable profile, as far as she could gather. Sensing at last from her carefully phrased queries that he was being a disappointment in the arts-and-culture department, George thought hard and came up with a glowing appreciation of the design of the new Alfa Romeo showroom in the rue Marbeuf.

It was Phoebe who caught her eye and, not too concerned to hide her amusement, reached across and patted George's hand affectionately. 'You won't find our George strolling along the Via dei Condotti showing off his suit or necking in a smoke-filled Berlin boîte!'

But George had realized at last that the two women were teasing him. Good-naturedly, he grinned and offered further evidence of the sophistication they were casting doubt on. 'You do me less than justice, Phoebe! I have adventurous friends in Paris. I was taken to a nightclub! Chez Joséphine in the rue Fontaine! Fascinating ... And someone dragged me off to the winter review at the Moulin Rouge. What was it called? ... All spotlights and spangles, I remember ... *Paris aux étoiles* – that's it!'

'It's not the fleshpots of Europe that attract George,' Phoebe answered Letty's unspoken question. 'It's the *people*. He has hankerings after becoming an anthropologist, Laetitia. He's been studying, making notes on the different races to be found in Europe. Alpine mountain men – grey-eyed Finns – red-haired Irish – George has chased them all down! What he's attempting to do is to trace the movements of the races westwards from the Indus Valley or some such. Am I mangling this too, too horribly, George? Research all done with dimension in mind. I'll bet you anything he can tell you to the inch the average height of the Parisian chorus girl!'

'As a matter of fact – I can!' said George, beginning to enjoy himself. 'They import most of them from England, did you know? Taller girls, you see . . . they can reach eight feet with feathered headdress. Laetitia could audition any day with great success.'

'Watch out, Letty! He'll whip out his tape measure, put it round your head, and declare you brachycephalic or dolichocephalic . . . I never know which is which . . .'

George hurried to correct this flippant assessment of his passion. 'I'm sure Laetitia knows her skull is a delightful, though by no means emphatic, example of the latter, Phoebe. Like yours, like mine. My father offers an example of the former, round-headed variety. Ancient British ancestry, I understand. But I don't, I assure you, categorize and judge everyone by the shape of his head! Don't, Phoebe, present me as a dilettante! There is a point to what I've been doing. I'm preparing a paper which I'm hoping will be taken up by *Nature*, a paper which will have the courage to refute a quite barmy theory – a *dangerous* theory – that's sweeping unchecked through the capitals of Europe. Perhaps you are aware of the National Socialist movement in Germany, Laetitia?'

Startled, Letty dropped her knife, and Gunning on her right silently bent to retrieve it.

But George was not expecting an answer and swept on: 'These thugs – what's the German for "thug", William? – are putting about the theory that there exists in central Europe a race of supermen, descended from a so-called "Aryan" race. Well – fine – they're welcome to entertain us with their vivid imaginings, so long as the rest of the sane world may be allowed to shoot them down with clear evidence that the whole thing is a preposterous invention. But we're not to be allowed that academic freedom if they have anything to do with it – Nazis, they call themselves. And what really sticks in the craw is the inevitable corollary that if one race (of which they claim to be members, though you'd be looking for a long time before you'd spot a blond, blue-eyed giant amongst them) is superior – then all others

44

must be inferior. This rancid theory condemns, by Nazi calculation, nine-tenths of the population to oppression and slavery – to the dustbin of history.'

Theodore coughed a warning. Phoebe wriggled with embarrassment at the outburst she had provoked in her stepson. Politics and passion were jarring notes at this very English dinner table. The swirling intrigues of the European capitals were kept well away from the shores of this sunlit island, Letty observed. Perhaps because it had problems enough of its own.

Gunning lightly defused the tension. 'Fighting oppression with a tape measure! Good man! We must all use whatever weapon comes to hand . . . Miss Talbot, I know, favours a Luger. But have you thought, George, that you could well be applying your skills and insight to a much worthier subject? Ancient Man! Now, I saw being unearthed this afternoon a skull – several skulls – which seemed to me to differ in some respects from the usual run. Long-headed, narrow facial features. Where on earth can they have sprung from? Perhaps tomorrow we might go and take a look?'

The arrival of an orange trifle in an elaborate glass dish further raised the spirits. Theodore looked round the table, gathering murmurs of appreciation, noting that even Letty was spooning her way through the offering with evident enjoyment.

'I fell in love with this dish in London,' he told her genially. 'I was introduced to it by Waldorf Astor. Ah! If I close my eyes I'm transported back to Boodles, looking out over St. James's Park.' He paused, evidently savouring a Proustian moment, eyes half closed but trained on Gunning.

'I think you mean Green Park, Theo. The Club at Number Twenty-four looks out on to Green Park,' said Gunning.

Letty's attention sharpened. Something was going on that she didn't quite understand. Some undercurrent was running between the two men facing each other from

45

opposite ends of the table. It was uncharacteristic of the suave and peaceable Gunning to contradict his host. And both men had got it wrong. You couldn't see either park from Boodles, Letty was quite certain of that. Not when she'd last looked. They were playing a game.

'Yes, of course you're right, William. Very handy for old Waldorf – he and Nancy live quite close by, I remember. Number four, St James's Square. Right-hand side. Wonderful house. Rather distinguished architect involved, I seem to recall . . .?'

'Couldn't tell you who the original seventeenth-century architect was,' Gunning replied placidly, 'but after it burned down it was rebuilt by Hawksmoor. I expect that's the name you're searching for, Theo? Jolly convenient place to park your motor, George, when you're next in London. Plenty of space.'

'You know that charming corner well, William?' Letty said, impulsively feeding him a line. From her research into his past she'd established that he'd been a member of one of the London clubs, though she'd forgotten which.

'Oh, yes! Blindfold, I could lead you from my club – that's the Army and Navy on the north side of Pall Mall (modelled on Sansovino's Palazzo Cornaro, did you know that? – rather overblown for my taste) . . . up St James's Street, across Piccadilly, up Old Bond Street to the Royal Institution of British Architects in Conduit Street. My stamping ground, you could say. Ah! London! Do I miss it? Only when a dish of Boodles Fool triggers a flash of homesickness. Otherwise I'm content to go on lotus-eating. Like you, Theo.'

Suddenly she had it. These two men disliked each other. Their hostility was disguised, transformed into a stately ritual. Not a dance . . . something more sinister – a bullfight! She looked to her left and saw Russell's dark head lowered, thick eyebrows gathering, aggression camouflaged with an interested smile. On her right, his barbs concealed by a cloak of unconcern, Gunning was playing to the crowd, his sword held out of view of victim and audience alike. Only Letty seemed aware of its presence. Only Letty had experienced its sharp edge. And at last she understood the seating around the table. The two opponents were at opposite ends, keeping each other in full view; the boys and the women were on the sidelines as arbiters, chorus, witnesses.

But Letty could not be content to sit by in a passive role. If Gunning had chosen to play matador to Theodore's fighting bull, she would be his picador, diverting attention and deftly sticking in a weakening pic at just the right moment. She recognized that this was not entirely selfless. Instead of the anticipated tears and recriminations of an abandoned woman, William Gunning would find a forgiving and unexpectedly friendly accomplice. Much more disconcerting! And perhaps, in the interests of tormenting him as he deserved, it wouldn't do any harm to pay extravagant attention to young George? She would demonstrate that she was heart-whole, confidence undented. But was George capable of holding up the other end of a flirtation? Letty caught the earnest flash of his grey eyes in the candlelight as he outlined his theory that the Basques of northeastern Spain could be descended from the Eteocretan race and she sighed.

She could swear that the young man hadn't noticed what was clear to everyone around him – that he was the very type of superman he was determined to discredit. There was about him a purity which would surely repel any attempt at romantic intrigue, however lighthearted. If George had called her a sea nymph, it was in poetic response to the clinging green silk confection she was wearing and not in lust for the flesh under it. His remark had been guileless. She had instinctively understood that. Like the *Achilles* statue in Hyde Park, whom he much resembled, she thought, hiding a smile, George Russell commanded attention. But, like that handsome warrior, he carried around with him his own pedestal, his own bronze shield, and his own bronze fig leaf. You could look up and admire, but she was not certain that there was blood coursing through those sculpted limbs. Ah, well, she would try. Any woman would try!

'Letty, can I tempt you to more pudding?' Phoebe asked, at once recapturing her attention and moving the meal along. 'There's the teeniest spoonful left.'

On hearing her acceptance (a polite compliment to Theodore's cooking rather than a desire for a second helping), Phoebe reached across the table towards the trifle dish but her trailing sleeve caught the neck of the bottle of Clos de Vougeot, which tumbled sideways. She gasped in dismay, watching in horror as the burgundy gushed dramatically across the white tablecloth. Dickie made a grab for the bottle and righted it, but the damage was done. All eyes followed as the blood-red trail oozed towards Theodore. All eyes lifted to focus on him. For a moment, Letty had an unaccountable feeling that he was in some odd way gratified by his wife's clumsiness. But she must have been mistaken, she thought, as he rose brusquely to his feet, face expressionless, voice cold.

'Well . . . Dimitri was right – I should have allowed him to use a decanter. Much more stable when there are awkward people about. But – in the modern way, I had thought to impress my guests with the sight of an incomparable label.' He sighed. 'The last of the prewar vintage I had left in my cellar. 1913. I *was* about to call for the cheese to accompany that excellent wine – a particularly good Roquefort – but we can't continue in this mess. Ladies – perhaps you would make your way to the drawing room directly, and gentlemen – we'll join them there for the coffee without delay.'

He made an angry gesture to the footman who had stayed frozen at his post, then he stalked to the door and held it open.

Hardly able to believe that she had witnessed such rudeness, Letty looked around the table for some guidance, unsure how to respond. As the newcomer, and a lady, it was certainly not her place to pick up the épergne and crown her host with it. Dickie and Stewart looked at each other, anxious and embarrassed, then turned to George for a lead.

George was staring, apparently hypnotized by the spreading stain, clenched hands grasping the table edge, lost to them. But not adrift. Across the devastation, Letty sensed a silent and gathering power, an energy just held in check. Watching him, there sounded in her memory the decisive metallic clunk of her brother's Luger as he showed her how to reload. She shivered.

Then she calmed herself. This man was, if she judged him rightly, a pacifist and a son who loved his father. George was not about to challenge Theodore over a wine spill at the dinner table. And yet he was not about to defuse the situation either, it seemed, lost as he was in his own dark thoughts.

Gunning was the first to throw down his napkin. Though it could just as well have been a gauntlet, Letty thought, admiring the panache of the gesture.

'A moment, Theodore,' he said firmly, not deigning to look back at his host, left stamping impatiently at the dining room door, but lightly collecting the attention of everyone still hovering at the table. 'A good meal deserves a good grace, wouldn't you say? Why don't we allow old Horace to give it an appropriate send-off?'

He bowed his head in a parody of the formal manner of a college dean at the conclusion of a dinner in Hall, and, clearly disguising a smile, intoned with clerical gravity:

'*Lusisti satis, edisti satis atque bibisti.*

Tempus abire tibi est.'

While Letty struggled with this, it was Phoebe with her throaty voice who was instantly up to the challenge of a translation. '"You've had your fun. You've eaten and drunk enough. Time to go now."' Dickie tittered nervously; Stewart allowed himself a deprecating smile.

'Phoebe, may I lead you on to the next pleasure?' said Gunning, offering his arm. Smiling up at him, she took it, and, chattering lightly, they went to the door without a glance for Russell. As they passed in front of him, Gunning bent his head to hers, denying her husband the sight of the tears beginning to trace a mascara-tinged course down her cheeks. His hand, as they left the room, was already moving to the pocket in which Letty knew he kept his spare handkerchief.

George came back to his senses and offered to escort Letty from the room. She conveyed what silent comfort she could by squeezing the arm offered and was relieved to feel an answering brief pressure. Unconsciously falling in with her schemes, he settled her in an armchair in the drawing room, kicking up a footstool for himself at her feet. When she refused coffee, pleading insomnia, he rang the bell.

A servant appeared at once. Surprisingly, after the parade of male employees, this was a young woman. Before his father could speak, George addressed her: 'Eleni, the gentlemen will all have coffee, I think?'

Four heads nodded agreement.

'But our guest, Miss Talbot, doesn't care for coffee at this late hour. Can you put together a tisane for her? Something soothing after the day she's had!'

Letty could just make out the woman's response in Greek before George translated for her.

'Dittany!' decided Phoebe. 'Eleni, brew up some dittany. It's extremely soothing. We could all do with something soothing . . . I'll have a cup, too. And you may serve it in the Wedgwood, Eleni.'

'Thank you, I'd like that,' said Letty. 'Though I have to confess I've never heard of dittany.'

'It's a Cretan herb,' said Theodore, rousing himself and stepping in as the authority on all things Cretan. 'Very ancient. Healing. Good for anything from arrow wounds to acid stomach, they claim. The list of curable complaints is endless: insomnia . . . nausea . . . heartache . . . Phoebe finds it invaluable.'

'*Origanum dictamnus* or *erotas* are its local names,' George told her.

'*Erotas?*' said Letty doubtfully. 'I say, does it have qualities an innocent girl should have warning of?'

George laughed. 'Well, you've guessed the root of the word. Yes – Eros, God of Love, but don't worry, it's quite safe. Eros merely makes a post-factum appearance in the rather charming story that goes along with it. Dittany is hard to come by – it's a shy herb that grows in the least accessible crevices of the mountain ranges. The sort of places a wild mountain goat would think twice about attempting. But it's much valued on the island and if a young man is so deeply in love with a girl that he thinks nothing of risking life and limb, he will climb a cliff face and gather a bunch for her. So that's where Eros comes in. It's a *proof* of love, not the cause.

> '*A branch of healing Dittany she brought*
> *Which in the Cretan fields with care she sought . . .*'

The sound of Gunning's voice, reciting John Dryden's translation of Virgil, was tormenting.

> '*Rough is the stem, which woolly leaves surround,*
> *The leaves with flowers, the flowers with purple crowned*
> *Well known to wounded goats, a sure relief*
> *To draw the pointed steel and ease the grief.*

'But have a care, Laetitia!' Gunning wagged a playful finger at her. 'In a bid to "ease the grief" you may find yourself one day in the hills on the point of accepting a gift of herbs from a golden, curly-haired boy. I warn you to take a look at his feet! He may well have cloven hooves!'

Chapter Four

Unable any longer to suppress her yawns, Letty excused herself before the rest of the party seemed ready to break up, making her apologies to Phoebe. Gunning was instantly on his feet, volunteering to light and carry an oil lamp for Letty, and with rather a bad grace she accepted his offer.

He took a lamp from a row on a table in the hall and busied himself with matches and wicks until he was happy with the result. He held it aloft and, passing the other arm through hers, walked her up the stairs talking about and occasionally illuminating the ranks of portraits and seascapes along their way.

The door of her room was already standing open, the flicker of candles dimly to be seen inside. Taking the lamp from him she thanked him briefly, made a play of stifling another yawn, and said good night, closing the door behind her.

As she turned from the door she was startled by a movement in front of the dressing table. Her heart lurched in her chest and she just managed to turn a scream of terror into an embarrassing squeal of surprise.

A dark figure of antiquity stood there, back to her, face reflected in the looking glass, eyes seeking hers. Dark-clad from head to foot, black hair curling down to her waist, the woman raised her arms in the slow stiffness of a cere-monial gesture. Letty recoiled, fearing to see the writhing snakes of a Cretan goddess twining their way about the apparition's arms. A candle guttered, and across the room

Letty caught faintly an ancient scent, a blend of orris root and perspiration. The woman was holding up to her neck not serpents, but a thick golden necklace which gleamed in the soft glow of the two candles set in front of her. The proud and lovely face stared back at Letty in the glass, amused and challenging.

Letty managed to gasp: 'Eleni? It *is* Eleni? How you frightened me!'

Eleni paid no attention, raising and lowering the necklace, head tilted to one side, admiring its effect. Finally she spoke in Greek: 'A beautiful thing! And valuable, I'd say. May I recommend that Mademoiselle does not leave it lying about? The servants are perfectly trustworthy but we have many Europeans through the house.' She put it firmly back into its case, clicked it closed, then handed it to Letty. 'Mrs Russell has a safe in her room. I'm sure for this she will be able to find a corner amongst her pretty things.'

Letty could just about follow, and tried to respond in the same language. 'I'm glad you like it. It was a present from my father. For my twenty-first birthday. A bit modern in design but I'm fond of it . . .' She soon faltered to a halt and filled in with English, which she was pleased to notice seemed to be readily understood. With Letty speaking in English and Eleni in Greek they found they were getting along with ease.

'Mademoiselle retires early? You catch me just finishing putting away the clothes. I have unpacked your things.'

Letty glanced around, noting that her trunk and small Vuitton suitcase had already been removed.

'These . . .' said Eleni, throwing a pile of creased and dirty clothes over her arm, 'will be washed and returned to you in the morning. And what kind of tea would Mademoiselle require on waking?'

Suppressing a giggle at the notion of such a mundane question from a dark figure of mythology, Letty replied, 'Any old English kitchen tea. Whatever you have.'

Eleni smiled, nodded, wished her good night, and let herself out.

Letty sank on to the turned-down bed, still disturbed by the meeting. Her nerves were stretched further by a tap a moment or two later on the door. Without waiting for a reply, Gunning stepped inside.

'Letty, are you all right? I thought I heard you scream?'

'Go away at once!' Letty bristled. 'I might as well be bunking down in Piccadilly Circus! How dare you barge in?'

'I just wanted to –'

'Leave! I'm about to grease my face.'

'It won't take a second –'

'It's not a pretty sight! Go! Now!'

'I have to warn you ... about the goings-on in this household.'

He'd managed to find the only words which would have held her back from ejecting him bodily from her room. Letty could never resist – even in an irritable and exhausted state – the hint of a scandal.

'Leave the door open and stand within a foot of it in plain view of the corridor,' she told him. 'If anyone approaches, you are to say you heard me scream and have dealt with the mouse I surprised under the bed. They do have mice in Crete?'

'They have owls, so I suppose they have mice.'

She took up a position ten feet away from him. 'Yes?' she prompted.

'Letty – you are to trust no one in this house,' he answered in a melodramatic murmur.

'Can't say I was intending to. But you're going to have to speak up, William, if you're intent on playing the Sybil, delivering awful warnings.' She found herself whispering in response to his urgency. 'And perhaps you'd like to explain why you waited five minutes *after* my scream to come to my rescue?' she said, raising her voice slightly. She would *not* be party to his games.

'I listened at the door, heard you talking to Eleni, and lurked in the bathroom next door until she'd left.'

Letty sighed. 'She frightened the life out of me! Does she normally creep about trying on guests' jewellery and fancying herself as Helen of Troy?'

'Eleni doesn't *creep* anywhere,' corrected Gunning. He thought for a moment. 'She glides. In her way, she's the spirit of the house. Nothing happens in it without her knowledge; sometimes I even think – things happen at her instigation. Look, there's information you ought to have . . .'

'I never took you for a gossip, William.'

'I've been here for seven months. It took me a while to work out what's going on and I made some gaffes early on. I'd like to save you the trouble of making the same mistakes.'

'You can fill in my race card, you're saying? A guide to the runners and riders of the House of Russell? Right, then – off you go.'

'I wish you wouldn't be so flippant.'

'Let's start with Eleni, shall we? What a figure! Straight out of the chorus of a Greek tragedy – a Maenad, would you say? Wouldn't much like to run into *her* on a mountainside! She'd shred you as soon as look at you! You'd never guess it to see her, eyes lowered, playing the servant, but with her voluminous pinny discarded, she's all bosom and swelling hips. She's actually beautiful, in a blood-chilling way.'

'You omit to mention the neat waist in between,' he reminded her thoughtfully. 'I had noticed and – I'll tell you – I'm not the only man to be aware of it.' He stirred uncomfortably, shifting his weight from foot to foot.

'Oh, do come in and shut the door. You've had a long day, I'm told. With a nasty surprise at the end of it. You may sit in that chair and rest your poor leg.' Letty knew all too well from experience that the discomfort of Gunning's war wound came and went as he exploited a situation. She pointed to the chair nearest the door and went to stand in front of him. 'Now, what is this nonsense about trusting no one in this house?'

'Eleni came to work here the year following the first Mrs Russell's death.'

'George's mother – Ilse, was it?'

'That's right. Eleni was a girl of fifteen at the time . . .'

'So she's only twenty-eight or so now?' said Letty.

'And became . . . I've no idea at what stage . . . very . . . er . . .' He paused and cleared his throat, '*close* to the master of the house, if you take my meaning. And I believe – still is!'

'Well, I never!' Letty was amused and dismissive. 'So old Theo keeps a servant-mistress, does he? How very Edwardian! And now I see why you dislike him so much, William. No fun to be had by anyone within a hundred yards of Chaplain Gunning, is there?'

'I don't judge people by their sexual peccadilloes or proclivities, Letty. You know that. You observe – rightly – that I have no fondness for the man, but my mistrust springs from quite a different source.'

'But how did you ever find out? These things are usually discreetly managed.'

'Well, I can't say a formal introduction was ever made. One day last summer, newly arrived and not knowing much, I was handed a message at the front door. It was for Eleni from her mother, who lives in a village down the coast. No one about, and the boy who brought it said it was quite urgent. I knew Eleni had rooms over the old coach house, so I set off weaving my way through the back quarters and across the courtyard, envelope in hand. But a kitchen maid spotted me and shouted at me through the window. She came hurrying out, wiping her hands on her apron, and asked where I was going. Bit of a cheek, I thought, but I explained. She snatched the message from me. 'I'll take it,' she insisted. Eleni was not to be disturbed, she informed me. Eleni, she added, was entertaining.

'I was a bit mystified. Some below-stairs jamboree going on? Someone's birthday? No wonder I could find no one about. But there was something about the girl's manner . . . challenging, peremptory, but inwardly laughing at

me . . . I was a bit miffed, to be honest – I hadn't then realized that Cretans, even the lowliest kitchen wench, look
you in the eye and don't have the word 'subservience' in
their vocabulary! So, I lurked – crossly! – and kept an eye
on the girl to be quite certain she delivered the envelope.
She climbed the outer stairs, pushed it under the door, and
hurried away giggling to herself.

'I thought no more of it. Strange Levantine ways, I
decided. Until some weeks later when I'd got a bit of Greek
together, I overheard two of the manservants gossiping.'
Gunning was uncomfortable with this. 'I say, Letty . . . not
deliberately *lurking*, you understand, not on this occasion
. . . I was in the square quietly sketching the Venetian elevation early one morning – the light was wonderful – and
the two blokes came out to smoke a clandestine cigarette –
Phoebe doesn't allow smoking in the house . . . she can't
bear it. Not even Theo's allowed to light his pipe in the
public rooms. In any event – neither man saw me. Their
talk was too colloquial and too salacious for me to catch it
all, but I did gather quite clearly that the housekeeper and
the master were . . . um . . . bracketed together in a sexual
equation,' he finished awkwardly.

'How jolly uncomfortable! Ugh! Fancy being *bracketed*
with Theo! Tell me: Do you think Phoebe *knows* what's
going on under her roof?'

'I've no proof and, of course, one can hardly enquire . . .
but I have a feeling she does.'

'Oh, poor Phoebe! No wonder she's so awfully skinny
and nervy. Looks like a girl in a Dr Williams' Pink Pills for
Pale People advertisement . . . She's lovely but almost
transparent. The ice blue dress she was wearing at dinner
wasn't much help! And she just pushed her food around
her plate. Did you notice? Do you suppose the hurt of her
husband's deception is eating her away?'

'It could be one reason why she hasn't the strength to
retaliate when he puts on a humiliating performance like
the one we've just been treated to.'

'Hmm . . . Whom did he think he was impressing with his victimizing of Phoebe over dinner just now? Why wasn't he firing a rocket at the footman who left the bottle on the table between courses? My father would have laughed, made a joke, and called for a fresh cloth and another bottle – of any vintage. He'd have reprimanded the servant later, perhaps. In private. And why did Phoebe marry such a man anyway?' Letty shuddered. 'He's handsome enough, I suppose, but I think he's deeply unattractive. He's so much older than she is – he must be nearly fifty, wouldn't you say?'

Gunning, all too conscious of his own advancing years, ignored this and said, *'Something's* gnawing at her, I'll agree, and it's grown more acute since she got back from Europe but – funnily – I don't think it's jealousy of Eleni. It's quite extraordinary, but they actually seem very easy together. And as to her reasons for marrying Theo . . . well, he leads a fascinating and involving life here, and he has many powerful and interesting friends. Phoebe plays hostess to some glittering people – crowned heads of Europe, stars of the silver screen, opera singers – they're all entertained here at the Europa. She has a diplomatic background – she's used to that sort of thing. And – though I recognize it's not *your* style, Letty – you who are known to appreciate the slim, cerebral type of man – some women do fall victim to that rather obviously masculine allure. She is herself a . . .' He hesitated, then finished firmly, 'very feminine lady . . . warm, responsive, pliant, and loving.'

'You mean she'd never be caught dead on a suffragette march or whacking someone over the head with a shovel? Well, you'd have to be – pliant, did you say? – to survive marriage to *that* man.' Letty recalled the man's callous treatment of his wife over dinner.

'You're too hasty, Letty. I've seen some quite surprisingly eminent ladies fawning over Theo! Rather an embarrassing scene last autumn when the Countess of . . . sorry! I'm confirming your accusation of tittle-tattling! He has rather a barbaric beauty, in fact. Stick him in a red silk caftan, touch of kohl around the eyes, and he could understudy for Feodor Chaliapin playing Ivan the Terrible, don't you think?'

'You don't mention his wealth?'

He hesitated, reaching automatically in his indecision to tug at a moustache that had disappeared months before. 'That's because I have no evidence that it exists. In fact I have evidence clearly to the contrary.'

'More eavesdropping, William? You can hardly expect the man to make you privy to his bank accounts! He does pay you, I suppose? Well, then . . . Wait a moment,' said Letty, collecting her thoughts together through her fatigue. 'Phoebe said something about . . . spending pots of Theo's money in Paris. Yes, she did. Rather dragged it into the conversation, I thought. Establishing that her husband isn't without a bob or two.'

'That would be like Phoebe. She makes it her business to provide a respectable cover for the man . . . whatever his enterprise. She has a good deal of money of her own. She wouldn't need to spend his. But I'm not so sure about Theo. And I have this from his son, no less. Information openly confided! George is very . . . unworldly. He's not mesmerized by money as the rest of the world seems to be. He's aware of its uses and he spends whatever he can lay hands on, but it's not a god for him and it's not something to discuss in an undertone in corners as the rest of us do. He'll not try to disguise the cost of that dear little motorcar –'

'He hasn't! I was shocked at his revelation!'

'In any event, George confided in me – discussing the Great Work his father's about to launch – that Theo is funding the publishing of the book entirely out of his own pocket. He's been covering the costs of his archaeological work for years and you and I both know archaeology's an expensive business for an amateur. In this world, you have to make a splash if you're to get anywhere . . . and Theo has much to make up for. At least he'd see it that way.'

'What do you mean? The man doesn't give the impression of inferiority of any sort.'

'Perhaps not. But Theo is acutely conscious that his background lacks polish – he could have done with a better grounding in the classics had he only known that, relatively late in life, he was going to be bitten by the bug of excavation. Evans – the man he clearly sees as his rival – was fluent in ancient Greek and Persian from a very early age *and* inherited a fortune from both sides of the family. If you're perceived to be well off in this little world, public funds are simply not available to you, however deserving and important your project. Poor old Sir Arthur discovered this. Evans had to sell his collection of coins and seal stones last year to make ends meet, having spent the family fortune on Knossos over the years. He doesn't even own the site any longer – or the Villa Ariadne, did you know?'

Letty nodded. 'It was in *The Times* last year. With typical generosity, he made them both over to the British School in Athens. A grand gesture by a grand old man.'

'Mmm . . .' said Gunning thoughtfully, 'and the news burst on a grateful world one day before his court case came up before the judge at the Old Bailey!'

'All a silly mistake, I'm sure,' retorted Letty briskly. 'And it's grudging of you to bring it up.'

'Come on! Evans was caught fair and square, hand in hand with a boy hawker in Hyde Park! The lad was seventeen and it wasn't apples he was hawking! Now – each to his own entertainment – but the timing of Evans's gift was interesting! But I make the point that excavation devours money. It demands tribute with the regular appetite of a Minotaur. Expenses have to be met – digging teams paid, officials bribed, artisans engaged . . . Have you any idea what Theo's paying *me*!'

'More than your qualifications would justify, even if it's tuppence ha'penny,' she said bitterly, and instantly regretted her pettiness. 'So – you're saying that this life

Theo supports on the island may be due to the generosity of his wife?'

'It could be. She inherited a fortune from her maternal grandmother before her marriage to Theo and another one from a doting old uncle last year.'

'How do you know all this, William? Oh, don't tell me!' she added quickly. 'You put on your confessional face and make sympathetic noises.'

He grinned. 'I can fool anyone but you, Letty. But I don't feel in the least bit guilty – Phoebe really needs someone to listen to her. Someone to be frivolous with. Someone to confide in. Though she's stubbornly loyal and I can only guess at her thoughts through her silences sometimes. I have the highest regard for her, Letty. She's a lovely girl. She could have chosen anyone. Theo can be charming, though he grows less so over time, I suspect. But five years ago, Phoebe married him and that, for me, silences all criticism. He was her choice and she's by no means a silly woman.'

'The most intelligent of my sex are occasionally capable of making a disastrous error of judgement,' observed Letty lightly.

He ignored her. 'So – one has to conclude that she loves the old blighter and not only provides the wherewithal for his hobby but presents to the world the flummery that he is the one with the moneybags.'

'Well, it seems to me that if what you say is true, all concerned are getting exactly what they want out of the situation,' said Letty. 'I think you can come off watch, William, put your knitting away and stop worrying.'

Gunning exclaimed with exasperation, 'You silly girl! You walk headfirst into a hornets' nest and say: "What a pretty buzzing!" There's something alive and growing here, something malicious, and I don't want *you* to be involved with it. You know what you're like, Letty! "Nasty, forward minx!" You meddle. Tragedy follows you around, and you won't need to whistle to find it snapping at your heels in this house. I'm anxious for you, can't you understand that?'

He held out his hands to her in some kind of appeal and, responding to words he had left unspoken, she moved forward to take them in hers.

'William, I haven't forgotten your concerns for me last year. I'll always be grateful. Truly. But,' she squeezed his hands encouragingly and released them, 'you're off duty now. Free of me. No need to worry.'

'Listen, Letty. No – *really* listen! I want you to promise me to take up at once and with no argument the offer Theo will make you very shortly. Whatever it is and wherever it is – just go off and get on with it. He's got several excavations on the go all over the island, and if I read him right he'll pick out one of little importance for you – a site that you can't possibly make a mess of – and send you off to it with a map clutched in your hand. Just pack your trowel and go. Distance yourself.'

Letty peered at him, searching his face in the glimmering candlelight. Why was he here, stirring up emotions she thought she had buried? This intrusion into her evening was trumped-up . . . unnecessary. And then the reason for his anxiety struck her. 'Ah! What you're really trying to say is, "Stay out of *my* hair," isn't it? "Distance yourself from *me*." Well, that presents no difficulty, as far as I'm concerned, but there's something else, I'm guessing . . . Are you going to tell me what's troubling you, William?'

'Not yet. No. I'm not about to voice suspicions that I can't back up with evidence. I'll just say, for the moment, that I'm uneasy, and the source of my unease is the volatile nature of the relationships between the characters in this house. There's a sort of tense balance at the moment – a balance that could be broken by someone stepping in with a clumsy insouciance.'

'Ah. Do I recognize myself entering, stage left?'

'Sorry! You're actually a breath of fresh, familiar air and I welcome it. But I'm not sure the troubled souls that flit about this place can take the glare of your sunny common sense.'

A banging door and the sound of laughter below alerted him. 'The party's breaking up. I'll creep down the back stairs and make myself scarce.'

He got to his feet and they stared at each other, unable to embark on further or deeper matters.

'Remember the mouse if you get caught,' she whispered unnecessarily. 'I'm quite certain I really did hear one earlier . . . scratching about somewhere . . .' She found she was not quite ready, at the last, to let him go.

He opened the door, looking up and down the corridor, then turned to her, smiling. 'I offer you a couple of lines I came across in *Medea* the other day: "*A man and a woman working in harmony, together make an invincible stronghold.*" Good night, Letty.'

'Good night, William. I'll see you on the battlements.'

Chapter Five

All the church bells of Herakleion were ringing out an imperious call to service on Sunday morning, as Letty guiltily stayed in her seat at the breakfast table and accepted a second cup of coffee. 'Ignore them,' Phoebe had told her. 'I'll take you to Evensong instead.'

The second summons was not so easily ignored. Theodore required the students to attend him in the library immediately after breakfast. All three leapt up and set off at once, Letty following the boys along to a spacious room on the ground floor at the rear of the house. The doors were standing open on a large courtyard, green with citrus trees and roses, and dotted with classical statuary. It was to this scene, unexpected in the centre of the city, that Letty's gaze was drawn. She was quite certain that the marble figure she caught a glimpse of was Artemis the Virgin Huntress, almost life-sized and playfully half hidden behind foliage. She was entertained to see that the goddess's extended, booted left foot and, likewise, her arrow, were pointing directly across the garden at the smooth bosom of an Aphrodite. The target, all gleaming, over-abundant curves, was standing in a clear patch of sunlight, admiring herself in a looking glass, oblivious to the threat from her sister lurking behind the laurel. Between the two, mocking their grace, stood a squat, rough-carved stone image of Dionysos. The God of Wine, drunken mouth open and carelessly about to shout out a secret, leered madly, his wild hair tangled about a crown of vine leaves.

In spite of the obvious care someone had taken to set out the garden, Letty found she had no instinctive urge to step into it and enjoy it.

Hesitating in the doorway, she looked about her at the library, admiring the coolly purposeful room, its walls lined with bookshelves, the centre occupied by a generous number of tables and chairs. A communal room if ever she saw one, and she calculated that Theodore Russell most probably had his own private retreat elsewhere in the large house. The lectern in pride of place, bearing an open copy of the first of Arthur Evans's volumes on his discoveries at Knossos, was sending out a sly message, she thought, and she smiled.

'There you are! Don't stand about – come in! Good breakfast? Phoebe look after you all right, did she? Good. Good. William and I have been hard at it since five o'clock,' Theodore announced. Looking at the self-satisfied pair, each with shirtsleeves rolled up, discovered bending amicably over the largest of the tables, Letty could well believe it. The two men appeared to be examining a map extended over the table and held down at the corners with potsherds.

'Now – who've we got?' Russell made a quick roll call: 'Stewart, Dickie, and Laetitia. Step forward, Laetitia, and look at this! It's your itinerary we're planning, miss. Crete not well served by map-makers, I'm afraid. Captain Spratt had a go in . . . when was it, William? 1865? And made a remarkably good fist of it – for his time. But not adequate for this day and age. What you see before you . . .' They crowded round to inspect the paper patchwork in front of them. '. . . is the culmination of my own attempts to pin down this mysterious island and reduce its four majestic dimensions to a simple – two.'

He waved a hand over the map, portions of which seemed to be printed, others hand-drawn and coloured, yet others blank. 'Underpinning all this are old Admiralty charts from before the War. Out of date when I made off with them, but I've personally sailed around and hiked across the island and made many corrections and additions.'

'Mr Russell, I can identify two dimensions,' said Letty, trying for an alert student's voice, eagerness just in control. 'Length – one hundred and fifty miles, width – thirty miles on average. But the other two . . .?'

'Height, of course, nitwit!' burst from him and, for a moment, Laetitia felt herself accepted. Russell recollected himself and went on in a more moderate tone, 'Even from your first view from the harbour –' he pointed to Herakleion – 'you can't have failed to notice the mountains. They run the length of the island, sticking up like the backbone of a donkey, and human life here has always had to seek out its niches in the interstices. River valleys, plateaux wherever Nature has created them, coastline, of course, but it's not a country that opens its arms to settlers.'

'And yet they came and continue to come,' remarked Gunning. 'It's a stepping-stone between three continents. Down here to the south you've got Egypt and Libya, to the north and west is Europe, and to the north and east is Asia Minor. And here, at the hub, caught between these widely different and vibrant cultures, is Crete. We don't know where the first inhabitants came from – George is in pursuit with his measuring sticks – but we do know that the very earliest remains of Stone Age Man are to be found using the shelter of the thousands of caves scattered all over the island –'

'Which brings us to the fourth dimension,' Russell interrupted. 'Time! And again – this goes deep and is difficult to measure. You are about to embark on the most stimulating and worthwhile study available to an archaeologist: no less than revealing to the world one of its earliest and most attractive civilizations. It was here, Laetitia,' he tapped a hairy knuckle over a red spot on the map which she had already identified as Knossos, 'in the Palace of King Minos that mankind learned to dance and sing and feast, to worship the Mother Goddess and Nature herself in peace and plenty; where he learned to respond to the beauty around him by recording his brilliant culture in the most glorious works of art of the ancient world ... or of any world.'

Enjoying the rapt attention of his audience, he strolled to a glass-fronted cupboard and took out an object which he brought back to the table cradled in his large hands. He set it down in front of Laetitia and waited to hear her murmurs of awe and appreciation. Into her silence he said encouragingly, 'Four thousand years ago, a Minoan artist carved in ivory the image of his Goddess. And here she is.'

The nine-inch-high figurine was carved from elephant tusk, making skilful use of the natural curvature of the material to convey the proud, stiff, slightly backwards-leaning stance of the Mother Goddess – or was this her priestess? She wore a high castellated crown and her long hair fell to her shoulders. Her skirt was flounced, the tiers edged with gold, and around her narrow waist could just about be made out a ceremonial apron. Her upper body was naked apart from thick golden bracelets on her upper arms. Downwards from her elbows wound more strips of gold which, on reaching her forward thrusting hands, reared up suddenly as snakes' heads, tongues flicking out aggressively. The Lady's expression was undimmed by aeons under the earth, still speaking to her worshippers.

Worshippers amongst whom she could clearly count Dick and Stewart. Their eyes never left the delicate figure, held firmly in Theodore's hands.

'I say ... may I?' Letty breathed.

'Of course.'

As she made to gather up the figure, Letty caught a nervous movement from Gunning; his lips tightened and he looked hastily away. To other onlookers, this was the nervous reaction of a man steeling himself to watch a woman he does not trust about to handle a precious object, but Letty knew the man and thought otherwise. Consciously or not – she could not be certain – he was sending her a warning.

With due reverence she lifted the ivory piece and looked at it closely, holding it firmly by its wide base and steadying it with one gentle finger atop its head as she'd been taught.

All four men waited for her response.

Her inspection complete, she turned the statuette upside down and peered at the base. She sighed.

'Ah. Yes. There it is: *Made in Athens*. I feared so. It's quite lovely, Mr Russell, but I hope you didn't pay more than ten guineas for it?'

She turned with a bright smile to the students. 'Not the work, sadly, of a Minoan Michelangelo but an Athenian craftsman – one of the Constantidis brothers, perhaps? There's a workshop just off Syntagma Square, where you can pick up wonderfully convincing . . . um . . . replicas.' Her voice trailed away encountering their shocked disapproval.

Dick broke the frozen silence. 'But it *doesn't* say . . . Oh, I see! She's joking! Laetitia – you m . . . m . . . mistake this!' He went on earnestly, crippled with embarrassment for her gaffe: 'I assure you – it is indeed a genuine antique. Excavated at a palace site fifty miles from here. If you would care to take a second look, you'll see that the ivory is worn away exactly as you'd expect in an object thousands of years old. Let me pass you a magnifying glass.'

'And the whole posture,' Stewart attacked from the left, 'is so typically Minoan . . . so familiar from wall paintings . . . the details of the dress so well observed . . . can we be surprised that the leading authorities on the island have all authenticated this particular figure? But perhaps we should now discount the expertise of the Germans, the Italians, the French, and the Americans, for here is Miss Talbot, freshly arrived, to set us all straight. Oh, dear! Gentlemen, I fear we've all been paying tribute to a *false* goddess!'

Letty felt her cheeks reddening. She looked about her for support or understanding but saw only male antagonism, dislike, scorn. Sympathy was the best Gunning could offer before he looked away. She felt herself surrounded and alone. *Only one thing to do, Letty!* Her brother's voice came back to her as he'd tried to explain to his little sister the tactics he used in aerial combat over Flanders. Three-dimensional pieces of choreography – however complicated, his manoeuvres always seemed to end with the same war cry: *À l'attaque!* John, she was certain, would have been yelling just that when his solitary De Havilland had run into a squadron of Fokkers. In late September 1915, with the war in the air still in its early stage of chivalrous combat, the German authorities had graciously returned his remains, and the leader of the enemy squadron had sent a letter saying that the lone Englishman had managed to shoot down four of his fighters in his suicidal attack before succumbing to a hail of machine-gun bullets.

À l'attaque! it was, then, since the enemy was massing and there was no safe way back to base. Laetitia's chin went up, her eyes narrowed, and she smiled a smile involving everyone in the room, assessing the strengths of her targets. Her brother would have picked off the weakest first.

'I'll answer your objection first, Dick, since it's the one most easily refuted by scientific – indeed, forensic – evidence.' Her forefinger trailed gently over the pitted surface of the ivory. 'Yes, I agree it looks as though it's been buried for centuries, but this process of decay can be simulated, speeded up, you know. Immersion in a jar of acid of the correct dilution will do the trick. A quick treatment, but somewhat crude and easily detectable. I understand the really professional way to do this, for those prepared to invest more of their time in the operation, is to bury the carving in the back garden and have the male members of the family urinate over the spot. It takes about a year. I think we have an example of such dedicated professionalism before us.'

'Oh, I say!' Dick could not find words to express his distress at her unladylike language.

'And Stewart's objection . . .' She placed the goddess on the table and, lining herself up with the figure, struck the same ceremonial pose: shoulders down, chest out, hands extended as if in protest. 'A fair copy, though any man with a working knowledge of a woman's anatomy will see at once the difference between the truly ancient version and this twentieth-century artist's view. The *breasts*, gentlemen!'

In confusion, four pairs of eyes shot to the safer target of the bosom carved in ivory.

'Minoan bosoms are high and rounded and virginal – think of apples – and they are well corseted. In the genuine museum pieces I've seen in Athens and Oxford and here in Herakleion yesterday, the lady is wearing a tight-fitting laced bodice with set-in sleeves. In the statuette before us you can see that the model used is rather . . . um . . . mature. And the artist, apparently uninspired by – or perhaps uninformed as to – the fashions in bodices has chosen to omit the garment completely. The unrestrained flesh produces the effect I observe you are now judging afresh. Pears rather than apples, are you thinking?'

Throats were cleared, feet were shuffled. Someone – Theo – snorted in disgust.

'And where is her pinafore?' If she was being tested, she'd give them both barrels in reply. 'It forms an indispensable part of the Minoan priestess's wardrobe, but here is merely suggested in a sketchy way. Could that be because a modern eye sees a pinny as a degrading, housewifely garment? Better left out of the design. And three tiers to the skirt? Wouldn't we have looked for seven?'

Her audience peered with renewed interest at the figurine.

'And the face?' she continued. 'The lady is quite lovely! An angel from a Gothic cathedral perhaps? A Byzantine Madonna? Next month's cover girl on *Vogue* magazine? Any of those. What these features are saying to me – a woman – is: This is no snake goddess. The faces of the genuine ones always strike me with awe and – yes – horror. You wouldn't want to have one on your bedside table! They are recognizably human and female but they convey no emotion I can understand. They are wide-eyed yet inward-looking, brutal, unapproachable. From another age. But this face is one I feel I know. The English mistress I had a crush on? That's it! It's Miss Carstairs saying: "Oh, come now, Letty! Do stop chattering!"'

'We are not the first to suffer, then,' Theodore rasped sarcastically. 'But we must thank you, miss, for sharing with us your female and sartorial insights. Could the editress of the Butterick Pattern Book have spoken with greater authority on flounces and sleeve settings? I doubt it. Will you put the lady back in the cupboard, William? And then, let us study the archaeological highlights of the island on the map.'

'It's a bit like a gold rush,' Dick explained to Letty. 'All the nations interested have set up national Schools of Archaeology in Athens and each supports its prospectors on the ground. Sir Arthur wasn't the first to dig at Knossos, you know. Lots of people had their eye on it – it was well known in local legend to be the spot where Minos had ruled in antiquity, and there was a local man – a Cretan – funnily enough I believe his name was *Minos* . . .

'Kalokairinos,' supplied Gunning. 'Minos Kalokairinos.'

'That's right. Thank you, Will. And this chap had been digging up all sorts of impressive stuff before Evans stepped off the boat. The old man was actually obliged to buy up the whole site in 1900 to get his hands on the excavation rights. Schliemann himself had been sniffing around, I understand. I suppose the world was lucky that the man who got ultimate control of it was a man of erudition and experience.'

'As well as of resources and connexions,' Gunning added. 'A man's reputation can rise or fall in an hour according to the whim or preference of a newspaper editor these days.'

Russell heard him and turned his comment into a challenge for Letty: 'I'm quite certain our Laetitia, modern young miss that she is, is already a skilled manipulator of the Gentlemen of the Press.'

'I think we all learned lessons when the Howard Carter Circus came to town,' said Letty quietly. 'Young King Tutankhamen was fortunate indeed to be unearthed by an excavator who knew how to secure the attention of editors on both sides of the Atlantic.'

'Unless, of course, the Pharaoh would have preferred to continue his sleep of centuries,' Dick suggested.

'Oh, come off it, Dickie!' said Stewart. 'No place for sentimentality in modern archaeology! You have to admire the skill with which it was all presented to the world – the drama, the flashlights, the wonderful artefacts, and all that nonsense about the curse! Showmanship, I dare say, but very effective!'

'And, contemporary with that civilization, and no less wonderful,' said Theodore, approving, 'here we are at the heart of the realm of Minos. The Palace of Knossos.' He pointed to the map. 'There are palaces, villas, and towns scattered all over the habitable parts of this island, but it is at Knossos that you ought to start your studies.'

Everyone nodded agreement.

'So I'd like you to begin, Laetitia, by taking the rest of the day off to go there and get your eye in. It's only a mile or two up the road – you can walk, though I recommend a donkey. Not many roads in Crete, you'll find, and the ones we have are damn dangerous. Can't imagine why that son of mine would bother to bring a motorcar here! There are fewer than fifty miles of metalled road available to him. Old Evans has a sort of glorified cocktail-bar with engine by Royce that he uses to impress his distinguished guests, ferrying them between the port and the Villa Ariadne. And there they run out of road. Everyone else gets about using the ancient track ways. Most of them laid down by the Minoans themselves. When you get to Knossos you should introduce yourself to the folk at the Villa Ariadne before you start poking about. You'll be expected. It's all laid on. There'll be people from the British School there but you won't be received by the great man – Sir Arthur is not in residence at the moment. He was there last year and plans to return, but his digging days are running out. He's approaching eighty, after all ... One must expect it.' A note of triumph gave the lie to the sighing sympathy in his voice.

'Now observe! The road past Knossos – just keep going along the Arkhanais road ...' Letty eagerly followed his pencil. 'And after a few more miles you come to the village where you're going to be based during the digging week – Kastelli. And it's here that your own excavation will be carried out. At weekends you will of course return here to us at the Europa. Lots of social events staged for you, I understand from Phoebe. Can't tell you how pleased she is that she's to have some female company in the house.' Had a trace of puzzlement crept into his voice? 'And after five days of roughing it out there in the country you'll be dying to get back. I'm starting you off with a small but skilled digging team – my best men. You will have under your direction eight diggers as your first team, plus any extras you may require to be recruited in the village.

'The foreman of your team is a Cretan – Aristidis. *Kapitan* to his men! He comes from the village so he's well known locally. Middle-aged and thoroughly reliable. Safe pair of hands. He speaks excellent English and will act as inter-preter as well as go-between for you and the diggers. Aristidis's enthusiasm for the sport and his ... shall we say, candour? ... you'll find, are the equal of your own, miss.'

He paused, his expression speculative and mischievous. He appeared to think better of pursuing his entertaining thought and continued briskly: 'Now ... we come to the selection of your team members.'

Letty noticed that the other men had fallen very still in anticipation of his next announcement.

'You'll be needing another European to accompany you. As your Deputy Director.'

Glances were shot from side to side, wondering, she guessed, who had drawn the short straw.

'I've decided that William would be the perfect choice. He can photograph and sketch any finds you may make, and his Greek is really rather good. Besides which, he it is who has been most closely concerned with the project development.'

Dick and Stewart sighed in unison. Gunning out-sighed them both.

'So – that's me, Mr Gunning, and Aristidis. And do you have a task for your three musketeers?' Letty asked.

'Four musketeers, in fact,' he said mysteriously. 'You will meet the fourth on arrival in the village. And – yes, indeed – I have a task. A plum! A gem! Do you see this mountain, Laetitia? It's quite close to Kastelli . . . an easy walk to what you might call the foothills – the lower slopes.'

'That's Juktas, isn't it? I saw it from the coast.'

'That's right. Juktas – the holy mountain, sacred to Zeus. Now, there has been a little sporadic, halfhearted digging done up there – a peak sanctuary exposed – and Arthur himself walked around surveying the area a year or two ago. From his reconnaissance he concluded that there were distinct possibilities. Things move slowly in Crete, I must warn you, Laetitia, and there are rules – stoutly upheld – and these William will be able to fill you in on – concerning digging by foreigners or natives and the disposal of finds. Written permission has to be obtained and all that. Thinking ahead, I obtained the requisite bits of paper allowing us to excavate a particular site on the slopes of Juktas. The whole legal procedure was greatly eased and speeded by the kind offices of Aristidis, whose farming family seems to own a large slice of the mountain.'

Gunning passed him a file and he selected a sheet of paper. 'I've drawn up and had traced for you a map of the area, marking on the exact location of the proposed dig. Matter of fact, I was up there last month, thinking and planning, assessing possibilities and, poking about as one does, I came across this . . .'

He felt in his pocket and, with a flourish, placed a small object in front of her.

'What do you make of this? Should numismatics not be your forte, Laetitia – there must be, after all, some limit to your areas of expertise – we can help you.'

She looked dubiously at the tiny coin, turning it this way and that, suspecting another trick.

'I've never seen such a one before,' she said. 'I can tell you it's not a Minoan seal . . . It's not even ancient . . . At a guess, I'd say it was Italian . . . Renaissance . . . so it would be safest to hazard . . . Florentine.'

'Close. Well done. It is in fact Venetian.'

He savoured her puzzlement and gave a slight smile. 'You're wondering what on earth a single Venetian coin has to do with a Minoan excavation? Think of the coin you hold in your hand as the end of the ball of thread that led Theseus into the heart of the Labyrinth where lurked the Minotaur – half man, half bull, wholly monster. This is where you begin. You have there, in that coin, a clue which will lead you back through the mists of Time. There you will solve a mystery that has tantalized travellers in this land since Antiquity. If all goes well, you will be the last in a glorious succession of historical researchers! Let me enumerate: Callimachus in the fourth century BC describes his quest; Ennius a hundred years later gives us the precise location; Cicero, Diodorus Siculus, Saint Paul . . . all laid a trail, and on to the Venetian explorers, one of whom left behind this evidence of his presence at the site. Along with precise details of its location. One only has to have faith and follow them, and the name of Miss Laetitia Talbot will be added to the scroll in the twentieth century.'

'Good Lord!' breathed Stewart. 'Sir, you can't mean . . .?'

'I do indeed. On Crete we're all familiar with the folk tale . . .' Theodore looked around him, and all except Letty nodded sagely. 'But is it merely a fable? Or, as Schliemann was to discover at Troy – is it a historical fact, cocooned in legend and buried deep, awaiting discovery? I refer, of course, to the Tomb of Zeus!'

75

His announcement was greeted with awed silence. No one looked in her direction. Theodore continued with the careful precision of a stalking cat: 'It's a notion I find rather piquant: that here, in this goddess-worshipping island, the stripling upstart god of the place, the Cretan Zeus, so long buried, should be resurrected by a woman.'

'A sort of Sleeping Beauty in reverse,' Stewart remarked. 'How are your kisses, Miss Talbot? Potent enough to wake the Thunder God?'

Chapter Six

Left alone in the library with Gunning with instructions to 'familiarize herself with the topography of the target area,' Letty listened to the footsteps receding down the corridor and heard the sudden release of male guffaws as they rounded the corner. She knew their laughter was at the expense of Gunning and, judging by the slight tightening of his shoulders, so did he. The other three were calculating his chances of surviving a season in the company of this arrogant girl who found ignorance no handicap to ambition. They watched each other steadily, Letty waiting for the familiar caustic sideswipe, but he didn't even wag an admonishing finger.

So it was she who broke the uncomfortable silence: 'The British School has a hostel for students somewhere near the harbour. They rent out rooms. Get me their address, will you, William, and I'll make arrangements to transfer myself and my things there as soon as I can,' she said calmly. 'I will not stay another night under that man's roof.'

'Your initial opinion of our host has not improved, I see?'

'It has not! What's the matter with the Cretans – reputedly such swashbuckling bandits – that they've left him alive so long? I can't put up with his nonsense for another day. So condescending! Does he reserve all that "Mists of Time over this Land of Antiquity" rubbish just for me?'

Gunning laughed. 'I had noticed he turns on the grandiloquence for you. It has the effect of setting you at a distance and marking you out.'

'A target, you mean?'

He shrugged. 'That would be going too far, I think. But you're certainly not treated to the peremptory naval tone he takes with the rest of us. I'd say he doesn't like you any more than he likes me.'

'But he speaks highly of you, William.'

'He'd never admit to making a poor choice. All his geese are swans – apart from you, of course. And I've helped him through a stressful time – got him out of a tight corner, dash it! But that's no reason to expect his genuine regard. My work here is really done. I had been waiting for him to pack me off back to England but then he unexpectedly renewed my contract. Actually increased my salary. And now I discover why!'

'Recompense for riding herd on the brash new arrival? Sending you off into the hills with me and getting rid of two uncongenial people at a stroke. Poor William! Fate, it seems, has it in for you – lurking around the corner to cosh you a second time? How unkind! But, you must have got to know the man well? You seem very close, at least when you're working . . . Tell me: Why is he obsessed with testing me? So unnecessary! It's not a struggle I can win.'

'But you mistake him, Letty! He wasn't trying you out just now.'

'Good gracious! You're not saying he really thinks that little figure is genuine?'

'He does. But so do several experts in the field. I'm not one of them! Stewart was overcaustic perhaps, but he spoke the truth. May I ask you, Letty, what made you so certain of your extraordinary analysis? Quite a surprise, your demonstration – illustrated as it was by a most entertainingly produced side-elevation! Dickie, for one, will never again be able to tooth a Cox's Pippin without a blush.'

'I just knew it wasn't right. Even before I held it. Difficult to say why.'

'You didn't seem to have any problems justifying your judgement?'

'I've spent the last six weeks in Athens undergoing a crash course on Minoan civilization with Andrew Merriman. He recommended me to Russell – he wanted to take no chances I was going to let him down. Andrew has many good friends there – professionals and amateurs – all experienced and all happy to talk to me on their favourite subject. And he didn't neglect my practical training.'

'I'm sure Merriman was thorough in all aspects of your instruction,' said Gunning coldly.

'I've been to museums and private collections – cabinets of curiosities have creaked open for me! I've been to excavations but also to goldsmiths and jewellers, forgers' workshops ... I've seen such things, William! Wonderful but alarming! I'm not sure I'd accept anything as genuine unless I'd turned it up with my own spade. When the reproductions are skilfully done and the materials used are not subject to decay – like gold and gemstones – well ... the only thing you can go by is intuition inspired by your own knowledge and sense of style. But it's never sufficient to say to a man, 'I've made my mind up in a second and I'm sure I'm right. Just believe me.' You have to go through the business of counting tiers and testing for tea stains. A useful lesson I learned from Andrew.'

'I trust you were adequately chaperoned for your forays into the Athenian backstreets?'

'Isn't that a bit stuffy – even for you, William?' she retorted. 'One has to be more circumspect than in London, of course, and I never went out alone. Andrew was usually available – I stayed with him and Mrs Merriman. They'd taken a house on the Lykkavettos.'

'Oh – Maud was there, was she? I'm surprised to hear she'd made the journey ... Athens? Not the place one might expect her to choose to spend the winter. How was she bearing up?'

'Her usual self. Getting better slowly; ensuring everyone around her suffered the effects of her mysterious condition. Do you know her?'

'I stayed with them in London last summer.'

'So that's where you went! Andrew didn't mention it. What an extraordinary thing to do –'

'Listen, Letty!' He seemed suddenly anxious to turn her back to her original request. 'I can tell you where the student hostel is, of course, but . . . this is a little difficult . . . surely you or your father has already – I'm guessing now – *invested* a certain sum in this venture? Can you afford to turn about and run for home before you've even got started?'

'Oh, come on – say what you mean, William! My father has *paid* for me to be here. He's donated funds to the Cretan-British Exploration Society, and some of this grate-fully received cash has doubtless made its way sideways into the pocket of Theodore Russell, who happens to be the Society's chairman. He makes no mention of it, naturally, but silently acknowledges the transaction by offering hospitality and underwriting the dig he's dreamed up for me. The knowledge that I'm funding this little jaunt prob-ably annoys him like anything, if what you have to tell me is true. But that's the way things are done in this world. I know the system. I use the system,' she said repressively. 'Oh, hello, Phoebe! We were just . . .'

Phoebe swept into the room bringing with her the sudden light of a summer morning. 'Theo told me I'd find you here, plotting and planning. I've just been hearing about your project. And you're off to the palace? How wonderful!'

She seemed invigorated by the sunshine – even her clothes suggested a renewed confidence: daffodil-coloured blouse tucked into black divided riding skirt and shining black boots. Her fair hair was freshly washed, fluffing up in an unruly way and lightly scented with lilies and sandalwood. 'It's going to be a warm afternoon. I thought we could have a picnic among the ruins. And, Laetitia, I've had another good idea – why don't we find George and ask him to lend us his car? Can you drive it, do you think? I should so enjoy swanning up to the Ariadne in a Bugatti!'

Letty was intrigued to see that she had dared to put on makeup even on a Sunday – the cheekbones were delicately rouged, the sweet mouth slightly reddened. All this for her benefit? Surely not? Phoebe's face was animated and clever, Letty realized in the sharp light of morning. Not elfin – there was too much mischief bubbling in the sideways glances. A sprite, Letty decided.

Phoebe turned her attention to Gunning. 'I don't know, William, if you were planning to spend the afternoon marching Laetitia round the site? I bet you were! Every inch of every level explained in precise order and in exhaustive detail . . . Oh, essential, of course – I know that – but she has all the time in the world to study the place. I thought today she should just be at leisure to enjoy it. To sit on the stones in the sun like a lizard . . . sniff the mimosa and the rosemary and dream a bit. No notebooks allowed! No guidebooks! In any case, you'd need to hire a spare donkey to cart that around with you!' She pointed a dismissive finger at Evans's thick *The Palace of Minos. Vol 1.* 'What do you say, Laetitia?'

Letty was instantly caught up by her gaiety. 'That's just exactly what I'd like! I can drive the Bugatti – yes. And there's just about room for a small hamper aboard. But do you really think George will let us take it? You know how possessive men can be about their motorcars.'

'Don't worry – George wouldn't refuse me,' Phoebe said with a slight smile.

'Then I'd better change my outfit,' Letty said doubtfully. 'Sunday picnic in tricky terrain . . .?'

'Desert boots rather than parasol, my dear,' advised Phoebe firmly. 'This is Crete, not Birdcage Walk.'

'Slow down! Slow down or you'll miss it! There's the carriage drive on your right. You go up between the pine trees,' Phoebe shouted and pointed.

They'd driven through the narrow bazaars of Herakleion and past the museum, joining the southern road where it wound down through the old moat and breached the ramparts. After a short halt at the gates for Phoebe to dole out a handful of coins to the flock of beggars who gathered around the car, they chugged on through untidy straggles of houses and out into open country. The recent rain seemed to have settled the dust; the driving was proving not to be the challenge Letty had expected.

Phoebe's call had come unexpectedly soon. 'Golly!' said Letty, braking and holding the car back to a docile rumbling approach. 'The Palazzo Evans already! I hadn't realized it was so close to Herakleion.'

'The Lodge at the end of the drive – the Taverna, they call it – is where the students are housed. You could have stayed there, Laetitia, but I don't think you'd have liked it. Trails of dirty socks everywhere, uncertain hot water, and a constant squabbling going on.' She caught Laetitia's quickly suppressed smile. 'So unlike the home-life at our own dear villa, of course.'

Fifty yards up the hill the land flattened out, and there ahead of them in a grove of sheltering trees was the Villa Ariadne. At last she was here, seeing it for herself, this bit of Arcadia talked of with a gusty sigh of nostalgia and a far-off look in the eye of everyone she knew who'd ever sampled Sir Arthur Evans's hospitality. The sighs were inevitably followed by stories of convivial parties, nights of deep drinking fired by raki and dark red Cretan wine, days of muscle-cracking exertion in the trench or on the tennis court, life lived against the stimulating beat of archaeological derring-do. Letty ached with longing to have been a part of it.

Here a changing cast of young and active scholars had helped to reveal to a fascinated world a society only hinted at in legend. Ancient writers had been confident that the empire of Minos had existed, had even pointed clearly to the slope near Herakleion as the centre of the culture, but no one had quite liked to believe in any of this until, in the first three years of the century, Arthur Evans in a series of swift and frenzied digs had laid it bare to the light once more. And here, to the villa he'd built on the hill commanding the excavations, one team had retired at the end of each day's work to cool off in the ground-floor rooms, to write up their accounts, draw profiles, argue and speculate and joke.

Constructed of sand-coloured stone slabs, large and flat-roofed, the Villa Ariadne occupied a perfect position overlooking the Palace of Knossos and the olive and cypress-covered slopes of the valley of the Kairatos. A garden had been contrived in the shallow soil, Edwardian in its formality but enlivened with pots of bright flowers and shy statuary placed amongst the shrubs by a discreet hand.

'Leave the car in the shade over there,' instructed Phoebe, 'and I'll go and see if anyone's at home. Back in a tick.'

Phoebe returned after a few minutes, accompanied by two middle-aged Cretans, obviously man and wife. 'No luck, I'm afraid. No royalty, no heads of state, no operatic tenors – not even an archaeologist, for goodness' sake! The curator's gone off to Rethymnon. But here are Kostis and Maria to greet you, Letty. They look after Arthur when he's here and they're going to provide us with tea when we've finished at the palace. I said four o'clock . . . I think that will be late enough.'

Letty was introduced to Evans's butler and his wife and, instantly catching on to their plans, Kostis whistled up two boys who seized the hamper from the car and set off down the hill. Phoebe and Letty followed after, Phoebe chattering nineteen to the dozen about the palace. She talked confidently about the excavations and about preclassical history, Letty noticed, intrigued. But Phoebe's information was not ponderously displayed: It skittered and bounced along the surface of what Letty guessed to be a depth of knowledge. And the deserted state of the Villa Ariadne had in no way dampened her mood, as one might have expected. Showing off and socializing were not, evidently, the reason for this outing.

They followed the boys down the road for about a hundred yards, crossed over and, passing the deserted guardian's house, entered the site from what Phoebe called the West Court. She gave directions for leaving the hamper in the shade, dismissed the boys, and stood scanning the terrain like a general. 'Deserted! Good! I hate to arrive at the same time as a charabanc-load of tourists, leaving piles of orange peel all over the place and yammering like monkeys.'

Letty looked about her at the vast slope, covered with a jumble of grey limestone walls and hummocks of stones stretching onwards down the headland towards the river, and her heart sank.

Reading her expression, Phoebe laughed. 'I know! How does anyone ever make sense of this maze? It's a palace surrounded by a town; it's a site two hundred yards long and two hundred yards wide. Buckingham Palace and its gardens would fit into it with room to spare, I'm told. Every inch packed with detail. And don't forget the third dimension – depth and height. Theo says some parts of the palace could have been as high as five storeys, most two or three. After your tenth exposure to all this, you may begin to have a glimmer of understanding, but today you're not even to try! Quite shamelessly, I'm going to show you the most dramatic bits – the Violet and Rose Creams of the Charbonnel et Walker assortment. Come on! Follow me – and keep your eyes looking straight ahead – if you start poking about in some of these holes, I know I'll lose you! I'm going to fire you with romantic enthusiasm for this place – others can instruct you as to the laws of stratification, destruction layers, *sondages*, cultural overlap, and all the rest of it.'

She paused before an insignificant piece of plaster-covered rubble wall and pointed. 'There, do you see it?'

Bemused, Letty peered and squinted and finally said, 'I see nothing significant, I think. Not really sure what I'm looking at.'

Obviously exactly the answer Phoebe was hoping for. 'And yet to me this dull little piece of walling brings the whole thing alive! Look. There. That's it. The patch of black . . .'

'Oh, I see . . . Charring – from the shape, it looks as though the end of a wooden beam abutting the wall has gone up in flames.'

'Right! And if you look beyond at the farther walls you'll see they have a coating of soot on them. You can tell which way the wind was blowing in the mid-1400s BC when the whole of the palace accidentally burned down – or, should I say, when someone put a torch to it? Yes, it was a strong southerly wind,' Phoebe said with emphasis. 'A wind that blows in Crete in the last days of April and early May.'

'The time of year Theseus is supposed to have killed the Minotaur and made off with the king's daughter, Ariadne,' Letty breathed, finding no difficulty in being the good pupil, 'setting fire to the palace as they fled?'

'Yes. Theseus! Legendary heir to the throne of Athens. Brave boy. Volunteered to come as one of the seven-yearly tributes of Athenian youths and maidens to be sacrificed to the royal monster that lurked at the end of the underground passages beneath the palace. A monster betrayed by his half sister. Ariadne gave Theseus a ball of thread and suggested that if he were to allow it to roll ahead of him he could follow it down into the centre of the labyrinth and – very important – it would guide him back up afterwards. I wonder how she felt, betraying her family and her homeland, handing the torch of destruction to an enemy? A foul deed when you think about it. She must have been very much in love, wouldn't you say?'

Phoebe fell silent and let the words lie between them, clearly expecting a response.

'Love! Huh!' Letty's tone was scornful. 'Why is love always the excuse for madness and villainy and deception? Whatever happened to self-control and common sense?'

The other woman appeared taken aback by her vehemence. 'Well, we all know that "*Cupid is a knavish lad, thus to make poor females mad.*" The fair sex can't help it, apparently. We're just the target of Love's arrows and – never forget – dear little Cupid never did learn to shoot straight. Or was he blind? I don't remember. Still, at least it can never be said to be one's fault.'

Phoebe paused for a moment and then, suddenly, smiled her understanding. 'I see. I think I see! There was I, imagining you'd come to Crete to dig up and reveal things, but now I begin to suspect you're here to *bury* something. Let me guess! You left some treacherous toad smarting on a northern shore? Some careless ingrate is even now wondering how he could ever have let you get away? How'm I doing?'

'You're miles off target!' Letty lied stoutly, then thought it only honest to make up for it with a half lie. 'There's no one at home I couldn't greet again with equanimity.'

'Oh, indeed! I shall have to ponder that remark! I tend to distrust sentences with a double negative in them. And girls who blush when they're delivering them. I rather think I don't believe you. A girl doesn't get to your age, Laetitia, looking like you do, without leaving a trail of broken hearts. Give me a week and I shall know all! Even if I have to trade a few confidences in return!'

'Well, naughty Ariadne got her comeuppance.' Letty was eager to divert Phoebe's attention back to the ancient lovelorn heroine. 'It wasn't two minutes before Theseus abandoned her on the isle of Naxos. And then he turned the knife in the wound by making the sound political decision to marry her younger sister Phaedra, who was not tainted by treachery.'

'Economically sound move, too,' agreed Phoebe. 'Funny the way the old myth-makers shy away from giving the real reason for their raids! It was lust for gold and greed for trade routes that sent the ancient Greeks to Troy, not the righteous snatching back of the abducted Helen of Sparta. Jason's romantic quest for the golden fleece was a clear piece of piracy. Theseus's monster-killing exploits were a dramatic vindication for naked aggression. The forceful Mycenaean newcomers conquered, allied themselves, perhaps even absorbed, the more ancient and peaceable civilization.'

'The thrusting young god triumphing over the tired old goddess?' murmured Letty. 'Is that what the story's telling us?'

'I think so. And it all started here!' Phoebe stamped on the hard-packed earth under her feet. 'There are terrifying deep places under here, not all discovered yet, I do believe. When the bull roared, this palace shook. Quite literally! And I've heard him roar! It's the legend-writer's way of referring to an earthquake. This region is very prone to them. Arthur was here the year before last, working in his room, and experienced for himself the quake that came in June. The Villa Ariadne stood firm and was unscathed, but what struck – and enchanted – him was the sound that preceded and accompanied the shaking. He swears it was just like the roaring of a bull, right under the palace.'

As she spoke she had been leading Letty eastwards into the centre of the site.

'And this huge space –' she pointed to a flat rectangle the size of a parade ground – 'is at the very heart of the complex. Do you remember what Theseus had come here to do, in the legend?'

'To be sacrificed to the Minotaur, though some say he and the other thirteen victims were made to take part in the sport of bull-dancing,' said Letty, enchanted. 'He had to learn to challenge the fierce creatures they kept here – half bull, half wild aurochs. The dancers were trained to seize the huge horns and use the bull's instinctive tossing motion to be propelled upwards and backwards in a somersault on to its back. If you were lucky, you'd spring off again and be caught on the way down and steadied on to your feet by one of your team – a girl or a boy, as both sexes performed. How many acrobats must have died, been gored to death or trampled! There's a fresco, I think, showing exactly such a performance? And I've seen lots of representations carved on seal stones and signet rings.'

'But none of them show pain or death,' remarked Phoebe, softly. 'Just lithe youths and maidens performing for a delighted audience with never a drop of blood! And the bulls were obviously revered. They were not put to death in the arena as they are in those disgusting Spanish displays. Nothing but sweetness and light at Knossos.'

'I do see that it's much more appealing to us on an emotional and imaginative level than the Egyptian civilization. No reference anywhere to war, violence, conquering . . . no stomach-churning lists of ten thousand foreskins and right hands lopped off as a symbol of victory . . . no fifty-foot-high statues of the supreme ruler to bow down to . . .'

'No. The only tangible reminder of the Ruler is a very human-sized throne carved in alabaster. You can try it for size before we leave! And there's another one, a little wider – no doubt to accommodate the more ample buttocks of the Queen! And here's where the royal party would have gathered,' Phoebe announced, 'up there on a balcony to watch the displays.'

Letty looked around her at the dilapidation surrounding the space they had entered. She tried to conjure up the wild excitement, the screams and the splendour. 'And this is where it all happened?'

'It could be. Something important to the Minoans went on here. Bull-leaping? Acrobatics? Dancing? Religious ceremonies? Imagine ranks of verandas and galleries built on to the houses surrounding the court.' Phoebe twirled, conjuring up the levels with her hands, spinning an animated townscape from her imagination. Letty smiled to see the outburst of good humour.

'All crowded with people. It must have looked like a cross between the audience at an East End music hall and the Delhi Durbar. And the extraordinary thing, Laetitia, is that we know what the audience *looked* like! Can you believe it! A Minoan artist painted on to still damp wall plaster a fresco showing what he saw with his own eyes.

Over there in the northwest corner beyond the staircase – do you see the reconstructed floor, there over the throne room – they've hung the portraits of the citizens. They're still here, you know! Come and meet them!'

They climbed a grand flight of stairs, admiring its tapering columns of deep red crowned with bulbous capitals of blue-black banded with gold, then turned right into a long corridor. After a few yards Phoebe led the way into a room finished in rough modern plaster. The walls were hung with a series of brilliantly coloured reproductions of Minoan artistry. Straight opposite the door, Letty recognized on entering, was an image she had long been familiar with from textbooks: 'The Ladies in Blue.' No goddesses these, inscrutable and terrifying – the three girls she smiled at were her own age, girls she felt she could have sat alongside and chattered with. Straight from the hands of their maid, shining black hair curling fashionably about their faces, bare-bosomed, bangled, the trio sat with a suggestion of fluid movement, friends, glad to be in each other's company, out for an afternoon of pleasure with much to gossip about. Letty wondered whimsically at whom their admiring and coquettish glances had been directed. At the latest star of the arena? The daring young stripling from Athens? ... *Rumour has it, my dear, that he is a king's son. Barbarian, of course, but a personage in his own land, they say.* ... Letty only hoped that Theseus, leaping for his life in the arena, had become immune to the sight of so much attractive flesh on display. It would have been fatal to be distracted by it when the bull came thundering in.

'I always think they must be sharing some salty piece of scandal about this fine young fellow over here,' remarked Phoebe, and Letty went to examine a painting on the south wall.

'It's called "Captain of the Black Regiment",' said Phoebe.

'Oh, yes! A fellow like that – he'd attract salacious gossip!' agreed Letty. 'What a cockerel!' She laughed to see the lean, wasp-waisted figure in its tight belt, gold anklets and diminutive yellow loincloth stepping out, two spears in hand, at the head of his squad of Sumali soldiers. An officer, judging by the horned skin cap he wore.

'The originals are preserved in the museum – but the colours and techniques are accurately reproduced,' Phoebe told her. 'And here are the two miniatures I wanted you to see – scenes of crowds gathered to watch the spectacle, whatever it was, that was taking place just below us in the main court.'

Laetitia looked in silence for a very long time, absorbing what she saw. Finally, she murmured: 'Between this artist and Henri de Toulouse-Lautrec there must be a gap of three and a half ... four thousand years? And yet they would have understood each other perfectly. They could have compared techniques! It's a piece of Impressionism, don't you think? In the front row of the gallery we have the poster girls, the larger figures of ladies in blue or yellow dresses with puffed sleeves, and they're doing what Minoan ladies apparently love to do – sitting about talking and gesticulating! And in the background a happy crowd – men and women mingling together. Not segregated as at a Greek or Roman theatre. It's amazing!'

Gratified by the obvious pleasure her guided tour was giving, Phoebe led her out and back into the courtyard, promising further delights. 'The Prince of the Lilies ... the Cup-Bearer ... the blue dolphins in the Queen's rooms ... the blue bird in the garden ... the first flushing lavatory in Europe ...' She seized Letty's hand in her enthusiasm. 'And you're off to start your own dig! I can't wait to hear how you get on! Perhaps you'll find something to rival this? Perhaps you'll have a simply *huge* success and put Theo's nose out of joint! Look, why don't we take out a little insurance? Come on! It can't do any harm!'

She led Letty over to the eastern façade and they slipped between two columns, out of the sunlight and into a dark chamber. No light wells here. Letty could just make out the flash of Phoebe's ring as she pointed to a looming shape in the centre.

'The household shrine,' she whispered. 'That pillar, rooted in the earth, represents the deity. It's a sort of altar top plugged into the underworld. This is where the court of Minos made their sacrifices and their offerings to the goddess. I always come to pay my respects.'

Letty's eyes were adjusting to the gloom and she saw Phoebe turn to the truncated pillar, bow her head, and touch the stone side with her right hand. She began to murmur quietly, her words not audible to Letty. Then she took something from her pocket, a white disc apparently, and placed it carefully on the flat top.

Letty was still struggling with her curiosity as they emerged into the courtyard again.

'A Bath Oliver!' said Phoebe, answering her unspoken question. 'I brought the goddess one of your biscuits. A new experience for her! The Palace Deity used to enjoy offerings of food and wine, so they tell us. A sort of Communion in reverse, if you think about it.'

She turned in the direction of the Royal apartments. 'Now, you're to have an audience with His Highness, the Prince of the Lilies! Come on!' But she came to an abrupt halt, staring anxiously in the direction of a confusing jumble of half-repaired walls to their right. She frowned and hissed, 'Tourists! Drat! Did you see them, Letty?'

'Er . . . no. I can't see anyone.'

'I'm sure I caught sight of someone. There's one person, at least, down there. A man, I'd say. I was thinking just for once we were going to have the place to ourselves. It was some chap in a panama hat. English probably. Double drat! I don't much want to have to stop and pass the time of day with a fellow-countryman.' Her voice sank to a stage whisper. 'We'll creep over to the throne room and skulk about until they've gone by. Follow me.'

For a light-headed moment, Letty felt herself back on a school outing, slinking off with an adventurous friend, making for a discreet corner. She could almost feel the clandestine packet of Craven A and matches tucked away in the pocket of her knickers.

The cheerful halloo stopped them in their tracks.

'Coo-ee! Phoebe! It's me!'

Chapter Seven

'Oh! Oh, I say! It's not a man at all – it's . . . yes, it is . . . it's Olivia!'

Letty followed her gaze and saw a woman emerge from behind one of the walls. She was tall and well-built, wearing trousers and a man's panama hat.

'Coo-ee!' Phoebe called back excitedly. 'Hello there, Ollie!'

The two women hurried across the courtyard to greet each other with an affectionate hug and kiss. Phoebe turned, blushing with pleasure, to introduce Letty. 'Olivia, this is the student I told you about: Laetitia Talbot from Cambridge. I'm just giving her my edited highlights tour. Laetitia, this is my good friend and bridge partner Olivia Stoddart. I think I mentioned that I travelled as far as Paris with her last December? That Stoddart. Or should I say – those Stoddarts? What have you done with Harold, Ollie? Left him basting the Sunday joint?'

'Oh, he's about the place somewhere,' replied Olivia cheerfully, taking off her hat and fanning her face. Olivia Stoddart was the kind of woman who was always cheery, Letty thought. Her straw-coloured hair had been tentatively bobbed by an inexpert hand and her skin, darkened by weather and early spring sunshine, flattered the watery green of her eyes under their sandy lashes. She exuded health and good humour. Flat-chested and angular, she could not have presented a more different picture of womanhood from the dark-eyed voluptuous beauties they had so recently been admiring. 'We bicycled up. Can't stand donkeys,' she explained to Letty. 'Awful little squirts – I always feel I should be carrying *them*. Boots trailing in the dust . . . one feels so silly . . . Harry? He's probably found some trench to fossick about in. Or dug up some herb he's never seen before. *Harold!*' she shouted in a voice that would have carried the length of a hockey field. '*Present yourself!*'

A figure kneeling twenty yards away broke cover and stood up reluctantly. He began to shamble slowly towards them. This was turning into just the kind of expedition Letty found annoying: enforced jovial time-wasting with two strangers she had no particular desire to meet. Not when her attention was claimed with such magnetic force by her miraculous surroundings. Not when the Prince of the Lilies was next on her calling list.

Harold Stoddart when he reached them was introduced as Dr Stoddart . . . 'If you fall over and break your ankle within a hundred miles of Herakleion, it's Harry who'll minister to you . . .' Phoebe prattled. 'We're all so lucky to have him on the island . . . I should have called him in last night to advise on your seasickness, Laetitia – he's wonderful with seasickness . . .'

Letty looked at the doctor and decided she was being unkind. Though no rival for a golden, almond-eyed Minoan in flamboyant crown of lilies and peacock feathers, Dr Stoddart at close quarters was a very presentable man. He took off his straw hat and smiled. Ah! Better than presentable, Letty thought. In fact, jolly handsome in a very English way. In early middle age, he had a pleasant face, with the friendly but guarded expression doctors seemed to acquire. His hazel eyes were warm, his thick chocolate brown hair was turning grey, and he wore a well-trimmed moustache. He transferred a clump of herbs to the hat he held in his left hand, dusted off his right on his trouser leg, and seized Letty's hand in a warm and gritty clasp.

'Fennel,' he explained. 'Doesn't grow everywhere . . . lucky to find it. I usually come across it up here. It's my theory – though I'm no botanist – that its great long roots enjoy a disturbed soil. They go deep and like it best when they're encountering no resistance. It makes an excellent tisane, did you know?'

Small talk apparently was not his speciality. Letty's opinion of the doctor continued to rise. 'No, I didn't!' she answered. 'Now tell me – would that be the root or the green feathery bit you use?' She peered into his hat. 'The seeds? Ah, really? Last evening, before retiring, I had dittany – prescribed by Phoebe. I see I shall have to try a different one every night,' said Letty and began to respond to his enquiries about her reactions to the brew Eleni had served up.

Phoebe and her friend, seeing them happily engaged in herbal conversation, rolled their eyes indulgently, linked arms, and began to stroll ahead along the paved courtyard. Phoebe turned and called back to them: 'Olivia's agreed to have lunch with us. We've brought a hamper full of good things, plenty to go round. Why don't we go and find it? I asked the boys to leave it over in Ariadne's dancing place. Harry knows the way, Letty, in case you get diverted by a herb or two.'

Letty was amused by the scene the two women presented, so similar was it in style to the friendship portrayed in the ancient painting.

Harry Stoddart seemed at once to understand her smile. 'Do I imagine it, or is Phoebe looking a little, er, brighter today? Silly question – as well as unprofessional! Forgive me. You can't, of course, be expected to have the slightest idea of what she normally looks like, Miss Talbot!' said Dr Stoddard. '(Call me Harry.)'

'You're Phoebe's personal physician?'

'Yes. Again, I apologize for my indiscretion.'

He didn't seem apologetic, she thought, and was encouraged to reply frankly: 'Well, even *I* noticed that she looked better this morning than she did last evening. In fact – and at the risk of flouting some ridiculous convention – I will say I was rather concerned for her when I arrived. I feel an awful tattletale even speaking of it, but she looked so pale and strung up and she didn't eat any of her supper. No one else commented on it or asked her how she was doing so I didn't think it was my place to bring it up.'

Into his encouraging silence she stumbled on: 'She didn't really have any breakfast either – just crumbled a piece of toast on to her plate. I tricked her into sharing an orange with me and she felt obliged to eat up her half, but that was as much as I could persuade her to have. She seems to be living on her nerves. I think you ought to be made aware.'

Harry coughed slightly. Ill at ease, she thought.

'Oh, I know! I'm embarrassing you! I'm meddlesome and I'm always sticking my oar in when it's not wanted. I'm sorry.'

'No! No! I'm interested to hear what you have to say. Truly,' he hurried to reassure her. 'Without breaching patient confidence, may I just say . . . I'm thankful – Olivia and I are both thankful (I know I speak for her) – that there is someone of Phoebe's own sex and age – more or less – in the house. Someone who would notice if there were any deterioration in her condition . . . someone who would have the sense to contact me at once.'

'Surely Theo or George would be quick to alert you if they sensed something was wrong?' Her question was delivered in a neutral voice but her eyes were watching his reaction closely.

The doctor was not a poker player, she decided. He looked away but not in time to conceal the scorn and impatience that flashed across his features. She decided she could like Harry Stoddart.

'You may not have had the chance to notice that the gentlemen in Phoebe's life are . . . shall I say . . . preoccupied with their own academic world. I honestly don't think they'd pay attention until she fainted in coils at their feet.' He fished about in an inner pocket and gave her a visiting card. 'At any moment of the day or night, Laetitia.'

She glanced at it and put it away in her pocket, nodding.

'If I'm not there Olivia will always substitute.'

Seeing Letty's surprise, the doctor smiled. 'We met in Mesopotamia during the war. I was an army surgeon and Olivia a Red Cross nurse. She's as competent in medical matters as I am – for all my qualifications.' He stopped and gazed around the site. 'You're an archaeologist, I understand? And all this is about to become your playground? I do envy you!'

'I wish that were so! No, this is my schoolroom. I look and learn here, that's all. They're letting me get out my bucket and spade in earnest tomorrow, but I must travel a little farther to use them. Over there!' She pointed to the lowering shape of Juktas in the middle distance.

'They're sending you off into the mountains? So soon?' The thought appeared to concern him.

'Just during the week – I'm to come back to Herakleion at the weekends.'

'Good – then we may look forward to seeing you regularly. There's quite a lot going on for such a small town. Many nationalities here. I think you'll find a lot of people you can like, Laetitia.'

A peremptory shout from Olivia drew them on towards a flat area in the shade of a cypress tree. There lunch for four had been spread out over a checked cloth.

'Ah!' sighed Harry. 'Idyllic scene! What a feast! Local cheese, good bread, olives, and red wine. And do I see pâté de foie gras?' He quivered with a simulated ecstasy that made Letty giggle. 'We lack only the trumpets! All this and the charming company of three fair-haired Graces. I do believe I've died and gone to Heaven!'

'Don't be so soppy, Harry! And don't tempt the Gods. Remember where you are!' advised his wife sternly.

Phoebe collapsed between the main course and the dessert.

Getting up to fetch spoons from the hamper, she stumbled and gasped. Letty thought she'd tripped over the picnic cloth and lunged forward to catch her. But it was

97

Dr Stoddart who leapt to his feet as her knees buckled and she lost consciousness.

Olivia went instantly into action, reaching for her pulse. 'Not surprised! Been expecting something of the sort. Silly old thing got up too sharply. She was sitting in full sun and will never put on a hat. Harry, carry her over into the shade. I'll get my smelling salts. Laetitia, fetch the water flask.'

'I think, Olivia, it may be something more serious than a swoon,' Harry said grimly. 'We'd better get her back to town as quickly as possible so we can find out what the real problem is. You say you drove here?' he asked Letty.

'The car's at the villa. I'll run and get it –'

'Would you? There's a quick way of getting up to the road from here –'

'Yes, of course,' interrupted Olivia. 'She can go along the Processional Way. Let me show you. Down here, Laetitia. Follow the paved road and it will bring you out right opposite the Ariadne. We'll haul Phoebe along between us, Harry and I, and meet you on the road.'

Phoebe was conscious and walking with support when Letty reached them, backing down the narrow Minoan roadway to save time. The Stoddarts had made their arrangements. 'Look – I think it makes sense if *I* drive her back,' said Harry, brisk and calm. 'Laetitia has no medical training and Ollie doesn't drive ... Would you mind awfully riding home on one of the bicycles, Laetitia? Can you ride a bicycle?'

'Can you drive a Bugatti?'

They nodded at each other and after a swift familiarization with the controls, Harry experimentally revved the engine and prepared to take off with Phoebe slumped in the passenger seat. A slim hand stole out and clutched Letty's. With a final effusive rush of apology, Phoebe murmured, 'Finish off the tour, Laetitia. Take your time. Get Ollie to show you the House of the Axes. I shall be sure to test you when you get back!'

Still holding her hand, she fixed Letty with a look full of meaning.

'We've had our fun!' she said, waiting for her response.

'We've eaten and drunk enough,' Letty said, the words of Gunning's grace coming back to her.

Phoebe smiled with pleasure and nodded.

'Time to go now,' she whispered.

Chapter Eight

After her friend's departure, Olivia seemed rather pre-occupied, Letty thought, and belatedly concerned, but the older woman assumed command of the clear-up and retreat with expected efficiency. In spite of Phoebe's wish for her to carry on with their plans, the heart, the reason, the joy had gone from the day. Letty was in no mood to be marched around the site by Olivia. Letty's suggestion that they call off the rest of the afternoon's entertainment and make for home was accepted with unflattering alacrity by her companion. The hamper was packed and left ready to be picked up by the boys from the villa. A note excusing themselves from tea was left tucked into the handle and Letty was assigned the lady's bicycle of the pair. Each wrapped in her own thoughts, the two women set off down the road to Herakleion.

'Stiff wind blowing in our faces! You're going to have your skills and endurance tested, Laetitia! Now come along – don't lag behind! Give it ten!' Olivia cried, clearly relishing the challenge and forcing the pace.

Letty got off her bicycle, exhausted, at the Stoddarts' substantial old house near the harbour, refusing Olivia's automatic and blatantly insincere offer of refreshment. She abandoned the bike and made her way back down the crowded streets she remembered from the previous evening, discovering, as she strolled along, and marking down for further attention, several smart boutiques. The house, when she entered, was cool and still, to all appearances abandoned. Letty rang the bell and Eleni appeared.

As far as Letty could make out from the housekeeper, the doctor had arrived with the mistress and had taken Phoebe to her own room. He'd stayed to check her over and administer a sleeping pill before he left. The mistress had a supply of her own but never used them. Exhaustion, he'd declared. No need for concern, but Mrs Russell was to be allowed to sleep and not be disturbed. This last comment was delivered as a clear warning for Letty. Mr Russell was not at home, she was told repressively, and the students were lunching in town with friends. Master George was out with the architect looking for bones. Eleni expected them back at teatime.

Tea and iced water were sent to her in the drawing room but, unable to settle, Letty soon went upstairs to her own room to wash and to change her clothes, write letters, and do what she'd been advised was the custom in Crete for women and foreigners – take an afternoon nap. Feeling she qualified on both counts, she gave in and indulged. She emerged from her room, fresh once more but restless and with a dragging concern for Phoebe. In spite of Eleni's warning, she found herself prowling down to Phoebe's room, which she'd been told was on the first floor but along the corridor and at the back away from the public rooms, overlooking the garden. All was still and silent. She found an impressive pair of gilded double doors and put her ear to one. She heard nothing. Remembering the doctor's concern and the charge he had laid on her to be alert to Phoebe's condition, her hand crept to the porcelain doorknob.

'Meddlesome!' she reminded herself. 'Don't do what you're about to do!' Then she reasoned that if Phoebe was, as might be guessed, fast asleep, she wouldn't notice that a kindly face had looked in. If she was still awake, she might well be pleased to see the kindly face. She might like to have a gossip or even be read to for a bit. The door wasn't locked. Letty eased it open a few inches and listened, ready to make off at the slightest sign that her presence would not be welcome.

A current of air through the doorway told her that the window over the courtyard must be wide open. She opened the door farther and looked for Phoebe on the bed against the right wall. The blue patterned toile de Jouy counterpane was rumpled as though someone had lain there briefly, and there was a dent in the pillow where a head had rested, but the bed was empty.

A breeze rattled the open shutters setting up a creaking and a slight movement on her left side, shielded from her by the half open door. Alert and concerned, she slipped inside and closed the door behind her.

And shut herself in with a horror.

Unable to blink or breathe, Letty stood transfixed and staring. All her senses were absorbing information that her brain was refusing to process.

The rush of air had stirred into pendulum motion a shape, a human form, that dangled, head at an impossible angle, eyes open and staring upwards at the rope looping over a gilded beam above her head. Below Phoebe's feet lay an overturned tapestried chair.

With a swallowed scream, Letty launched herself forward and seized Phoebe by the legs, hoisting her upwards, fighting to release the clutch of the rope on her neck. Struggling to hold up the slight frame with one arm, Letty fumbled for the pulse in the frail right wrist. Remembering with frustration that she had never had any luck in locating even her own pulse, she reached up and felt for a heartbeat.

Nothing.

It was the hardest thing Letty had had to do in her life: Relinquishing her support of the body was to admit that Phoebe was indeed dead. With a shudder and a moan, she let go and dashed across the room to tug violently at the bell pull that dangled by the bed head. Then she flung the door open and called for help, hurrying along the corridor to lean over the balcony, looking down the stairwell to the black and white tiled floor of the hallway on the floor below. She was weak with relief to hear her name being shouted back.

Two men had entered the hall, and it was William Gunning's voice that called up to her. 'Letty? Is that you? Letty – what the hell?'

In seconds he was at her side, accompanied by George Russell.

'Phoebe! In her room! I think she's dead!' she moaned, pointing.

George shot off without a word, leaving Gunning to fold Letty briefly in a comforting hug. When they joined him, it was to see George repeating Letty's instinctive gesture, bearing the weight of Phoebe's body, thrusting it upwards in a compulsion to counteract the dragging finality of death.

'Cut her down, for pity's sake!' he said through gritted teeth. 'Knife in my right pocket, Will!'

But Gunning's own army-issue clasp knife was already in his hand. He reached up and sawed through the fibres where they strained against the beam. Released, Phoebe's featherlight body, slumped in George's arms, was carried over to the bed and placed gently on the counterpane.

'Did someone ring?' The staccato Greek syllables rang out into the silent room with the force of machine-gun bullets.

'Eleni! Thank goodness!' said George. 'There's been an accident. Phoebe needs attention. Get Dr Stoddart at once, will you? Send a runner. Tell him it's of the utmost urgency.'

Eleni's eyes raked the room, noting the company and resting, lingering, on the pale face and broken neck from which the frayed rope still trailed its way across the pillow. She turned and disappeared as suddenly as she had arrived.

'How long before . . .?'

'If he's at home he can get here within ten minutes,' George told Letty. 'Nothing he can do, of course. Nothing anyone could have done. She chose a time when the house was empty.'

'*I* was here,' murmured Letty. 'I was in my room. If I'd come down sooner . . . I was told not to disturb her.'

'People who are seriously bent on doing away with themselves work to ensure seclusion.' George said it gently. 'She probably left those instructions herself. But why? Why would she do this? "Suicide while the balance of her mind was disturbed." That's what they say, isn't it? But, really, that answers no questions. Poor old Pa! He'll be devastated. Horrified! Where is he, by the way? Anyone know?'

William and Letty both shook their heads. 'Eleni just said he was "not at home". He could be anywhere. Surely you know, George?'

'"Not at home" could mean anything. He sometimes tells Eleni to say that when he's having a sleep in his room. That's next door.' He pointed to a door in the west wall. 'But sometimes when he's working at something in his lair –' He looked uncomfortable, then explained: 'Pa has a study on the ground floor. His own private domain. Full of books and treasures of one sort or another. No one is encouraged to enter. Even if they could get through the door – it's stacked high with his things.' He drew himself upright. 'I'd better go down and check. I should be the one to break this ghastly news.'

'Poor, poor Theo! Did she leave him a letter, I wonder?' said Gunning. 'People who commit suicide normally do, you know.'

They all looked about them. Letty saw it first. 'On the dressing table. Look. Under the paperweight. There's an envelope.'

She went to look at it and, without touching it, turned to stare at the two men, uncomprehending, startled. 'But it's not addressed to Theo. The name on the envelope is *George*.'

His exclamation of surprise went unheeded, drowned as it was by the shock of hearing a rumbling and a stirring from the adjoining room. Through the door they heard the unmistakable sounds of a man just swimming back to consciousness. An ear-cracking yawn was followed by a cheerful bellow.

'Phoebe!' Theo called out. 'Pheeb, old gel! You there? Why don't you come and plump up my pillow, eh?'

The lascivious invitation was unmistakable.

Chapter Nine

Unable to deal with the further drama that seemed about to explode over their heads, Letty started to make for the door mumbling: 'I shouldn't be here . . . sorry – must leave this to you, George . . .'

'No. I'll go with you,' said George.

'Better if you stay. I'll take her downstairs,' said Gunning and both men started after her.

They were all stopped in their tracks by a sound at the partition as the handle rattled and the door began to swing open. 'That's if you're in a mood to, of course . . .' Theodore said, catching sight of Phoebe's body on the bed. 'An hour or two tête-à-tête with little Miss Know-It-All could leave anyone feeling a bit limp . . . Good Lord! What the hell's going on here?' he burst out, catching sight of the three figures frozen in horror over by the door. 'Would any-one care to tell me what you're all doing in my wife's bedroom?'

He advanced into the room, filling it with his dark pres-ence. His bulky frame was clad, improbably, in a dark blue embroidered satin robe of some eastern cut, and they all recoiled from the menace of his suspicion. His eyes flicked from one to the other and finally turned to rest on the lifeless shape of his wife. He stared for a very long time, taking in the obscene trail of rope from her neck to the counterpane. His howl of rage and incomprehension rang through the room and was unbearable.

'Stay! You all stay exactly where you are and tell me what's happened!'

He stormed towards the bed and clasped Phoebe's body in an embrace, gasping with emotion. 'Will someone speak!' he said finally. 'What's happened to her? Who's done this?'

George gulped and began: 'She did it herself, Pa. I'm afraid she took her own life. Letty discovered her body . . . about . . .'

'Ten minutes ago,' Letty supplied softly.

'William and I were just back from the coast when we heard Letty calling out. We dashed up here but – but – there was nothing we could do. She's been dead a while, I'd say, but the doctor will have a view, no doubt. Eleni's sending for him now. Awfully sorry, Pa. Just tell us what we can do. Anything.'

'For a start you can get the police. Inspector Mariani – contact him. She didn't kill herself! Why would she? I don't believe it – nor should you!' Theodore looked around him desperately. 'Where was she hanging? I take it she *was* hanging?' He fingered the rope around her neck. 'Good Lord! This is the cord from my old dressing gown. The one I keep on the back of her door.' He pointed to a dark brown monk-like garment suspended from a hook, then turned his gaze back to her still features. One large hairy hand reached out to close her eyes and mouth, and he bent to kiss her brow.

'She gave no hint . . . she didn't confide . . .' he started to say, and then looked wildly about him.

With sinking hearts they watched as he caught sight of the envelope on the dressing table.

'Ah! That may tell us more,' he said. With an aggrieved look at Phoebe's contorted face, he went to gather up the letter. Before he could tear it open he saw the name written on the front and looked at them, puzzled and affronted. 'It's for you, George. Why the hell would she be writing to you before she died?' Grudgingly, he handed the envelope over to his son. 'Only one way to find out, I suppose.'

The tension was too much to bear. Letty tried again to sidle to the door, murmuring wild excuses. Gunning attempted to follow her.

'Are you deaf? I told you to stay where you are! Both of you!' shouted Theodore. 'We don't know what we're dealing with here, and I may need witnesses if a crime has been committed under my roof – which I am quite certain it has. You must understand that.'

'I say, Theo, er, if we're being punctilious, perhaps you should confirm, before any tearing takes place, that this is Phoebe's handwriting?' said Gunning.

'I can. Unmistakably her neat girls'-school script. Let's ask George. What do you say, George?'

George shrugged his shoulders in a helpless gesture. 'Not sure I'm familiar enough with her writing to give a firm opinion.'

His father glowered. 'Come now, my boy, you've seen your name written often enough on her cheques. With her signature at the bottom. Why suddenly so coy?'

'Hardly "coy", Pa! Devastated . . . dislocated . . . wishing myself a thousand miles away. Wondering what sort of horror is waiting for us in this envelope. If you insist, I'll open it. Better do it carefully, though.'

He took the knife Gunning silently offered him and slit the envelope along the top. He peered in. 'There's no note in here,' he said, puzzled. 'Just a . . . What is this, William? . . . A page torn from a book? It appears to be a sheet of ancient Greek . . . poetry? No . . . a play, would you say?' He handed the folded paper to Gunning and looked carefully again inside the envelope, finding nothing more.

Exchanging a look with George, Gunning unfolded the sheet. As he silently read, Letty drank in every shiver of emotion that disturbed the familiar features, understood them, and prepared herself for further racking disclosures.

'Well, man?' said Theodore impatiently. 'Am I to be allowed to be privy to my wife's last thoughts? Or do you want me to summon the cook and the bottle-washer to take a look first?'

'Sorry, Theo, sorry,' said Gunning and passed it over like a hot potato.

Theodore read avidly, then, shaking his heavy head, thrust it back at Gunning.

'I don't understand. What on earth are we meant to make of that?' He looked once again at Phoebe's body and, with a grunt of disgust, reached over and tucked the rope out of sight under the pillow. 'Poor lass! Perhaps she *had* suffered some sort of a brain fever. Didn't know what she was doing? Where's that damned doctor?'

He sighed and began to pace about the room. Finally: 'Look, while we're waiting, why don't you identify that piece of nonsense for us, William? Can you translate? Looks like a play to me but my ancient Greek was never much good.' The admission clearly made him uncomfortable. Another reason for his dislike of the classically educated Gunning, perhaps, Letty thought.

Gunning offered the text first to George. 'Would you like . . .?'

George shook his head, dismissive and distancing.

'Very well, then,' said Gunning heavily. 'Just tell me to stop if this looks like being disturbing. For anyone. I recognize it. It's a passage from a play by Euripides.'

'A play? Which play?' Theodore wanted to know.

'Um . . . it looks like *Hippolytus*.'

At the name, Letty's knees buckled with dread and she went to sit down on the twin of the tapestried chair which still lay on the floor. If her suspicions were to prove correct, Gunning was about to embark on a feat of bull-dancing that would demand the fast footwork and suppleness of an acrobat in the arena of Minos.

'Get on with it, man! Do I have to ask you again? What is it saying?'

The bull had entered the arena, snorting.

'It's a section not far from the beginning of the play. We're still in the exposition phase, where Phaedra, Princess of Crete and now the second wife of Theseus of Athens, is telling the chorus why she's decided to kill herself. It goes something like this . . . will an approximate translation do? The gist of it? Very well. Phaedra says:

'"When love wounded me, I wondered how I could best endure it. My first thought was to stay quiet about this sickness and keep it hidden.

'"My second thought was this – I planned to overcome my madness through self-control and thus to bear it more easily.

'"My third course – since the first two were gaining me no victory over the Goddess of Love – was to decide on death.

'"This was the best plan – no one could deny that. I knew that the act and the sickness brought disgrace with them and besides, I was well aware that I am a woman – and must be an object of loathing to all men.

'"It is right that the most despicable of deaths should fall on the woman who shames her marriage-bed with a man who is not her husband."'

There was a silence interrupted only by the sudden cooing of a pair of doves in the courtyard. And the sound to Letty's ears was a mockery, a gloating comment, chilling and unbearable. These were Aphrodite's birds, her sacred symbols and messengers. Exclaiming with outrage, Letty strode towards the window.

'Here, use this,' said Gunning guessing her intention and as she passed him he slipped into her hand a potsherd from his pocket. She located the lovebirds perching in the wisteria below and hurled her missile along with a muttered and very personal curse in case the Goddess of Love still thought she held sway on this island.

Even before the squawks of indignation had died away, Theodore spoke: 'Remind me, William,' he said in the tone of a Lord Advocate, questioning but totally chilling, 'of the nature of the lady's problem. I refer, of course to the ancient Greek lady.'

'Um . . . Phaedra, who was very much in love with her husband, King Theseus, suffered a sort of rush of blood to the brain and imagined herself in love with another man.

All brought about by the jealous and vindictive behaviour of Aphrodite, who had thought herself slighted in some way. Probably one too few oxen sacrificed that week or the wrong colour ... something of that kind. It didn't take much to bring the wrath of the gods down on your heads in those days ...'

'And Theseus was unaware of his wife's state of mind?'

'Completely. He was miles away at the time. Consulting an oracle, I believe.'

'One might question the efficacy of the oracle. And she carried out her threat?'

'Yes. She hanged herself from a beam in her bridal chamber.'

'Mmm ... the remaining point of interest would seem to be, then, the identity of the man she was in love with,' said Theodore harshly, 'the man she died for ... the man whose image was before her eyes when the noose tightened and cut off the light. Well? ... Well?' he demanded again into Gunning's awkward silence.

'The play bears his name.' Gunning was cornered but not ready to give up on his defensive skirmishing. 'It was Hippolytus.'

'Ah, yes. Hippolytus. And what more do you have to tell us about the eponymous hero, this fornicator?'

'He was the son of the Amazon queen, the beautiful fair-haired Hippolyta. The young man was handsome, but he was utterly virtuous and had dedicated himself to the service of Artemis, the virgin Goddess of Hunting, who was, of course, his mother's favourite deity ...'

Theodore was not to be drawn aside into the thickets of mythology. 'Impeccable parentage on one side – and the *father* of this paragon was ...?' He was pressing Gunning with the quizzical tone of a schoolmaster shepherding an uncertain pupil along a predetermined path.

Gunning sighed. He said resignedly, 'Theseus, King of Athens. Hippolytus was the son of his first marriage.'

Theodore turned slowly to stare at his son. 'Ah. George? Or should I say – Hippolytus? What have you to say?'

Chapter Ten

'It was all a piece of nonsense, Mr Russell!' Letty burst out. 'A dreadful misunderstanding! In the play, I mean. Hippolytus wasn't guilty of anything! Horrid, horrid boy – impossible to like him – an unsympathetic prig of the worst kind, but a complete innocent! He declares that he was so uninterested in all things carnal he didn't even like to look at dirty pictures on vases – he had what he called a virgin soul. He never looked twice at Phaedra even though she was lusting after him . . . oh, I mean . . . That's how the tale goes . . .' she finished lamely, recollecting that further details of the murky saga of lust, blame, vengeance, and death could only make matters much worse.

To her surprise, George went to his father and enveloped him in a hug. 'Letty's right, Pa. It *is* all a story. A disgusting and dishonourable story! No one came out of it well. No one!' He held his father by the shoulders and looked him in the eye. 'I've no idea why Phoebe should have left this envelope and addressed it to me. You have my word that there has never been any feeling between my stepmother and myself other than warm and proper regard. If there had been – I swear to you – I would have been the first one to die.'

Seeing the purity of his profile and the tears starting down his cheeks, Letty believed him.

More important, so did his father. Theodore clapped him on the back murmuring, 'You've never lied to me, lad. And you're not lying now. But I swear I won't rest until I know the truth of all this.'

* * *

Dr Stoddart came in panting, bag in hand, distraught, in time to witness the scene of filial affection and consolation. But he barely noticed; his attention was all for the dead woman. He took a moment or two to pull himself together, then in a clipped professional tone he commented on his routine examination as it progressed. He shone a torch on to the dilated pupils and commented on the cyanosed state of the lips and tongue. He eased the noose away from her neck and examined the pattern of the bruises in the flesh. Guided by Letty, he checked the beam where she had been found hanging and looked carefully at the monk's robe on the hook behind the door. Finally, he announced that on initial examination the death appeared to be due to compression of the neck, apparently self-inflicted and achieved by hanging in the manner Miss Talbot had described. He would, however, wish to have the body conveyed to the city hospital where further examination might be carried out. He assured Theodore it was the usual routine. The police would have to be notified, of course, before removal. Had anyone thought to . . .?

Theodore and George left the room to make arrangements, Harry Stoddart saying he would stay by the body. As Letty and Gunning reached the door, Stoddart called after them. 'I say, Miss Talbot? Laetitia? Would you mind awfully waiting behind a moment or two? Women's matters . . . Could use a bit of help . . .' he finished limply.

This was the last thing Letty wanted to do. She had been longing to creep away into some corner with William to talk about and mourn for Phoebe. Though she had known her for only a few hours, she had thought the young woman could become a lifelong friend. Her sudden loss was devastating. She saw her own desolation reflected in the downcast eyes of Dr Stoddart, but there was something more there, surely: anger, perhaps?

'I could do with a nurse,' Harry told her, 'but I'm not going to summon Olivia. Those two were quite close, you know. Olivia's tough, but I fear this would be too much for her to bear. Can't be easy for you, I understand that – I oughtn't to burden you with this and I wouldn't ask if I didn't take you for a level-headed young lady who had become fond of Phoebe. But, you see, there's things about this death I'm not happy with. I want you to look and see if you can see what I'm getting at.'

Puzzled, Letty went to stand by the bed.

'Help me turn her over, will you?' he asked. 'She's as light as a bird. I can probably manage . . . There. Thank you. Now . . .' He selected a thermometer from his bag. 'I'm going to check the body temperature. Impossible to take an anal temperature with the family standing around . . . You may look the other way if you're squeamish. Fine . . . Now, you say you handled the body when you found her – I want you to tell me in what state of stiffness her limbs were.' While Letty recounted her impressions Dr Stoddart bent and prodded. She helped him to take off Phoebe's boots and peel down the silk stockings she'd worn to prevent chafing. The doctor checked the condition of her feet. 'Slight discolouration – hypostasis setting in. Here – do you see? That bluish-red blotching around her ankles.'

Letty looked and exclaimed. 'I see it. And are those blisters on her feet?'

'Yes, they look like blisters to me.'

'Oh, poor Phoebe! She didn't complain . . . not once . . . and it must have been agonizing walking round Knossos with me!' It was this small detail that caught Letty out and finally threatened to submerge her in a flood of emotion.

'New boots, would you say?' The doctor smiled sadly. 'How she loved her boots! She brought several pairs back from Paris. Not all, I'm afraid, entirely suitable for Crete.' And finally: 'I'm going to remove the noose. Please watch me do it and you'll be able to bear witness for the inspector if he asks you.'

Stoddart inspected the knot before he turned his attention to the neck. 'Efficient,' he muttered. 'A running knot. Did Phoebe know about knots? We must find out. Abrasions on the neck . . . such a fragile little neck . . .' He turned aside and for a moment Letty thought he was going to break down but he recovered himself and went on. 'She died quickly . . . broken neck. People can linger, you know, caught up in a noose. Usually it's the lighter ones who have problems.' He cleared his throat. 'In fact, I would have expected her, with such little body weight, to have strangled to death in the rope with all the unpleasantness that implies. Drawn-out asphyxiation. But I'd say her neck broke almost at once.'

Letty appreciated that he was offering what consolation he could and in terms she would understand, and was grateful for it.

'You say the chair was overturned? Just as we see it now?'

Letty nodded grimly, thinking she could see where his thoughts were leading.

'I say, Laetitia, I wonder if you'd mind . . .' His request was so distasteful he could not voice it.

'Of course I'd mind, but I will. For Phoebe,' said Letty, gritting her teeth.

She took the noose, replaced the chair, and stood on it underneath the beam. 'Let's remember that Phoebe is – was – a good three inches shorter than I am,' she warned and reached upwards demonstrating the length and position of the rope where it had been secured to the beam. 'There. Do you see? I can attach the rope here . . . slip the noose over my neck – no, don't worry! – then . . .' She grasped the beam in both hands, kicking the chair out from under her feet before jumping back to the floor. 'Well, there you are. That's exactly where I found it. She could have done it as easily as that.'

'And the obvious solution,' said Stoddart doubtfully. 'But tell me, Laetitia – you were with her for most of the morning – did she give any warning of this? Was she depressed? Weepy?'

'Not at all,' answered Letty. 'She was cheerful, positive, full of life. Even what my aunt would describe as *un peu surexcitée*.' Letty struggled to crystallize her half-formed impressions of Phoebe's mood. 'She was looking forward to something. Mind not quite on the present . . . as though she were going on holiday the next day.'

'Mmm . . . I think I'd agree with that. You know, Laetitia, I'm not sure we have the full story,' said the doctor. 'Come and look at this.'

He pushed up the hem of Phoebe's divided skirt.

'Didn't think it was quite the thing to draw attention to this, with her grieving family standing about. There's bruising. On each leg. Very faint. I think the marks didn't have long to develop – they would have ceased forming the moment her heart stopped beating – incurred preceding death, at any rate. I think it wasn't just luck that snapped her neck so quickly. I think she had help. Someone prepared her for death and then when she was hanging and the chair pushed away, the assistant pulled sharply on her legs. It's a well-known executioner's trick when the, er, the procedures are going too slowly. She was wearing her shiny boots so, to get an adequate grip, that second person had to reach higher around the thighs, you see. That could be a thumbprint there and another over the other side. One violent tug from below would be sufficient.'

Letty looked around the room for the hundredth time. 'Doctor, there's no sign of a struggle. Phoebe wouldn't have just let someone do that to her. She'd have fought back, hit out, bitten, wouldn't she?'

Stoddart extended the dead woman's hands. 'Take a look. The nails are unbroken. No sign of skin or flesh under them. No scratches. I'd say she didn't defend herself.'

'She could have screamed, overturned the furniture – made a noise that alerted her husband. Theodore was having his siesta right next door – through there.' Letty pointed. 'You can hear quite clearly what's going on in the next room – we all heard him yawning when he woke up. A scream would certainly have been quite audible. She'd have left some sign of attack by an intruder, surely?'

'Not, sadly, if she was sedated,' he replied, heavily. 'I gave her a sleeping pill before I left her. She didn't want it. . . . If only I hadn't been so bossy . . . if she'd been awake, this might not have happened.' Again emotion was threatening to get the better of him.

'Why was she still wearing her boots?' said Letty, hoping to divert him. 'Her feet must have been killing her.'

'Oh, yes, that's a point. First thing a woman does, isn't it, when she's alone in her room – kick her boots off? She was still wearing them when I left her. I escorted her up here. Eleni was buzzing about with glasses of water and so on. I examined Phoebe and checked there was no life-threatening condition, gave her a pill. We sat right there in the chairs on either side of the table and talked for, oh, about ten minutes. When I saw she was beginning to fade I rang for Eleni and left. I wasn't keeping a close eye on the time – no reason to – but it must have been about half past two. And you discovered her at?'

'Five o'clock.'

'I took her temperature at five-fifty, and it's always a rough measure. She's slender and so would lose heat more rapidly than the average person . . . and the room is of average to cool temperature. Must get the ambient temperature taken. The police will do that. Perhaps. Allowing for a loss of one point five degrees per hour, I'd say she died round about three o'clock. Bit before? Bit after? Very soon after I left her, at any rate. As though someone was waiting for the effects of the pill to kick in. Someone close at hand.'

He looked, distraught, at the body and muttered to himself, Letty's presence almost forgotten. 'I shouldn't have left her alone. I shouldn't have left her here. It wasn't safe.'

Stoddart shuddered and glanced around him at the communicating door and the open window, and when he spoke again to Letty it was in the same stricken whisper. 'I was uneasy the whole while. Can't explain why. You know the sort of feeling . . . chill on the back of one's neck . . . current of air . . .' He looked thoughtfully at the window.

'I heard nothing suspicious. It was perfectly silent . . . too silent?' He frowned in an effort to give a more logical, a more scientific reason for his apprehension. 'No sound of snoring from next door. Even the doves . . .' His voice trailed away. 'The doves that normally perch in the tree outside – we heard nothing from them. Had someone scared them off? Was someone lurking, do you suppose, in or near this quiet house? Waiting for me to leave her alone and unprotected?'

A scraping sound below the window made him fall silent. They stared at each other, hearts pounding, waiting for a repetition of the noise and hoping there would be none. 'Those wretched birds back already?' Letty quietly suggested. But after a few seconds the stealthy scratching sound came again. A loose piece of masonry clattered to the paved courtyard. The scraping took up again, louder, more rhythmic, coming closer.

'We have an intruder,' mouthed Stoddart. 'Leave this to me.'

He advanced on the window and Letty scurried after him. A head appeared and with a shout of surprise, Stoddart leaned over and hauled a panting Gunning over the sill.

'Thanks, old man,' said the latter, collapsing in a heap on the floor. 'Should have called up in case you were still here, but didn't want to alert the rest of the family . . . sure you'll understand.'

Letty could contain herself no longer. She took hold of Gunning as he got to his feet, grasped him by the lapels of his jacket, and gave him a good shaking. 'Idiot! You fool! What on earth are you thinking of, climbing up like that? You could have killed yourself!' Reddening, she turned to the astonished doctor and muttered, 'Mr Gunning has only one good foot – was wounded in the war – but he makes no allowances for his condition. One day he'll go too far.'

Stoddart looked uncertainly from one to the other. 'One foot? Good Lord! Would never have guessed. You two know each other?'

'Miss Talbot saved my life last year. She rightly objects to any attempt on my part casually to throw it away again,' Gunning answered, dusting off his knees. 'No danger!'

'Glad to hear it but, look here, man – what on earth are you up to, frightening the life out of us?'

'Just showing how it would be possible to gain access to this room without passing the dragon Eleni in the hallway,' replied William. 'Sneak down the alleyway off the avenue, through the coach house that George uses for a garage, if it's been left unlocked – it has! – and you can get into the courtyard. Then you encounter the ancient wisteria conveniently writhing its way upwards. As good as a staircase! It was a piece of cake! And if *I* can do that climb, every citizen of Herakleion – and his granny – can do it.'

'Would you care to explain why it occurred to you to stage this little demonstration?' asked the doctor, who had already, Letty guessed, worked it out for himself. Perhaps Stoddart needed the reassurance of hearing his own suspicions endorsed from an independent quarter.

Gunning did not let him down. 'Because I'm quite certain that Phoebe didn't take her own life. Because I think, as I suspect you do, Doctor, that we may be looking at a case of murder.'

Chapter Eleven

With the doctor's instruction – to stay in the drawing room until summoned by the police inspector – ringing in her ears, Letty headed with determination for the front door.

'Letty!' Gunning seized her by the shoulder. 'Where are you going?'

'Out of this house! *Out!* It hardly matters where. I want to get away from this gloomy place. There's malice seeping under every door, evil lurking round every corner, and there's always a rustling along those dark corridors.'

'That'll be the draughts and the long skirts the servants wear – they rustle, you know.'

'Well, I've had a considerable shock to the system. I want to walk in the sunshine. I want to breathe fresh air and get my thoughts in order. A less sensitive soul may not have the same need – you can wait on Inspector . . . Mariani, was it? If you want to.' She dismissed him with a nod and turned away.

'You can't parade about by yourself without an escort. Not in Herakleion. The women in this town still go about wearing head scarves and veils and long black dresses, both Muslim and Orthodox Christians. Discretion is expected, even with foreigners. I'll come with you. Look – there's a hotel in a square near the seafront that's used by Cook's tourists and the like, off the boat and in transit for Egypt. We'll go there and get a pot of tea or something. You're still trembling, Letty. A cup of Assam with lots of sugar in it is what you need.' He gave a short bark of a laugh. 'If we were in the trenches, I'd prescribe a half-pint of rum each to numb the pain.'

Through her self-absorbed daze, Letty began to notice that Gunning was subdued. He was clearly wrestling with his emotions, and she was ashamed for her own insensitivity. The man had known Phoebe for months, not mere hours. His loss must be greater than any Letty could feel.

They walked on in silence to the hotel where they settled on the tea terrace amongst a chattering crowd of Europeans. All around them they heard a swirl of French, Italian, and German, as well as braying English voices, and they sank gratefully into the camouflage of colourful summer clothes and straw hats. They sat quietly, unable to offer each other comfort, alone with their distress.

Letty finally broke the silence. '*He* did it, don't you think, William?' she asked impulsively. 'But how to prove it? Not sure how I can do it but I think I'm going to try!'

'Not sure which "he" you have in your sights, Letty.'

'Theodore, of course! Lying asleep in the middle of the afternoon while your wife gets murdered right next door? Is that likely? All that yawning and huffing and puffing! I wonder if the police will be taken in? Judging by the way he asked for a certain officer to be fetched, the fellow's probably in his pay anyway.'

'Hang on a moment! Theodore quite often *did* retire to his room in the afternoon. And always on a Sunday. It's a Cretan tradition. They call it *mesimerianos hypnos*, and so alien is it from the habits of our cold home climate we can only translate it by using another foreign word: *siesta*. I remember one day an urgent message came for him from one of his digs. Nobody about, so I went up to deliver it myself. Deep sleeper. It took me quite a while to rouse him.'

'Can you be sure he was *alone*?' Letty asked sharply, thinking of Eleni.

'I don't think it would be quite the thing for the master of the house to conduct his clandestine affair behind a door communicating with his wife's bedroom. . . . But I bow to your greater experience of bohemian life.' He stirred uneasily and leaned across the table. 'I told you about the ... er ... arrangements over the coach house. And the lair George referred to, on the ground floor – no one's allowed to go in there except Eleni – to clean it, of course.'

'Ah. I see. But who else would profit by Phoebe's death, William? If he depended on her for her money, and if she'd suddenly decided she'd got fed up with him and intended to do a bunk, he might have thought his best plan was to kill her and pass it off as suicide. It could have been done on the spur of the moment – perhaps he was lounging in his room and heard her come back early with the doctor. ... There's a keyhole in the door – he could have watched and listened.' She shivered. 'Dr Stoddart said he had a feeling he was being observed – that someone was waiting for him to leave. And taking advantage of her stupor, Theodore could easily have strung her up. Let's not forget that he's a navy man. He'd know all about knots, wouldn't he?'

'Every man under the age of fifty – and that includes yours truly – knows about knots, Letty. Has known since he was in short trousers! Ever heard of the Boy Scouts? The hangman's noose was one of the first we learned. With ghoulish glee! It's really a wonder to me that there haven't been many more accidental and experimental hangings.'

'I know what you're up to. You're playing devil's advocate, William.'

'Someone has to put the brakes on when you're in full flow! You allow your instantly formed dislike of Russell to sway your judgement, which, in any case, I seem to remember, is far from infallible.'

'I can be impartial! And just to demonstrate my flexibility, let's change roles for a minute, shall we?' She hesitated for a moment. Then: 'That suicide note,' she said, 'if we may call it that. Now, if Theodore is as ignorant of ancient Greek as he purports to be, how could he have been familiar enough with a text of Euripides to select the very passage where a wife makes a statement of her guilt and declares her intention to kill herself? That's what I'd want to know. Unless, of course, there was a useful translation on the opposite page. Would you have any idea?'

'I know there wasn't one,' said Gunning, and Letty looked at him in surprise. 'I recognized the page. The print and the paper. It was torn from my own book.'

'*Your* book?'

'Phoebe was interested in that sort of thing. She liked to give the impression of being a fluffy-headed flapper, but there was much more to Phoebe than that. We had long conversations about mythology, ancient literature. She expressed an interest in the play *Medea*, and I lent her my old school text. It contains three plays of Euripides – *Medea*, *Hippolytus*, and . . . what was the third . . . not one of my favourites – *Alcestis*. Pure text, I'm afraid. No crib on offer apart from my scribblings in the margins. But she would have read it. She certainly didn't return it. It's probably on her bookshelf right now. With a page missing.'

'And your name on the flyleaf? Oh, dear! You'd better watch out, William! If they discover it and come after the only man in the household who acknowledges an acquaintance with ancient Greek, they'll slap the handcuffs on you. All the same, I'm not yet ready to cross Theodore off my list. I shall have to think my way around this.'

'I wish you wouldn't.'

'Well, perhaps the police inspector will be more willing to listen to my suspicions.'

'Stop this! For a clever girl you can be remarkably foolish! Think! If Phoebe's death is indeed murder, the murderer is still at large and, one must presume, in the vicinity. He could kill again. And what more likely target than a bouncing blabbermouth waving a list of suspects in her hand? If the inspector asks for a statement, you will give him the bare facts, Letty, unadorned by any of your baroque flourishes. Antagonize no one.'

'Then I'll reserve my flourishes for you. Tell me – what sort of man may we expect the Guardian of the Law to be in this city?'

'Well, don't expect a crack Scotland Yard sleuth. There's not much crime on Crete. Knifings amongst sailors in the waterside taverns, sheep rustling, revenge killings in the course of family feuds. Cretans have a strict sense of honour, and anyone infringing on it is likely to meet his Nemesis sooner or later. And Nemesis will probably have a face he's familiar with, will clasp him warmly with one hand while the other sticks a knife between his ribs. But that's about it. The perpetrators are usually well known, instantly denounced, quite often summarily dealt with before the affair even comes to the ears of the authorities.

'You'll observe that most of the Cretan men, especially in the country, go about armed to the teeth. At the very least they'll have a silver-hilted dagger stuck into their cummerbund. Often side by side with a pistol of some ancient design and dubious state of reliability.' He winced. 'Not the sort of thing you'd want in proximity to your vitals! The shepherds out in the hills are not the curly-haired cherubs of myth – they're hard, moustached men apparently made of the same limestone as the crags they leap about on, and they sit on guard with a blunderbuss across their knees. They revere weaponry and don't hesitate to use it at every conceivable opportunity. The women as well have been known to take up arms in the defence of their homes.'

'Good gracious! Is there no official force to keep order on the island?'

'Keep order? Over Cretans? I can as easily imagine Agamemnon being chased over the hills by the Keystone Kops!' Gunning shrugged. 'But there is a gendarmerie force that attempts to keep order in the country areas, and a smarter sort of police judiciaire that swaggers about town liaising with the embassies. Their main duties are checking that the luggage of departing Europeans doesn't contain the valuable contents of some ancient grave or other. And *that's* a heinous crime out here – smuggling artefacts out of the country. The authorities are much more vigilant than they used to be. Scandalous to-do last year at the port! A distinguished archaeologist was attempting to make off on the ferry with a rucksack containing a particularly delectable piece of ancient pottery. When challenged and threatened with a search, his outraged response was to defy the officers and chuck the bag and contents into the harbour!'

'What a villain! My sympathies are entirely with the authorities! Did they let him get away with it?'

'He comes and goes and we don't hear the clank of manacles. But their control is increasingly effective, I have to say. So, if you're thinking of picking up a seal stone and having it made into a hat pin, watch out! They'll be on to you!'

'I'll bear it in mind. But what about a murder? How will they deal with a murderer?'

'You must expect them to parade a portly, epauletted, gold-braided servant of the Law, such as it is in this remote outpost of the Greek State. Rather out of his depth and grumbling that his Sunday's been disrupted.'

'So, the town's hardly a hotbed of crime and intrigue, then?'

'This is a peaceful time but these huge walls have, at least four times in the last hundred years, enclosed a killing ground; they have witnessed ethnic massacres, burnings, lynchings – horrors I won't attempt to convey over a Sunday cup of tea.'

He glanced around at the bristling Venetian fortification. 'A shelter or a trap, depending on the blood that flowed in your veins, the shape of your head, and the length of your nose. The Turks used to have a curfew. They closed all the gates every night, shutting everyone in. And then, one day they went on the rampage. They shut the gates at noon and by the end of that day more than a thousand Christians were dead. The branches of the plane tree above our heads were heavy with the hanged corpses of young men. The basin of the fountain over there where that little girl is paddling was running red with blood. Most of the Turkish population fled back to their homeland when the Great Powers – that's us plus Italy, France, and Russia – came stamping in saying: "Enough's enough! This land belongs to the Cretans. You Turks are to hand it back."

'But some Mohammedans remain living where they ever did. And some families in the long centuries of peace had intermarried and, awkwardly, have both Muslim and Christian antecedents. The flames may have been doused, but the embers glow still. And in addition, drifting about on the surface, you have the European community, mostly diplomatic, commercial, or academic. Not many incidences of violent crime there! Inspector Mariani is going to find himself challenged.'

'Mariani? An Italian name?'

'After the bloody turmoil of 1898, with Turks and Cretans still growling at each other like fighting bull terriers on a lead, they imported with great success a crack corps of carabinieri from Italy to keep the peace. This Mariani may be a son or even grandson of one of these. The orderly thing to do would be to bury the evidence quickly, without undue fuss, I suppose. I'm not sure how important the suicide of a foreign woman would be to the police inspector.'

'And that's exactly what I was expecting to hear you say!' said Letty. 'I know it's all going to be swept under the carpet or under six feet of earth, but I won't leave it there, William! Phoebe was a mystery to me and I can't begin to grasp her essence any more than I can grasp a ray of sunshine through the leaves, but I liked what I saw in the brief glimpse I had. She was warm and bright.'

'True enough ... the light and the colour have gone from that house now she's dead. She struggled against the shadows.'

'And she wasn't expecting to die! Just before she left, she said to me: "Get Ollie to show you the House of the Axes. I'll be sure to test you on it when you get back." She was holding on to my hand ...' Letty stumbled and her lips began to tremble. She reached out her hand blindly and Gunning's handkerchief was instantly thrust into it. With a growl of sympathy he moved to the chair by her side and put an arm around her shoulders, murmuring remembered priestly words of consolation.

Letty shrugged him away. 'Spare me all that "Time the Healer . . . gone to a better place" nonsense, William!' she said briskly. 'Perhaps the elder spirits of this place are breathing on me with their sweet, foetid breath, but I can't leave Phoebe dangling as a suicide, unexplained, unavenged. She's waiting about somewhere, shocked and displaced and angry. "I'll be sure to test you when you get back," she told me, and I'm certain she's doing just that. I won't forget it. And I promise you, William – I intend to give her an answer. Not just any answer that will satisfy the living – I mean the correct ten-out-of-ten answer.'

Gunning sighed. 'Very well. I give in. Suspect number one's Theo. Who's next on your list?'

'I suppose that we ought not to forget that there are staff about the house. Eleni, for one. She was flitting about with glasses of water, according to the doctor. Nothing easier than to slip in and knot up a noose –'

'Odd that she should have waited for years before succumbing to an urge to murder her mistress, don't you think?'

'Mmm . . . and *hanging* someone like that . . .'

'Know what you mean,' he said, answering her thought. 'It's not a female method, is it? Poisoning perhaps . . . a quick push downstairs . . . Either of which she could have done at any time over the last five years. No. Hanging's such a pre-meditated, dramatic end. A see-what-you've-driven-me-to shout of despair from the dying – of either sex.'

'From Phaedra onwards,' Letty murmured. 'And I don't suppose it was an innovation in *her* day. Always a length of rope and a beam around, from the very beginning. But, William, I could accept more easily that Phoebe had staged her death herself if it weren't for those marks on her thighs that alerted Stoddart.'

'Marks? What marks?'

He considered her account and then, hesitating, suggested quietly: 'Have you thought there might be an alternative explanation for this? Come on, Letty, woman of the world that you are! If Stoddart declares them to be finger and thumb prints, I'm prepared to accept that, but I do wonder if, in his innocence, it hasn't occurred to the good doctor that there is an activity other than murder which could have left traces in that region?'

Letty's eyes widened in horror. 'That she'd been attacked – raped – you mean? Oh, Good Lord! Remember the note Phaedra held clutched in her dead hand? It accused Hippolytus of just that – rape. I didn't mention it at the scene. No point in pouring oil on a fire already raging.'

'No. I noted your discretion and was thankful for it. But, look, whatever it was, it needn't have been quite so gross ... just overenthusiastic, perhaps? And Phoebe bruised easily. That paper-thin skin of hers – about as tough as a butterfly's wing, I should imagine.'

'You're implying that she endured an act of sexual congress whilst wearing her boots?'

'It's not impossible.' His voice was determinedly steady.

'But you heard Theodore waking up. Erotic urges stirring, wouldn't you say?'

'Siestas. That's the effect they have on the male constitution. Particularly in hot climates,' Gunning explained. 'But I take your meaning. Unless he had superhuman gifts in that department, it quite obviously wasn't her husband who'd ... um ...'

'No. Clearly. We'd better examine the other men in her entourage,' Letty interrupted, judging the discussion bordered on impropriety. 'I think it might be easier if we first *eliminated* the men around her who could not possibly have done it. So that's George out of the running. Even if he weren't a saint anyway – he has the cast-iron alibi of being in your company all afternoon, William. "Out looking for bones," Eleni said – with a slight frisson of disgust, I thought.'

'A saint and a priest together?' mused Gunning. 'Impeccable company, you'd say ... vouching for each other ... but you'd be wrong!'

'Wrong? In what way, wrong?'

Gunning stirred uncomfortably in his seat, poured out another cup of tea, and drank half of it, thinking furiously before he replied. 'We did indeed go out after bones – the skulls I talked about last night, do you remember? George was keen to come along with his tape measure. The skeletons were holed up in a cave near the shore about three miles down the coast, according to the map. The Cretans would say a distance of two cigarettes. We walked there. And very fascinating it was, too, but when he'd finished taking his notes George seemed to get a little restless ... kept looking at his watch. I was sketching and not about to be put off, so I told him I had a good further hour's work to do and would quite understand if he wanted to get away and do something less boring. Just being polite, you know – and I was quite surprised when he accepted, rather too readily, I thought, to set off back by himself.

'But the odd thing was – when I got to the city gates, there he was, chatting with a crowd of beggars. He rejoined me as though he'd only been away for a minute and we arrived in each other's company back at the villa at – well, you know when.'

'Five past five,' said Letty. 'So you're saying that George was on the loose for ... an hour?'

'Longer. I wasn't really paying much attention to my watch. It's not very reliable anyway. You learn to do as the Cretans do and keep an eye on the sun to run your life by. The sun and a packet of cigarettes will get you through the day! But, nearer three hours. I'd say – though not on oath – that he left me in the cave at a little before two o'clock. We met up at the gates at half past four, had a drink in a *kafenion*, and wandered back. George is always very considerate about my leg when we're out together. He didn't push the pace. I think he sensed I was a bit sore and weary.'

They both fell silent, absorbing the meaning of all this. Finally Letty said: 'So Saint George moves into second place on my list. Well, second equal, I should say.'

'Equal?' he asked, puzzled.

'Sharing the slot with one William Gunning! If George is suddenly without an alibi – then so are you, William. You must see that.'

Her tone had been light, but abruptly she realized the significance of her teasing remark.

'What's your problem, Letty?' he asked, picking up her change in mood.

'Not *my* problem. Yours, perhaps? I was just remembering . . . From something Phoebe said, I got the impression that she was in love. Had fallen in love, and she wasn't thinking about her husband.' Letty made an effort to recall the laughing conversation in the bull court. 'It was something she said about Ariadne . . . wondering what it had felt like to betray her family for love, understanding her . . . excusing her. I could swear now, with hindsight, that she wanted me to pursue it – you know, in a girls-together speculative sort of way. I was too slow to understand, I think. And I certainly didn't pick it up. Killed it dead, you might say.' She sighed. 'Too preoccupied with my own problems. If only I'd shown a bit more interest in *hers* it might all be much clearer. Poor Phoebe! Do you suppose she'd fallen for someone? And was dying to talk about it? Someone around her, here in this town, that she was sighing for?'

She frowned and bit her lip. 'Oh, no! She couldn't have been . . . Oh, sod it!' The crude expletive escaped, betraying the depth of her sudden anguish. 'William, please tell me – Phoebe wasn't planning to run away with *you*, was she?'

Chapter Twelve

'With me? Good Lord! What a perfectly disgraceful suggestion! The fact that I lost sight of my companion for an hour or two, to any reasonable person, would not constitute grounds for suspicion of immorality and a capacity for murder! Laetitia, I despise you!'

He caught the attention of the waiter and asked for the bill. Letty had never seen him so angry.

'Calm down! I'm just trying to see it with the eyes of an impartial investigator,' she said defensively, and at once went on the attack. '"Why not?" people might think. "Here's a devilish handsome man, newly, well, nearly newly, introduced into the household. Cultivated, amusing, her own kind and countryman. Decorated war hero . . . a man with a past . . . Any woman might have her head turned . . ." That's what *they* could say. It might be a while before they discovered that he was a charlatan, deceiving and not to be trusted the length of his own ruler . . . that's if it *is* his own ruler . . .' she finished rudely. 'I mean – what do you suppose they'll conclude if they discover you're not what you pretend to be?'

'I am exactly what I say I am,' he said stiffly.

'And what exactly *are* you telling the world? That you're a renegade ex-priest, wanderer, and confidence trickster?' she said, unable to suppress her bitterness. 'You're not an architect. Never were. Nor are you an archaeologist – you just peered over my shoulder into the occasional trench last year.' The words sounded sharper, more angry than she intended, the unsuppressable symptoms of the hurt his leaving had caused her.

'I have the same qualifications as yourself, miss, to be an archaeologist, which is to say – none at all.'

She was not surprised by the coldness of his reply but Letty blushed with fury.

'You need no scroll, no mortarboard with tassel dangling on the left to declare to the world that you have sat for three years in lecture rooms to make you an archaeologist, Miss Talbot.' She flinched at his scorn. 'You have none such yourself, I understand? No disgrace: Nor has Theodore – Schliemann was self-taught, as is Howard Carter. Dig, discover, record efficiently, and you're an archaeologist. Not that I am claiming to be such. Your accusation is unfounded and unkind. As to your other fraudulent charge – the same applies. Anyone may call himself an architect. Didn't you realize? An engineer – now, that's another matter! But in our society anyone who fancies he has the talent may put up his brass sign and begin to draw. He'd do well, of course, in the interests of public safety, to obtain the services of a professional engineer if he's attempting anything more adventurous than a decorative cornice, but there you are . . .'

'But how do you know so much about it, William? How on earth did you ever convince Andrew Merriman – who is nobody's fool – that you were an architect?'

'You could say it runs in the family. I had a brother. An older brother, James. He was studying architecture. He made me test him on his assignments. I worked through his course with him.' His information was coming as though dragged from him, in staccato bursts. Was this the creaking of invention she was hearing or the dredging to the surface of memories deliberately repressed? She felt a passing twinge of guilt when she remembered the many occasions she'd talked to Gunning with nostalgia for her own happy early years spent with her brother. She had never asked him about his own. Too late now to make polite reparation.

'By the time James received his degree I knew almost as much about architecture as he did. I tramped London in his wake, listening to him raving about Wren and Hawksmoor and Soane. I have a retentive memory. I also have a ruler which has his initials carved on it.'

Letty could not meet his eye.

'But I didn't deceive Andrew. I colluded with him! He can be very . . . puckish . . . as you know. He thought it would be a great joke to pass me off on to a man he had no liking for – Theodore. And I rather think it suited him to mark my card and start me on a new career. Merriman likes to cup people in his hands and launch them like a bird into the air. Perhaps you've noticed?'

He paused, challenging her to reply, but she was silent, dealing with her embarrassment.

'For *that*, at least, I shall always be grateful to Andrew,' he went on. 'Our mentor has a knack of bringing out the best in people. He convinced me I could do it and, Letty – I *can*! I produced the goods for Theo. I wouldn't have stayed on if I hadn't been able to do that.'

'I do wonder, though, whether Theo has found you out – all that seemingly casual questioning at supper last night was a bit pointed, wasn't it?'

He shrugged. 'You're right. And let me thank you for your unexpected support. It quite put him off balance. I must have said something that alerted him, and if he's any sense – and he has a lot – he'll have run a check on me in London. He can't, however, at this stage, with his book ready to go into print, denounce me in a fit of righteous indignation and rip out the illustrations.'

'When he's accepted the situation,' said Letty, 'you watch: He'll decide his best plan will be to take his cue from Andrew and put all his authority behind you – present you as his discovery. You said it, William – all Theodore's geese are swans. I shall expect to see you paddling elegantly down the academic stream when you return.'

'Letty? Did you mean what you said . . .?' He started to speak and thought better of it, trailing away in confusion.

'The bit about your appeal for the opposite sex? Cultivated? Amusing? Devilish handsome, did I hear myself saying? Just quoting opinions I've overheard.' She allowed herself a long, deliberate look at his face. 'Yes, you know, they might have something there. The Levantine air seems to agree with you. The darkened colour gives your eyes an even more devastating depth of blue . . . your new haircut's a bit on the short side – a touch of the Knights Templar, perhaps? – but it suits you. And those Cretan tall boots and corduroy breeches are quite devastating. Not sure about the baggy black shirt . . . And the human bone – a metatarsal, is it? – sticking out of your breast pocket might put the ladies off, but – well – yes – I can quite see how some women might –'

But, apparently too angry to stay and hear another word of her nonsense, he pushed back his chair abruptly and stalked off. She put down a handful of coins on the table and hurried after his retreating figure.

Eleni opened the door the moment they knocked and told them to go up to the drawing room, where they were awaited by the Herakleion police. The master was with them, she added.

Gunning made their excuses to the inspector, claiming that Miss Talbot had needed to take a walk in the fresh air to recover from the shock of her discovery. Miss Talbot murmured her own insincere apologies for her moment of feminine weakness. Mariani, a surprising figure, stepped forward and bowed slightly. 'I wonder, Mr Russell, if I might be allowed a few minutes' conversation with the lady and then the gentleman alone? Could you arrange this?' His tone was deferential, his voice low and with the slightest Mediterranean accent.

'Oh . . . right-oh. We'll make ourselves scarce, Kosta, and leave you to it.' He turned with a warning glower to Letty.

'As you hear, the inspector speaks excellent English . . . or French . . . or Italian . . . whatever you care to throw at him from your repertoire, miss. I leave you in his capable hands.' He made for the door, gesturing to Gunning to follow.

As he turned to leave, Gunning pushed a handkerchief into her hand. 'In case feminine weakness should strike again,' he muttered.

Letty took a long look at the inspector when they were left alone and decided that she would do well to take Gunning's advice and stick exactly to the letter of her evidence. Straight down the line. Those clever dark eyes would catch her out if she elaborated or twisted anything, she thought. She'd been completely taken in by Gunning's exaggerated sketch of a musical comedy character, and smiled to see that this man was young – early thirties perhaps – with an athletic figure. He was wearing a smartly tailored grey suit but, 'strip that away,' she thought, round-eyed with admiration, 'put him in a yellow loincloth with a spear in his hand, and I'd know him!'

Responding at once to her inspection of the region of his thighs, he apologized for his appearance with a neat, dismissive gesture: 'You will take me for one of the *makrypantalonades*, Miss Talbot.'

'The . . . long-trousered ones?' Letty hazarded a guess.

'Yes. City slickers, I think you would say. And you would be right – not all Cretan men go about in baggy woollen *vrakes*! And this is a Sunday, you understand. I am not on duty. However – this case, and it distresses me to refer to such a tragedy as 'a case,' is one in which I take a personal interest. I was acquainted with Mrs Russell . . . a charming, charming woman. Such a loss. And such a shock for the household, of which I understand you to be a recent member? I'm sure I need not detain you for long. Shall we sit down and begin?' He indicated two high-backed gilt chairs and they settled opposite each other. She noticed that he had given her the chair facing the window with the westering sunlight shining in her eyes.

The inspector took a notebook and held it on his knee. 'I have the outline of the circumstances from Theodore,' he said, 'and I'm told that you were the unfortunate one who discovered the body. Please tell me how this came about, referring to times whenever you can be sure of them.'

She accounted for her day from the moment Phoebe had met her in the library until she had left the house with Gunning. He made meticulous notes and then finally: 'A most clear narration, Miss Talbot. And it corresponds in all respects with the statement of the housekeeper, whom I have already interviewed. One or two points . . . Could you sum up your impressions of Mrs Russell's mood, her temperament, as it struck you when you became acquainted with her?'

Letty talked about Phoebe's apparent frailty and her lack of appetite, the concern she had expressed on her behalf to the doctor. She mentioned the doctor's own concern and Phoebe's collapse during the picnic. She added, and heard the inconsistency in her own statement as she spoke: 'But she was very cheerful this morning. I remember telling Dr Stoddart it was as though she was looking forward to something. And – she talked of what we would do when we got back home. We were going to discuss the excavations at the palace. She'd appointed herself my tutor for the day and was going to check I'd taken it all in.' She fixed the inspector, whose pencil was poised, hovering over the page, writing suspended, with a meaningful look.

'And you were present at the discovery and opening of what I will call the "suicide note"? Tell me more about that.'

Letty told him.

'You stayed behind to help the doctor to complete his examination? Why was this?'

'He wanted a little female input. Help with her clothing, someone to witness the degree of . . . oh, what did he say – hypostasis – that's it. And there were tasks he couldn't perform without causing embarrassment and grief for the members of her family or, indeed, the rest of the household

136

who knew and loved her. I'm sure you'll understand, Inspector. Being freshly arrived, uninvolved, female, and – most pertinently – on the spot, I was the obvious choice to render assistance.'

'Ah. Yes. Dr Stoddart must have found you a very useful substitute for a nurse, Miss Talbot. Not surprising that, after this valiant effort, you needed to take a breath of air. Well, I think that's all I need to know. For the moment. You have given me a clear and objective picture of the day's sad events.' He closed his notebook and – unexpectedly – smiled. 'I understand that you are to go off adventuring with a spade tomorrow? Digging about on old Juktas? Disturbing the last resting place of the Father of the Gods? Never forget, Miss Talbot, that Zeus is the brother of Poseidon the Earth shaker. Some say they are two halves of the same god. He – or they – may not take kindly to having the sleep of centuries disturbed. If I feel the ground stirring below my feet I shall know whom to blame!'

'Oh, I wasn't expecting to go off straight away! If I'd thought at all. Not with all this going on!' protested Letty. 'Not with Phoebe's death still unresolved.'

'May I recommend that you go?' he said, and Letty instantly recognized this for the command it was. 'All is arranged, I hear. And there are others dependent on the schedule being adhered to.' He softened the forcefulness of his suggestion by adding with a smile, '. . . If you can bear it, of course? And you will be no more than . . . oh . . . ten cigarettes' journey away from Herakleion.' He stood and offered her his hand. 'I will send a runner for you if your presence here should be necessary. And you will be returning in any case for the weekend. Would you now summon Mr Gunning for me as you leave?'

Letty loitered unashamedly outside the door while Gunning was interviewed, even put her ear to the gilded panels when the coast was clear, but heard nothing more than the indistinct murmuring of the confessional, certainly not the snap of handcuffs.

The door opened after only ten minutes – a fraction of the time the inspector had taken to speak to her, she noticed. She caught a startled Gunning by the hand and tugged him down the corridor. 'Come to the library, William, and explain to me why you're still at large!'

'Now tell me,' she said when she'd closed the door and window and placed two books, randomly selected from the shelves, open on a table in front of them, 'did you reveal that George went AWOL for most of the afternoon? . . . William?' And, seeing his confusion: 'You *didn't*! I bet you didn't! But why not?'

'It never came up,' he said tersely. 'I answered the inspector's questions . . . told him nothing less than the truth. He asked me what time George and I had arrived back at the house and I told my story from that point. He didn't seek to know what I'd been doing earlier. He'd obviously already spoken to George. If he asks me – I'll tell him,' he finished defiantly.

'Defending Saint George? Well, I can see why you wouldn't feel able to tweak the inspector's sleeve and hiss: "Hey! Here's something you ought to know! Take this down: The man Mrs Russell's note involved in her death was actually gadding about town for the best part of three hours out of my vision at the crucial time . . ." Difficult thing to do – point the finger at someone you're fond of. You *are* fond of George, aren't you, William?'

'Quite obviously,' he answered sharply. 'And I respect him. I got to know him well last autumn before he went off to Europe, and my opinion hasn't changed. I've been closely involved with all types and conditions of men, most of them under unbearable stress. I think I can tell a good 'un when I come across one, and George is one of the best. "A golden man", they say in the village. He wasn't involved in Phoebe's death, I'm certain of it. I don't think he even understood the significance of that suicide envelope – it was not a note, remember, Letty. I think he was aghast and astonished like the rest of us.'

'But you heard Theo's comment as plainly as I did – Phoebe was apparently in the habit of passing him cheques. Perhaps she'd got fed up with underwriting her husband's expenses and supporting her stepson into the bargain. That Bugatti wasn't cheap, you know.'

'And in a fit of pique George climbed up the wisteria and hanged the golden goose, are you saying? Then he arranged to incriminate himself by leaving a supposed suicide note just where everyone would look for one? This isn't a parlour guessing game, Letty, and I want you to stop this silly speculation. It does you no credit to smear the reputation of people who are not yet known to you.'

'Can you say you know George as well as all that? He seems to me a pretty inscrutable character. I've never met anyone like him before.'

'Listen – George is not a taker of life. My faith in him is as simple as that. He couldn't begin . . . He's a defender and saver of life, if anything. And any life! It's slow progress going out into the town with him, I can tell you – he stops to berate anyone he catches beating a donkey. Any creature's pain he seems to feel as his own. I've seen him rescue a cat from tormenting boys and then kneel in the dust to talk to the villains. The neighbourhood dogs fawn on him and escort him about the streets.'

Gunning paused in his eulogy, uneasy, wondering whether to confide further. 'I think I can account for the cheques that so worried you, Letty. They weren't for his own use, I suspect. He's involved with something he doesn't want generally known, and you must promise, Letty, that you will try to curb your tongue and not pass on what I'm about to tell you!' He waited for her nod. 'George – with, I do believe, the support both moral and financial of Phoebe, who was as good-hearted as himself – is the driving force behind the rescue mission for lepers.'

It took a moment for Laetitia to absorb the word with its medieval associations of death, despair, and exclusion. 'Lepers? Great heavens! Do they still have them out here?'

'I'm afraid so. In large numbers. But you won't see them about the streets anymore – not for the last twenty years. They've been herded together from all parts of Greece and the Aegean as well as Crete, and sent to finish off their existence on an island to the east of here. It's called Spinalonga. They live in the old Venetian fortifications, building their own houses from whatever materials are to hand, dependent on the charity of people like George. He's helped to organize a daily handout of bread, rebuilding on the island, and a medical service. It's a hellhole but it's a shelter of sorts where they can organize themselves into some sort of civilized life. He's constantly over there working with them, with absolutely no regard for his own safety. And he's been doing it from a very young age. One of his objects in going to Europe was to grill the medical world and find out where they'd got to in working on a cure for this disgusting disease. He's knowledgeable and he's impressive. You can imagine the effect his storming into a meeting, claiming to represent the unfortunates of the Aegean, would have!'

'Clatter of tumbling ivory towers heard for miles around, I shouldn't wonder!'

'You should hear him on the subject of "experts"! "Sitting on their bloody arses – holding symposia, listening to the sound of their own voices while there are people here on Crete, good people, crumbling and falling apart!" He doesn't always talk like a saint,' said Gunning, smiling faintly. 'The best saints swear fluently.'

'I had no idea,' said Letty softly. 'Isn't it very dangerous? I mean – he must realize he risks infection himself?'

'He doesn't talk about it much, for obvious reasons. People still believe that leprosy can be transmitted by physical contact, with all the ease of influenza. Perhaps they're right. The villagers note that family members often fall victim. There are grandparents, parents, and children from the same family in isolation over there, sent away into exile as soon as their symptoms become evident.

140

Sometimes – and this is the most heartbreaking thing – a child will be sent over by itself, separated forever from the rest of its family who are unaffected, and left to the care of the other outcasts there on the island.'

'What you say is truly appalling,' whispered Letty. 'I don't wonder that Phoebe should have involved herself with this. It must have touched her deeply.'

'From her first week of living here, George says. He was escorting her while she explored along the coastline of her new home when she witnessed a sending into exile. At the centre of a wailing crowd, a small boy, no more than eight, was being torn from his mother's arms and hurried into the ferryboat to make the crossing to Spinalonga. Hideous scene! Phoebe demanded to know what was going on – what was happening to the boy. The upshot was, George told her exactly what went on, then confessed his involvement. Phoebe began at once to encourage him and, with the underpinning of large amounts of her cash, to extend his interest.'

'Is George in danger, William? Is he in contact with the sick?'

'Frequently. He makes no social distinction between lepers and the rest of us. He's one of those who maintain the disease is not transferred by contact. And he cites his own impeccable state of health in evidence. But, get him in a corner, and even he admits that physical proximity does, time after time, seem to be a factor. And yet, there are people like himself, like the island doctor, like many nurses and workers in leper hospitals who've been in contact for years with pus and gore and sores of every description and remain unaffected. I've seen him shake their hands, exchange hugs and kisses with the little ones. "They like to be touched," he'll tell you, "to feel that they aren't ghosts to the rest of us."'

'You argue on both sides?'

'The truth is, Letty, nobody knows how leprosy spreads. What they do know is that there isn't a cure. Once contracted, isolation and a lingering, painful death are the only possible outcome. So – any man confiding that he spends his days in the company of lepers is likely to find his friends shuffling uncomfortably away from him in short order.'

'But you don't shuffle away, William,' said Letty. 'You would never abandon someone close who needed you?'

He looked back at her steadily. 'No,' he said. 'I would not.'

A thudding of boots down the tiled corridor made Letty pull her chair away from Gunning's. They both looked up innocently from their unread books when the door banged open.

'Aha! Getting in a little practice for a season of intimacy – with Minoan culture, I see,' said Stewart with heavy innuendo. 'Been all over the house looking for you. Aren't you the lucky ones – getting away from all this doom and gloom! There's a welcoming party formed up on the square outside waiting for you. At least I *think* they're welcoming!' He mimed cutting his throat. 'You must decide for yourselves. Theodore's laid it on. You've got to hand it to the man – in the thick of all this grief and drama he thinks of his guests. The chap who'll be running the dig for you has turned up with some of his merry men to say hello. And to fix a departure time for tomorrow, as he's eager to get this little junket under way as early as possible. They've been loitering about the place all day. The sooner you start digging, the sooner they start earning. They're all waiting to get a look at the new director. So – jump to it! Off you go – I'll put your books away . . .' He glanced at the titles. 'Good Lord! What's this? A closet lepidopterist, Gunning? And Miss T., I see, is halfway through the *Erotokritos*? In the seventeenth-century Cretan? I say, well done!'

Laetitia could have sworn the eight men lounging in the shade of the plane tree had arranged themselves

142

deliberately with a thought to the effect they would produce on a female stranger. For a moment she was torn between clapping with delight and taking cover in a cowardly way behind Gunning as she hesitated on the steps.

The men in the square had all the self-mocking dash of the chorus of *The Pirates of Penzance*, she thought. All were in Cretan dress. Baggy dark blue *vrakes* were tucked into high boots; gleaming white wide-sleeved shirts were confined by body-hugging embroidered waistcoats. Around their waists were wound lengths of mulberry silk, and tucked sideways into each cummerbund was an assortment of weaponry; ivory-hilted daggers and silver pistol butts gleamed in the folds. All had luxuriant moustaches and thick hair under fringed black kerchiefs twisted around the head at a jaunty angle. The packs they wore casually slung over their shoulders were woven and brightly coloured, crimson, purple, and orange.

Their leader wore a cape thrown negligently over his shoulders. He swaggered forward, putting out his cigarette, on seeing them. Impossible to slouch in such a getup, Letty thought, admiring. All you could do was stride to centre stage with the panache of a Cyrano de Bergerac.

Gunning was swept instantly into a whiskery embrace by this man, whom she took to be Aristidis, and the hugs and backslappings were repeated seven more times as they all greeted him. The moustaches grew less formidable as Gunning progressed down the line until he arrived at the youngest man, who sported a very creditable Ronald Colman. A good deal of banter followed until the moment came for Gunning to introduce her. He managed this in Greek with a bit of prompting from Aristidis.

Eight pairs of lively dark eyes considered her with undisguised curiosity. They were friendly; they were not deferential as an English digging team would have been. She would be looking at this crew for a long time, she thought, before she saw anyone tug a forelock.

'We are delighted to meet you, Miss Laetitia.' Aristidis made her name sound like a sneeze. His men grinned appreciatively. 'We come to greet you and show ourselves so that tomorrow morning in the thick mist of dawn you will know you start out with friends and you will not fear you are being kidnapped by brigands. The supplies have been going out to Kastelli all week and all that remains is to move the people out to the site. I have hired horses for yourself and Kyrie Gunning. Englishwomen, I know, do not like donkeys.'

She murmured a few polite phrases in reply and then the talk clicked back into Greek once more. It was Gunning who was consulted, informed, and advised. The conference broke up with laughter and noisy good-byes, and in seconds the team had swirled away, leaving Letty amused and intrigued.

'Did they dress up just for me?' she asked Gunning.

'Not at all!' He was laughing at her. 'Sunday best shirts, perhaps, but otherwise their everyday gear. If you'd looked closely you'd have seen that those dashing breeches were worn and much patched, the boots resoled many times, the cummerbunds and armament hand-me-downs. Most of them are shepherds and farmers. They work, travel, and sometimes sleep out on the hill in the same outfits.'

'Ah, that explains it,' said Letty, waving a negligent hand in front of her nose, 'that feral odour.'

'Those men have hiked ten miles under a hot sun over rough terrain just to come and get a look at you, Letty! A bit strong for you, is it – the honest stink of a working man? Are you regretting already the bay rum and lavender water of a London drawing room? It's not too late for you to turn your delicate nose to the north and beat a retreat.'

'Not at all, William. You mistake me. I expressed myself badly. I was thinking, rather – the enticing scent of a herb-covered mountainside, underlaid with the sweat of a vigorous man in his prime and, floating over all, a tantalizing top note of Balkan tobacco. My senses are telling me a wolf pack has recently passed this way.' She shivered and

144

had little difficulty in conjuring up the shiver: 'Alarming –
but exciting!'

The tight line of his mouth told her he was trying not to
laugh. 'Balkan tobacco, eh? I can see,' he muttered, 'that I
must get in a supply of Sobranies.'

Chapter Thirteen

As she stood waiting with Gunning on the steps, luggage at her feet, Letty was relieved to be escaping the brooding stillness of the dark house at dawn. She had, nonetheless, a moment of trepidation as her escort loomed into view down the mist-shrouded street. The cavalcade approached as quietly as a file of six donkeys, eight mules, two horses, and eight men could manage, and their silent purposefulness contrasted with the noisy joviality of the previous evening.

At the sight of them, lines of poetry that had thrilled Letty as a child with their sinister meaning came back to mind. Shivering with sudden chill, she whispered the chorus of 'A Smuggler's Song' to Gunning:

> '"Five and twenty ponies
> Trotting through the dark
> Brandy for the Parson
> 'Baccy for the Clerk
> Laces for a lady, letters for a spy . . ."'

He smiled, leaned close, and added, '"And watch the wall, my darling, while the Gentlemen go by!"' The warning of a Cornish father, suddenly aware of smugglers abroad below in the street.

The men, now in black shirts and short woollen cloaks, were each leading a mule, its wooden saddle covered with a scarlet blanket. The two horses, sturdy-looking animals, were led forward for her and Gunning. Lean brown hands snatched away their bags and the luggage disappeared into the donkey file. Greetings were hushed, movements and gestures spare.

Holding her horse steady by the head as she prepared to mount, Gunning touched her shoulder. 'You'll be all right, Letty. You're with friends.'

They were well beyond the city gates and clattering down the Arkhanais road before Letty broke the silence. Drawing level with Gunning, she asked, 'Didn't Theodore mention a fourth member of the team? Who is it we're to meet in the village?'

'I'll leave it to Aristidis to introduce you when we arrive. It's his surprise!'

She knew he would say no more. 'Then tell me about Aristidis. Theo sings his praises. Another goose or a swan, would you say?'

'For once Theo does not exaggerate. If he's had any success on the island – and he's had considerable – he has Aristidis to thank for it. The man has an uncanny ability to sniff out productive sites. I've seen him do it. He can stand and survey a tract of countryside for a few minutes and then point and say: "I'd dig there, if I were you." And he's invariably right.'

'Well, he has lived here all his life. I should expect a native to be familiar with the terrain.'

'There's more to it than that. You should understand, Letty, that Aristidis is more than a clerk of works . . . the gaffer. He is truly interested in the world of Cretan archaeology and extremely knowledgeable. He has a natural ability and enthusiasm. If he'd had a sliver of the advantages that Theo and Arthur Evans have – money and connections – he could have been the authority on the Minoan age. He was raised in a village and was practically illiterate –'

'Was?'

'He just about knew his numbers and letters when he left the village school, but he wasn't content to spend the rest of his life herding the family goats. He took a job in the city and educated himself to an impressive standard. He was driven by an intense interest in his island's culture. Many of the villagers combine this interest with a phenomenal memory. I've heard – I've actually sat through – a recitation by a very old man of the hills, quite illiterate, of the *Erotokritos*.'

'The book I was pretending to read in the library?'

'Yes! Bad choice! Their national saga. And you saw the length of it! It's a thousand lines longer than the *Odyssey*! You can imagine the bardic stamina required to memorize that. A constant supply of the local *raki* seems to fortify them. Three glasses are my limit, I'm afraid! They think I'm rather a weed.'

'Yet they seem to like you?'

'I take the trouble – not that it is a trouble, it's a joy – to learn their language. I enjoy swaggering about in boots. And I find much to admire in their character and in their history. They have a good deal in common with the English – we're both an island race – sailors, soldiers, odd sense of humour, fiery, honourable, generous, irreverent – I could go on! They'd appreciate all our heroes – Robin Hood, Francis Drake, King Arthur, Thomas à Becket – name whom you like.'

'Toad of Toad Hall?' Letty suggested with a smile.

'They'd love his dashing style! It's hard not to think of Cretans in heroic terms; they're men you'd choose without a second thought to fight shoulder to shoulder with.'

'That's quite a eulogy coming from you, William.'

'I love them,' he said simply.

'Surely they have *some* faults?'

He frowned. 'Well, yes, they're human like the rest of us. They have quick tempers – it goes with the pride. And they're as fierce as they look! They'll readily seek vengeance for injuries done to them or their family. So stay on the right side of Aristidis! It shouldn't be difficult – he's easy to admire.'

'And one hundred per cent Cretan.' She smiled, watching Aristidis dash by, cloak flapping, as he spurred the length of the convoy, shouting abuse at the men at the rear. They responded with a laugh and returned the abuse, but, she noticed, put in an extra effort to do as he asked.

'In fact it's more like seventy-five per cent Cretan. His paternal grandfather was Turkish, a Turk who married a Greek girl. Quite a lot of that went on during the two hundred years of Ottoman occupation. And, before that, four centuries of Venetian rule. Acculturation and miscegenation occurred. And it's been going on since the Stone Age.'

'And it hasn't finished,' said Letty thoughtfully. 'Look at George. English father, German mother, but born here on the island. What on earth does that make him?'

'I don't think he gives it a thought!'

'Well, I rather think, if he had to choose, he'd decide to be Cretan. In spite of the drawbacks. What did you say – quick temper and pride? And didn't someone else say "All Cretans are liars"?'

'It was my least favourite saint – Paul – who was responsible for spreading that nasty little calumny,' he replied angrily. 'But he missed the point! The original statement came from a philosopher from Knossos, in fact – Epimenides. Himself a Cretan! And so –'

Letty laughed. 'The old logic problem? A paradox? If a Cretan says that all Cretans are liars – then he's presumably lying himself?'

'You have it! The humourless Paul wouldn't have seen that!'

'I think there's a rather unphilosophical interpretation of the charge. I'd say Epimenides was making a sweeping and tetchy statement about his countrymen and, in a superior way, excluding himself from the lineup. Do you know what he actually said?'

'Not sure anyone does. His works have disappeared. We just have quotations from other writers to go by.' He paused for a moment, suddenly thoughtful. 'But I can give you a taste and, Letty, you may find our man has something important to say to you, down over the centuries.

149

Good Lord! I wonder . . .? He's talking about Zeus. Listen
. . . something like this:

'"They fashioned a tomb for thee, o holy and high one –
The Cretans, always liars, evil beasts, lazy gluttons!
But thou art not dead: thou livest and abidest forever,
For in thee we live and move and have our being."'

Letty mulled this over for a moment, then asked: 'And
when was he saying all this?'

'Oh . . . about 600 BC?'

'So it's been common knowledge for centuries that the
Cretans claim Zeus to be mortal. They build a tomb for him
on his death. Or do they? Are they lying about that too?'
She reined in her horse and sighed. 'This is a wild-goose
chase, isn't it, William? We're being sent away to play
where we can't do any harm!'

'Very likely. My suspicions also.'

'And at just the time I would have wanted to be in
Herakleion. We ought to be there, William. Standing witness for Phoebe.'

'Some things just have to be left to the family, Letty.
There'll be funeral arrangements to make, her people in
Paris to be informed and summoned. Believe me, there was
little you could do at the Europa but get in the way.'

'I'm not sure the family can be trusted to pursue the
truth of her death. And Harry Stoddart must have felt
the same. Why else would he ask *me* to help him examine
her body? Because he sensed that I am the one person in
that household, recently arrived and impartial, who retains
an open mind.'

'Impartial, eh? Well, if it's any consolation, I formed a
good opinion of Inspector Mariani during our short interview. I don't think he's in Theo's pocket and I didn't get
the impression that he was going to let the matter rest
"under six feet of earth" as you put it. I promise you that
we'll go back to the villa at once, should it become necessary.' He glanced back at the troop riding behind and

grinned. 'Aristidis and I have devised a useful messenger service between Kastelli and the city. A sort of donkey express! And, look at them, Letty! You've got a skilled team with you – the best! Even if you don't manage to dig up the King of the Gods, you'll have learned a good deal.'

'And enjoyed *your* company for the length of the digging season,' she said. 'Something to be thankful for?'

The little convoy paused at a roadside *kafenion* five miles into the journey, and Letty tactfully distanced herself from the male company, waving a dismissive hand at Gunning, who was evidently torn between dutifully staying with her and joining the men in the café.

'It's quite all right, William. When in Crete . . . I wouldn't want them to take you for my poodle, so go and join them. You'll find me over there under that fig tree when you're ready.'

She made herself comfortable at a table out of earshot of the company and, lulled by the murmur of male voices punctuated by the occasional shout of laughter and the distant tinkling of bells as goats moved about in the surrounding hills, she felt guiltily at peace. The sun was well up, warming her bones and coaxing scents from the tussocks of herbs that seemed to seize a handhold in every crevice. The eye was enchanted by the colours, springtime yellow and purple, and Letty thought she recognized mimosa, bushy rockroses, and wild iris. She picked a spray of rosemary and ran it through her fingers, bruising the slender needles and breathing in the astringent perfume.

She must have started to nod off, she thought, minutes later, and shook herself fully awake as a more aggressive scent assaulted her. Coffee! A small white earthenware cup was being waved tantalizingly under her nose. It was accompanied by a frosted glass of chill water. 'William tells me you enjoy Greek coffee, Miss Laetitia,' Aristidis said. 'And this is wondrous coffee. *Metrio* – not too sweet. I hope that is what you like.'

151

She sipped and sipped again the sticky black brew. 'Wondrous indeed! One of these and I'm ready for anything!'

He smiled his pleasure and settled down on the chair opposite. 'Then I will ensure you are served coffee every morning in Kastelli. I added a kilo or two of beans to the supply list,' he added with quiet satisfaction.

'No one's told me, Aristidis – am I to stay in a hotel? Or a guest house?' she asked.

A short bark of laughter greeted her question. 'None such on offer in a small village like Kastelli, I'm afraid. But you will be comfortable and welcome. Don't worry – all is arranged.'

'I'm prepared to sleep on a pew in the church or on a schoolroom floor like my pioneering predecessor if I have to,' Letty told him lightly. 'I was thinking of Miss Harriet Boyd, the American archaeologist.'

'Oh, that was twenty years ago, and we have had good warning of your arrival, miss. We can do better. I met Kyria Boyd,' he confided. 'I was a very young man away from home for the first time, earning money where I could, and she gave me a job digging on one of her excavations. I was promoted to classification, and when she returned the following year she remembered me and made me a foreman. My interest in archaeology began with her. An exceptional woman!'

'She certainly is,' Letty agreed. 'And she owes her start to Arthur Evans, who pointed her in the right direction and smoothed the way to her first dig.'

Did he pick up the slight question behind her bland comment? Aristidis considered for a moment and then said carefully, 'I wonder if you have noticed that the so-obliging Dr Evans directed the eager but inexperienced Kyria Boyd to a very remote part of the island – far from his own centre of operations at Knossos? And – the site he encouraged the lady to explore was an Iron Age site. Not nearly so fascinating to the world as a Minoan one!'

Letty laughed. 'Dr Evans' prejudices are no secret! Harriet Boyd struggled against two drawbacks in his eyes:

She was a woman and an American. But she was nobody's fool. It wasn't two minutes, I understand, before she had abandoned the recommended site near Kavousi, wandered a mile or two down the road, and discovered Gournia! Hailed in the English press as "the Cretan Pompeii". But you were on the spot! Tell me – do I have that right?'

'Almost! Miss Boyd didn't "wander". She listened to advice from the local people and followed her own sure instincts. And they led her to Gournia. A whole Minoan town! The oldest town in Europe. We had to hire a hundred extra workmen to do the digging. Roads, houses, shrines – even a palace – were lying there just inches below the surface. You must take time to go and study it! There are still lessons to be learned from the experiences of Miss Boyd.'

And from Aristidis too, Letty thought, enjoying the show of pride and enthusiasm.

'And after that, Aristidis?' she asked. 'What did you do?'

'I worked with Miss Boyd for as long as she continued to return. Then for whoever was undertaking an interesting dig. Evans, of course, and lately Mr Russell.'

'I'm surprised Mr Russell could spare you,' said Letty. 'I understand him to have no fewer than three enterprises on the go at the moment.'

Aristidis shrugged. 'You are my punishment,' he said with a cheerful grin.

'I beg your pardon! I'm sorry to hear that!' Letty exclaimed. 'But I don't understand what you can mean?'

He grunted and looked over to the *kafenion*, perhaps regretting his bold statement, perhaps hoping for Gunning to intervene. 'I have had a falling-out . . . a disagreement . . . with Mr Russell. And this is his way of showing his anger. He sends me off to dig under the direction of a woman, and an inexperienced one at that. He thinks this will be a lesson to me and I will return begging forgiveness and professing eternal loyalty.'

Letty was not sure how to respond to this second-hand insult. 'I should very much like to hear how you managed so to upset Mr Russell, if you feel you can tell me,' she invited.

'Ha!' His black eyebrows gathered into a formidable line. 'It was in the matter of payment,' he confided. 'Mr Russell was in a hurry to finish a project before the end of last season. He hit upon what he thought was a clever way to make the men work faster. He divided the force into three teams and at the end of each day offered a bonus to whichever team had shifted the largest amount of earth, regardless of quality or quantity of finds produced.'

'And you objected to this cavalier attitude to excavation?'

'I did. I made my views clear! I withdrew my team – the men you have working with you now.' He waved a hand back to the café. 'They too are being punished. They are good men, most of them my cousins. They objected, as I did, to the sight of others not so careful, shovelling up and barrowing away tons of earth with little regard to the possible contents.'

'Well, you needn't be concerned,' Letty assured him. 'I intend to introduce no such dubious methods. I do worry, though, about supervision. I shall be on hand myself each day, of course, to keep an eye on things, but I know that many of the finds associated with the Minoan civilization are small in size – seal stones, rings, statuettes – all of which might possibly find their way off the site and into an antiquary's shop by the back door if proper supervision is not exercised. I've seen all too many of these items on sale in Athens.'

She paused, assessing his reaction to the speech she'd been advised to deliver. Andrew Merriman had been full of indignation at the scale of pillaging of important sites. Her teacher had warned her that on Crete, where the artefacts tended to be small enough to slip easily into a pocket or a saddlebag, they frequently fetched up in private collections and antiquarian boutiques. 'And keep an eye out, Letty,' he'd told her. 'It's not only the diggers who are tempted.'

Aristidis nodded, pleased, evidently, and not affronted, to hear this stated clearly from the outset. 'Sadly, this happens. But these men are all known to me and perfectly trustworthy. If we should have a bit of luck and find it necessary to take on extra labour, there could possibly be a problem. Do you have thoughts as to how to overcome the temptations?'

She had no doubt he had his own method and intended to implement it. But she played along and gave the answer which would have satisfied her mentor.

'I should like to offer a reward slightly in excess of the going rate at the antiquary's for any small finds,' she said. 'This, on top of the fair weekly wage I have agreed, should be clear and a sufficient incentive. And, I would like to think, the assurance that the objects so declared will be guaranteed a permanent place here on the island. Cretan remains will stay here where they belong.'

Aristidis nodded vigorously. 'Your terms are more than fair, Miss Laetitia, they are generous. My men will give you their best work. And if they can be rewarded openly and honestly for using their sharp eyes and experience, all the better.'

Seeing the men beginning to leave the café and head for their tethered mounts, he stood and smiled down at her. Briefly, Letty tried to decide who had been interviewing whom. She wondered if she had passed the inspection. How different all this would have been in England. There she would have had no direct contact with the men who got their hands dirty. All communication would be conducted through a string of intermediaries – the deputy director, the site foreman, the gang leader. She would have surveyed the activities from the nearest vantage point from the shade of her parasol. Letty silently thanked the groundbreaking – in more ways than one – Miss Boyd for the positive impression of western womanhood she had left behind. She vowed to build on it.

At least she was not encumbered with the Edwardian lady's petticoats and high lace collars. She had taken

Gunning's advice and set aside the trousers she had hopefully brought with her. Not acceptable, apparently, to Cretan eyes. He had approved the ankle-length riding skirts – two serge, three linen, and all brown – she had had tailored in Athens, and the men's boots scaled down to her size by a London bootmaker. The purveyor of footwear to the adventuring aristocracy had understood her problems at once and come up with several pairs of surprisingly comfortable, though tough, boots. Not elegant – and she felt a stab of grief as she thought of the salty comments Phoebe would have made. But at least they were guaranteed snake-proof. And that was a primary concern for Letty. She would be a figure of fun if she appeared in this rig in Piccadilly, but here in this rugged landscape among these rugged people she thought she would pass muster.

The village, when they approached, was an enchantment for Letty. Surrounded by a bounding convoy of small boys, who'd rushed out on sighting them to act as their riotous escort, she reined in her horse and stared in delight.

Gunning and Aristidis drew up alongside.

'I've seen this place before!' Letty said. 'In the museum the other day. Haven't you noticed? In one of the display cases, there's a dozen or so painted pottery plaques – tiny little things not much bigger than mah-jong tiles – and they're pictures of Minoan houses. Put them side by side and you could make up a street, a townscape. I longed to take them out and play with them! Two or three storeys high, flat roofs, dressed stone façades, timber frames, mullioned windows . . . yes! Here they still are!'

She swept a hand over the village square where the grander houses gathered. More modest houses climbed the slopes away from the centre, along winding streets that marked immemorial trackways. In the centre, old men seated at café tables drank their coffee, tormented their worry beads, or played card games. To Letty's eyes they all looked exotic. Most wore the island costume; some sported a red fez at a jaunty angle; all wore baggy boots. They paused their gossiping to stare as the cavalcade went by.

'What you say is true.' Aristidis nodded, charmed by her appreciative outburst. 'And the patterns go deep. Two years ago, old Manoli's house collapsed in the earthquake – the earth sheared away from under it and you could see layer on layer of buildings – all the same materials down to the very lowest slice of the cake, which is what you would call Minoan. I examined it as closely as I could before they rebuilt it, and there was very little difference between the ancient, the medieval, and the modern.' He smiled. 'Except that it would only be fair to say the Minoan remains were more solid, the stone better dressed. We found the remains of a wine vat and an olive press. Nothing, it seems, has changed much in four thousand years in this corner.'

'And the people?' said Letty, smiling at the slim brown boys who, in their impatience to parade strangers through their village, were tugging at bridles and whacking at the donkeys' rears.

'You must decide,' replied Aristidis.

The audience was mainly female, Letty thought, as they clattered up to the village square. Heads bobbed shyly out of sight behind windows; some, bolder, peered round doors. One or two even gathered on the edges of rooftop terraces to wave a greeting.

At last Aristidis called a halt halfway up one of the sloping roads out of the square. 'And here we must leave you, Miss Laetitia, in the care of the fourth and most vital member of your team!'

Chapter Fourteen

An elderly woman was hurrying, arms open in welcome, down the cobbled path towards them.

'And here she is! My mother,' Aristidis told them. 'Maria. Your ... what would be the word, William? Watchdog?'

'Chaperone,' supplied Gunning. 'Without which you could not possibly run your operation. Aristidis does not exaggerate his mother's importance, Letty! But she's also your hostess. You are to stay here in Maria's house. I will be lodging with Aristidis and his wife and children at the other end of the village. Very proper. The sexes are rigidly separated on the island. Unmarried people simply do not go about together unchaperoned. The villagers will find our relationship difficult enough to understand as it is.' He leaned towards her and said confidentially, 'I must ask you, Letty, to avoid showing me any public signs of affection or intimacy for the duration of our stay. They would be shocked by any such demonstration.'

'You know, William,' she drawled, 'I find more and more to admire in Cretans. I now add good taste to the list. And here's one Cretan I shall certainly like,' she said, watching Maria greet her son.

The small, straight, black-clad figure waited with quiet dignity for Letty to dismount and approach. Her face, Letty thought, had all the colour and texture of a polished walnut shell. Her large dark eyes, which retained an unquenched beauty, were not merry and insouciant like her son's but watchful. It was a face that showed calm after a good deal of tumult, even suffering perhaps, and Letty reflected that this woman, who must be now over sixty, had lived and raised her family through a calamitous time on the island.

'Miss Laetitia, you are welcome to my house and to my village. My grandsons will take your things inside, and if you will come with me I'll show you to your room.' She spoke slowly and listened, encouraging, to every halting syllable as Letty replied, using her small store of polite phrases.

Suddenly the hesitantly delivered words in a strange language were insufficient to express Letty's gratitude for the warmth of the welcome, no adequate response to the eager curiosity. Impulsively, she reached out her arms and hugged Maria, planting a kiss on each wrinkled cheek. A burst of laughter and a reciprocal hug greeted the gesture. Unexpectedly, Maria turned to Gunning and said, 'You did not tell us how beautiful your new English mistress was, William. Now I understand why you were not so unhappy to leave the city and Mr Russell's employ!'

Gunning replied in equally fast Greek. 'She is indeed lovely, Maria. And I warn you – my new English mistress understands what you say though she does not yet speak the language with much fluency. But a week or two swapping gossip with you and she'll be yattering at the washing trough with all the other women before we know it.'

Again, Letty was surprised by the ease with which Gunning had adapted to his surroundings. She was impressed too by the open affection and intimacy he seemed to receive. Things were easier for a man in this most masculine of societies, she decided. But survival here could only stand her in good stead when she returned to England.

After a hasty good-bye from Gunning and a reminder that she was to present herself at the site at four o'clock, the party clattered off, leaving her alone with Maria.

Letty followed her host through a gateway and into a courtyard, its paths lined with pots of basil, mint, and rosemary. The centre was filled with a medley of lush-leaved trees, lemon and orange, their golden fruit gleaming amongst the dark foliage, and, skirting these, rows of salad crops, most unknown to Laetitia. The small space spoke of meticulous husbandry; every square inch was producing something useful or lovely.

Maria slowed, acknowledging her guest's interest. 'Kastelli is known as the village of gardens. We are fortunately placed here. We have good soil, and water in abundance. It runs down from the snowfields on the mountains and most houses have their own spring or well.' She pointed to a fountain where the carved head of a god – another Dionysos, Laetitia guessed – shook his wet stone locks and opened wide his laughing mouth to spout a clear jet of cold meltwater into a basin. By the door to the house stood a bench shaded by an overhanging jasmine tree. It was covered in woven cushions, each, it seemed, the preserve of a scrawny ginger cat, blinking with suspicion at the stranger.

They entered the cool interior. Letty's senses, already seduced by a hundred different sounds and scents on the journey, were teased with a fresh palette. She wrinkled her nose in appreciation of a savoury smell from her childhood. Something delicious was simmering on the cooking range.

'Hare?' she wanted to ask. 'Could that be hare, stewing in the pot?' But her vocabulary was not up to it and the best she could do was 'rabbit'. It seemed to work. Maria tilted her chin in the emphatic Greek 'no' and gave her the word for 'hare'. Letty repeated and learned it. She understood the next piece of information, which was that the dish would be produced at supper time. Lunch would be on the table in half an hour. Maria hoped Laetitia liked cheese and salads? Today she had prepared some *spanakopita*, because no one disliked the spinach-and-goat-cheese pastries.

Letty settled in the place indicated at a polished wood table covered with embroidered mats and received the welcoming glass of cold water and a saucer of sweetmeats. As she sipped, she looked about her. Pride of place was accorded, largely because of its uncompromising demands on space, to a loom where a length of tough and colourful peasant cloth was stretched, halfway through its production. The rest of the furnishings were sparse: four chairs, a decorated bridal chest, divans along two walls providing seating or sleeping places, racks of pottery, and a large and lovingly polished sideboard. Along its length, a lace runner accommodated a cargo of silver-framed family photographs.

'May I look?' Letty asked politely when she had finished her drink.

'Certainly. You will see faces that you recognize already, I think,' Maria said, waving her towards the sideboard.

'Oh, yes.' Laetitia started on the right with the most recent exhibits. 'I know Aristidis. And this must be his wife . . .'

'Dafni,' supplied Maria.

'And his two daughters and two sons – and I've seen *them* before. Two minutes ago! They were carrying my baggage in.'

'The best grandsons an old woman could wish for!' Maria smiled happily. 'Nikolas and Stephanos.'

'And Aristidis's father?' Letty asked delicately. She had assumed Maria to be a widow but had noticed that widows, in any country, never seemed to resent an enquiry about their lost husbands.

The smile faded a little and took on an element of pride. 'Here he is,' said Maria, picking up a posed studio portrait of a handsome bearded man. 'Ioannis. My son looks much like him, don't you think?'

'He does indeed.'

Aristidis's father was in traditional dress and, apart from the old-fashioned fez he wore, where Aristidis favoured the piratical black kerchief knotted over his brow, she could have been looking at the same individual. The illusion was strengthened by the fact that the age of the man

161

in the photograph appeared to be the same as that of Aristidis in the present.

'Ioannis was thirty-six when he died,' Maria said. 'Four years younger than my son is now. It hardly seems possible! Aristidis was only a child when his father died. But he has never forgotten him.'

Good manners and lack of Greek discouraged Letty from indulging her curiosity further, but she had reckoned without the Cretan love of giving and receiving news and stories. Maria, correctly interpreting her guest's continued interest in the portrait in her hands, explained further: 'My husband died in 1898. At the end of August. Many hundreds of us died that summer.'

Letty made a silent calculation. 'The rebellion against the Turks? Was he caught up in that?'

'Yes. The rebellion. Ioannis was killed. A most unjust death.' The dark eyes filled with tears but her chin went up. 'My husband was *palikare*! A fine strong man. A fighter for freedom. My sons – all *palikares*. My grandsons also if their country should ever call on them to fight will be *palikares*.'

Letty thought she was getting the flavour of the Cretan word.

Maria sighed and looked with pride at a large framed print on the wall. Letty recognized the features of Venizélos, leader of the independence movement, politician, prime minister first of Crete – his home country – then of Greece itself. His handsome but sombre features did not look out of place in the family lineup. He could have been anyone's uncle. The eyes twinkled behind the scholar's eyeglasses, the balding head was well shaped, the beard and moustache were greying at the edges. On an English wall he would have been thought the epitome of Victorian respectability.

'Eleuthérios Venizélos,' said Letty. 'My father took me to hear him speak when he came to England seven years ago. He came over to accept an honorary doctorate.' Though not an immediately attractive prospect for a sixteen-year-old girl, Letty had told herself that anyone given a Christian name which meant 'Freedom' probably deserved a sympathetic hearing. She pronounced again 'Eleuthérios,' enjoying the sound of the light syllables dancing on her tongue.

'My sons would fight to the death for *eleuthérios*,' pronounced Maria. Letty was left wondering whether she meant the politician or the ideal and decided there was probably little distinction.

The most recent photograph, the least posed and obviously snapped by an amateur, showed three men standing with a show of pride for the camera, arm in arm on the edge of a trench. An archaeological dig was going on in the background. On the left Aristidis, on the right William Gunning, and between the two, Theodore Russell.

'Ah,' said Letty, laughing and eager to use her new vocabulary, 'three *palikares* in a row!'

Maria gave her a swift sideways look. 'Two,' she corrected. 'Would you like to come up to your room, Laetitia? The staircase is over here and you have the whole of the floor over the living room. When the weather turns hot you can go on to the terrace and catch the cool air coming down from the mountain.'

Letty made at once for the ladder. Maria followed her to the roof, happy to comment on the wide views and name the features of the landscape from the tiny offshore island of Dia, just visible to the north, through the flat, olive-covered plain of the Kastron Letty had crossed that morning to the herringbone pattern of the vineyards surrounding the village and, dominating the scene and drawing the gaze, Mount Juktas.

'The Holy Mountain,' said Maria.

Letty was silent, overawed and dismayed by the huge bulk. Brutal in its grey limestone, unsoftened by any green vegetation, the mountain beetled its brows at her. She could make out one or two zigzagging goat paths straggling up its flanks and guessed that where the goats might just be tolerated, a strange, soft city girl would be easily shrugged off. Looking beyond Juktas to the gleaming snow slopes of the far higher mountain of Ida to the west, she chose a defiant response. 'Well, *holy* – I couldn't possibly say – but – *mountain*? It looks much more like a hill to me. And a rather ugly one at that.'

Maria smiled. 'When you're halfway to the top, you'll ask yourself whether it is a hill or a mountain you're climbing,' she said simply. 'For us who are born in its shadow it is holy. It gives us water, pasture, a sense of place, and, in the past, protection. In times of trouble our ancestors would make for the caves on the summit, and the defences they had built up around the shoulders of the mountain would be the place of their last stand against the Invaders from the Sea. Aristidis has found these walls. Kyrie Evans has explored the summit. He found a sanctuary on the northern peak, there, do you see? A hilltop shrine he said had been lost. Not lost to the boys of our village! Some of the lads made quite a lot of money by selling Evans their collections of rings and seal stones. Many of them they'd found up there.'

'Offerings to the gods? I've seen some of them in the museum,' said Letty.

'Evans did not acquire the best,' said Maria with a trace of triumph. 'The women of the village wear these stones around their necks as a charm – you will see many. They bear pretty carvings – usually of animals. We call them "milk stones" because they increase the flow of milk when a woman is nursing. And, of course, no amount of piastres or persuasion is going to tempt a woman to give up her milk stone!'

'Do you have one such?' Letty asked.

'Indeed, I did have one,' said Maria. 'But I handed it on to my daughter-in-law when Aristidis married. It was a very special stone – she will show you – red with a fine carving of a mother goat and her kid.' She laughed. 'Very appropriate! And very effective! It was found by my great-grandfather up there on the mountain and has been passed down in the family.' She confided, 'Every woman should have one around her neck ... for good fortune. Who knows? Perhaps you will be granted such a find if Juktas is in a generous mood?'

They both turned to the forbidding grey mass shouldering the village and Letty shivered. Maria covered her hand with hers and spoke softly, 'Take heart, Laetitia. The mountain was holy before ever the warrior Greeks arrived from the mainland bringing their aggressive young god with them. Zeus was born; he lived and ruled with thunderbolts to maintain his capricious authority; he died. But the king of the gods had a mother, and perhaps she outlived him? Perhaps her gentler spirit survives somewhere in a fold of these hills?'

Letty smiled, not quite sure that she had been able to follow all that was said, but grateful for the older woman's understanding.

'But the best thing for recovering one's spirits is a good meal,' said Maria, reverting to practicalities and conclusively winning Letty's heart. 'Come to the kitchen. We will have our lunch and then rest. And when your men arrive to take you off again you will spring around like a goat on those rocky slopes.'

Too wound up to waste any time sleeping, Letty passed an hour reading through her notes and the flimsy copies of Gunning's typed documents. The preparations must have been embarked on weeks before, and had been thoroughly done. She would have expected no less. He had researched the history of the site and set out a summary of all the known previous archaeological forays into the area. Objects claimed to have been found locally were listed with their provenance and present location.

The digging team was identified, the specialities of each man noted; the local conditions and resources were set out right down to the names of six village girls who were willing to act as pot-washers if called on. Equipment was itemized from donkeys to paper clips. She smiled to see that the measuring stick was reported to have been freshly painted. Only Gunning, the photographer, would have thought of that! Bleakly, Letty wondered what there remained for her to do. Apart from financing the whole expedition, it seemed – very little. The hilltop vantage point called, evidently. She almost checked her list for: *1) Lace gloves: 2) Parasol: Director, for the use of.*

She leafed through the file looking for a location map but found none. She looked again. Surely the meticulous Gunning would not have missed such a fundamental item? She taxed him with this the moment he rode up with Aristidis to escort her to the mountain.

'Don't worry! We have one!' he told her cheerfully, taking an envelope from his pocket. 'It's all very hush-hush! Theodore is careful in the extreme about the security of sites. And rightly so! You don't want word to get out – a good deal of premature amateur tomb-robbing goes on. Aristidis and I have looked it over and we think we know where we're going. There's a very clear marker for our patch – a range of dilapidated goat sheds in one corner. That will come in useful as the site and finds office, perhaps. Depends on its condition.'

He passed her the map, eager to be off. 'It'll take half an hour to reach it.' Checking the sun, he added, 'And as it's on the northern slope, we should get a good two hours of useful angled light.'

They stood in a row silently surveying the designated site, passing the map from one to the other, turning it this way and that, no one quite ready to be to be the first to speak out. Letty narrowed her eyes and surveyed once again the one-hundred-yard-long tract of land ahead of them, every dry hummock outlined by the late afternoon sun. The thin soil was almost bare of vegetation. Very little would struggle to grow on such hard-packed terrain.

'Tell me, William,' she asked, breaking the awkward silence, 'did *you* have a hand in drawing this up?'

He replied thoughtfully. 'Well, no. You have seen that

Theo rather prides himself on his expertise with maps. And the initial exploration of the site was all his. I was not consulted.'

'And your family owns this land, Aristidis?' she said, turning to him.

'Yes, we do,' he said. 'All that you can see on this slope.' A wide gesture embraced the spur of hill on which they stood. 'Unproductive as you see, untouched for generations. Animals graze here occasionally, but that's the extent of it. The goat sheds are at present unoccupied and have a stout roof.' He pointed with slight embarrassment to the unlovely constructions that sprawled higgledy-piggledy down the slope. They were in varying states of repair, from the one or two which appeared weatherproof and useable to the last insignificant outlier, apparently no more than a mass of crumbling masonry, half buried under the soil.

'We can use them to sort and store any finds we may make. I will have them guarded at night.' He shuffled uncomfortably. 'Should it prove necessary.'

Letty pulled herself together and said crisply, 'Well, gentlemen, we are aware of our strategy; let's think about tactics, shall we? A foot survey of the ground may tell me otherwise in the next few minutes, but my first thought is that tomorrow when we have the men on site we'll start with an exploratory dig – no, no! Not for remains,' she said hurriedly, seeing them both stiffen with disapproval, 'but to establish the position of the spoil heap.' They relaxed and exchanged a shifty look. She pointed to a flat piece of ground on the perimeter of the outlined plan. 'I have my eye on that, but a trial trench will establish whether we're looking at barren earth and therefore a suitable place to tip our scrapings.'

Gunning and Aristidis nodded.

She took back the map and studied it. 'Now, according to Theodore Russell, he made his find – the Venetian coin – thirty yards to the north of where we're standing.' She set off, pacing out the distance. Arriving at the spot she kicked about in the dust and moved three stones into a line as markers. She continued her stroll around the perimeter of the site, eyes constantly flicking to the horizon, taking in the unchanged aspects of the scene. The two men watched her with a disturbing lack of enthusiasm. They offered each other cigarettes, they drank from their flasks. They waited for her to return.

Her tour finished, she rejoined them. All uncertainty apparently gone, she spread the map on the ground, kneeling and inviting them to pore over it with her. 'Your pencil, William? Got a good thick drawing pencil in your pocket, have you? Thank you. Well, now. Look closely. This is my initial finding.'

The pencil hovered over the discreet cross in the centre of the outlined site, which indicated the find of the ancient coin. 'Now – X marks the spot, you see.' She swiftly drew around it a child's version of a treasure chest, complete with skull-and-crossbones insignia.

Aristidis began to chuckle. Gunning snatched the pencil from her fingers and, in a few quick strokes, added the scrolled and tattered edges of an ancient treasure map. He drew in an arrow pointing to the north-northeast in the direction of Herakleion and wrote in an attempt at medieval script *Here be Dragons*.

'Of course, it may well all look different in the morning,' Letty said, 'but for now, I'm thinking we've been sent to a piece of land barren in more senses than one. I'll try a few *sondage* trenches in the prescribed manner but, honestly, I'm not very hopeful.' She sighed and swept another long look around the hillside. 'If Zeus had a hand in choosing his resting place, I somehow can't imagine that he'd have picked out this spot. It doesn't speak to me with the spine-chilling voice of the god. And, I observe that you two are not exactly a-quiver with religious awe! I'll tell you what – I have a feeling that the King of the Gods is not particularly pleased that we're here! Do you see his thunderclouds in the west?'

The light was slanting down through a gap in gathering purple clouds, seemingly whirling down at them from the heights of distant Mount Ida. Aristidis squinted up at the sky. 'Let's get the horses. I reckon we have twenty minutes before the heavens open,' he calculated. 'And I think we're in for a bad one. You won't get much sleep tonight, miss, with Juktas growling at you!'

Laetitia spent hours of the night awake, from time to time climbing the ladder to look out on to the mountain, deafened by crashing thunder, fascinated by the lightning that flashed around its summit, silhouetting the swaybacked crest of the mountain. She would not have slept much anyway, she thought resentfully, since the digging team, cousins and brothers, had gathered with Gunning at Maria's house for what seemed to be a party. A lyre player had joined them, and his music and chanting grew louder in direct proportion to the number of glasses of raki he consumed.

Peering down from her floor, Letty watched the pitcher of brandy circulate, punctuated with bottles of red wine and plates of *mezedes* to keep the strong liquor in its place. Poetry and songs floated up. She thought she heard Gunning attempting his own version of a lilting *mantinada*, a spontaneous and witty four-line song. His effort was rewarded by an outburst of laughter and applause, and she wondered crossly what he'd made up.

The garden was grey and chill, the sun just a promise below the horizon, when Letty struggled out of bed the next morning. She crept downstairs to find no signs remaining of the drunken revelry. Maria called a greeting from the stove, where she was grinding coffee beans, and announced breakfast in ten minutes. Ablutions were carried out in a small bathroom behind the house but on her way, Letty paused to scoop up handfuls of water from the fountain. No water had ever tasted or would ever taste as good, she decided. Strong coffee and bread hot from the oven went some way to restoring her will to live, and she was booted and spurred and waiting by the front door when her team arrived to collect her.

Annoyingly the men showed no signs of wear and tear from the evening's celebrations, just a quiet purposefulness. The horses slipped on mud and loose stones dislodged by the outburst of rain which had poured down gullies from the summit of the hill. At least it would make the digging an easier task, Letty calculated as they were joined in the valley at the approach to the goat track by the diggers with their supplies of spades, shovels, baskets, and wheelbarrows. A gang of boys were already on the mountain, come to join in the excitement. With a pang of foreboding, she wondered if they would still be eager to associate themselves with the activities at the end of the day. Or would they have trailed away in boredom as the layers of yet another unpromising trench were exposed?

While Gunning supervised the tethering of the animals and the stocking of the equipment, Letty stood with Aristidis on the spot they had occupied the previous evening. She decided to speak her mind. 'We're wasting our time, aren't we, Aristidis? I can hardly spell out why I think so, but all the evidence of my senses is that we will find nothing of interest here. Russell's malice couldn't possibly run to annoying ... shaming ... fooling every member of this party, could it? Surely not? Do I find myself the unwitting – and undeserving! – piggy-in-the-middle in a very masculine crossing of swords? I must know!'

All Letty's past experience of male ill will came to mind – ill will ranging from unemphatic and unconsidered derision to open enmity – and a rising despair and anger were evident in her voice.

'I would put nothing past that man,' he answered. 'And you are right to suspect that he would not welcome a noteworthy discovery by a protégée – and a female one at that. Some men take pleasure in bringing forward their pupils, sharing their knowledge, encouraging them and rejoicing at their success. Russell is not such a one. He sees any other man's achievement as a loss to his own esteem. Poor man! He leads a tormented life!'

They stared on together at the featureless landscape and sighed.

A joyful shout and a cry of '*Baba!*' made them turn their heads. Aristidis's oldest son, Nikolas, was running towards them. He thrust the small object he was carrying into his father's hand, chattering excitedly in Greek.

Aristidis's smile grew broader. 'If you want to know what's under the ground hereabouts, you should start your enquiries with the village boys,' he told Letty. 'Worth more than a dozen *sondage* trenches! Nikolas is saying that he and the gang were about here early this morning, poking about. The boys know the ways of the mountain. It's their playground! They know the rain loosens interesting things sometimes and brings them to the surface. And last night's deluge was especially productive. See what they've found!'

He put into her hand a small metal object. The unmistakable gleam of gold showed through the mud. Catching the boy's excitement, Letty lifted a fold of her cotton skirt and gently began to clean the gold ring. When she was satisfied she had done as much as was safe she took a magnifying glass from her satchel. 'Heavy signet ring. Gold, with a very broad circular boss and what looks to me like a very accomplished design,' she said, not quite managing to keep her voice level. She held it up to Aristidis and offered the glass. 'A beautifully executed picture of a bull.'

Aristidis gave a low whistle. 'A bull caught in a thicket by the horns. There are two men, one on either side, approaching. One carries a net, the other a rope.'

'It's Minoan, wouldn't you say?'

He nodded. 'It could be Mycenaean – the subject would seem to say that . . . it's very male – no doves, flowers, or goddesses in froufrou, which is more common. But the workmanship at any rate is Minoan.' He raised his head and yelled for Gunning. 'Come and join us, my friend! It seems the King of the Gods has decided to leave his calling card!'

Chapter Fifteen

Gunning opened his eyes wide on seeing the ring and grinned. 'Lead on, Nikolas!' he invited, and they set off to follow the boy.

'It's not far – down here, the other side of the sheds,' Nikolas announced, and bounded off in a direction diametrically opposite their designated area. After only a hundred yards or so along the goat path, the character of the land changed. The surface became more uneven; tall-growing herbs appeared here and there, rocks projected from the surface of the field. But, above all, it was the siting that claimed Letty's attention. They had come out on the opposite flank of the northern spur, and it was at this point that the green, cultivated land of the valley rolled upwards and lapped at the edge of the limestone slope. She had the sensation of standing on the deck of a vast ship. The edge of the rocky outcrop curved round in front of her like a prow. Ahead was the brilliant blue of the Aegean leading onwards to the mainland and, poised invitingly, the first stepping-stone to the Cyclades, the island of Dia. The morning mist heaving gently over the plain in between enhanced the impression that she was afloat and her sails filling with a southerly wind, set for Greece.

'I haven't been up here for years,' muttered Aristidis. 'But of course!'

Suddenly she could see what he was seeing.

Scattered over the field, four small boys were standing importantly to attention. Set there by Nikolas, it seemed, as the moment they appeared, each one raised a hand. Living site markers of finds made that morning, she suspected, and admired the disciplined stage-managing that had worked to keep four energetic lads in their places. But she was noting also with a surge of triumphant insight other markers scattered around the site. Tufty fennel plants appeared to be thriving here. Dr Stoddart's herb lore, remembered from their stroll around Knossos, came back to her and she wondered whether she had guessed the secret of Aristidis's alleged magical diagnostic powers. Well, as far as she was concerned, it could remain his secret.

She leaned close and whispered. 'I think we're looking at a promising site here, don't you, Aristidis? I like it! Look – it's covered in my lucky herb! Fennel!'

He smiled back at her, surprised and approving. 'You admire it, too? Such a useful plant! Are you aware? – I think you must be! – that its roots penetrate the soil to quite a depth. And, of course, there's nothing they enjoy so much as a *disturbed* subsoil. A soil concealing ancient walls, tombs, grave shafts –'

Letty could stand still no longer. 'Shall we? I see Gunning's already started!'

He had headed straight for the boys, listening to each one's story, examining objects proudly presented on grubby palms, exclaiming and congratulating. To her surprise, Aristidis caught her quickly by the arm, instantly apologizing and pointing to the path at her feet.

'Take care, miss! Fennel roots are not the only things that slither down holes in the ground. Those trails you see on the path there were left by snakes. Another sight that points to something interesting under the earth. They like to hide themselves in fallen masonry. I will have the site combed and the creatures removed. There are men in the village who can do this.' He handed her the twisted shepherd's staff he always carried over his shoulders. 'Just in case. I can see that the idea of vipers does not deter you.

Perhaps this will deter *them*. Bang it on the ground or bang them on the head.'

Letty was thankful to take the offered staff.

An exhausting hour later, they gathered back in the shelter of the goat sheds. The boys had been rewarded for any finds they wished to turn in, and these were already nestling in a tray awaiting cleaning and identification. One boy only had been reluctant to hand in a particularly handsome seal stone in agate with a carving of a cow and its suckling calf. When questioned by Letty, with Aristidis's help, he had shyly explained that his mother was about to give birth to her fourth child and she'd always had what he described as 'troubles'. He wanted to keep his find and give it to her. He looked away in some distress when his friends gleefully counted their coins and made outrageous plans for spending the money, starting with a trip to the village confectioner's. Letty admired his determination.

Her slight nod to Aristidis was instantly interpreted. 'Here, son, take this,' he said, counting coins into the lad's hand. 'Miss Laetitia insists you have half the value of the stone, and it is a very good one! You will keep it, of course, and give it to your mother, but, by declaring it and revealing the place you found it, you are helping the excavation and that should not go unrewarded.' He spoke loudly and firmly for the benefit of the other boys. Then he turned to Laetitia with a smile and a shrug and confided: 'I do not spoil them, miss! The amount they received was carefully judged. They are happy, but not so overwhelmed they will broadcast to all their classmates that you are . . .'

He hesitated and Letty supplied the words: 'A soft touch?'

'Yes. That! I explained to them that you are not a trader buying these things to have as your own or sell on at a profit, but to give them to the Cretan museum where they and their own children may visit them whenever they wish.'

When the boys had gone whooping off back to the village, Gunning approached with Russell's map outspread and a serious expression.

'And where do you suppose all this leaves us?' he asked. 'Consent to excavate isn't easy to obtain, you know. It's going to take months to redraft and reapply! And, in the meantime, the whole of the country will be hearing stories that you've discovered El Dorado up here, Letty. In spite of your optimistic version, Aristidis, I don't think we'll be able to keep the lid on! Might as well pack up and go home,' he grumbled.

'No! No!' said the site manager cheerfully. 'This is my land also. I give permission! And look – there has been a slight misunderstanding. I am sure it can be no more than a misunderstanding, though perhaps *not* one made by a clerk in the Office of Archaeological Development . . . But watch! If you do this . . .' He took hold of the map and turned it up and over, pivoting it on its corner. 'There now, do you see? We have the goat sheds – no longer in the southeast corner but the northwest. But still my goat sheds and still my land, extending down here over this so interesting stretch. This is not the original map he's given us – it's a tracing and we all know how mistakes may be made with tracings. I'm sure that if we were to tax Mr Russell with this he would be mortified that such an error had cost us a few hours' work. And then he would have to congratulate us on our quick thinking in – literally! – reversing his error. Would he not?'

Before he'd finished speaking, Letty had grabbed a pencil and was sketching in a trial trench to establish the new site of the spoil heap.

While the men worked on this, she and Gunning walked over the site, planting markers in the places where the boys had made finds and hunting for evidence of the Venetian explorer's original investigation. Puzzled, they had to agree that it was undetectable.

'The rain?' suggested Letty. 'A shallow scraping by Theo might well have been obliterated by the winter's downpours . . . he didn't tell us exactly when he was here. And a dig over four hundred years distant is hardly likely to show up. We'll take it for granted, shall we? And just go ahead and excavate. I have good feelings about this place. And at least it has a soil covering we can get our spades into. There could be something under there. If only we had an idea what we're looking for. A tomb? Could be anything from a simple shaft grave to a marble mausoleum.'

'A *tholos* – a beehive-shaped tomb? A simple pot filled with cremated remains? Both have been found on the island . . . I must say –' Gunning perched on a rock and held his drawing board across his knees – 'now I come to sketch this I could more easily imagine a Viking burial taking place up here. Some old warrior king being laid to rest where he can still command a view of the sea lanes, wouldn't you say?'

'Oh, yes,' said Letty. 'But I think this place was import-ant to people right back into prehistory.' She hit the ground with her staff, rattled a furze bush, turned over a stone to ensure there were no lurking horrors beneath, then settled down next to him. 'And perhaps particularly in very ancient times. The early farmers who lived here were pro-tected from invasion by the miles of ocean surrounding them, but in case unwelcome visitors got through and pulled their boats up on to the beaches near Herakleion and showed signs of moving inland, they'd be spotted from up here.'

'Better view from the summit?' Gunning suggested.

'But a shorter and easier run from here to take a warn-ing message to the village. Halfway up a mountain can be a much more strategically useful position to occupy than a summit. You can see all you need to see from here, your communications chain is easier to maintain, and it's sheltered by the bulk of the mountain behind you. Much more comfortable than standing about, teeth to the wind, on the top. I think we should prepare for several layers of occupation before we reach bedrock,' she said with anticipation.

She remembered suddenly she was talking to a clever man who'd managed to live through four years of all-out warfare. There was nothing she could explain to Gunning about survival tactics and defence systems. Trenches, redoubts, communications – these had all been life or death to him. But he listened, smiled and nodded, and bent his head to his drawing board.

Letty leaned over, admiring the swift strokes of his pencil, recognizing the economical conventions for rock, soil, and vegetation she'd seen him use in Burgundy. He never showed any sign of irritation or discomfort when she peered over his shoulder, tending rather to involve her in the process with his comments as a drawing master might. She was more likely to hear an inviting: 'Come and see this, Letty!' than a tetchy: 'I say – do you mind!'

'You're quiet, Letty. Am I getting this wrong? Or are you having second thoughts?'

'No, no! I was just thinking about Phoebe,' she replied. 'I was looking forward to getting back to the Europa to share the news of our discoveries. She was so eager to hear. I can't believe she won't be there, William. It's ridiculous – I only knew her for a day or two but . . . but . . . she flashed across my world like a shooting star. It's a cliché – don't tell me! – but sometimes a hackneyed old phrase is exactly the one you reach for – for the good reason that it says exactly what you want. She was gone in an instant but the light she gave out stays on in my mind's eye.'

'Quite agree,' he said gruffly and busied himself with a piece of hectic cross-hatching.

Unsatisfied by his response, she persisted, determined to communicate her feeling of loss. 'So much I was looking forward to . . . it's . . . it's like missing the boat train, hearing that Christmas is cancelled . . . She was snatched away in the middle of a conversation and I'm still waiting to hear her answer.'

He remained silent, his pencil moving swiftly over the page.

'You know, William, it was Phoebe I was really going to be reporting to. Not Theodore. Oh, he would have – *will* – read the written accounts, assess the scale drawings, and assign dates to each stratum as we uncover it, but the real story of the dig I'd have kept for her. Those keen, clever boys this morning . . . the shy, loving one so determined to hold on to his stone – she'd have wanted to hear about that!'

'I'm sure she would.' Gunning was refusing to be drawn down into her grief.

'Her death turns all this poking about among the dry bones of the past into an irrelevance, don't you think? Here we are, along with eight good men and true, all armed with spades and raring to go . . . but I'm wondering – what are we doing here in this strange place, William? Seeking to unearth a foreign god, buried thousands of years deep. If he existed at all. And Phoebe, so alive I can still hear her laughing, is lying scarcely cold and not yet buried. Demanding . . . deserving answers.'

'Know what you mean. You needn't go on.'

He turned his head away from her. Hiding his emotion? Letty was instantly contrite for her self-indulgent outburst. Gunning had known Phoebe for several months. They'd had time to grow close. It was thoughtless of her to trail her own distress in front of him when he was struggling to deal with his own. Letty sensed that there had been a warm relationship between the two, and was not surprised by the notion. Women were drawn to Gunning. She'd noticed it early in their acquaintance, while affecting to find it inexplicable. She remembered wondering about the attraction out loud to her friend Esmé.

'You're asking what might be his special qualities?' Esmé had seemed very ready to give the problem her serious attention. 'I mean, apart from his good looks, charm, wit, and chestful of medals? Well . . . let me try to think beyond those . . . You know, Letty, it could be that he's so jolly *mysterious*. Oh, I know you've ferreted out enough information

on him for an entry in *Who's Who* or even a slim mono-
graph, but he's no clear rushing stream is he?'

Esmé, the aspirant student of psychology, was always
prepared to abandon scientific vocabulary to indulge in
female chatter and speculation. 'I think of him as a deep
pool. Half the surface is in sunlight, the other shadowed by
the overhanging branches of a tree.'

'Just the conditions to encourage a heavy growth of
pond life,' Letty had sniffed.

'If you like. And what's wrong with that? It's not a barren medium we're considering and women sense that.
"Here are possibilities!" they think. "There's something
stirring in the depths of those blue eyes and – who
knows? – perhaps *I* shall be the one who is granted a
glimpse of it."'

'Well, I've had a glimpse,' Letty told her friend. 'And I've
learned to look the other way. You'd think blue eyes could
only be serene and cool but Gunning's can *scorch*.'

'Well, you must have done something desperately
annoying,' said Esmé. 'I don't recall him scorching any of
the available ladies you paraded for him when he was
staying with you and Sir Richard before you went off to
Burgundy. Sophie Carlisle, I know, was very interested . . .
and Patty Templeton was embarrassingly keen –'

'That'll do, Esmé!'

Had perhaps Phoebe joined the circle of Gunning's
admirers? Perhaps she had found Gunning's company a
welcome change from that of her forceful, self-absorbed
husband?

'Do you suppose she really existed – Phaedra? The
younger daughter of the king?' she asked Gunning, unable
to switch her mind from Phoebe's preoccupations. 'Do you
think she might have watched Theseus performing in the
bullring and fallen in love with him? What must she have
felt when her older sister ran off with him?'

'Oh, yes, indeed, I do believe she existed,' he said, willingly distracted by the question. 'Why not? It's time we
began to accept the myths and legends as more than folk

179

stories. There was a time, after all – and not so long ago – when no one seriously thought there had ever been an early Cretan culture. And when the first signs of it came to light, archaeologists casually referred to it as "Mycenaean". It took strong evidence unearthed by the spade to make everyone understand that Agamemnon and his stout lads were newcomers, adventurers. His descendants seized on a moment of weakness and invaded the island. They imposed their warrior culture on a much more ancient and graceful one. If I had to choose between them – no contest!'

'But you'd wonder why we hear so little in ancient writings about Crete and so much about the early Greek states of the mainland?'

'The victors write the history, tell the tales. Negative propaganda. All sides attempted it in the recent war, remember? The masculine Greeks – Hellenes, I suppose we should call them – whichever city they came from, and perhaps it was Athens? – when they mentioned the vanquished at all, dismissed Minoan culture as effete, goddess-worshipping hedonists, ruled by a king, but a king who was much less noteworthy than his scandalous mother, wife, and daughters. I don't think it's quite fit for an innocent young girl to hear what they are reputed to have got up to, but I think we can take it that what we have is an upstanding Hellene's disgusted propaganda: "See what happens when you let the women get above themselves!"'

He paused to whittle his pencil back to sharpness. Studying the point, he added: 'And let's not forget that it was the descendants of the Mycenaeans – warrior societies themselves – who hit on the means of preserving their national histories by writing them down.'

'Those hundreds of clay tablets Dr Evans discovered – they reveal a language, surely? How tantalizing! When someone's deciphered them we'll know much more about our Minoans. Though from their appearance . . .' She frowned. 'So fragmented . . . they don't strike one as containing a body of literature. Are we looking at a Cretan *Iliad*? Hymns to the Gods of Homeric style?'

Gunning chuckled. 'Much more likely to be someone's laundry list.'

'So nothing for it but to go on digging.'

'This is why I'm so intrigued by the possibilities of this site, Letty. We may find some explanation of what happened on this island over three thousand years ago. Why did the palaces burn? Why did such a powerful and peaceable civilization come to an end? Were the invaders, bringing their god Zeus with them, any more than piratical adventurers? Did they carry off Phaedra to marry the King of Athens in a symbolic union between the two cultures?' He grinned. 'One last question – where's archaeology been all my life?'

'You can understand why Theodore became so obsessed with it.'

'Oh, yes! I'd really like to despise him but I find I can't. If I were an envious man, I could envy him. I can understand all Theo's enthusiasms.'

Letty was silenced, swallowing suspicions which threatened to choke her.

'Oh, look! We're getting the thumbs-up from Aristidis,' he said. 'Your spoil heap has got the green light, it seems. Let digging commence.'

He looked again at the space before them and Letty, to her own surprise, was prompted to make the sign of the cross. 'Just taking out a little insurance! Well, you can never be sure what deity's lurking about and this place has a . . . would the word be "numinous"? . . . it'll do . . . numinous feel to it. There may be spirits to placate!' she told him.

'Then this is what you do.'

He stood up, marched forward a few paces, selected his spot, and struck the ancient pose of salute and dedication she'd seen on figurines in the museum, left arm by his side, the back of his right hand held to his forehead. 'But if you were thinking of offering up a white heifer before we start, you can forget it,' he called back. 'My sacerdotal skills don't run to knife work.'

'All the same . . . it mightn't be a bad idea to make your-self agreeable to the god of this place,' said Letty. She looked out to sea and scuffed about in a patch of loose limestone at her feet, needing to make closer contact with the earth. Almost to herself she murmured, 'He's here, you know.'

Chapter Sixteen

'He's here!'

Olivia Stoddart had rushed into her husband's study, for once not pausing to knock. Harold, at his desk, looked up in puzzlement.

'Inspector Mariani's here. Were you expecting him so soon? He has a file in his hand.'

'Calm down, Ollie! Yes, we might well expect Kosta to be bringing us the results of the autopsy, and I'm sure he'll want me to have sight of the report before he goes public with it. By which I mean ... before he tells the Russells what the findings are. He'll pass it in front of me as her family doctor, but not entirely for professional good manners. He'll want me to comment in case there's a glaring error. Act as medical backstop. Michael Benson was scheduled to do the autopsy. Sound physician. Trained in London with Spilsbury. We're jolly lucky to have him on the island. I'm not expecting any problems. Now – is Kosta by himself or has he come mob-handed?'

'There's Kosta and two constables. Can't imagine why he always needs an escort. A provincial doctor and a retired nurse hardly constitute much of a threat, I'd have thought.'

'I think our inspector enjoys doing a bit of swaggering! Creating an impression. Got his sights on higher things. And I don't disapprove ... very able young man. Another one the islanders should be thankful to have.'

'Well, I sent the men to the kitchen for refreshment. I didn't fancy the idea of them standing about, shuffling their feet with boredom. They'll have a happier time gossiping by the stove with Despina.' She glanced at the clock. 'It's near enough to teatime. I've asked for it to be served to the three of us in the drawing room. I hope that suits you?'

'That'll do well. Go back to our guest and I'll join you in a minute. And – Olivia! – do stop fluttering!'

Harold looked anxiously after her and wondered again what emotion it was that was pushing his habitually competent wife – so calmly prosaic as to be infuriating at times – to this sustained show of nervous tension. He'd enquired solicitously, commiserating with her on the loss of a close friend, said all the right things in the shocking circumstances, but still her demeanour worried him. He began to wonder just how close the two women had really been. Should he be concerned? A strange friendship, people must have thought: Phoebe a ball of glinting quicksilver, Olivia a bar of iron. Inflexible and obdurate perhaps, but iron had been known to shatter under stress. The right kind of stress, effectively applied.

He'd privately thought it a mistake to encourage the association – bound to end in some sort of disaster and, of course, he'd be the one left carrying the can. And he'd said as much. But the death of Phoebe was not the disaster he'd envisaged. Could Ollie's nervous state be occasioned by some confidence the younger woman had rashly shared with her? Surely not?

Harold breathed deeply, bracing himself for the coming encounter. He conjured up the worst possible scenario in preparation. He rehearsed a few defensive phrases. Professionally, nothing good could come of it, he feared, and, on a personal level, it could herald a complete unravelling of the fabric of his life. He tightened his tie, tugged down the sleeves of his tweed jacket, and set off for the drawing room to meet Inspector Mariani.

They settled, pleasantries over, tea politely tasted and then set aside, the Stoddarts together on a sofa opposite the

184

inspector, who had drawn up a chair magisterially facing them. In his uniform, glinting with a cargo of gold frogging, the young man was impressive.

'Why don't you just read it out, Kosta . . . er, Inspector?' Harold suggested. He reminded himself that this was no informal soirée and they were not conversing across the bridge table. 'Then we are all three considering each point at the same time. Save passing the thing around. All that "I say, could we just refer back to section three, para six above" stuff! Can be very tedious, you know!'

'Of course.' Mariani smiled genially. Judging by the way he held the sheets of the report in his left hand with a pen at the ready in his right it was exactly what he'd planned to do.

He set off reading quickly through the routine phrases which, he was aware, Stoddart knew by heart. Clipped and efficient, not a word of the autopsy report was superfluous, nor yet were there any omissions. Harold nodded sage approval as he listened to his colleague Benson's account. 'Good man, Benson,' he murmured at one point.

They worked their way through the brief analyses of the state of the decedent's heart, lungs, stomach, and other organs. Nothing noteworthy here. There was even a toxicology report. Again, all was normal. Benson had, in his opening phrases, mentioned that the cadaver appeared to weigh at least one stone less than one might have expected for Mrs Russell's height and age, but this was the only thing that fixed his attention.

Mariani's voice indicated that at this point they were to leave the security of the well-worn phrase, the reassurance of the 'indicates nothing untoward' part of the report.

Harold glanced at his wife. He really had no idea how she would react to the details of the death, which he knew were coming. He'd forbidden her to go to the morgue to see Phoebe's body, and wondered whether that was wise. Ollie had been a battlefield nurse in Mespot, for God's sake! She'd worked at his elbow, seeing horrors no woman should ever be exposed to, and without a murmur. But her patients were young men, fighting men, unknown to her, and Harold guessed that the sight of her friend – never a pretty one where hanging and asphyxia were involved – might be overwhelming. He'd been impressed by the cool practicality that young archaeologist woman had shown ... what was her name? ... Laetitia Talbot? That was it! Sharp-eyed little thing. He'd thought for a moment she'd noticed, but she'd been easily distracted. And, unworldly English miss that she was, was it likely that she'd have spotted it?

'Better to remember Phoebe as she was, Olivia, my dear,' he'd advised. And, rather to his surprise, Ollie had obeyed.

The cause of death was compression of the neck resulting from complete suspension of the body from a noose. Blood vessels including the carotid arteries had been completely closed, and also the air passages. Cerebral anoxia resulted, followed by loss of consciousness ... hyoid bone fractured and dislocation of the spine consistent with a drop from a height had occurred at the atlantoaxial joint ...

Olivia leaned over and whispered, 'So she didn't suffer, Harold. Something to be thankful for.'

So far, so predictable. Harold nodded reassuringly at the inspector as he paused between paragraphs.

'The next point is of interest as it may answer our questions regarding the bruising on Mrs Russell's legs,' said Mariani.

He passed a diagram and a photograph to Dr Stoddart. '*It is impossible to determine,*' he read out, '*the timing of these bruises, from clinical inspection alone, and information as to their origin should be sought from other sources. They could have been caused premortem but, equally, they may be the result of brusque handling of the corpse by others (in an effort to save life? To release the corpse from suspension?). Pressure of – say – fingers, applied with the force of emergency, could have caused blood vessels to rupture after death in areas already engorged with postmortem hypostasis and ooze blood into the tissues.*

186

Visually, the effect of this would be indistinguishable from ante-mortem bruising.'

'Miss Talbot and George Russell each manhandled the body,' Stoddart interrupted. 'So that's inconclusive . . . unless . . .'

At a glance from the inspector, he fell silent.

'I think, if I continue, you'll find the next paragraph goes some way to answering your concern. May I?'

The pathologist added that there were no signs of an attack of a sexual nature nor evidence of recent sexual activity.

The smallest sigh of relief from Olivia went unnoticed by the inspector but was picked up by Harold.

'So.' Mariani riffled through the papers. 'We are almost at the end, and to this point – no surprises.' He selected the last typed page and looked it over again in silence. The Stoddarts, watching keenly his expression, were uneasy to see it grow increasingly sombre.

'Mr Benson made an additional discovery which he includes, as he says: "*. . . since this evidence may well determine the outcome of the deliberations of the coroner. It could be a factor in ascribing the cause of death to suicide or to homicide, a decision which will be made by others, in another place, at a later date. The condition cannot, of course, be described as directly causal in her death, yet could well prove to have been a factor."'*

'And he continues . . .'

Mariani stopped, marked his place with a finger, and looked Stoddart in the eye. Without emphasis, he enquired: 'At what moment, Doctor, did you become aware that Mrs Russell was pregnant?'

Chapter Seventeen

An astonished silence stretched endlessly between them. Olivia broke it with a whimper and she reached into her bag for a handkerchief.

Harry, seemingly mesmerized by the keen stare of the inspector, could only struggle to hold his eye and swallow nervously. Finally he took a deep breath, unhooked his gaze, and murmured: 'Pregnant? Did I hear you rightly? Well, at no moment. I'm sorry, Inspector, I was not aware. This comes as a considerable shock to me. I hope you can understand that.'

'You were her general practitioner, were you not? Surely the first to hear of the suspicion of the condition?'

'She never confided in me ... perhaps she hadn't realized herself ... Of course! That must be the reason. She was *losing* weight, not gaining ... it wouldn't have occurred to her ...'

'I'm no expert, and you will correct me if I have this wrong, but there are other more obvious signs of pregnancy, I believe,' said Mariani delicately. It was clear he rather wished Mrs Stoddart had not insisted on being present at the interview.

'The cessation of her monthly, er, ladies' problems? That can happen if a woman loses weight – through stress perhaps. It's called "amenorrhea".'

'That pathologist's mad,' said Olivia firmly. 'She wasn't pregnant. She'd have told me.'

Without a word, Mariani passed a photograph over.

Olivia looked hastily, passed it to Harry, and buried her head in her handkerchief.

'How many months are they saying?' Stoddart asked, studying the photograph.

'Three months. No less, perhaps a little more. Difficult to be precise,' Mariani summarized. 'Could the weight loss have affected the development of the foetus? I put the question, Doctor, because it occurs to me that the coroner, as a layman, may well require a professional opinion in the matter.'

Stoddart nodded his understanding. He would be prepared.

Olivia came snuffling up from her handkerchief. 'Well, that proves that this is indeed the nonsense I've just remarked on! Three months? That takes us back to the last half of December. There! I told you! Phoebe was in Europe! For the whole of that month. At her father's funeral. Theodore did not accompany her. He was here on Crete.'

The two men exchanged glances, teetering dangerously on the edge of hysterical laughter, each willing the other to explain.

Finally Mariani said softly, 'Forgive me, Mrs Stoddart, I know we are speaking of your friend but believe me – a husband is not always . . . not entirely an essential element of the equation.'

'You wilfully misunderstand! This is *Phoebe* we're talking about! Let me explain! You should know that my husband and I were together with her – travelling companions – in the role of chaperone almost – except that she didn't need one! – for most of the time she was in Europe. On the ship she stayed in her cabin suffering from seasickness. As did I! It was a particularly bad voyage, wasn't it, Harry?'

'It was indeed, Olivia. You suffered terribly, I know.'

'And when we got to Paris we stayed in the same hotel. When she was not with us she was with her family. Phoebe

189

was – oh, how would you describe it, Harry? – devastated by the death of her father, whom she loved very much, and a little uncertain being by herself. She's – she was – a woman who had always been surrounded by a crowd of loving people, family and friends, and she was uneasy when she was left alone. Am I getting this right, Harry?'

Harry agreed, still in a state of shock to equal his wife's. It occurred to him that when all this got out – and it soon would in this small city of chatterboxes and sensation-seekers – it wouldn't do him a great deal of credit professionally. He could imagine the remarks behind cupped hands: 'Couldn't spot a three-month pregnancy! What sort of doctor is that!'

'You see, Inspector, if Phoebe had been . . . involved . . . with someone in that way, we would have been the first to suspect. Wouldn't we, Harry?'

'I don't think it would have escaped your notice, Olivia.' He hurried to add: 'I'm certain she would have confided in you, my dear.'

If he had had doubts, the inspector kept them to himself. 'At all events, let us accept for the moment the recorded evidence of the pathologist, shall we? I was wondering, Doctor, how her loss of appetite and weight may be connected with her condition? Do you have a theory?'

'If she had reason to believe that she had conceived and that the child was not her husband's and, further, that it would become very evident – in three months' time – that he was not involved because he was thousands of miles away at the crucial time, she might have been deliberately starving herself to put off the moment when the pregnancy would show. She may have thought that, if she could by this means skew the appearance of the bulge by – shall we say a month? – she was home and dry. And when the child appeared a month prematurely – some first babies are notoriously laggardly – she could present it as her husband's.' He looked down thoughtfully at his fingers for a moment. 'With the collusion of her luckless physician,

which I have no doubt she would have sought eventually
. . . in her own good time. Poor Phoebe!'

'But who, Harry? It's madness! Who? You must have
some idea!'

Harry, crimson in the face, turned to his wife and said in
glacial tones, 'Olivia! Be silent or leave the room! You can
only make matters worse by your fervid speculation!'

He waited for her resentment to subside, then, 'Is that
all, Inspector?' he asked, firmly. 'You're satisfied? You have
nothing more for us?'

Mariani studied him before replying. The doctor was sitting on the edge of his seat, poised to flee from the room
as soon as he could politely do so. The inspector's instinct
was telling him that Stoddart had been expecting more.
Mariani paused for a moment, taking his time, reviewing
the sheets, unwilling to release the couple until he was
satisfied, thinking furiously. He was not aware that anything had escaped his attention. With only a trace of reluc-
tance he told them he'd finished. The coroner's enquiry
would be taking place on Friday afternoon, and would
they please hold themselves ready to attend?

'This report leaves us, or leaves the coroner rather, with
the usual five choices. I think we can discount the first two:
natural causes and accident. He will have to examine the
evidence and hear testimony from witnesses to decide
between: suicide, murder, and undecided.'

Harry Stoddart wasn't really listening. They'd missed it!

If there was any relief at all to be derived from this
appalling scene it was that Phoebe's secret – the first of her
two secrets, he now acknowledged – remained still that, as
far as the authorities were concerned.

He'd wondered whether to attempt to persuade, even
coerce, his colleague Benson into turning a blind eye. But
Harry had often thought that if you just let things alone,
they found their own level. The less you meddled, the
better. And now he was relieved to hear that no action

from him had been necessary in the end. Benson had, in all good faith, missed it! And the awful knowledge would go to the grave with her. The doctor knew how to keep his mouth closed.

But he saw clearly why Phoebe had had to die.

Chapter Eighteen

The sun was warm on her back as Laetitia stood facing her site. She started out once more to walk her way across it, eyes on the ground for the most part, but constantly her gaze was tugged upwards and out to sea.

With a sigh of impatience, Gunning followed after her.

'Who exactly are we worshipping here, William?' she asked. 'A god of the earth or a god of the sea? Zeus or Poseidon?'

'Zeus Enalius? Or Poseidon Cthonius? Interchangeable roles? They seem here, dizzyingly, to come together. And perhaps with a third element? Their descendant Hyakinthos?' He waved an arm over the countryside. 'The young god of green vegetation . . . fertility. Yes, all three, I'd say. They exist together – as far as they exist at all, of course.'

'And you realize, William, that this splendid site may have been no more than an open-air place of worship. A peak sanctuary. A holy place, but not necessarily one where you would have put up a building. We may find an altar or some such at best.'

'Cold feet, Letty? I can understand why you might hesitate . . . But, look here – are you ever going to say the word? The men are straining at the leash – why have you sent them away to the sheds?'

'An hour's reconnaissance, carefully done, is worth a week's badly directed digging,' she reminded him crisply. 'There'll be more than an altar here. I've noted remnants of a Minoan roadway (now a goat path) linking this site and the sanctuary temple that Arthur Evans excavated last year right up on the topmost peak. They wouldn't have bothered with a road link up if this weren't also a site of some importance. And digging? We don't need to plunge straight in. No one digs until the snakes have been removed. I risk no man's safety. There's plenty to be done in the sheds, and we'll be glad of it once we get under way.'

His disapproving silence made her smile. 'Oh, all right! I'm aware that morale must be kept up as well as hands kept busy. This team knows what it's doing and the men are keen. We'll start on a small *sondage* pit just to keep everyone happy. And I've decided where to put it.'

She beckoned Aristidis and asked for two diggers to be sent for.

'Trial pit? Over there where I've set a marker. Just a whisker off the centre of the site. And far enough from the slope behind us to be out of the course of boulders crashing down in the winter. You can make out the southerly limit of the safe area if you look. Halve the distance between that point and the cliff edge and we may have something. I thought we'd begin the excavation proper in squares. It's not a vast site.' She consulted the plan Gunning had drawn up. 'A hundred yards or so? By about fifty? We can start from the middle and work our way outwards without tripping over ourselves coming in, if you see what I mean, and be guided as to direction by the significance of whatever we turn up. We'll use ten-foot squares with a two-foot barrow balk.' She glanced up at the slope behind them. 'Impossible to know how deep we'll have to go. I'm guessing there's been quite a buildup of soil washing down over the centuries. Unlike our first site, which was wind-scoured and bare. It may be patchy. And we shall have to be prepared for evidence of earthquake disruption in the strata. Control pits along the site will be essential.'

Eagerly, Gunning checked his camera and his drawing pad.

Tuning in to the Cretans' love of occasion, and much enjoying their sense of fun, Letty called the men to be assembled. She ceremonially removed the first spit of earth herself and, to enthusiastic applause, handed her spade to one of the men. 'I declare the excavation begun,' she said, wagging a minatory finger, 'but let's not expect *too* much, shall we? I don't want to see tears before bedtime.'

Before bedtime, the first piece of elegant *kamares* pottery was being tenderly placed in her outstretched hand by a digger whose eyes shone with mischief and triumph.

'Thank you, Demetrios,' she said. 'We'll get the rest of this out tomorrow, now we know it's down there. Too dark to do careful work at the bottom of a six-foot shaft! This seems as good a moment as any to call a halt for the day. We're losing the sun. Aristidis! Can you shut the site down now, and if anyone's interested to see how far we've come I'll be at the sheds looking over the finds.'

An hour earlier, the last canvas bag, writhing ominously, had been carted off site by a team of men from the village who had worked silently and attentively over the ground. They'd promised to return the next day for the stragglers at a time when the serpents would be out and about.

All the men came back to hear Aristidis talk about the day's production and watch him demonstrate and explain the finds. They crowded into the goat sheds, noisy with question, remark, disagreement, and debate. 'For every two Cretans, you'll hear three opinions,' Gunning had warned her, and the opinions of eight of them were being aired at top volume. At last, leaving a night guard of two behind, they began to walk off to their homes.

Gunning drew Letty to one side and for a moment his expression was almost indulgent. 'Had a good day?' he asked simply, confident of her reply.

She nodded. 'And it'll be better tomorrow. Six seal stones, twenty clay animals, the remains of about a dozen vases all in sherds, and, best of all, this gentleman!'

Laughing, she held up a six-inch-high bronze figurine. Carefully cleaned, the rough natural texture left by the bronze-smithing spoke reassuringly of Minoan workmanship; the portrayal of the human figure was simple and natural, the work of an artist. She held in her hand a neat-waisted Cretan standing to attention, adoring his goddess, left arm by his side, right hand raised to his forehead. 'You must have been standing almost above him, William, when you struck this pose! How could you have known?'

'My party trick,' he said lightly. 'These are ten a penny in Crete. Strike the ground and one pops up. He's lovely, but I'd say the most significant things we've got are the body parts.'

Letty went to look at a tray labelled in English and Greek – LIMBS. Nestled in sawdust were a dozen or so small and rather roughly modelled clay representations of arms, legs, and feet. 'No torsos,' she commented. 'Or heads. What do you suppose these are doing up here?' Carefully, she began to pick them up one at a time to examine them.

'I think we've hit on a shrine of some sort. You've seen Celtic or Roman offerings at holy springs and so on? Engaging the goddess's attention in the matter of health problems? 'Having awful twinges in my arthritic old legs, Lady. How about a spot of help in this department? And just so you know what I'm on about, I'm offering up a model of the parts in question.' '

'This one's a puzzle, William. Look! It's a miniature pillar with a rounded bit at the top like those at the palace. Help with *architectural* problems being sought, do you suppose? Some poor chap's structure threatened with collapse?'

'Um. Problems of elevation and support of a kind, I should say.' He paused, trying to decide whether a comment on the piece she had picked up and was studying closely would be appropriate. 'The object you've got in your hand right now is a male member. Very rare.'

'A what? . . . Oh, yes, of course.' Letty didn't give him the satisfaction of a blush but continued to examine the artefact for a calculated moment before replacing it and selecting a pair of clay legs. Four inches long, they were slim and carefully modelled and quite obviously female. From the knees to the feet they were pockmarked, she was sure quite deliberately, to indicate the nature of the ancient disease.

'Gangrene? Snakebite? Varicose veins?' Gunning offered. 'We should ask Stoddart to take a look at these. He might be able to diagnose some Minoan ailments. Why not? I've no reason to suppose they've changed vastly over the centuries . . . Mmm . . . an interesting study, there. One could – Letty? Letty! What on earth's the matter?'

Blinded by tears, she could no longer fight down the response of grief, triggered by the sight of the pathetic little legs. She thrust the votive offering into Gunning's hand. 'It's Phoebe's legs, William,' she whispered. 'Oh, gosh! It brings it all back! And I thought I was being so tough and efficient, playing the nurse . . . You didn't see . . . She walked all over the site with me at Knossos that morning . . . her boots were new – not broken in – but she never whimpered or complained. She stumbled a bit and I had to help her over a wall or two, but I thought it was because she was feeling a bit feeble. But when the doc and I took her boots off and the silk stockings she was wearing under them, like a cavalryman, her feet and ankles were so terribly sore. I feel quite dreadful that her last hours were spent trying to hide the pain – pain she was putting up with to entertain *me*!'

Gunning was turning the clay legs this way and that, lost in thought. 'Tell me again, Letty, if you can bear it, exactly what you saw. The marks on Phoebe's body. All the marks.'

Strangely, the obvious thing to do, it seemed, was to take back the Minoan model and use it to demonstrate and describe. Letty pointed to the three-thousand-year-old clay ankles, talking of blisters and blood flow and the purple tidemarks of hypostasis – all she could remember of Dr Stoddart's twentieth-century vocabulary – and she heard Phoebe's laughter. Phoebe would have been charmed by the resonance. She would have been the first to hear the click that linked the present indissolubly with the past. 'They're still here, Laetitia!' she'd said in the Palace, her imagination conjuring up spirits unseen by Letty. And here, in this bleak spot on the shoulder of a mountain, perhaps they were beginning to reveal themselves.

Letty shuddered. It had been a long day. 'What's wrong, William?' she asked, concerned to see he was still holding the votive piece. 'What are you thinking?'

'Something impossible.' His words were disjointed and slow in coming, as he struggled to order his thoughts. 'But, with your permission, I'll take this object to show to Dr Stoddart. His remarks may well be interesting. No – don't ask. I shall have to think about this. I've had a notion so disturbing . . . Look, I'd rather not discuss it. Not yet.'

Chapter Nineteen

The coroner's court was declared open at ten o'clock on Friday morning and Gunning and Laetitia slipped into their places, still breathless from their dash down to the city from Kastelli. Summoned by runner the day before, they had preferred to make an early start that morning rather than give up precious digging time the previous day to travel back, and Letty was having some difficulty in pulling the two sides of her life together. Her head and her heart were still on the breezy promontory on the slopes of Juktas.

She looked with misgiving at the coroner. If this scene were being played by English rules, she was contemplating a gentleman combining the decisive authority of a judge and the opportunities for curiosity of a policeman. A layman, but a man charged with a duty to weigh evidence and make a decision that would, at the end of this day, either close the lid on Phoebe's suicide or unleash whatever hounds Inspector Mariani chose to whistle up in pursuit of her murderer.

To her surprise, the elderly Cretan chosen for the job, Professor Sokratis Perakis, addressed the assembled company in English. In a few words he had made plain his scholarship, outlined his task, set out a timetable, stated his objectives, and taken account of every person in the room. From the way he consulted his pocket watch, Letty guessed he was not a man who planned to be late for his lunch. The morning session would close at one and proceedings would restart, he announced, at three o'clock precisely.

George, pale and disoriented, came over before the inquest opened to sit by Gunning, and the two men exchanged a few soft words. Including Letty in the conversation, George leaned over and whispered, 'Professor Perakis! They've rolled out the big gun for this, it seems. Good man. A bit idiosyncratic but – sound.'

The gathering consisted only of family, immediate witnesses, and a stranger sitting next to Eleni – a woman so like her she could only be her older sister. Here for moral support, Letty guessed. Evidence was heard first from Mariani, resplendent in uniform and crisply authoritative. Dr Stoddart followed, calm and thoughtful. Theodore, dramatically dressed from head to foot in mourning black, gave a resonant performance outlining the events of last Sunday afternoon as he had witnessed them. Laetitia, the first to discover the body, gave her account and was asked a few sharp questions. George also, as second on the scene, was called to give his evidence.

Though rather quenched, he spoke in a calm voice, replying without hesitation to the questions. Even struggling with his grief, he was impressive, Letty thought. The coroner took him through the events of Sunday afternoon, nodding and noting the clear terse answers. Answers delivered with raw honesty, with a gaze so assured it could have locked with that of owl-eyed Athena and the goddess would have looked away first.

Yes, Charles St George Russell had spent the afternoon in the company of the architect Mr Gunning, returning with him to hear Miss Talbot's screams from the first-floor landing.

The coroner stifled a yawn and scratched on his note pad. Letty managed to stay still and silent throughout the account, trying to control her dismay. She even managed not to throw an incredulous glance sideways at Gunning. Of the two men she had a liking and a respect for in this sorry business, one was lying. But was it the saint in the box or the sinner on the bench at her elbow?

Gunning followed, speaking economically and saying much the same thing as George. His brief contribution appeared not to draw much official attention. Finally, after a further swift consultation of the pocket watch, Eleni was called on.

Undaunted by her surroundings, she stood, a regal figure, black-clad and beautiful, and granted the suddenly alert coroner five minutes of her time. Yes, all had proceeded as the doctor and Miss Talbot had said. She herself had been alone in the house from midday when she had dismissed the last of the staff. It was the custom for the family to wait on themselves on a Sunday, though when there were guests – and Miss Talbot was freshly arrived – she, Eleni, generally stayed on. The master had retired to his room.

'Ah, but which one?' Letty had thought, with an unkind look at Theo.

And Eleni had been peacefully polishing the silver in the pantry when the doctor and the mistress had returned unexpectedly early in the Bugatti just after two. She had rendered what assistance she could – fetching fresh water to Mrs Russell's room – and had been dismissed by the doctor with orders not to disturb the mistress as she'd taken a sleeping pill. Miss Talbot had arrived nearly an hour later. She had gone to her own room, and the next event was the ringing of the bell in the servants' hall at five o'clock to summon help. Mr George and Mr Gunning had arrived immediately afterwards. Eleni had at once sent a runner to fetch the doctor.

Professor Perakis adjusted his gold-rimmed pince-nez and scanned a sheet in front of him. He made several ticks with his pencil. The coroner thanked Eleni for her evidence and followed her with admiring eyes as she swayed back to her seat, as did every man in the courtroom, Letty noted crossly. Her companion, the older woman, welcomed her fussily back to her seat, clucking quiet encouragement.

Five minutes before one o'clock the coroner passed out to each of the principal players a copy of the autopsy

201

report, with a request that they would make themselves familiar with the contents, which would be discussed when the enquiry resumed later. By this action, Perakis declared with authority, not only would time be saved but, in consultation with the grieving family, the embarrassment of a public reading would be avoided.

Letty detected Theo's hand in this. Perhaps the professor was a bridge partner? Or was this a demonstration of the idiosyncrasy George had warned of? she wondered, and raised an enquiring eyebrow to Gunning, who shrugged.

The coroner informed them with a bland smile that he had no objection to this. If any of the gathering thought otherwise, would they make known at once their objections? He raked the gathering with a basilisk stare. No one took up his challenge. George glanced at his copy briefly, then whispered to Letty and Gunning that he would go to his father, take him home, and look through the no doubt distressing document with him. He'd be delighted if they'd come back for lunch. They were expected; all was prepared and they would be very welcome.

They both tactfully declined, assuring George that they could pick up some lunch at the hotel on the seafront.

There they asked for and were led to a discreet table, a large one, at the back of the dining room where they would not be observed. A not unusual request, Letty judged, as the waiter scurried about creating a screen of potted plants between them and the rest of the diners. After ordering dishes of salad and cheese and olives, in which neither was very interested, they spread out the sheets of their autopsy reports and began to read, sharing a comment or two as they worked through it.

'Those bruises on her thighs. It would seem quite possible that they were made by *my* fingers and thumbs, then, William?'

'Or George's. He hoisted her body up rather violently, I remember.'

They read on steadily, keeping pace with each other through the pages until, suddenly, Gunning grunted in

202

surprise. Letty gasped at the same moment. They looked at each other in concern over the table.

'Did you have *any* idea about para six page ten?' Letty whispered.

'Of course not! Did you?'

They fell silent, their thoughts running down the same channels.

'She was on her way to or in Europe for the whole of December,' said Gunning. 'She was at her father's funeral on the twelfth and she spent the rest of the month in Paris. She was in the company of her friend Olivia for most of that time. Though the Stoddarts left her with her family in the boulevard des Capucines over Christmas when they went off to Surrey. Ah!'

'Some old flame reappearing in her life, do you suppose?'

'Could be. She wasn't inclined to share details of her love life with me. Other people's – yes. She was a woman who was always delighted to gossip – but she was very reticent about her own. If, indeed, she had one. I mean, an illicit one.'

'So. The child wasn't Theo's. I'd guess she was hoping to pass it off as his, wouldn't you? It would account for her starving herself. No one suspects a woman who's losing weight to be, er, you know. It's what I'd have done.'

'All the same – a strong reason for committing suicide, I'm thinking. Suppose Theo twigged? Very unpleasant scene of a Dickensian nature could ensue . . . mother and babe cast out into the winter snow . . . "Never darken my door again, you trollop" and all that.'

'Oh, pouf!' Letty could hardly contain her anger. 'Shall we try to remember what century we're in – and who's paying the rent? Phoebe, if what you tell me is true, could well have ejected Theo! And let's not lose sight of the fact that this person she is avowedly so keen to avoid upsetting is actually himself *bracketed* with –'

'Shh!'

Letty held her tongue impatiently, anxious to deliver her broadside, while the waiter poured out a glass of lemonade. 'Morally he had no hold over her,' she persisted. 'And she had the financial clout to tell him to go hang – oh, you know what I mean ... These things are not the problem they used to be – she could have not simply walked out but *driven off* in style, taking her lover with her. In a smart little green sports car!'

'What the hell are you getting at? Speak plainly!'

'We both know who was in Paris at the time in question. And perhaps we can acknowledge the reason for the generous present. I bet they chose it together.'

He glared at her, not even deigning to respond. Letty pressed on. 'When he was travelling in Europe, George went to a nightclub. He told us over dinner on my first night at the Europa. He went to Chez Joséphine. But he also said he'd seen the winter review at the Moulin Rouge. Now, that starts in December. So that places him in Paris at the *crucial* time. It would have been possible. The question is – if all this is so, why on earth would she kill herself?'

'Do you really need to put the question?'

'Well, I do, actually. She might have killed herself, but never her baby. Phoebe was in love. A woman doesn't kill herself and the unborn child of the man she loves – not when she has the means to support them all. She could have changed her identity and taken a villa in Antibes. Plenty of widows about with young children, wives of military men who never seem to return from ... oh ... the North West Frontier. Women with mysterious pasts! She could have made a life outside or inside society. With a protector or by herself. A life of her choosing. A better life. I for one would have preferred it,' she finished defiantly.

'You're thinking Theo found out – goodness knows how – perhaps she even told him? That she confessed all before doing a bunk? And the thought that his wife has not only deceived him but has deceived him with his own son and – poisoned arrow this – is expecting his *grandson* – was too much for him to accept?'

'The very stuff of Greek tragedy, I'd have said. And the sheet torn out from the play and left as a suicide note? Doubly appropriate, it would now seem. But who left it? Who really wrote the name 'George' on the envelope?'

'I've been thinking about that. Phoebe gave regular amounts to him for the purpose I've already outlined. She always put them in such an envelope. They were not exactly hush-hush – everyone knew – they appeared on the hall table with the post sometimes. It wouldn't have been difficult to get hold of one.'

'George was roving about town that afternoon out of your sight, William. He could have returned, entered through the coach house, nipped in through the back door, and gone up to Phoebe's room. She could have told him the news. Perhaps the doctor had just confirmed it? Harry told the coroner he had no idea but – do you think that's likely? He looked a bit shifty to me when he was denying all knowledge. I don't think he's a very accomplished liar. George may not have been prepared for it, may have been totally unable to cope with the situation. Perhaps this was all the result of an unfortunate slipup in Paris. Wouldn't be the first. Christmas, you know – the champagne flows. Perhaps the saintly George was undone by the titillations of all that female flesh on display at the nightclub? All banana skirts and bottoms! And now, three months later and hoping all was forgotten, Phoebe throws this bomb at him.

'He may have refused point-blank to do what she was asking him to do. Perhaps running away with his step-mother was the last thing he wanted? He's unaccountably fond of his ghastly old father. When Phoebe began to fade with the effects of the sleeping pill, he decided to do away with his problems and make it look like suicide.'

'That still doesn't account for the suicide envelope,' Gunning objected. 'George is a bit strange but he's not stupid. And – I told you – he's not a murderer. I won't listen to another word of your nonsense. In fact, I'll give you a bit of nonsense of my own and see what you make of it.' He narrowed his eyes. 'George, according to your fantasy, rejects Phoebe. He is in no way prepared to disgrace his father, throw up his life here, and flee with his stepmother under a cloud of sin. He storms off. Left alone with her secret, abandoned in a foreign land by the man she loves, about to lose everything familiar along with her reputation, and with the additional burden of what society will regard as a monster-child, she takes the only possible way out. She hangs herself. And, in a Phaedra-like spurt of animosity for the man who's just deserted her, she plans retribution from beyond the grave. She tears that incriminating sheet from the play, writes the name of the now despised culprit on the envelope, and makes her exit. Leaving a tidy little time bomb behind her. The explosion can only involve the two men she hates: Theo and George . . . Well? What have you to say to that piece of nonsense?'

'I have to say it's ingenious and perfectly feasible. And, whatever the motive for the note, it could have caused the most appalling ructions between the two. Good Lord! I wonder what the Russell men are making of the autopsy document? They must be reading it at this moment! How dreadful! Just imagine what will happen when Theo links George's presence in Paris with paragraph six! I can hear him now: "So! *Hippolytus*, what have *you* to say?" And I don't like to think of the next gruesome scene in that tragedy.'

But Gunning, struck by a fresh thought, was riffling through his pages, rereading sections, hunting for something he was clearly not finding.

'What more are you looking for? Phoebe's condition is the only surprise in the report, isn't it?'

He thoughtfully put the sheets in order, folded them, and tucked them away in his pocket before replying. 'Yes, it is,' he said. 'And thank God for that! Look, I think we can order our coffee now. And there's plenty of time for a pastry to fortify you for the afternoon session.'

Gunning seemed unaccountably relieved, but Letty could not relax. She was struggling with a residual concern, with a gathering feeling of foreboding. 'Are you thinking, William, that we ought to have done as George seemed to want? That we should have gone back to the Europa with him?'

William nodded. 'Yes. I'm afraid so. He seemed quite insistent that we go. I should have given him my support.' He looked at his watch. 'Too late now, do you suppose? We can hardly turn up, grinning, for the coffee.'

Letty reached out impulsively and squeezed his hand. 'You *have* supported him, William. You've been a good friend. You've done more than you should. But I must remind you that *my* loyalties and interest lie – and always will until this is sorted out – with Phoebe. I've made a vow to her and I'm not about to break it. If I have to throw George to the lions to establish the truth – I will.'

'I'd say it's the bull he'll have to confront, wouldn't you?' said Gunning bitterly. 'Look – I think, if you don't object, we ought to go to the Europa. Right away. Just call in casually, you know ... say we're picking up a few papers ... anything.' He jumped to his feet, alert and concerned. 'We're going to the arena.'

The house, when they pushed open the front door and made to walk into the hall, was in turmoil. Stewart cannoned into them, obviously on his way out. Dickie was striding about biting his nails. In the dim depth of the back corridor, a maidservant yelled and sobbed and was silenced by a gruff male voice in Greek.

'William! Thank God!' said Dickie.

Surprisingly Stewart also seemed pleased to see him, and halted his outward rush to seize him by the arm and haul him inside.

'We don't know what to do! They're killing each other! You've got to go in and stop them!' implored Dickie.

'Perhaps we're too late. Listen! George has gone silent. He may be already dead!'

A crash and a torrent of angry words exploded from the direction of the library.

'Ah! Still at it! Well, thank goodness for that! Alive at least! They came back just after noon, friendly enough, talking as they usually do, and went straight into the library. It was all quiet for about half an hour and then all hell broke loose!'

'Theo gave that roar,' said Stewart. 'You know the one I mean?'

Gunning nodded.

'And he went on and on . . . like he does when he's roused. Only this was . . .' He exchanged glances with Dickie.

'Excessive. Unnatural. Terrifying,' Dickie supplied. 'And then George shouted back at him. And that's when we *really* got the wind up! I mean – George never answers back, does he? We couldn't make out what they were saying – well, kinder not to listen . . . family business prob-ably . . . Not meant for our ears.'

Letty sighed with irritation. 'Couldn't you have just barged in on some pretext? Or were you waiting for the blood to start flowing under the door?' she said and was ignored.

'And then the noises started,' said Stewart. 'Sounded like furniture being thrown about. Screams and yells. It calmed down for a bit but just as we were about to breathe again it started up once more. Can you do something, William, before they kill each other? Eleni's not here. *She'd* have settled them straight away. Nobody knows where she is.'

'She's stayed in town,' said Letty. 'With her sister. I'll go in.'

She started for the library and had reached the door and flung it open, Gunning at her heels, when George burst from the room and pushed past them, unseeing. He was bleeding from a scalp wound, his face an unrecognizable mask. Pale and shaking, he shouldered his way along the corridor, cannoning blindly off the walls. Dickie and Stewart flattened themselves to the sides to allow him space to crash by. Letty shuddered as she sensed a rush of poisoned air following in the young man's wake.

She shook off Gunning's restraining hand and entered the room at his shoulder. The elegant room she'd known was wrecked. The lectern and the tome it had supported had been thrown to the floor. The copy of *The Palace of Minos at Knossos* was lying open, broken at the spine, one of its pages ominously stained with blood. A whole book-case had been wrenched from the wall and its volumes littered the carpet. The cabinet of curiosities was lying on its side, the glass panels in splinters. Its precious contents had spilled out on to the floor, like a child's discarded toys. And in the centre of the wreckage the lowering dark figure of Theodore, seeking a victim. Letty almost gagged on the thick odour of anger and hate.

'Get out! All of you! How dare you barge in here?' It was more alarming to realize that he was not out of his mind with rage but acquiring a modicum of composure and reacting rationally, if aggressively. Letty saw that his face was glinting with tears dripping unregarded down his cheeks.

'Delighted to oblige, old man,' said Gunning affably. 'Just thought you could do with a little help in here. Bit of a rumpus, what?'

'I'll get you a cup of tea, Theo. I've never seen a man more in need of a cup of tea,' said Letty easily. 'And perhaps a ginger-nut with that? I shall have to do it myself, I think – you've scared the living daylights out of the maid, and she's run home to her mother. Now, tell me: Earl Grey or Ceylon?'

Theo looked at her in astonishment and dashed a hand awkwardly over his face.

'But first things first – here,' she said, holding out a handkerchief. Gunning's own, he recognized. 'Let me posh you up a bit.' She advanced on Theo and, murmuring comforting nannyish sounds, began to dab at his face. With a howl that went through them like a band saw, Theodore lost what little control he had left. He grabbed hold of Letty and bent his head to her shoulder, weeping uncontrollably.

By the time they had managed between them to move Theo along to the drawing room, he had calmed sufficiently to launch into a tirade against his son.

'The traitor! He was in Paris over Christmas! You heard him say so,' he shouted accusingly at Letty. 'Denies it all! Well, wouldn't he, the liar? She spoiled him! All that cash – going to a good cause – huh! I shall have his accounts scrutinized. I'll get my man on to it at once. And the sports car! What an indulgence! And now we know what she was paying him for! Bloody gigolo! I've disowned him. He's no longer my son and you're the first to hear it. I'm going straight back into that courtroom and I'm going to tell the coroner all! The world will know I've been harbouring a strumpet and a snake in my bosom for goodness only knows how long!'

'No, you're not, Theo.' Gunning's tone was one Letty had not heard him use before. He was not expecting to be disobeyed. 'You're going to stay right here, take a few pink gins aboard, and calm down. We'll go back and make your excuses. Everyone will sympathize and no one will be surprised. You did your stuff this morning. And I'll find out what George has done with himself. I ought to go after him.'

'Listen! Do you hear? *That's* what George is doing with himself!'

The Bugatti engine roared below in the street as the car emerged from the old coach house and turned into the avenue heading for the centre of town.

'What else would we expect? Running away as usual! Leaving someone else to clear up his bloody mess! Where does he think he's going? I hope he drives off the pier and straight into the jaws of Hades!'

* * *

The coroner raised an eyebrow at the absence of two of the witnesses but made no further comment. A roll call revealed that Eleni also had apparently decided to miss the afternoon session. Showing a shrewd anticipation of the squall in the Russell household and taking evasive action, Letty thought. Finally, Perakis launched into a swift and accurate summary of the autopsy and sat back, sighing.

'I think, ladies and gentlemen, this report makes all clear. It was difficult to ascribe the death of a well-placed and happy young woman to suicide. Mrs Russell had everything to live for, as they say in these cases. Sadly, her condition, the unaccounted-for and clandestine pregnancy, a child engendered by an unknown man, we must guess, somewhere in France in the month of December last, gives us an entirely understandable motive for taking her own life. She could no longer endure the shame she was about to bring on herself, her husband, and her family. In spite of her attempts to tinker with the progress of the pregnancy, she must have been aware that it was about to become evident at any moment, and this knowledge it was that sparked her suicide attempt.

'Her successful attempt. Successful because the tools of the grim task were immediately to hand: the rope – from her husband's own gown . . .' He paused and sighed again. 'Symbolic perhaps of the lady's remorse. The beam – of her bridal chamber. A classical echo. The knot – a skill learned, her husband tells me, as a child, sailing on the lakes of her homeland. The note she left, the speech of Phaedra, sums up her feelings of shame for her illicit love and tells us clearly why she chose not to go on living.

'A sad case. A deeply sad loss. But I have to bring in the verdict of suicide.' He scanned the court, assessing the effect of his decision. 'It is the custom on these occasions to reach for a well-worn formula: The victim took her own life "while the balance of her mind was disturbed". Frequently used as a comforting anodyne for the family. On this occasion I will not be entering such a phrase in my findings.

'I believe Mrs Russell to have been fully in control of her emotions. And, though her action was, by the lights of her own religion, sinful, it was prompted by a clear desire to divert the opprobrium which her conduct must inevitably have brought down on her family and to atone for her shameful behaviour and loss of honour.' He shook his head. Then he murmured, 'A sinner, undoubtedly, but a sinner who seized on the one way left to her to clutch her sin to herself, by this means preventing the poison from spreading to those close about her.'

The elegant figure of Inspector Mariani stood in wait for Laetitia on the steps of the courthouse. He greeted her and then neatly separated her from the accompanying Gunning, leading her away from the dispersing crowd.

'Miss Talbot,' he said when he judged that they would not be overheard. 'A grudging and ill-deserved tribute we've just been treated to, if you don't mind my saying so? I would have said: "*Now boast thee, Death, in thy possession lies a lass unparalleled.*" Are you engaged for the next hour or so, or may I beg your services?'

'My services, Inspector? Why, yes. I was just going to return to the Villa Europa. Mr Russell isn't feeling well . . . there may be things I can do . . .'

'Perfect.' He smiled, offering his arm. 'We'll go together. I think you guess, mademoiselle, that the verdict of suicide is not one that satisfies me any more than I suspect it satisfies you. I would like you to come to Mrs Russell's room with me. I am quite sure that that is where the answer lies. And I think you can help me find it. Would you mind?'

Chapter Twenty

The right mudguard of the Bugatti hit the wall of the city gate and clanged to the road, causing tumult in the ranks of the mule train coming through in the shadows on the other side. George accelerated away from the scene, unaware of the uproar, dashing the streaming blood from his eyes, seeing nothing but the road ahead. He shook his head to clear the dizzy confusion but the motion loosened a pain and sent it knifing across his forehead.

He honked his horn to scatter the crowd of beggars gathering in anticipation at the welcome sound of his engine and shot past them, their astonished faces on either side of the car an irrelevant blur.

Clear of the city, he pressed his foot to the floor. The car surged forward. Only speed mattered to George. Speed intoxicated. Speed saved and purified. It separated him from the pain and ugliness, the deception behind him. His mind was no longer befuddled; it was thinking with absolute clarity. It was poised somewhere above his body, all-seeing, as in a nightmare, whipping him on and shrieking a warning.

It had caught sight of the Furies behind him, awake after all these years and giving chase. Hunting him down. The Eumenides, the so-called Kindly Ones. Ha! Savage avengers, ruthlessly dealing out death to sinners who broke the natural familial laws. Monsters born of the blood of the castrated Uranus. No wonder they scented a victim. They were in pursuit and closing fast, demanding just retribution. George pictured them: Alecto, Megaera, and

Tisiphone, three women, grotesquely tall and black-clad. Their snake-hair writhed; red eyes blazed, exultant, in white faces as they swooped the last few yards, leather bat-wings creaking.

He blinked hard and blinked again, his lashes sticky with blood, focussed on the next bend, and skidded around it, reaching at last the precipitous coast road. There was only one place of safety left to him. It lay ahead. Not far now. To hell with his father! He'd do what he should have done years ago. The right thing. If he could outrun the Furies.

He rounded one more bend and yelled in horror. They'd outflanked him! A trio of black-clad women stood in the middle of the road. They turned with the dreadful precision of slow motion, white-faced masks of tragedy confronting him, and he thrust up a forearm to fend them off.

At the last second before impact, he instinctively wrenched on the wheel. The Bugatti, screaming in outrage, ploughed across the yards of rough ground beyond. It charged, nose first, down the side of the cliff, somersaulting three times before crashing into the sea below.

Chapter Twenty-One

They entered the house to be greeted by a hissing from the first floor. Dickie's anxious face peered over the banister at them. 'Up here,' he said. 'Be quiet – I've just got him off to sleep.'

He was closing the door to the drawing room with exaggerated care when they joined him. 'Hello, Laetitia . . . Inspector. It took four large ones! William told me to keep pouring them and I did. But it got worse before it got better. The language! The sentiments! Never heard anything like it. Raging against poor old George. Stuff you'd never believe! Treacherous, sneaky, slithy tove, according to Theo. No son of his! Womaniser, should have been strangled at birth, castrated even! Funny – Theo hadn't a bad word to say about Phoebe in all this . . . Which is a bit strange, if what I'm guessing happened, happened? Wouldn't you say? But, more pertinently, what did the coroner have to say? Er, Stewart went off to the courtroom . . . .' Dickie shuffled his feet awkwardly. 'I lost the toss and had to stay behind with Theo. We haven't heard the verdict yet. He says he's not interested in hearing but I bet he is!'

Mariani silenced his effusion. 'Suicide. It was judged to be suicide. Look, Mr Collingwood, go back into the drawing room, if you would, and keep watch on him. If he comes round, simply tell him the result. Tell him also that I am in the house and have gone to Mrs Russell's room.'

He paused at Phoebe's door and ushered Letty into the stuffy room. The silence was broken only by a fly buzzing madly on the ledge of the closed window. Mariani went over, raised the window, and shooed out the fly. He opened the second door and left it standing ajar.

Letty stood uncertainly at the threshold, her eyes straying to the beam and seeing again the horror she had confronted days earlier. All was as it had been, down to the indentation on the counterpane where Phoebe's body had lain.

'We've missed something,' said Mariani.

'I have the same feeling,' she said. 'I wish I could help, but . . .'

He gave her a slow smile. 'I think you can,' he said. 'I can ask none of the other inhabitants of this house. They have their secrets and will not reveal them to me. They have their loyalties and would lie to me without compunction to protect their interests. But you, mademoiselle, so freshly arrived, have not had a chance to form allegiances, acquire prejudices. I believe you to be a clever and honest woman and one whose sole motivation might be judged to be to do right by the deceased. Am I mistaken? Do I assume too much?'

'No. You're quite right, Inspector.' Letty's chin went up. 'I could have got very fond of Phoebe and, in fact, I've sworn an oath to myself to work out what really happened to her. And if I can do that working *with* the police instead of getting up their noses and under their feet, well, that's nothing but good news.'

He smiled again. She was on the hook. Mariani knew there were more ways than one of getting cooperation. The thumbscrew approach was not always the most productive. He was conscious of the intriguing effect his large brown eyes and long lashes had on European women, and though he judged this one to be less susceptible than most, it would be foolish not to push his charm as far as it would go. He noted with some amusement that she hadn't considered for a moment the social implications of her situation – alone in a bedroom with an attractive man. The uniform, of course, defended against any suspicion of impropriety, but Mariani was aware that any Greek girl would have insisted on being accompanied by a male relative – and her grandmother. He wondered briefly whether to summon up that architect the Englishwoman seemed to trust – Gunning – for the sake of appearances.

But Miss Talbot was moving around the room with complete unconcern, inquisitive, eager to get on.

'Shall I look over her things first?' she said, going over to the dressing table. 'Women leave quite a lot of clues about themselves in front of their mirrors, you know.'

'We already have an inventory but by all means – cast an eye,' he said easily.

'Nothing unusual here,' she said, poking about. 'Some very good makeup. All bought in Paris. Rouge, lipstick, mascara, eyebrow pencil. Hairbrush and nail file. Not much in the way of equipment – no eyelash curlers, not even a pair of tweezers. Really, a modest collection. This is the only thing of significance, don't you think?'

She pointed to a flacon of perfume. 'The best. Caron. From the rue de la Paix.' She put out a finger and stroked the red silk tassel fastened around the neck of the elegant Baccarat bottle. 'And have you noticed what it's called?'

The inspector came over and picked it up, removing the stopper to wave it about under his nose and sniff at the contents.

'No! This is what you do. May I?' She took it from him and put a forefinger over the neck, tilting it slightly. Slick with scented oil, her finger traced a line along the base of her throat. 'Something woody – chypre, sandalwood? And something flowery – lilies and roses!' she murmured. 'It needs the warmth and chemistry of skin to release its true scent. And this one is very romantic, wouldn't you say? I recognize it now – it's the one she was wearing the day she died.'

Alarmed that the inspector was responding to her unintentional invitation by leaning towards her, nostrils flaring, she turned and briskly replaced the bottle on the dressing table. 'Creamy yet spicy. And perfect for Phoebe.

It was created during the war years. A gift that a soldier going off to battle could offer as a memento to the woman he was in love with. It's called *N'Aimez Que Moi*. "Love only me",' she whispered. 'I wonder who gave her this? She's used very little of it. Perhaps it was a gift from her Christmas lover?'

She moved to the escritoire. 'All neat and perfectly ordinary,' she said. 'Writing paper, silver pen, envelopes of the kind the so-called suicide note was put in . . . blotter. Did you check the blotter? Oh, sorry, of course you did.' She tilted the used sheet to the light and pointed to a section in the top corner. 'Here. She's blotted the name "George". The sheet isn't badly used so it must have been changed, let's say, less than a week ago.'

'Last Wednesday, according to Eleni.'

'So there we are. Phoebe did address that envelope and very recently. I wonder . . .' Letty took one of the unused envelopes, opened the flap, and licked it. Then she pressed it down firmly and put it back on the desk. She went to the wardrobe and checked the clothes, searched under the bed, and emerged red-faced but having found nothing of interest. The contents of the adjoining bathroom were orderly and unsurprising. Phoebe's medicine cabinet contained only plasters, an emergency bandage still in its wrapper, and a half-used and ancient bottle of Dr Collis Brown's Chlorodyne. The top, when Letty tried to unscrew it, proved to be rusted on to the bottle. 'Well, this hasn't been opened for a decade, I'd say. Phoebe wasn't one for patented cures, was she? Not even an aspirin! Right – I think we could inspect the envelope now.'

She picked up the envelope and gently ran a fingernail under the seal. It sprang up at once. 'Thought so! It's been a damp season. The glue on these things has been pretty poor since the war – Lord knows what they use these days. I always have a pot of cow gum by me when I'm sealing an envelope. Anyone could have –'

'Removed the original contents and substituted a torn-out page,' said Mariani, beginning to betray his excitement. 'And resealed it.'

'We found it underneath a paperweight. That would have ensured it stayed stuck down.'

'I'll take a sample. But now – you gave me at the beginning of all this a vivid picture of the scene of discovery. I want you to reconstruct, if you will, what may have taken place here *before* you arrived. Imagine for me, conjure up with a woman's insight, what might have transpired between Mrs Russell and her doctor.'

Instantly involved in the game, Letty went to the door and mimed entering. She closed the door after her and with a hand invited the imaginary Stoddart to take a seat at the table. 'That's where Harold *says* the consultation took place. Sit down here, Inspector, and be Dr Stoddart.' She settled in the matching wicker chair opposite. 'Though I noticed, from the door before I came in, that there was a slight indentation on the counterpane. I thought at first she'd been having a rest and perhaps got up to change. But she could have lain down for an examination. It's possible. Anyway, they talked. We can't be sure how much he knew about her condition . . . I mean the real reason behind her fainting and swooning and sickness. She could have been deceiving *him*, too. As he told us in court.'

'To go back to what we know to be fact,' said Mariani, 'the upshot was that Stoddart gave her a sleeping pill and left her here. Now – tell me – did he have his medical bag with him that day?'

'No. He was out with his wife, having a picnic or something . . . No, he had no bag. And they came back in the Bugatti and there were certainly no medical supplies in that.'

Mariani picked up her hesitation. 'Picnic, you say?'

'Odd, that . . . Phoebe and I were to have a picnic, but the Stoddarts hadn't brought anything with them. Not even a sandwich or a flask of coffee. They were happy to share the spread Phoebe had got together . . . and why would they not? It was quite a banquet! Good Lord!' she

219

exclaimed, remembering. 'There were four plates, four sets of cutlery, and enough food to feed a battalion in the hamper.' She looked at Mariani, excited by her memory. 'She'd *planned* it, hadn't she? Arranged with the Stoddarts –'

'With one of the Stoddarts at least,' he cautioned.

'– to meet there and join us for lunch. She pretended it was a chance meeting. Did she pretend also to faint, I begin to wonder?'

He raised a questioning eyebrow.

'She collapsed, practically into the pudding. She'd been very wobbly all morning . . . I hadn't realized that her feet and ankles were terribly sore and I thought it was just another stumble, but it was more than that. She lost consciousness. And the doc drove her back in George's Bugatti. I cycled back with Olivia. We must have arrived, oh, half an hour after them and then I walked back here from the Stoddarts' house.'

'Did you come straight back here after leaving Olivia?'

'Well, no. It was a Sunday. I loitered, enjoying the atmosphere, watching people parade about in their Sunday best . . . it's all very exotic for me, you know! And the shops. I looked in quite a few windows on the way back down the avenue.'

'You came by the main road?'

She nodded. 'It's the only one I know. I had only arrived two days before. I didn't – and still don't – know the byways.'

'Or the shortcuts,' he murmured.

'So. Phoebe is given a sleeping pill. It had to come from her own supplies. Did you . . .?'

'Of course, mademoiselle.' He rummaged in his briefcase and took out an evidence bag. 'This bottle. It was in her bathroom. The label declares that it contains the usual amount of twenty pills. Prescribed a year ago. These are rather a strong formula and doctors never prescribe in large quantities for obvious reasons. This bottle contains nineteen. The doctor says he gave her one pill that day.'

220

'Phoebe didn't like to take drugs. We know that. Harold knew that. He said he sat here at the table and watched her take it. Eleni brought a glass of fresh water ... Right ... I'm Phoebe. I'm upset ... cross ... nervous ... I have things to do ... decisions to make ... A letter to write to George? If ever I needed to keep my wits about me it's at this moment. I don't like the idea of sleeping pills anyway. Now – Phoebe was right-handed.'

Mariani watched as the young Englishwoman held an imaginary glass in her right hand and an imaginary pill in her left. She put the pill to her lips, pulled a face, and swallowed from the glass. Under cover of replacing it with a flourish on the table, her left hand went casually to the cushion of the wicker chair and felt about beneath it. It came up a second later, a white pill pinched between thumb and forefinger.

Mariani said something unintelligible in Greek.

Letty looked closely at the pill, seemingly amazed to find it in her hand. 'It's got a trace of lipstick on it – do you see? Phoebe pretended to swallow it, palmed it, and hid it in the easiest place.' Her voice betrayed her distress as she spoke again: 'This is worse than I feared. You know what this means, Inspector? Phoebe went to her death fully conscious. She was in complete possession of her senses when the noose went round her neck.'

Chapter Twenty-Two

'She knew what she was doing! Good Lord! Old Sokratis Perakis had it right!' said Mariani, taken aback. 'She *did* commit suicide. There were no signs of a struggle, no resistance had been put up. And if she was fully conscious, she could have resisted. Anyone would have.' He was muttering to himself, reasoning aloud. 'Her husband, through there,' he pointed to the door standing open, 'would have heard something. Would surely have been alerted and come running?'

They looked at each other, unwilling to share their thought. 'Unless he was in the room with her at the time, with his hands around her throat,' Letty managed to hold back from saying.

They both jumped on hearing a tap at the door and the embarrassed clearing of a throat. Mariani strode over and flung the door wide open to reveal the boot boy, pressed into service to deliver a message.

'Excuse me, sir . . . lady,' the lad mumbled. 'There's a gentleman below who urgently wants to speak to the master, but Mr Collingwood won't let him up until you say it's all right. It's the mistress's lawyer come all the way from Athens.' He thrust a card into Mariani's hand.

Mariani didn't hesitate. 'Mr Russell is not to be wakened. Send the gentleman up here. I will have a word with him. Thank you.'

'Would you like me to . . .?' Letty began to say politely, edging to the door.

'No, no. Stay here, Miss Talbot. We'll receive him together.' He passed her the card.

'A Frenchman,' she said. 'Offices here in Herakleion. Also Paris and Athens.'

'Monsieur Dupleix.' Mariani beamed, taking the hand of the puzzled lawyer when he appeared. 'I believe we have met before. Do come inside and I'll present you to a young lady, a compatriot and friend of the deceased who was in her confidence. Miss Talbot is helping me in my researches.'

M. Dupleix was most uncomfortable, and it took all Mariani's easy charm to persuade him to enter. He was young, like the inspector, but had none of his confidence. Letty noticed that as soon as his prey was inside, the inspector stationed himself in front of the door, which he closed gently. 'I came the moment I got the news,' Dupleix said defensively. 'I was in Athens when the telegram reached me. Dropped everything and came back on the next boat. Thought it might be urgent. But, of course, I should be addressing myself to her husband and her immediate family. Have we had the funeral yet? Families like to hear the will read straight after the last slice of funeral fruitcake's disappeared, you know. Haven't missed it, have I?'

'No, no. It's scheduled for next week. It was decided to allow time for some of her relations to get here from Europe. Don't worry, Monsieur Dupleix, you are in good time! Take a seat, will you?'

Uncertainly the lawyer sat down on the edge of the chair Mariani indicated, clutching his briefcase to his chest and looking up with suspicion at the imposing figure of the inspector.

'You have the will with you?'

'Yes, the final version. I have it.'

'*Final* version? Tell me, monsieur, when was this arrived at?'

The man clearly wanted to tell him it was none of his business.

'You may not be aware, coming straight from the port, that a murder enquiry is in progress,' Mariani lied smoothly. 'I believe Mrs Russell to have been the victim of a murderous attack. She was hanged, monsieur, from that beam.' He pointed dramatically and Dupleix shuddered. He began nervously to tug at his moustache. 'I am collecting evidence,' Mariani explained, 'and the contents of your briefcase may well be material to the progress of my enquiry. I'm sure I don't need to spell out why.'

Dupleix held his case more tightly to his chest. It was clearly going to take force to separate him from it.

'Now. I would not like Mr Russell to think that anyone had jumped the gun, set aside the protocol . . . I would not like you, my friend, to have to admit to any illegal or even careless lapse. So I will ask – and Miss Talbot will bear witness to my request' – Letty tilted her head and smiled, obliging and demure –'that you keep your documents to yourself, to be shown to whomever and whenever you judge proper.' He made a gesture conveying light unconcern. 'I am not requiring that you show them to me.'

Dupleix began to relax. Letty waited for the blow to fall.

'But I must insist before you leave this room that you give me an outline of the contents – an oral résumé of Mrs Russell's last will and testament will suffice. A simple statement of the main provisions will satisfy me and will help enormously in the pursuit of the guilty party. I'm quite certain you would wish to do all that you can to bring about his unmasking and arrest? No?'

The lawyer considered his position. He weighed his options. He looked again at the athletic, smiling menace before him, camouflaged in reassuring blue serge and gold braid. He made his decision.

'She changed it a month ago,' he finally answered. 'She called at our office and did it there and then. Seemed extremely certain of what she wanted.'

'Which was?'

'You may be aware that my client was a rich woman? Legacies from –'

Mariani nodded and with a brusque gesture invited him to get a move on.

'She had maintained control of her assets on her marriage to Mr Russell. He was, I believe, frequently consulted, but had no legal interest in her financial affairs. Though he did benefit in –' He caught himself, reconsidered, and carried on. 'The upshot is: Instead of her wealth passing immediately and entirely to her husband, half her fortune now goes straight to her younger sister, Alice, who is married and living in Paris. Of the rest . . . a sum is to be invested in a trust in her husband's name and payments made to him from it at monthly intervals. The residue – by no means a negligible sum – is to go to her stepson, Charles St George. No strings, no conditions; he may dispose of it as he wishes. Yes . . . Master George Russell is about to discover that he is now a very well-off young man!'

'Indeed? And can you assure me, Monsieur, that no one but yourself was aware of Mrs Russell's revised provisions?'

'She did everything necessary in my office, as I've said. My secretary and my clerk witnessed the signing and, of course, were given no view of the document other than that. Mrs Russell kept no copy of the will at home and was very clear as to her wish for absolute discretion in the matter. As far as I know she had kept it a close secret. Which it still was until a moment ago,' he added resentfully.

'You have been most helpful, Monsieur Dupleix. I will remember that,' Mariani assured him. 'And now, may I recommend that you return to your office? And await further instructions from the family? Mr Theodore Russell is quite unable to deal with anything for the present. Distressed, indisposed . . .' he murmured.

'Drunk as a skunk, the boot boy said.' Dupleix shrugged and made a dash for the door.

Chapter Twenty-Three

'A *marrying man*, that's what my old ma would have called *him*,' said Gunning.

'Great heavens, William! I never realized you had a mother,' said Letty.

'And I'm afraid it's what *I* shall be expected to become if I'm observed bringing you here alone with such frequency. Did you notice the waiter dashed forward with a potted palm the minute I put my foot over the doorstep?'

'Where would you have preferred to confer? In the wrecked library? In the drawing room with Theodore snoring on the chaise longue? Your room or mine? People just assume we're tourists from one of the boats. A kind uncle taking his niece for a pastry. Oh, speaking of which, I'll have one of those little Cretan cheese-and-cinnamon things.'

Gunning ordered *kalitsounia me kanella* for two and a pot of Darjeeling.

'You're confusing this with your last job, I think, William. Last summer, you were supposed – you were *paid* to ensure I didn't get into trouble of an amorous, or any other, nature. You are no longer employed by my father, so you can jolly well come off watch.'

'I'm sorry. Old habits . . . I got used to trying to fend off the beasts of prey.'

'He's not a beast of prey! William, you're mad! *Kosta* – the inspector – is a very respectable, educated, and honourable man.' She couldn't prevent herself from adding, 'And dashed attractive! Cretan Christian name, Italian surname – that's a seductive blend . . .' George may have proved to be a damp squib when it came to tormenting Gunning, but here, most unexpectedly, was the unwitting policeman filling the role nicely.

Gunning sighed. 'I say again – Mariani's a marrying man. All Cretan men are that. A bachelor is almost unknown on this island. It's a wonder he's got to his age – thirty would you say? – still unattached. He's got mistresses all over Crete, I shouldn't wonder, but it's high time he settled down. His career demands it if nothing else. He's ambitious, and someone like you would do him credit – actually smooth his path – on the international scene. Mariani would be Head of Interpol in three years with you at his side.'

'You let your imagination run away with you, William. There's no danger, I'm sure. But perhaps we shouldn't tell him quite yet that I'm a rich woman. Think what happened to poor Phoebe! Now – give me a moment to nibble this cake and I'll reveal to you the contents of her will. Phoebe Russell continues to astonish us, you'll find!'

'Good Lord!' Gunning's surprise at her account of her session with the inspector was very satisfying. 'Well, I never! Seems morally correct to me – don't you agree, Letty? – that the lion's share of her fortune goes back to the family whence it came? But as to the rest . . . Theodore is going to be devastated to receive nothing more than a grudging annuity. More ructions to come from that quarter, I fear! I'd like to know the reason behind all that. And even stranger – the generous gift to George. She must have trusted him.'

'Without conditions, too. He could just go out and buy a string of racing cars if he wanted to,' said Letty, disapproving. 'Where *is* George?' she asked, struck with sudden anxiety. 'I didn't like the look of that head wound his father inflicted. Someone ought to go and find him, check that he's all right.'

'I was prowling the streets while you were dallying with the inspector. No trace of him. His car was seen making off towards the harbour. He could be miles away by now. All we can do is wait for him to come back again.'

'I'm not so sure. A wound like that – he'll have taken it straight to the doctor, won't he? Come on, William. You know the way. That's where we'll start. Let's go and bother Harry.'

The door of the Stoddart house down by the harbour was opened not by a maid but by Olivia herself. It creaked open a reluctant inch or two.

'Yes?' The single word conveyed such a depth of inhospitality and suspicion that Gunning took a step back, and words of stumbling apology were already leaking from him when Letty firmly put her foot in the door, the assertive action belied by the cheerful smile on her face.

'Olivia! It's only us! We need to see Harry. Rather urgently, I'm afraid. Tell me – how are you both bearing up? It's been quite a day one way and another, hasn't it?' She started to peel off her gloves.

Olivia's face was blotched with red – anger or grief? – impossible to tell. Her watery green eyes were swollen and she had clearly been weeping. She was twisting a damp handkerchief nervously between her hands. Clearly, Letty and Gunning were the last people she wanted to have in her hallway.

'You can't see him. He's in his study and has asked not to be disturbed by anyone. You'll have to leave.'

'Don't be silly, Ollie! Harry won't at all mind seeing us. It's about George. George Russell. And it is, as I say, very urgent.'

'Matter of life and death,' Gunning added dramatically.

Olivia hesitated. Finally, her nurse's instincts overcame her truculence. 'I'll give you five minutes. That's all,' she said ungraciously. And, with a surprising swirl of resentment, in a voice rising out of control, 'Oh, by all means, go in and annoy him! Why not? Kick him in the privates! Take a paper knife to his knick-knacks! What do I care?'

Harry, when they hurried to his consulting room, looked up and cringed, obviously fearing just such an attack. He was righting a fallen hat stand and in some disarray, but he waved his visitors to chairs by his desk and took a seat behind it. Letty looked about her with dismay. The scene in the library at the Europa had been devastating. A battlefield. This consulting room could in no way be compared with that, but emotions had been unloosed here also. Ink had spilled from an inkwell, ponding over the desk and dripping on to the Turkey carpet; a framed photograph had been knocked from the mantelpiece, the glass splintered.

Curious to see whose features had incited someone to smash a heel down over them, Letty took a wider than necessary track to her seat and noted the subject of the photograph as she passed by.

Aurelia.

Strangely, not a picture of a person but a ship. The steamship *Aurelia*. The kind of trashy souvenir handed out by the captain at the end of a cruise, received with gushing thanks, and instantly thrown away with the rubbish. In this austere, panelled room it was puzzlingly out of place.

'George Russell? You've come about George Russell?' Harry seemed surprised and relieved. 'Haven't seen him since this morning – in the courtroom. Why do you ask?'

'We're very concerned for him ...' Gunning gave a résumé of the scene at the Europa, outlining the reason for the altercation and describing, as best he could from his brief glimpse, the serious nature of George's wound.

'Hit him with a volume of *The Palace*? Good God! Weighs a ton! And he drove off? In *that* car? I understand your concern. Better check the hospital. The boy's most probably a casualty by now.'

Stoddart looked exhausted, Letty thought. His wife had been giving him a rough time and the coroner's court had been a strain. If ever wifely sympathy was called for, this was the moment. What could have got into Olivia? And what was the reason for those crude and desperate suggestions she'd thrust at them? Letty eyed the paper knife on Harry's stationery tray, almost fearing to see blood on it. And – knick-knacks? What on earth did Olivia have in mind?

And then the shock of realization ran through her. Her mind had seized on the last dozen pieces of a jigsaw and slotted them home with gathering speed, one after the other.

She was sitting opposite the man who had murdered Phoebe. And she was going to make him confess.

She put a restraining hand on Gunning's knee as he made to rise and leave. He instantly, without quibble, sank back, waiting to hear from her.

'Such an unfortunate family, the Russells,' she remarked. 'How many more disasters? And how unfair that George should be found guilty of being the father of that poor babe! Surely the true father must be in Europe and well away from the scene? No man with a shred of honour could stand by and see another being destroyed by an unjust accusation! I do not think George could possibly be responsible . . . nor does William. What about you, Doctor? Does this strike you as a reasonable proposition?'

'Well . . . no . . . Actually, George would be the very last person who'd come to mind . . .'

'We should be looking elsewhere for the man in Phoebe's life. For her Christmas lover. "N'aimez que moi", he told her in the rue de la Paix.' Letty sighed. 'And that's just what poor Phoebe did. You should be aware, Doctor, that I visited her room again just now with Inspector Mariani. We made some interesting discoveries.'

Stoddart slumped at his desk, waiting for the blow to fall.

Letty got up and strolled to the broken photograph. She picked it up gingerly and examined it. 'Ah, yes, a memento. Carefully framed. Happy memories? Not, it would seem, for someone? It's been stamped on. Is this heel mark Olivia's?'

She put the photograph down on the desk and resumed her seat. 'We've concluded that this affair of Phoebe's could well have started on her journey to Paris. On the boat! She had taken a first-class cabin, of course. And you'd need the comfort and privacy if you were going to have a prolonged bout of seasickness – or spend a week curled up in your lover's arms. Phoebe told me you were 'wonderful with seasickness.' I wonder, Doctor, if you ministered solely to Phoebe that week? Olivia was obviously completely taken in by whatever stories you concocted to account for your absences.'

'Didn't need to "concoct" anything. Ollie was the one who suffered – she spent most of the time groaning in her cabin, begging to be left alone. She understood I was doing the rounds of the ship, ministering to the suffering.'

'And the affair continued in Paris. You all stayed at the same hotel. Phoebe chose to spend her time there rather than in the comfort of her family home. She must have valued the anonymity – and the proximity of her friends.'

'Ollie did a lot of shopping . . . Christmas coming up, you know . . . She was rather pleased to get rid of me,' the doctor said dismissively. 'Our interests were never the same. She understands that I like to go off round the museums. Not her cup of tea.'

'You are admitting that the child conceived in December was yours?'

Stoddart's head drooped, his reply was almost unintelligible. 'I had no idea until Sunday! She dropped her bombshell in the car on the way back to Herakleion. She sent me a note, arranging the meeting at Knossos. It was getting increasingly difficult to plan time together. Ollie made it very awkward. Oh, not that she suspected anything – she didn't. They say the wife's always the last to hear . . . and she wouldn't have believed any such gossip. She'd have laughed! Doesn't regard me as love's young dream, exactly.

Problem was – Ollie seemed to think it was *her* Phoebe was keen on seeing.'

He studied his fingers for a moment. 'Phoebe's mad idea, that! Get close to Ollie and it would be a good cover for our ... um ... And now it's doubly backfired! Ollie isn't a woman who makes friends easily, and when Phoebe started to make overtures she was thrilled and flattered. And now she's dead and Ollie's worked out who the Parisian Lothario was – she feels twice betrayed. *I* deceived her. *Phoebe* deceived her. And I'm not certain which of the two offended her more. I'm not going to get out of this alive,' he mumbled in misery.

'Why did she arrange to see you that morning, Harry?' Gunning asked.

'To tell me she was pregnant. It was beginning to show and she'd have to come clean. She wanted me to pack and leave for Europe with her straight away. I couldn't.'

'Why on earth not? Sounds like a good offer to me,' said Letty to provoke him.

'And give up my profession forever? I'd have been struck off! And doctoring's what I do. It's the only thing I've ever wanted to do. I've very nearly finished my research here on the island and I'm about to publish the results. I could be a world authority on ... Oh, never mind! To go away with her would have meant giving up everything, and for an uncertain future. Suppose she found a younger model next year and left me high and dry? Many more seductive blokes to be found in Paris. Not so much competition here.' He shot an assessing glance at Gunning. 'At one's time of life ... well, one begins to lose confidence in that department, I'm sure you'd agree, old boy.'

'Nothing wrong with Mr Gunning's department,' Letty snapped, impulsively.

'Oh, indeed?' He looked from one to the other, speculation beginning to dawn. But he had weightier matters on his mind and, to Letty's relief, did not pursue his thoughts. 'Er – very well – I'm a coward. There, you have it.'

'A coward and an adulterer,' said Letty in a neutral voice. 'Yes. But are you also a murderer? Did she threaten to expose you, Harry?'

'You didn't know her well. Phoebe would never have done that! She would have protected my good name. And – no – I didn't murder her. Nor did anyone. She committed suicide. I'm very clear on that now all the evidence is in. My rejection was part, I don't doubt, of her motivation and to that extent I am culpable. We heard the decision in court. Leave it alone, Laetitia. Let the dead rest in peace.'

Letty's eyes went to the paper knife and she allowed herself a moment's fantasy.

'You flatter yourself, Doctor. I don't think being rejected by you would tip a woman like Phoebe over the edge! She'd have laughed and got over it. She'd have fled to Europe and remade her life.'

Gunning had been very silent. Suddenly, he began to make the movements a man makes when he's about to stand and take his leave. 'Look, really, Letty – you have your answers – nothing more to be said, I think.' He put his hand under her arm, hauling her to her feet. He turned to Harry casually. 'One more thing, before we leave you in something like peace. A bit of medical information – would you mind awfully?'

He reached into his pocket and put the Minoan votive offering on to the desk in front of the doctor. 'Something very wrong with these legs. Are you up to a diagnosis of a condition three thousand years old? Or perhaps you've seen something very similar recently?'

Stoddart turned grey and his jaw dropped. He gasped for breath, unable to speak, and Letty said urgently, 'Get Ollie! He's having a heart attack! Oh, William, what on earth have you done?'

Chapter Twenty-Four

'No! No! For God's sake, don't call Ollie! I'm quite all right,' Harry croaked unconvincingly. 'Rather a shock. Just pass me that glass of water, would you? Thank you, my dear.' He stared at the pale clay legs in revolted fascination, making no move to examine them. 'Silly of me to react like that. Got so used to hiding it . . . but I suppose it doesn't really matter anymore. How on earth did you ever manage to – She didn't leave a journal, did she . . .? No, she wouldn't have been so careless. . . . How did you find out?' he asked again.

Letty could only glance from one to the other, deeply puzzled.

'It was Letty's sharp observation,' said Gunning, baffling her further. 'She described to me the condition of Phoebe's legs. Skin macules, lesions, ulcerated in places. Like the ones on this model. And all hidden under the boots she insisted on wearing. Letty was alarmed to see her stumble around Knossos. Assumed she was in pain from blisters but, of course, she was in no pain. Probably numb from the knees down. But muscle weakness would have led her to drag her toes, to trip. There were symptoms, however, that she couldn't hide from the world. In the seven months I was living in the household, and constantly in her company, I couldn't help noticing that her skin deteriorated, became blotchy . . . she lost her eyebrows. Skilfully pencilled in, it was hard to spot.'

'But there were no tweezers on her dressing table,' Letty murmured, still mystified.

'One of the early signs, I understand, of Hansen's disease?'

At the name Stoddart gave a bitter smile and, in an echo of Mariani's quiet but deadly accusation, said, 'When, Doctor, did you become aware that your patient had leprosy?'

Letty reached for Gunning's hand, unable to speak.

'And the answer to that is – unbelievably, unprofessionally late in the day,' Stoddart continued. 'Her family remains unaware. She herself had no idea for a long while. She dismissed the first signs as a mild skin complaint . . . was looking forward to stocking up on all manner of cosmetic unguents when she got to Paris . . . was planning a visit to an Alpine spa . . . We'd – we'd been intimate for two or three weeks before I began to suspect. Devastating, of course. All relations of that sort had to stop, naturally.'

He looked at the clay legs and, finally, reluctantly, reached out to examine them. 'An ancient disease. It's mentioned in Pharaonic Egypt, nearly four thousand years ago. And, yes, these show the symptoms quite clearly. Poor soul! Alexander's soldiers brought it back to Macedonia with them; the Romans imported it from the Middle East. All those centuries of suffering and there's still no cure.'

'None? Are you quite certain?' Letty asked desperately. 'William – you gave it a name just now . . .?'

'Hansen's disease. It's named after the Norwegian who, last century, identified the bacterium that causes it. Gives it a certain scientific flavour, doesn't it? Belies the ugly truth of the matter. Leprosy. It's still leprosy. We don't know how it's caught and we don't know how it's cured. The only certainty is death – following on exclusion from society, lasting anything from one to forty years. Phoebe knew all too clearly what her fate was. She'd taken an interest in George's efforts to improve things in the leprosarium on the island, even accompanied him on occasions, though she would never admit it to me – or anyone – for quite obvious reasons. But – Phoebe being Phoebe – loving, demonstrative, heart on sleeve – I'm quite certain she wouldn't have held back the hugs for the children. I blame George when it comes down to it – you know what he's like – believes himself unassailable, even by disease. Or is he one of those men who courts death? I've come across them in the war. I expect you have, too?' he said, exchanging a glance with Gunning.

'Oh, yes,' said Gunning, remembering. 'The "Follow me, chaps! Everything'll be all right!" type. And no one can understand why *he* always returns unscathed while his men litter the battlefield. Sometimes he really is as brave as he appears – is it a kind of numbness or a genuine feeling of God-given invincibility that protects him? Is it an antidote for fear?'

'Perhaps it's just what it appears,' said Letty, fed up with the pair of them. 'A determination to do the right thing whatever the odds. To offer your life to protect what you hold dear. The fact that the gods don't choose to take you up on the offer in no way diminishes it!'

'But this time, one of the peripheral victims of this careless bravery was Phoebe. Why? How? It's not the easiest thing, contracting leprosy. It's hardly the 'flu,' Gunning reminded her brusquely. 'One sneeze and you're infected. That's not the way it happens – but you'll correct me if I've got that wrong.'

'I told you – we don't know. For thousands of years medical men have been saying that!' Stoddart's voice was desperate. 'I could burble on about genetic variation in susceptibility, transfer of bacilli via nasal droplets. *No one knows!* Perhaps if the disease struck London or Paris or Vienna, someone would come up with something. But still we wait. And still the patients crowd into the leper hospitals. Cut off, barely cared for, their lives suspended, waiting to die.'

'Phoebe wouldn't have wanted to do that,' said Gunning. 'Spend the rest of her days knitting leprosy bandages.' He looked speculatively at Stoddart. 'She was asking you to run away with her to Europe, wasn't she,

Doctor? But not to live with her and raise a child. To find medical care? Some discreet sanatorium somewhere?'

Stoddart nodded miserably.

'A terminal and hideous condition, a baby on the way – a child for whom there could be no future – and a lover who washed his hands of her,' Letty said softly, her heart aching. 'Too much. Yes, the noose and the beam would have made sense. Professor Perakis had it right, but for all the wrong reasons. What did he say? She died to "prevent the poison from spreading to those close about her". He couldn't have known just how pernicious the poison.

'But the thing that tipped her over the edge, that turned her brittle cheerfulness into utter despair, was your betrayal,' she finished bitterly. 'Your abandonment.'

'I say! That's rather harsh. I've admitted my part in all this, but do bear in mind I've sworn an oath.' He began to quote: '"*I swear by Apollo the Healer, that I will use my power to help the sick to the best of my ability and judgement. I will not give a fatal draught to anyone if I am asked, nor will I suggest such a thing. Neither will I give a woman means to procure an abortion,*"' he said, murmuring the ancient oath of Hippocrates.

'Phoebe asked you for that? An abortion? And you refused?'

'Out of the question. Against all my principles.'

'Interesting piece of moral correctness, that venerable oath,' Gunning said. 'But you quote selectively, Stoddart. You're silent on a further paragraph: "*I will not abuse my position to indulge in sexual contacts with the bodies of women or men whether they be freemen or slaves . . .*" Pity you didn't observe all the conditions with equal rigour.'

Even Letty flinched to hear his condemnation. The doctor sat, head bowed, still as a stone.

Letty picked up the votive offering and put it in her pocket. 'Come on, William. We were looking for George, do you remember?'

'I say – you're not intending to bother Mariani with this, are you?' Stoddart asked. 'I haven't even told Ollie. The fewer the people aware, the better, wouldn't you say? We don't want to start a panic . . .'

His desperate voice followed them to the door, unregarded.

'All the same,' said William, as the front door banged behind them and they hesitated on the pavement, 'and considering the weight of guilt he carries – that was quite a performance from the doctor!'

'Performance? What do you mean? Wasn't he telling the truth?'

'Oh, yes. Every word he spoke, I think, was the truth. It's just that not every word of the truth was spoken. It's all right, Letty. It wasn't Stoddart who murdered Phoebe. But I'm sure he thinks he knows who did.'

Letty had a sudden and vivid memory of the doctor's reaction to the sound made outside the window of Phoebe's room. 'At the time, he genuinely believed there was someone lurking about, you know. He was very tense, all senses twitching, while I was in the room with him. Expecting someone to burst in, you'd say. And when he heard you climbing the tree – somehow it was no more than he expected.'

'In the circumstances – wound up like that – I'm lucky he didn't knock my head off . . . Great heavens! What on earth's this?' He pivoted to look up the street in the direction of the noise of a clattering cart and men's voices shouting in fear and concern. 'Oh, no! This couldn't be – Oh, no! Letty – bang on the door again! Quickly! Get the doctor out!' And he raced off towards the sinister cortège.

Letty's urgent knocking and her voice, shrill with apprehension, finally managed to bring Harry Stoddart to the door, just as the cart with its hideous burden stopped in front of it.

The panting spokesman addressed the doctor, though what he had to report was evident enough. 'Car crash . . . coast road . . . He was only yards from the turnoff to the village. Car went right over the cliff into the sea, throwing him out. Bones broken ... unconscious but still breathing ... He'd have still been there unnoticed if it hadn't been for the women. My wife was on the road home with her sister and her ma and they saw it all. We've been very gentle – pulled and pushed the cart ourselves, two up front and two behind. Didn't want to risk donkeys or wait for them to harness up. We know who it is – it's young Master George.'

The man leaned over the pale features and murmured, 'Hang on there, lad! We've done it! *You've* done it! The doctor's right here. He'll see you're all right.'

And their confidence was not misplaced, Letty thought, seeing a different doctor from the hopeless figure they had just left. Instantly in charge, unsurprised, the battlefield surgeon was on parade, swiftly beginning to check what he could there and then in the street, his skilled hands moving with authority.

Tenderly, under Stoddart's direction, four men lifted the improvised stretcher of willow boughs, bearing George from the cart. They'd covered him over with a scarlet saddle blanket and it was impossible for Letty to make out how badly he was injured.

Stoddart paused to catch Gunning by the arm. 'His father must be informed. Could you go back to the villa and break the bad news straight away? I think Theo ought to come at once. I'll summon Olivia to help with this.' And he hurried inside ahead of the stretcher.

Gunning exchanged a few words with the rest of the village men before they set off, hearing further details of the accident and their fears for the young man's condition. Letty could make out that Gunning was thanking them and saying that if George survived, it would be due to their care and speed. He promised them that he would bring news of George as soon as there was something to report, most probably in the morning.

'Thank God those men were on the spot,' said Letty, hurrying along beside him. 'They saved his life. Aren't you going to give them a reward for doing what they did?'

'Heavens, no! They'd be offended. George is one of them. I shall go to the village sometime later. I'll take a bucket of raki with me and we'll have a night-long party with a good deal of heroic storytelling. And I pray that George will be of the company.' His grim features belied the positive tone of his voice, adopted, she guessed, to jolly her along. 'But now, Letty, we have an impossible duty to perform. We've got to go and find out what state Theodore is in. We may even have to shake him awake. And then we must try to find the words to tell him his son's life may be hanging by a thread.'

On Crete, even the gods may die. Letty shuddered, remembering.

Chapter Twenty-Five

'He's dead, surely?'

Theodore Russell stared at the motionless body laid out on the treatment bed in Dr Stoddart's surgery. Letty had been afraid that he might refuse to see the son he had so recently and so vehemently disowned but he had agreed to go with them to the Stoddarts', the sombre news cutting through his gin-induced fog.

His emotion at the sight of the bruised and bloodied face and closed eyes was betrayed by an unnaturally quiet tone and an occasional mistimed gesture.

'Who did this?' He spoke again, breaking the silence. 'Some other poor bugger whose wife he seduced?'

'Russell!' Harry brought him up swiftly, indignant and disapproving. 'Your son has had a motoring accident. I insist that you moderate your language and adjust your response in the presence of the injured. And I say – *injured*. Your son is not dead.' For a moment, Letty had a glimpse of the man Phoebe might have loved: forceful, calm, and principled. Before he compromised his honour.

'You're wasting your time. He's a goner.' Russell turned to leave.

'No. No. I've given him a sedative. He'll be in considerable pain. There are broken limbs – ribs and a cracked skull. I can't yet say whether there's cerebral damage. It's possible. I'm going to do what I can here and give him a chance to stabilize. He ought, perhaps, to be taken to the hospital, but I don't want to risk a further jolting through the streets. Or a change of surgeon. Really, there's nothing

241

they can do for him that I can't do. We're well equipped here.'

'No one is well enough equipped to bring him back. I can see that. It's a hopeless case. You don't have to wrap it up for me, Doctor. Where did it happen? Was he fleeing to the harbour? Running away from his betrayal?'

Letty decided there were two ways of dealing with Theodore. She rejected her preferred plan to wallop him behind the ear with Stoddart's paperweight and chose the second. 'As a matter of fact he wasn't fleeing, Mr Russell,' she explained in a kindly tone. 'He'd left the town and was heading towards a village on the coast . . . what did you say it was called, William? Mournia, that's it. He would certainly have died up there if he hadn't been spotted by some village women. Just driving away his anger, I suppose, until he ran out of road. And, yes, since you are the one who injured him, you're probably right to blame yourself. But, Theo, when you know the facts that have recently come to light, you may forgive yourself as I'm quite certain George will forgive you.'

Gunning looked at her, sending a question and a warning. She persisted, ignoring him: 'George is *not* guilty of the offence you ascribed to him,' she said firmly. 'Doctor Stoddart has been raking through his recollections of Phoebe's time in Paris and –'

Doctor Stoddart stiffened. 'I say! Miss Talbot! Laetitia! I spoke in confidence –'

'And it will be respected, Doctor!' She smiled reassuringly at him and carried on. 'George was indeed in Paris that month with friends, but never managed to meet up with Phoebe. Their itineraries overlapped for only a day or so, and on those days she was engaged with Ollie and Harry.' She dropped her voice. 'You wouldn't expect the doctor to name names even if he could remember, but he believes there is question of an old acquaintance from the war years – Phoebe's previous life – who resurfaced at the funeral,' she improvised. 'We have the doctor's assurance that George was in no way responsible for poor

Phoebe's condition. Just an unfortunate coincidence. Will you confirm this much for Mr Russell, Doctor?'

'It wasn't George,' Stoddart spoke up. 'Couldn't possibly have been George. And I'll swear to that on my honour. And in a court of law, should you wish it.'

Theodore took a moment or two to absorb this, then went to grasp his son's cold hand.

'Speak to him,' said Stoddart surprisingly. 'Say something. Anything. Sometimes they can hear you, you know. Men at death's door will occasionally come round and answer a question you've spoken over what you thought was about to become a corpse. I was once roundly ticked off for my barrack-room language by a devout young Methodist who recovered consciousness two days after my outburst. It's worth a try.'

Awkwardly, Theodore began to mutter: 'Forgive me, George. Bloody awful temper. Short fuse . . . act first, think later . . . you know what I'm like. Understand, old man, that you weren't involved in this to-do with Phoebe at all. 'Nuff said? What? Look here – I'll go to Mournia and see those you'd want me to see. Say what you'd want me to say. And I'll try to get it right this time.' He looked around almost furtively, wondering if he'd said too much.

'Well done!' said Letty, briskly. 'I'm certain he's heard that.' She took Theo's place at the bedside and kissed the unconscious man's marble cheek. 'We've got you! You're safe now. It's all going to be all right. You're not to worry about a thing.'

The cook had done well, considering, Letty thought, enjoying the scent of herbs that rose from the dish of lamb stew when the lid was lifted. With all the turbulence at the Villa Europa, she was surprised that he'd managed to put together a creditable dinner for the five remaining members of the household. Eleni had not returned after the inquest and it was clear that Theo was feeling bereft of the two female presences in the house. Every time the door opened, he looked up in hope instantly disappointed, and in spite of her dislike and mistrust, Letty felt for him.

'Thank you – we'll wait on ourselves now,' he told the footman who was preparing to spoon out the stew, then waited until he'd left before continuing. 'Laetitia – if you wouldn't mind?'

'Eleni sometimes takes the weekend off,' Stewart explained with a show of exasperated eye-rolling. 'Goes to stay with her mother and sister. You'd have thought that at a time like this she would have considered it her duty to stay on and make herself available.'

He was silenced by a glare from Theodore and an icy assurance that he could safely leave domestic arrangements to the master of the house.

This was bidding fair to be the most uncomfortable meal of her life. Theo was self-absorbed, Gunning uncommunicative, the two students baffled and awkward, and where one would have looked for the bright good humour of George and the lively, inconsequential chatter of Phoebe, there were two empty places silently reproving them.

The shadows of the house had crept closer. What had Gunning said on her first evening? '. . . *something alive and growing here, something malevolent.*' The dark presence had not, it seemed to her, been appeased by the double sacrifice. Did George count as a sacrifice? He was still hanging on to life, after all. Fancifully, she wondered whether, once on the hunt, each of the three Furies demanded her own victim. Were the red-eyed goddesses even now savouring the prospect of a third? 'Whom will you choose, Tisiphone? Eeny, meeny, miney, mo . . . Catch a sinner by his toe . . .' Or *her* toe. Letty glanced around the table. She decided that, of the group, Dickie was most probably the only one who might be immune to their malice.

Theo, she suspected, was capable of the blackest of misdemeanours; Gunning had confessed to her last year that he was in very bad standing with any divine authority minded to roust out sinners, hinting at transgressions too dire to mention; she blushed at the memory of her own bad behaviour, which she had thought forgiven by Magdalene, the saint she had adopted in France; and Stewart – well, no one could reach Stewart's pitch of cynical nastiness without having annoyed a divinity or two.

She shivered and began to dole out the *stifado*. 'Mmm . . . smells delicious! Garlic and mushrooms in there, with thyme and rosemary, I think. Help yourselves to pasta, will you?'

Theodore recovered himself for a moment and, remembering the reason for her presence in his house, stirred himself to ask: 'You are eating well *chez* Aristidis, I trust? His mother has the reputation of being an excellent cook. I understand she makes the most delicious mulberry raki on the island.'

'The most wonderful food, Mr Russell! And I do notice that the islanders are the healthiest and most long-lived people I have ever come across. I was overtaken the other day on the steep slope up to Maria's house by an old goat of a man who, I was to discover when I enquired, is ninety next birthday.'

'And, tell me, how goes it with your dig?' He went on to ask sensible, uncritical questions about the progress and managed to listen to most of their answers. Gunning and Letty both replied happily, skating lightly, in deference to his shaken state, over his attempt to hoodwink them by the misleading mapping of the site. Instead of the 'You double-dealing fiend!' Gunning might have hurled at Theo, Letty heard him say, almost teasingly: 'I say – you'll never guess what those twerps in the planning office did! Reversed the map! Did you ever hear the like? No – no harm done. Aristidis twigged in no time. He put us back on track.'

'We sank a *sondage* pit right where you put your cross, Mr Russell,' said Letty. 'And it gave up wonders! Two more, north and south – the same result. Goodness knows what lies between them! Holy site, quite obviously. Temple? Burial of huge importance? We should know by the end of next week. It's all terribly exciting!' Hating her tone of false jollity, she had to admit that it seemed the only way to lull Theodore into a state of mind where he could just about function in a civilized way. A trick Letty had learned from her nanny. When over-excitement or tears threatened, Nanny's response was to invoke the mundane, even the infuriatingly patronizing. 'Time for hopscotch, I think, dear.' The beaten track, the road most travelled, the hopscotch square was sometimes what was called for.

A footman entered silently to light the oil lamps standing in a row on the sideboard behind Theodore. In the sudden flare, as Theo turned his head to thank him, Letty saw his silhouette cast on the wall opposite and she caught her breath. She recognized there an outline she had become familiar with: the rugged shape of Juktas. An Achaean warrior lying on his funeral pyre. The beard she had taken for a naval cut was even more of an affectation than she had supposed. She saw it clearly now for what it was – a copy of the aggressively jutting and sculpted beards worn by Greek fighting men on ancient black-figure vases.

With a rush of insight accompanied by pity, she saw that this man who had so disturbed and antagonized her was a man perpetually seeking acceptance. Not happy to be himself, the incomer, the English gentleman, Theodore Russell was emulating the likes of Colonel Lawrence, a man who had so admired the Arabs he had adopted their dress and customs. Her own great-uncle Hubert had vanished into tribal territory on the North West Frontier with the son of a local chieftain and had emerged years later speaking Pashtun and more Afridi than the Afridi. And he'd never been happy again, declared all the aunts, in any society.

Here Theodore sat, looking for all the world like a Levantine pirate, involved emotionally and professionally – and, she had to think, financially – with the life of the island and yet he would never experience the same easy acceptance as his son. Penniless, foreign-looking George was welcomed and loved wherever he went.

The students, subdued and not quite understanding the currents flowing about them, made their excuses as soon as they politely could at the end of the meal and went to their rooms.

'Look – don't rush off, you two,' Theodore told Letty and Gunning. 'I have a proposition for you. If you've nothing better to do – why don't you accompany me on a little outing tomorrow morning? Short trip out to the coast. We can take the horses. I keep a Ford in the garage but hardly ever use it. You see so much more from the back of a horse. I thought we could go and find the site of the accident – see if we can work out what pushed him – literally – over the edge.'

Though this was probably the last thing either would have chosen to do with their Saturday morning, both replied warmly, accepting the strange invitation. They fell silent, sensing that there was more he wished to say.

Battling his uncertainty: 'But that's not all. I'd like you to come with me to the village. That's where he was heading.'

'Ah, yes,' said Gunning. 'George has friends there. They'll be wanting news of him.'

'George has unfinished business there. You heard the promise I made him? Something I have to do on his behalf. Whether he recovers or not. I know what he would want. And it shall be done!' he said with sudden resolution. A grim smile broke through. 'I have a good deal to atone for . . . You're to keep me up to the mark! It won't be easy and I may try to back out at the last moment.'

Briskly, with a return of his old vigour, he rang for staff and made arrangements. Letty found herself dismissed with a jarringly cheerful: 'Tomorrow morning at eight, then? In the stables?'

'Hey, don't rush off!' Gunning called after her as she strode ahead of him down the corridor.

Letty turned a strained and anxious face to him. He held up his oil lamp and looked at her carefully.

'You're upset. Anything I can do?'

'Nothing. But thank you. I've suddenly had quite enough of this grim place, William, and these grim people. I can't be easy here. Tragedy has broken over our heads, but I have a feeling I can't squash that there's more to come.' Suddenly losing all confidence, she was aware that her voice had become plaintive: 'I don't want to stay on . . . I just want to go back to my own world, William . . .'

'Back?' he asked. 'Back where? Back to Cambridge or back to Athens? Where is your world, Letty?' And, gently: 'I'll take you. Wherever you want to go. You know that. You only have to ask.' But, as though regretting his show of sympathy, he added lightly: 'I spent a season running at your stirrup last year, playing the *preux chevalier*. Seems to have become a habit, you know. For here I still am, trailing about after you.'

She was unable to reply, silenced by a dizzying sensation that she no longer knew where her place was, certain only that, wherever it might be, William Gunning was, inconveniently, at the centre of it.

The accident site wasn't difficult to spot. Skid marks on the road and torn turf where the wheels had fought for purchase on the lip of the chasm were clear markers. They dismounted and Gunning held the uneasy horses back as, in shuddering curiosity, Letty and Theo lay on their stomachs peering through the gorse bushes and over the cliff edge. The boom of the waves was deafening, the drop vertiginous and made more sickening by the glimpse of green metal far below, hidden for a moment by the crashing surf, then tormentingly revealed.

Theo drew back and got to his feet, muttering, 'You think that's terrifying? The next hour will bring worse.' Unable to decide whether he was speaking to her or to himself, Letty stayed silent and she remounted, ready for the final half mile into the village.

When they turned around the shoulder of the cliff, the road gave out and the track way took on its ancient aspect.

It wound its way down into a cluster of houses snugly occupying a valley bottom.

'A fishing village?' said Letty uncertainly. 'But I can't see any access to the sea ...'

'No, not fishing. Not much farming goes on, either. It's a village of craftsmen. Has been for generations. Basketwork, smithing, potting, leather work – you name it – the men and women of Mournia can turn it out.'

He reined in his horse to contemplate the pleasing arrangement of white two-storied houses, the central square of the village clearly marked out by its cluster of Cretan plane trees. The sheltering brown slopes, which a half mile farther on would rear up as aggressive cliffs, splintered into the shapes of a Braque painting.

Letty had a feeling he was wasting time, loitering, beginning to regret bringing them along with him on this strange mission. It was at just this point he might have refused the challenge he had set himself, turned his horse, and made off back to Herakleion. 'When I was in Egypt,' she started to say, ignoring Gunning's histrionically slumping shoulders, 'I saw a wonderful frieze showing representatives of different races bringing tribute to the Pharaoh – you know the sort of thing, Persians bearing perfume, Sudanese pulling along giraffes – Well, the hieroglyph for one of the races of men was deciphered as the "Keftiu". Andrew Merriman believes these men were the ancient Cretans and we ought properly to call them not Minoans, but Keftiu. And do you know what they were carrying as presents to the King of Egypt? Luxury craft goods! Pottery, jewellery, and baggy leather boots! I wonder if they were made here?'

'Good Lord!' said Gunning, amused. 'This is where I have *my* boots made. There's a man in the High Street who can accommodate my left foot to perfection. To think the Pharaoh and I share a bootmaker!'

They rode through the surprisingly noisy streets. Theodore seemed to know his way about, Letty noticed, as he led them with no hesitation through the warren of narrow cobbled alleyways, loud with clanging of metal, shouts, and laughter. Smoke reeked from chimneys and sparks flew from dark interiors of forges; men and women sat at the open doors of their workshops or houses, all busily engaged in producing something lovely or useful. Blankets and swathes of woven cloth hung from poles over house fronts – a different range of colours in use here, Letty noticed. In this village all was green and blue and brown, the colours of the sea and hillsides, whereas in Kastelli they burned a fierce red and orange and purple. Several of the villagers looked up and greeted Theodore shyly with a nod and a smile. One old black-clad lady raised her gnarled fingers from her embroidery to make the sign of the cross as he passed.

Having tethered their horses, they continued more easily on foot. They settled down at a café table by the Byzantine church and Theodore ordered coffee and cold water for the men and a glass of lemonade for Letty. As they sipped their drinks, one or two men going by exclaimed and came over to pat Theo's shoulder in a gesture of sympathy, murmuring a few soft words before moving on. Letty didn't doubt that George's story had gone the rounds of the village in no time.

After a while, Theo pointed to a house that had already claimed Letty's attention. Larger than the others fronting the square, it had an air of faded elegance. The style was Turkish, she thought. Sheltering walls offered a welcome privacy from the rest of the village, their austere intent softened by a curtain of tumbling bougainvillea; stout gates, standing open, led into a courtyard. Letty could just make out the start of a line of huge pots overflowing with bright flowers and could imagine a fountain splashing in the unseen centre.

'A lovely house,' she said. 'Do you know the owner?'

He nodded and sipped his coffee, on edge, uncomfortable with their presence.

Somewhere close by a cracked bell struck nine and suddenly, with shouts of encouragement and instruction from several female voices from the interior of the house opposite, two small boys dashed out carrying shopping bags. An elderly woman in long black skirts hurried to the gate to call after them: 'Make that *two* kilos of tomatoes and don't forget to check that they're ripe, Andreos! If there's any change you can spend it at the cake shop, but don't tell your mother!'

Letty found the comfortable domestic scene strangely moving and reassuring after the high drama she had lived through under the Russells' roof in the past nine days.

'What beautiful boys!' she said, admiring the slender dark-eyed pair. 'Like something off a Cretan fresco!' To her astonishment, Theodore stood, oblivious of his companions, with eyes for no one but the boys, and without a word went to meet them. When he arrived within a few feet they looked up and saw him. Their faces burst into smiles of recognition and they rushed towards him calling '*Pappou! Pappou!*'

Gunning and Letty exchanged confused glances. '*Pappou?*' said Letty. 'Is that what they're saying? Oh, Good Lord! That doesn't mean what I'm thinking it means, does it? Can those boys possibly be . . .?'

Gunning was too astonished to reply at once. When he could collect his thoughts he said, 'No. It doesn't mean "Daddy". That would be *baba* – or *papa*. You heard Nikolas calling to Aristidis, remember.' He considered for a moment, unsure how to continue. 'Lord Almighty! I've had this hideously wrong! Theodore's not their father. He's their *grandfather*.'

Chapter Twenty-Six

They watched in fascination as the boys came to an abrupt halt a stride in front of Theodore. Letty had been expecting them to rush towards him and clutch him by the knees as she would have done at the same age but, while continuing to smile expectantly, both held themselves still and silent, waiting for his response. He bent and shook their hands and patted their heads, murmuring to them in Greek. He put his hand in his pocket, took out some coins, and selected one for each boy. They thanked him politely and seemed to be asking if they might spend it at once. Theo made a show of careless generosity, Letty thought cynically, most probably for their benefit, and, with a promise to see the boys again before he left, he dismissed them to continue on their way to the shops.

'You will have guessed, William, because I have long suspected my household has few secrets from you, that the house over there is where Eleni lives. And those are her children.'

Gunning made no reply. It was obvious to Letty that his insight had been vastly overestimated by Theodore. Not even William had had an inkling of what was going on. She herself was still trying to untangle the skein of intrigue and, unable to attack the central issue head on, began to skirt around the periphery, hoping that, if she asked the right questions, or any questions at all, explanations would be offered and everything would become clear. 'Doesn't Eleni find it hard – working with you in the city all week and only seeing her sons occasionally at the weekend?' was the first question that came to mind.

Both men looked at her in astonishment. It was Gunning who spoke first. 'Boys of that age in England are sent away from their parents for weeks, years on end, occasionally taking tea with them in a Lyons Corner House, two Saturdays a term, with a visit to the zoo thrown in if they're lucky. At least Eleni sees them nearly every week. And their father also, I suspect, makes time to visit. As last Sunday, Theo? The day Phoebe died, George and I came out to examine the skeletons in a cliff cave a mile or so from here. He disappeared for three hours before rejoining me at the city gates. I'd guess he came here. To see his sons? He'd want to see his sons after six months' absence, wouldn't he?'

At last it had been spoken. The relationship was out in the open.

'We were dismal together in that grim old house a year after George's mother died – you can imagine,' Russell said. 'Just the two of us, George's English tutor, and a mostly male staff. I decided to bring a little female colour and influence into that masculine environment. Eleni and her older sister Kalliope had lost their father in the troubles. Mother left without family to support them and barely able to cope. No income . . . orphanage looming for the girls. By then Kalliope was old enough to be married off and she escaped destitution, but Eleni was only fifteen. I was told her sad story, took pity on the child, and offered her respectable employment at the Europa – maid of all work – bit of female company for young George, who was thirteen at the time.'

Hearing the naiveté of his words, he hurried on in his eagerness to justify his actions. 'With my obsession for all things Cretan, it was my idea that she would teach him the language. I was anxious that my son should at least feel easy getting about on the island – since he refused to be sent away to Europe for schooling.' He gave an amused snort. 'Huh! The lad has always thought of himself as

Cretan, in spite of his looks. All that blond hair and those grey eyes . . . much more of the Hellene about him. He could have stepped down off a Parthenon frieze . . . He always said the same thing when I pointed this out to him: "It's a melting pot, Pa, and I'm just the latest ingredient."' Something like a look of tender recollection flitted over the stern features. 'To sighs of relief all round, Eleni moved into quarters at the villa, under the nominal chaperonage of the old cook, the only female staff we kept in those days, and the wife of our butler. Cretan women are not generally employed outside the family home, you understand.'

He gave Letty an assessing stare. 'I will speak bluntly because I do not take you for a prim miss, miss! Attractive girl, Eleni. She hadn't been long under my roof when I – I attempted – I unwisely . . .'

He hesitated just long enough to afford Letty the satisfaction of an interruption: 'If it's a blunt phrase you're searching for, Theo, why not say – you attempted to seduce her?'

'Yes. Something like that. No matter. She roundly turned me down.' The beard jutted defiantly. 'I didn't insist. I'm not quite the beast you take me for.' He allowed a pause for concerned objection or polite agreement, then plunged on into the silence: 'You can imagine, however, my dismay, when a couple of years later I discovered that her relationship with my son had . . . had . . . developed . . .'

Gunning's feeling shudder told Letty that not only had the man had a mother, he had also at one time been a fifteen-year-old boy.

'. . . developed . . . blossomed into something quite extraordinary.'

'I really can't see why you'd be surprised, Theo,' said Gunning, exasperated. 'George was fifteen – a big boy for his age, I shouldn't wonder – and Eleni seventeen? An explosive situation. And, knowing the strength of the characters involved, I think you would always be looking at a *Romeo and Juliet* scenario rather than . . . shall we say? . . . Prince Hal and Doll Tearsheet – *tragedy*, not comedy, brewing under your roof.'

'She was so damned good at her work!' Theo exclaimed, in an attempt at self-justification. 'Efficient, forward-thinking, intuitive. The staff came to depend on her. I trusted her. It wasn't long before she was running the household. She made our lives easy.'

'"Harbouring a snake and a strumpet in your bosom", isn't that what you said, Theo? You'd been through all this before, hadn't you?' said Letty with belated insight. 'You were ready enough to believe George a sinner because he'd betrayed you before. And in the most hurtful way – with the helpless, dependent girl you'd fancied for yourself!'

'Not so dashed *helpless*! Eleni is clever and she's damned manipulative! By the time she was eighteen, she was pregnant with the son of the Young Master and had made herself an indispensable figure in our establishment. Well, you can imagine, I did the right thing by them. I offered any amount of discreet help – which was rejected. My son refused to countenance her being sent away or, indeed, any threat to their child. Said he'd run away and marry her. And many other hysterical threats were made. Like a chapter out of a melodrama! Dickens would have rejected it as far-fetched! But George never spoke lightly in his life. Oh, no. He would have done it. The upshot was – if I wanted to retain my son, I would jolly well have to retain his paramour. Against my better judgement, I capitulated.'

'And you gave him enough leeway to make the mistake a second time?' Gunning commented.

Theo gave a bark of cynical laughter. 'Not like me, you're thinking? To be caught out like that twice? George is single-minded, headstrong, and infuriatingly righteous. Even when he's discovered sinning – up to his armpits in the honey pot – he has the knack of making you think *you're* in the wrong for catching him out. At all events, I think even he knew he'd gone too far. He agreed to be shipped off to Europe for a few months to stay with a cousin of mine. Man of the world, if you understand me.

George came back having learned some essential principles of modern life and . . . so far, so tolerable.'

'And with his record for amatory intrigue, you allowed yourself the liberty of jumping to the conclusion that he'd had an affair with your wife – before all the evidence was in,' said Gunning.

'You saw them! For God's sake, man! Always muttering in each other's ears, in corners. Sighing affectedly over dusty old texts. Going off on expeditions to the coast. Rambles along the cliffs . . . *You*,' he rasped accusingly, 'were very nearly as bad! Quite the Sir Lancelot, were you not? But I can't say I blame you. Men were attracted to Phoebe. She couldn't help it. She was warm and loving and . . .' He gulped and ran out of words.

'And made every man she spoke to feel he'd been singled out for her attention,' said Gunning, remembering. 'And with Phoebe it wasn't just a finishing-school trick . . . you know – "one hundred and one ways to attract and keep your beau". I do believe she had no veneer – she really understood our problems, our prejudices, our enthusiasms. We told her things we'd never even admitted to ourselves. She made us laugh and forgive ourselves.'

'Made me feel like the third wheel on the bicycle sometimes. You and George both!' grumbled Theo.

Letty was beginning to find the turn in the conversation disturbing. She decided to bring their heads back round to the course. 'And this house, this discreet situation, was your response to your problems of miscegenation and acculturation?' she asked, trying for a neutral tone.

Russell took her question for a serious enquiry. He replied thoughtfully. 'Yes. Not as smooth and easy as you might think, looking at it. Impossible to be discreet in a village – or even on the island. You have to find other ways of ensuring goodwill. The people here are of a religious bent. Their faith survived centuries of Ottoman rule, so it has deep roots, and they have far higher moral standards than we have back home. The relationship between the two would have been incomprehensible and much to be condemned had it not been for two factors.

'George let it be known that he was to marry Eleni as soon as this was possible ... He was convincing because he was himself convinced that this is what would happen. It wouldn't surprise me to hear that word's got out that he *has* married her – it would be the outcome all were looking for. You see, the Cretans are nothing if not romantic – puritanical they may be, but they love a happy ending to a romance as much as my great-aunt Honoria. And this one had all the makings of a fairy tale – well, half a dozen fairy tales. Cinderella, who is really the Princess Aretousa, gets her man, her Erotokritos, in the teeth of opposition from the wicked King Iraklis. You will recognize *me*, I think, in the scenario.

'And just to ensure George's presence was welcome in the village, generous donations were made to the school and the church. Money well spent in more ways than one. With the padre and the schoolmaster in our corner, we were well on the way to acceptance.'

'Acceptance,' echoed Gunning. 'Quite the most difficult state to attain on this island. Suspicion of foreigners goes deep, and who shall blame them? After the years of oppression they suffered?'

'And it's never easy, sailing in as liberator, you know. I was on the *Griffin* – junior officer – sent out to teach the Ottoman a lesson in '98.' Theodore grimaced. 'Candia was a powder keg! But with a little decisive action, we defused the situation. We'd had seventeen British soldiers massacred by the Turks. Well, if you tweak the lion's tail, you're likely to get your head bitten off. To be expected. Hard decisions have to be made. We bit back. Exacted just retribution. Seventeen of the Turkish ringleaders were apprehended and strung up on the hanging tree they'd used themselves for executions. Desperately unpleasant, of course, but it sent the right message.

'Cretans duly grateful, naturally. And, under patriotic pressure from the inhabitants, the man they were all clamouring to see – Prince George of Greece – eventually arrived from the mainland aboard a British ship to greet his people and reclaim the island. I was there when he stepped ashore. Stirring times! I'm honoured to have been able to play a small part.'

'So, with the reputation of the British navy behind you and the chink of cash in your pocket, you achieved some sort of acceptance?'

He became aware of Letty's frosty reception of his explanation. 'Quite. But the best card in our deck was one even you could not possibly sniff at, miss! And quite un-calculated. The lads themselves. You've seen them.' His expression softened. 'Andreos and Teodoro. They're strong, lively, witty boys. Good boxers, too. I've had them taught. Important to be able to hold your own on the quarterdeck or in the playground, don't you know. I'm thinking they might enjoy a naval career . . . But, as I say, they're very impressive. They have their mother's striking looks. And,' a smile of satisfaction twisted his lips, 'it pleases me to think – something of their grandfather also, wouldn't you say?' He paused, concerned to hear their response. 'And they appear Cretan to the bone. They fit in. They're accepted for themselves.'

'You're not planning to ship them off for an English edu-cation, then, Theo?' Gunning asked.

'Good Lord, no! They'd refuse to go anyway. With their parentage to contend with – I wouldn't stand a chance. Their roots are here. Their aunt Kalliope – their highly respectable aunt Kalliope – uncle and cousins live just up the road. Their grandmother – you saw her just now – is a rock and has largely brought them up. No, they wouldn't want to move away.'

'But for the present – let me be clear about this – George and Eleni remain unwed?' Gunning asked.

'Yes, that was part of the bargain. I agreed to underpin this domestic setup here – and by that I mean buying the house and paying the bills – as long as they agreed to hold off making the relationship official. As the alternative was a runaway marriage and life of poverty together, I imagine it was Eleni who talked George into accepting my terms. I suppose I was playing for time ... hoping all the while that my son would see sense, that Eleni would lose her attractions, that he'd meet someone of his kind and his class. Wouldn't have done for him to find himself, hands tied and encumbered, when Miss Right sailed over the horizon.' He gave a wicked smile and cocked an eyebrow at Laetitia. 'Someone like yourself, miss? Well, why not? Wouldn't have been bad! But I could see that was never going to work. Women don't seem to view my son as a marriage prospect. Good-looking, athletic chap though he is, they don't even seem to be attracted to him.'

'You're right. I had noticed it,' said Letty. 'George carries a sort of immunity with him. Eleni has rendered him untouchable by any other woman. He doesn't quite qualify for the virginal Hippolytus – but very nearly! But Theo – aren't you going to go inside and tell her the news of George? We sit here knowing he's still alive – she must be uncertain even of so much. I really think you ought to –'

But Theodore was already making his way across the square.

'Perhaps we should order more coffee,' said Letty, joining Gunning on his side of the table. 'This could take a while. Crikey! Did you have any idea?'

'Lots of ideas,' said Gunning, shaking his head, 'and all the wrong ones! Poor old George. I sensed he had troubles but I didn't guess of what magnitude. It's funny, you know – there's a real split here – I mean back at the Europa – between upstairs and down. I'll swear none of the students, guests, or other European hangers-on had a clue what was going on. But the servants did! That kitchen maid with her embarrassed giggles and her "entertaining the master" stuff – she knew! Any of the man-servants would have known but they never let on. I can admire that!'

'Do you suppose Phoebe was aware?'

'She and George were pretty close, you know. I think he would have confided in her. She knew how to keep a secret.'

'And how would she have reacted?'

'Knowing Phoebe, I would expect her to have thrown herself wholeheartedly into the intrigue. George's children, had she met them – and I'll bet you she did! – would have engaged her full, loving attention. And, Letty, this makes the terms of her will more comprehensible if you think about it. She did her duty by her family and, grudgingly (wonder if he knows yet?), by her husband, but she left a good deal to George. And I think you said – with no strings attached. I had supposed she meant him to use it to make the life of leprosy victims more comfortable, put it towards research, that sort of thing but, the way things are – he could equally well use it to assert his own independence and support his family himself.'

'I'm sure that would have been her intention,' said Letty. 'But for that to happen – George must stay alive.'

She was struck by a sudden chilling thought. 'William? I can't imagine that George has ever bothered to make a will.'

'Not the first thing on your mind when you're a twenty-four-year-old bachelor in perfect health – and having no resources of your own to worry about.'

They fell silent and watched as Andreos and Teodoro returned with bulging shopping bags and a train of village boys of all sizes, chattering excitedly. After some good-natured skirmishing, the gang settled down on the marble ledge below the central fountain and looked on expectantly as the older brother unwrapped a large confectioner's box full of pastries. He passed it around and each boy made his choice. Then he handed the box to Teodoro, who repeated the process until it was empty.

'Well!' said Gunning, touched by the scene. 'Baklavas all round! Those boys have certainly inherited one of their father's qualities. They're as open-handed as George! I wonder if Theo realizes his contribution has just been used to treat the lads of the village?'

'William?' Letty's voice was uncertain, full of misgiving. 'What on earth do you suppose would happen if George were to die on Stoddart's operating table? Those poor boys! What future would they have without their father? Do you suppose they've been told how ill he is?'

'He's not going to die, Letty! He's a strong fellow and he has much to live for. He'll fight back.' Gunning's attempt at reassurance did not convince Letty and, she suspected, did not even convince himself. 'But yes, I see where you're headed . . . The money he's just inherited would pass on to his next of kin. Not to those boys because they're, I presume, illegitimate. No, it would go to his father. To Theodore.'

Chapter Twenty-Seven

'I shall pray for her,' said Maria. 'And for his boy. He is not a good man, but I can feel sorry for any man whose wife dies and whose only son is injured in such a short time.' Aristidis's mother was holding the photograph of the three diggers in her hands while listening eagerly to Letty's account of the weekend's proceedings, her eyes on Theodore Russell in the centre, her voice betraying decision but not a note of sympathy.

They were sitting on either side of the table on Sunday evening, sipping a glass of Maria's homemade mulberry raki, and Letty could feel her revelations becoming more outspoken with every sip of the strong spirit. She made an effort to remember that some of her information was undoubtedly confidential and not meant to run the length of the Cretan grapevine. But gossiping was proving so seductive, she thought she had probably been lured into going too far. And Maria was the perfect audience, listening without interruption, absorbing and asking just the right questions to draw out the story. Certainly by tomorrow morning the affairs of the House of Russell would be common knowledge in Kastelli, traded over every doorstep.

'You don't like Aristidis's employer, I think?' Letty inquired blandly.

'My son dislikes him and does not trust him,' said Maria, and Letty smiled at the simple reply. No further explanation was needed. The son's judgement was clearly enough for the mother.

'Have you ever met him?'

'I don't care for the city and never go there . . . but I went to my niece's wedding at the Cathedral of Saint Minas last month. While we were gathering in the square before the ceremony, an elegant man walked by with his pretty wife. Such a striking couple – he so dark, she so fair – I asked Aristidis who they were. He told me that the gentleman was his employer, the Englishman, Russell. The one who has treated him so badly. His wife I understand to have been a good woman. Aristidis spoke warmly of her.'

Maria filled up Letty's glass and offered a dish of mezedes. 'Englishmen are so very different, one from the other, Aristidis says.'

Letty pursed her lips. The son of the house was certainly Maria's porthole on the world outside, and she acknowledged that anything she confided to the mother would be, at the soonest possible moment, relayed to the son. The trouble was, Letty thought with rueful amusement, that she was rapidly heading in the direction of dependence on Aristidis herself. In the short time they had worked together, he had already established himself as a trusted and knowledgeable figure. Never in her way but always at her elbow when she needed him, never patronizing, always encouraging. Theodore must have been mad to antagonize such a valuable foreman.

'He has nothing but praise for *this* man. Gunning,' said Maria, pointing to Gunning's grinning face. 'I think William has your respect and affection, too, Laetitia,' she added subtly, with a slight question in her voice.

'Gunning? Respect and affection? Not in the least!' said Letty. 'He is a useful and well-informed professional chaperon, a man who is in my father's confidence. But he is not a man who inspires affection and, indeed, I know very little about him. He's an army man – very much a man's man, I'd have said. He doesn't easily get along with women. Not had much practice, I suppose. He finds me very irritating and I think him awkward and overbearing.'

Maria listened to this churning outflow, trying to understand. 'I see. I think I see. But he is quite a good-looking man, wouldn't you say so?' she persisted, twinkling. 'I may be elderly, but I still have an eye for a handsome man and I have good judgement. I cannot understand why such a fine fellow would be still unmarried at his age. It would not be so, here on the island. Perhaps it is on account of his injury that he goes unclaimed?'

'Injury? Oh, his foot, you mean? I forget about it, he makes so little of it. No, I don't think it can be that. There are so many spinsters and widows in England left behind by the war, any unattached man putting his head over the parapet is pounced upon and marched up the aisle. It is really very strange that even Mr Gunning should have managed to avoid matrimony for so long. I understand him to have spent the years after the war travelling on the continent instead of doing his duty and returning to plunge into marriage with some unfortunate girl.'

Maria looked bemused. She reached out and put her hand over Letty's. 'I think the girl he chooses will be fortunate,' she said, nodding wisely. 'And I've decided to do something about it. I am making a list of suitable candidates. You know him better than anyone, I think ... you must help me. We'll start with Angeliki. My young friend Angeliki is recently widowed and beginning to look around. She still has her looks, even after six children, and it would be a blessing for her to find kindness and culture after the ten years she spent married to that wild boar of a husband.'

Maria burst into triumphant laughter at the agonized and betraying expression she had provoked.

Aristidis was full of pride next morning as they stood together on Juktas surveying the dig. The extra men they had hired to work at the end of the week had cleared the site of concealing grass and most of the shrubs, though any protruding stones had been left in place. Tapes had been stretched from pegs outlining the plots they had agreed should be dug, and the men were standing by with picks and shovels and wheelbarrows ready for the off.

The first of the *sondage* pits had revealed such a wealth of finds, they had decided to extend their luck by extending its sides and follow the intriguing suggestions of masonry walls where they led. Stone ledges had come to light, pottery sherds and what Letty thought might prove to be a small shrine. She was confident they had prepared well. All was ready. At least, not quite all. Where was the recorder and photographer?

Gunning strolled on site, a shepherd's twisting staff carried across his shoulders, his two hands hooked over the ends in the island manner. One of the men shouted a derisive comment and burst out laughing. Gunning instantly went into a parody of a swaggering Cretan walk, provoking more amusement and some crude suggestions. He responded by lowering the stick and swinging it in his hand like a cane, moving into a Charlie Chaplin routine. He tipped an imaginary bowler, he tripped over his stick and landed on his behind in a wheelbarrow.

This was a side of Gunning Letty had not so far caught a glimpse of, and she suddenly understood that this was a sample of behaviour learned in the trenches of Flanders. The sight of a padre fooling about would have been a boost for morale, perhaps the only incitement to laughter for days, in that hellish place. And these men liked him. Following on his performance, they'd gone smoothly into action, each with his appointed task, each with a smile on his face. They felt free one minute to seek his opinion, the next to deride his ignorance. An easy relationship. And one she could never, whatever her wealth, influence, or talent, emulate. She felt a familiar flash of anger.

Well, physical activity had always been a release for frustration. She grabbed a pick and a spade and made for an outcrop of stones breaking the surface a few yards away from the main dig, thinking to sink a test pit of her own and leave the rest of the oiled machine to run on without her. With a sharp memory of Knossos and Phoebe she pulled up a root of feathery fennel to clear her way, and began to dig. The stones she removed seemed to have been cut and used as part of a wall or a building of some sort. No pottery fragments came to light, in fact, nothing of interest as in the other pits. She glanced around and decided that if she was right about the position of the main activity site, she was now working on one of its outlying areas.

She was on the point of giving up and slinking away when a change in colour and texture was revealed by her slicing spade. Terra-cotta. A man-made object. Intrigued, she knelt and peered more closely. She took a trowel from her pocket and poked the enrobing earth away from it. It fell away cleanly, and she put out her hands to grasp the artefact and gently move it with the idea of drawing it from its bed in one unbroken piece. Heavy and some eighteen inches long, the tubular shape came away with surprising ease, revealing a hole, beyond which lay another terra-cotta pipe of the same diameter. Sewage system? These were well known in the palace at Knossos. Sanitary engineering of a quite sophisticated quality had been undertaken there. But up here on a hilltop in the wilderness? What would they need to pipe away?

With her fingers she began to clean off the earth, fascinated to see that what she held was a decorated pipe. And therefore probably not meant for sewage or water overflow dispersal. What would you call this decoration in pottery terms? She racked her brain. Repoussé? Not quite right. Appliqué, that was it! Gunning would know for sure. Or Aristidis. She stood and held up the heavy pipe and waved in their direction, hoping to catch their eye. Strips of the terra-cotta clay had been moulded into thickish ropes and attached with fanciful Cretan sinuosity to coil around the body of the cylinder. Not even the arty Minoans would bother to do that for something utilitarian that they intended to bury under the floor, surely?

Perhaps it was a container? She raised the open end to

her eye to look down the length of it, certain that there was something inside.

A hard body crashed into her from behind with a shout of warning, knocking her off balance. With one fist Aristidis smashed the pipe from her grasp, a split second before the occupant shot out with the speed of a hurled lance, mad eyes seeking a target, pink mouth open wide, sticky white fangs gleaming, head darting in attack.

Chapter Twenty-Eight

The terra-cotta crashed to the ground, shattering into fragments on the jagged surface of a rock. The snake fell and instantly rounded on Aristidis, who had put himself between the reptile and the paralyzed Letty. Gunning was suddenly at her side, seizing her by the waist and hauling her, rigid with shock, a few feet off. They watched, helpless, as Aristidis lashed out at the snake with his shepherd's staff and finally caught its neck in the forked piece at the end. The snake writhed and thrashed in impotent fury but Aristidis calmly took the knife from his waist, bent, and in two swift strokes sliced off its head.

Demetrios hurried over with a shovel and deftly began to scoop up the remains. He pointed to the bright orange stripes and the V behind its head. '*Ochendra*,' he commented. 'Leopard snake. You're lucky to have your nose still, miss!' He went off to the cliff edge to dispose of the horror.

To her mortification Letty could not keep a limb still. She shivered, her teeth chattered and yet seemed clenched together, and no sounds would come, not even the pitiful wail she needed to express. She had revealed to no one her acute fear amounting to phobia for snakes and had hoped that, striding about with unconcern, as she did, in her boots, the men would take her for fearless and the snakes would give her a wide berth. Gunning put both arms around her, murmuring soothing nonsense, and held her closely, one hand firmly behind her head, pulling her face into his shoulder.

Finally, 'Hell's bells! What on earth was that?' she managed to gasp.

'That was, as Demetrios says, a leopard snake. Poor creature! You disturbed him. Don't take it personally – he was just defending his home.'

Without releasing her, he stuck out a foot and turned over one of the broken pieces of pot. 'A snake tube. That's what you unearthed. They've been found on temple sites all over the island. The thought is that snakes were offered accommodation in these kennels and probably fed as well. A diet of milk and honey cakes, they say. Most likely they were de-fanged and used in religious ceremonies. Earth spirits. Chthonic beings. And just like the human inhabitants, your modern snake makes use of the ancient facilities if they're in good working order. It's my theory that the practice of keeping house snakes up on the Athenian Acropolis may have descended from the Cretan custom. And the goddess Athena, to whom they were sacred, perhaps a memory of the ancient mother goddess . . .'

His voice was reassuringly professorial. 'He's talking to calm the baby,' Letty thought. 'Well, I have to think it's working.' The warmth and the scent of his skin under the rough shirt were calming and the pounding of his heart intriguing. She could see no reason to break away. Odd that the danger threatening her had been averted by Aristidis with heroic panache, but her distress had needed to be assuaged by Gunning's presence. He was not a comforting man to her; he was barbed and slightly inimical – at best, awkward – but, standing here in his arms, within his defences, what she felt was a rightness, and more than that – the excited joy of a homecoming.

He was making no attempt to move away and the moment had been prolonged beyond what was socially acceptable. She was struck by the memory of one of Gunning's sly comments: 'Oh, dear! William! Could you possibly be offending the men by this public demonstration of affection?' She turned her head to see if they were observed. The men had gathered into a group, passing around cigarettes. They were talking loudly to each other, reliving the moment with gesticulations, already embellishing the story – and every man was facing tactfully away towards the sea.

'I'm sure they understand it to be nothing more than what it is – a public demonstration of first aid and essential comfort,' he replied and then, hearing the hurtful dismissiveness in his gruff voice, his arms tightened again. 'So – have a little comfort!' When she turned her face back towards him, he gently touched her nose with the tip of his forefinger. 'Nice nose. Awfully glad you didn't lose it.'

'Well, whatever we've got here, it's not the Tomb of Zeus,' said Aristidis at noon on Friday. There was no disappointment in his voice, rather intrigue and excitement.

They had finished a light lunch supplied by Maria, standing about on the site rather than leave off to eat in the sheds, and Letty was gathering together the remnants of the meal into a basket. The men went back to busily finishing off in their trenches, leaving everything ready for a start again the following Monday. The sides were plastered with white labels marking out the changing strata, numbered from one onwards as the digging revealed them, down to base level. From here a further set of labels in red, many of these with question marks added, worked their way back up again from the very lowest stratum, which someone had hopefully labelled 'Neolithic,' signifying the succeeding layers of civilization.

'Not entirely sure we've got that right, Letty,' Gunning had said doubtfully. 'We might get old Theo out to take a look. He's hot stuff when it comes to pottery dating. He'll know. Best we can do for the moment is be certain we've recorded everything correctly.' He was hurrying along the balks from one square to the next, sketching and photographing, establishing continuity between them and producing suggestions for further work based on the evidence unearthed.

'No tomb, no body, not even any charred remains in a cooking pot. But what we do have promises to be magnificent! William! Come and show Laetitia your sketch. There . . .' Aristidis laid out Gunning's drawing on the ground, put a boot on it, and pointed with his staff. 'Tell me what you see.'

'A three-bayed something or other,' said Letty, feeling her way. 'Unusual, would you say, for an outdoor site?'

'But not unknown.'

'Right . . .' Letty gathered her thoughts and spoke firmly: 'What we have would appear to be some sort of temple, not just an open-air altar. A proper building, one storey high, as Gunning has established from the foundations and thickness of the walls. Lime-plastered walls, painted in dark red and white – must have been very striking! Beams of Cephalonian pine as at Knossos. It offers three good-sized rooms . . . what are we saying, William? . . . four yards wide? Central one a little more spacious than the east and west rooms? A plethora of potsherds in situ on what may be a stepped altar in the easterly room – let's call it number one. The rooms have doorways out on to a wide corridor to the north. Here . . . Now if this corridor proves to have been colonnaded, we've got rather spectacular views over the Aegean. Age? You have an opinion on this, Aristidis?'

Aristidis had an opinion.

'Minoan architectural style and decoration, probably contemporary with the main palace building we see standing at Knossos today,' he said. 'I'm saying Middle Minoan III. Walls of fine masonry, gypsum dado to the lower courses, signs of wooden columns. *Kasellas* – floor cists – just emerging in the eastern room. . . . Could be very interesting. Mason's marks very similar. Carvings of the double axe and the horns of consecration link it to the religious aspects of the Palace at Knossos. But I see evidence of rebuilding – after some disaster, perhaps? Earthquake? Conquest? More likely. The upper layers show evidence of

271

a Mycenaean presence. The conquering mainland Greeks were here.'

He went to a finds tray and took out a small ivory carving. Letty leaned over and looked again with satisfaction at the object that had taken her breath away when it had risen from the soil. On a flat disk of ivory was carved in profile the perfect head of a Mycenaean warrior proudly wearing his helmet of boar's teeth.

'What did old Schliemann say when he dug up the gold mask at Mycenae?' Gunning came over to take a look. '"Today I have gazed on the face of Agamemnon." Well, there you are, Letty! You can say today you have gazed on the face of Theseus! With probably just as much respect for the truth! Telegraph the London *Times* with the news, why don't you?'

He paused, puzzled by her silence. 'What's up? Not happy with what we've got? Goodness, girl! What *will* it take to set you on fire, I wonder, if this won't do it? Oh, yes . . . The Tomb! You were really waiting for a body to be exhumed, I think? A male skeleton ten feet tall? I wonder what the toe bone of the King of the Gods would sell for on the black market? Or were you expecting a chryselephantine statue in silver and gold?'

She skewered him with her disdain. Since the shameful episode with the snake, he had kept his distance, occasionally, as now, closing in just long enough to annoy her with a sharp comment. Regretting his show of concern and redressing the balance, most probably, but she wondered if the demonstration was aimed at her or put on for the benefit of the men.

'Yes, William. Yes, I won't deny it. I came expecting a burial. Unless Theo has been lying to us all along, with, of course, Callimachus, Ennius, Cicero, and all the rest of those old boys ranged up alongside him in the dock, there *is* a tomb of some sort here. I don't believe the myth would have survived all those centuries without some concrete – or perhaps I should say kouskoura rock – foundation for it. I'm still hopeful.'

She dismissed him with a nod and a smile, picked up her basket, and walked off towards the goat sheds. She'd discovered that sharp words between them disturbed the crew and it was becoming her practice to walk away and avoid any public disagreement. After a short exchange with Gunning, Aristidis followed her, taking the basket from her hands and walking companionably along in step.

'I too am still hopeful, miss. I'm sure you're right about the temple building and no burial may be expected in its precincts. This tongue of land is not large . . . I think we should be using our heads before our spades to locate the tomb.'

'Agreed,' she said, turning to survey the site. 'Let's imagine, then, the structure over there in the centre. We've found vestiges of a circular perimeter wall and can project the course of that out to about there . . .' She pointed. 'So we must look in the area outside that.'

He put down the basket and they stood with their backs to the goat sheds, looking at the unpromising outskirts, boulder-strewn and tussocky.

'Remind me, Aristidis, from the few burial sites discovered on the island – how were the corpses aligned? Any pattern? I mean, if we were thinking of, let's say, Celtic burials in Europe, the bodies would have been laid out facing the rising sun. Feet to the east, heads to the west.'

'It is the same here,' he said.

'Well, these are not *gods* we're considering, shall we agree on that? If someone was buried hereabouts, then he was a person like us. Human, not divine. Whoever it was, he died and was buried.' She gave him a steady look. She had learned never to take anyone's religious principles for granted, had discovered for herself that the roots of ancient beliefs were deep and tangled and sprang occasionally and disconcertingly back to the surface.

Aristidis nodded his understanding.

'Let's assume his followers thought they knew what would please the dear departed. And that would be to lie looking in this direction.' She waved an arm to the east.

'That would be at right angles to the temple. Their under-takers or whatever they used might also have considered the dead man – for it was undoubtedly a *human*, however impressive his credentials – might like to look out over his temple.'

Aristidis lined himself up as she suggested. Then he turned, threw out his arms, and gave a burst of derisive laughter. 'You realize where that plants the King of the Gods? Firmly in one of my *goat sheds*!'

Letty looked over her shoulder and, amused, joined him in his laughter. They both saw it at the same moment and fell silent abruptly. They looked at each other, startled.

Aristidis began to speak in short bursts, in a voice lacking its usual confidence. 'Forgive me! What a fool! I should have seen it! I can only plead over-familiarity. I can say – this has been my playground for decades. I have worked here, I smoked my first cigarette here . . . I . . .' He stopped in some embarrassment and Letty knew he would have continued had he been talking to Gunning. 'Every inch is familiar to me and therefore unregarded.'

'But you see what I can see?' she pressed. 'The little stone building, almost buried to the lintel at the end of the run? It looks to me like a stunted French *bori* . . . a shepherd's hut?'

'A shelter. During the bad times, it was slept in by *palikares* on the run. Everyone knows about it. It's too small and unhealthy to put the beasts in there. You'll find it ankle-deep in cigarette ends . . . and other things less salubrious. Please, Miss Laetitia, I beg you not to enter.'

While he spoke they had begun to move quickly towards the unimpressive little beehive of a shack. As they walked, Letty looked around her, assessing the possibilities of the site. 'A wonderful wide view over the plain below. Yes, if I were on the run, I'd think this was the place to be for a good lookout. No one could leave the village without my seeing them. And I have noticed, Aristidis, that the human voice carries in a quite extraordinary way between this

274

spot and the valley below. Easy enough to arrange signals or even shout messages to and fro.'

'Which has proved useful at times of war, certainly, but has more often these past years been a source of embarrassment.' Aristidis gave a smile of boyish mischief.

They had reached the building and, talking calmly to disguise her excitement, Letty took a moment to absorb the changed perspective. She stood with her back to the vestige of a doorway, looking towards the east. 'And in Minoan times, the times of our temple, from this open doorway, you'd be looking straight down the colonnade. Far enough away so as not to pollute the holy space, near enough to keep a spirit eye on processions and ceremonies. Check the priests were offering up the right colour of bull ... that sort of thing ... In its unassuming way, it offers a commanding position.'

Aristidis began to clamber over his despised property, slapping it with his hands, seeing it with fresh eyes. 'Look at the lintel! It's been carved out of the living rock! So heavy that was probably the only way they could get it up there. Then it's been propped by these two massive flanking stones. All masonry straight out of the hillside, you'll notice. Four yards – would you say? – in diameter ... circular layers of stone courses, not all that well dressed. One might have assumed – one did! – that it was the work of unskilled shepherds. What have you seen?'

'We'll see it more clearly in slanting light ... this evening? But I could swear there's an indentation, a straight line running across the field from here to the temple complex.'

'*Dromos!*' he exclaimed. '*Dromos* – the pathway. A long disused pathway. We farmers have always approached – well, as you see, by this path here on the opposite side.'

They stood grinning at each other in deep satisfaction. 'Will you go and tell Mr Gunning?' said Aristidis.

'No,' said Letty. 'I'm sure he'd rather hear the news from you. But – tell him to drop everything and send a digging party over at once. We've got hours of today left and it's a very small building.'

When he left her alone, Letty turned to the dilapidated stone hut and addressed herself to Zeus. 'Well, hail, King of the Gods! If you're in there, mate, let me tell you – you're about to see the light of day again! And – may I ask you not to start hurling thunderbolts about and quaking the earth in a fit of pique? You know what you're like!'

She swallowed, suddenly hearing her words replayed and shuddering at their unfeeling flippancy. Her *lèse-majesté*. The gods didn't take that lightly! She risked being turned into a laurel bush or even worse – something small and disgusting. Gunning might yet come along and, all unknowing, uproot her or put a foot on her. And he'd never have the satisfaction of knowing. Letty reined in her unruly fantasies. She thought she would never have been able to explain to anyone but Phoebe the ancient compulsion that made her run back to the lunch basket and ferret about in it until she found what she was looking for. She returned and stood awkwardly in front of the hut.

A spoken formula was called for. Her mind skittered over the word 'prayer', discarded it, and settled on 'sentiment'. Knowing nothing suitable, she dredged up an imperfect memory of a translation she'd worked on at school. The closing lines of *Medea*. 'Six out of ten. Rather too free an interpretation of the text.' It would have to do.

'Olympian Zeus, all powerful!
Controller of Man's destiny!
What we mortals expect to happen, rarely comes to pass,
And it is the unexpected that lies in the hands of the gods.'

'Greetings, er . . . Sir . . . and please accept a small gift. It's all I could find, but perhaps not unwelcome after all these years.'

Finding a fissure in the rocks just before the entrance, she stood astride it and held out her hands. From her left, she poured out the remains of a bottle of red Arkhanais wine and with her right, she upturned a jar of honey, watching until the last drop had slipped down into the ground.

A libation. Well, it couldn't do any harm. And he might be glad of the sustenance.

The diggers were organized to work in pairs, one digging, one shovelling, the numbers restricted by the small space available inside the beehive. All were eager to find something substantial before they went off to their homes. Aristidis had lined them up and called for volunteers to work an hour or two overtime until the last of the light. Every man had stepped forward. Four – keen young men with no farms or flocks to run – had offered to return the next morning. Catching Aristidis's look of pride in his team, Letty understood that there was more than the prospect of a few extra piastres to be reckoned with. The men desperately wanted an opportunity to outsmart Theodore Russell. This would undoubtedly please Aristidis, their respected Kapitan, but they had pride of their own to be restored. And there was something more, which she recognized from the gleam in their eyes, from their concentration and the lapse of habitual banter, as a deep concern for the job in hand. They would have worked through the night without the lure of piastres. Their enthusiasm matched her own.

'Double overtime for any man who stays on – whether he digs or not,' she announced boldly.

Aristidis, whose first impulse as overseer was prudently to question this, hesitated, then nodded, a victim also of the general fever.

Gunning's hands, Letty noticed, were tense with the effort of restraining himself from snatching the spade from the diggers. And Letty herself was unable to keep still and detached, moving around, supervising more closely than necessary the sieving of every shovelful of soil that came out of the little building that Aristidis had firmly renamed a '*tholos*'. A tomb.

The wind dropped and children's voices raised in the excitement of a game floated up from the valley. The slanting sun was throwing a gauzy veil of copper-gold over the whole headland, and the sea was a perfect mirror of the azure sky when the moment came.

Chapter Twenty-Nine

A conical structure sixteen feet high and twelve at its base had been revealed by the efforts of men working around the exterior and excavating down to its foundation layer of three-foot-long limestone blocks. The pairs working inside, whose area of operation was more constricted and consequently more backbreaking, relieved each other frequently and settled freshly to throw the dirt and detritus of centuries into a wheelbarrow in front of the entrance. The floor level dropped steadily but little of interest was revealed. Spiro's grandfather's spectacles saw the light of day again to much merriment; three tobacco tins and a packet of postcards from Port Said followed, but nothing of archaeological importance.

Not until, to joyful exclamations, reddish pottery sherds came to light, alongside a handful of dull faience beads. Aristidis pounced on these and, shaking his head in disappointment, pronounced them – Roman.

'Roman?' Letty asked without thinking. 'What would *Romans* be doing up here?'

She resented their presence. Pushing their eagle noses into everything . . . Roman – a word to stir the blood at any other time and in any other place. But on a Minoan peak sanctuary? No! Here, Roman traces were an aberration, a distraction. The thought was instantly squashed by the imagined reproving and scientific voice of Andrew Merriman. 'Open mind, Letty! Open mind!'

'Who knows?' Aristidis shrugged. 'Perhaps it was Saint Paul having a picnic? Come to make certain that if there *had* been a Zeus, he was well and truly buried? No – it was tomb robbers, I believe. Undoubtedly these are their traces. I think this building must have been the subject of robbery from the very earliest days. I must ask you to prepare yourselves for disappointment. I expect it all started with the Minoans themselves. Any grave goods would have been noted at the time of the burial, as with the Egyptian Pharaohs, and quietly removed when everyone was looking the other way.'

One of the digging pair stuck his head out through the doorway. Through the layer of dirt, Letty recognized the bright eyes of Demetrios. 'Kapitan! We're down to original floor level. Nothing under our feet now but bedrock. What do you want us to do?'

Before anyone could commit himself to calling a halt, there was a squeal from inside the beehive. The voice of the youngest digger was heard calling to Demetrios to help him and chattering excitedly with Gunning, who had squeezed in with his measuring tape. They listened by the doorway, peering into the gloom and seeing nothing when, after a moment, Demetrios's shaggy head reappeared, grinning. He held out an object in his right hand.

What had she expected? Gold necklace? Silver altar cup? Not this, at least. Brown with age, but recognizably – an upper leg bone.

Letty blinked to see the size of it. Two feet long and three inches in diameter, it was the leg of a giant or a god, she thought. Then, hastily pulling herself together, she tugged at Aristidis's sleeve. 'Didn't you tell me one of these blokes is a butcher in his real life?'

He was there a second before her and already turning to call out: 'Spiro! Come over here, lad, and cast an eye on this, will you?'

Spiro jumped to his feet, pleased to earn his piastres, and looked knowingly at the bone. 'Horse,' he said, seizing hold of it. 'Shall I chuck it away?'

Shouts and oaths from all around persuaded him to think again.

'Grab a basket and stand by to receive more of the same,' shouted Gunning from inside. 'Bones. Collected together on something I can only describe as a sort of pottery serving dish of medieval proportions . . .'

'Where, man?' Aristidis yelled back. 'Exactly where? It's important now! Mark where you find them! Is the plate decorated?'

Gunning came to the lintel and peered out. 'The wall opposite the entrance, backing on to the rock face,' he said. 'There's a pile of – what did you decide – horse? – bones on a platter in the centre right up against the rear wall. Decorated – yes! Geometric: spirals, wavy lines, rosettes, that sort of thing. Nothing out of the ordinary.' And then . . . 'Christos is just getting it out . . . and there's a further one piled up also, in a sort of niche built into the rock. Obviously an offering any tomb robber can well resist! Not attractive! But – interesting. Wouldn't you say – interesting?'

Aristidis could contain himself no longer. He pushed himself into the hut, flinging out the diggers and Gunning in swift succession, and came out a minute or two later, holding bones in each hand.

Spiro did his bit. He enjoyed the limelight for a little longer this time, selecting a piece and turning it this way and that before pronouncing: 'Jawbone. And what a jaw! Cow? No! Much too massive. More like an ox or a bull,' he said, turning them this way and that. 'Yes, bull, that's what this was. Big old feller! But what's he doing down there in bits?'

'I'll tell you what!' said Aristidis. 'Marking a grave. Animal sacrifices. Two animals. A bull and a horse mark the spot. And they would only have been offered up to a personage of the highest importance – someone of the royal blood. Or a god! It may have been well and truly robbed in ancient times, scoured clean, you might say, but I think we've found it! The so-called Tomb of Zeus!'

His positive tone sounded unconvincing, even to Letty's ears. They had made a find of some archaeological importance, they knew that – burials of any sort were a rare discovery on the island – but their expectations had run higher. Looking around at the drooping shoulders and the hastily averted faces, Letty wondered crossly whether this might not just be a further piece of calculated tormenting by Theodore, and decided she was being unfair. Not even he could have predicted this emptiness following on such a surge of hope. Could he? She reined in her thoughts. She recognized in herself the quality Gunning had objected to – an over-readiness to blame him for everything based on very little but her instinctive dislike.

Gunning was looking anxiously at the sky. 'We've missed something!' he declared. 'I'm sure of it. Hard to explain ... it's something architectural that's nagging at me ... something to do with proportions. Hang on a minute, will you?' He began to encircle the tomb from the outside and then put his head inside again, measuring with his eye.

'Look, Aristidis, I'm just going to burble out loud and you must tell me to shut up when it becomes unbearable! Those bones were still piled neatly – they hadn't been moved. Not worth the effort even if any intruders had noted them. They were centrally placed on the rear wall. Round the back, on the outside and in a position corresponding to the place of the bones, the diggers have taken all the earth covering off. And there's a sort of slab that you could take as being just a natural piece of limestone. But – take a look and see what you think – I think it's been dressed. It's a crude little building but this stone has had some attention from the mason, you'd say ...'

He spoke into the air as Aristidis and Letty scampered off to have a look. They returned a moment later, bursting with comment yet politely leaving Gunning to finish his interrupted sentence.

'And it all leads me to wonder whether we might be contemplating a bit of Minoan cleverness? They must have learned a few tricks from the Egyptians after all, with their close cultural contacts. Could even have been the other way around, I suppose?' he finished, flirting with a further

282

will-o'-the-wisp idea. 'I think there may be a side chamber, carved out of the rock. This kouskoura's not very resistant . . . carves easily. If there is, wouldn't you guess that's where the burial proper was located? And the odds are that it's undisturbed.'

The men murmured quietly to each other, gripping their spades, ready for the next onslaught. But: 'There goes the last of the useable light,' said Aristidis, coming to a decision. 'If we hang on any longer, it'll be dark before we get back to the village and I'll have your wives to reckon with! I agree with all that you have to say, William. However – we'll just have to test the strength of our theory by the morning light. If you have no objection, I think I'll double the guard tonight?'

He called the men together, a bone-weary but still spirited crowd, to go over in a few words their achievements and set out his hopes and expectations for the next day's dig. Eager now to get back to their own firesides to tell their tales and recover for whatever tomorrow might bring, they made their way back to the goat sheds to clean equipment and leave all ready.

Dutifully, Letty stayed behind with Gunning, who'd settled down at his drawing board, insisting on bringing his records of the last few hours' excavations up to date without delay. The light had been too difficult for supporting photographs and he was anxious to produce an adequate set of sketches. In the end, she had snatched the pencil from his hand and called a halt.

'William! I am not paying *you* overtime, you know. You may stop work now.'

'Whatever makes you think I'm working for *you*?' he said coldly, pausing to snatch back his pencil and sharpen it. 'Pass me those lamps, would you, Letty? You're off now, are you? You'll have to step out a bit to catch up with Aristidis. Here, take my flashlight. There's still a bit of juice left in it.'

She sighed with resignation. Then she set off by herself in the twilight to follow the well-known path back down to the village, hearing the merry shouts and conversation of the men half a mile ahead and lower down the hillside.

Laetitia was distracted from her path by the stunning beauty of the headland. She had never lingered there after sunset but found herself lured past the temple remains and on, almost to the edge of the precipice, tracing the deepest indigo of the eastern sky, through an arc over her head and on to the bronze glimmer that still outlined the rim of the western sea. In the distance she could make out the lights of Herakleion and closer, in the valley bottom, lamps were being lit in the village houses. A chorus of women's voices was raised, musical calls summoning children inside, shouts announcing that supper was ready, fetching in men from the gardens, reassuring, ordinary, and ancient. Somewhere on the hill behind her a goat bell tinkled and from the olive groves below was answered by the *coo-coo-vay* of the Little Owl of Athena.

And then the nightingales came onstage. Two of them, calling to each other, as far as she could work out. From this height it sounded like an inspired duet, improvised on the wing over a lemon orchard, a love-lure, liquid and enchanting. The purity pierced through her, bringing shivers and tears and she stumbled, whispering, through a few lines of Keats's ode to the bird:

> '*The voice I hear this passing night was heard*
> *In ancient days by emperor and clown:*
> *Perhaps the self-same song that found a path*
> *Through the sad heart of Ruth, when, sick for home,*
> *She stood in tears amid the alien corn . . .*'

'Bloody birds! Shatter your eardrums! Disputing territory, I shouldn't wonder,' said Gunning's voice in her ear.

'Probably just as well we can't understand what they're saying to each other!'

'Well, I love them! The nightingale's song is so pure it could quench your thirst!'

'I wish you'd come away from the edge, Letty, you make me nervous.'

He grabbed her by the arm and tugged her some feet away over to a slab of rock still warm from the sun and, with a cursory 'May I?' he sat down beside her.

So far things were working out as she'd planned, but she remembered that with William Gunning nothing was ever predictable. Any other man of her acquaintance who'd caught her interest would be moving smoothly to whisper in her ear, hold her hand, drape his jacket around her shoulders, and, under cover of it, pass a tentative arm around her waist. It would all lead, at the very least, to a kiss. And here was the man who'd occupied her waking thoughts for the past year hauling her about and subjecting her to a rant against nightingales. Perhaps if she could just keep quiet for long enough he would explain himself. Even confess that he'd got fond of her.

The unexpected hug the other day had settled two questions. Firstly – her own feelings, about which she had remained confused. She had wrapped her arms around him and held him gladly, not wanting to be separated from him. A fragile thing on which to base your hopes, when your head told you with certainty and frequency that this was a man quite unsuitable for the involvement you had in mind. He was much older than she was – fifteen years, perhaps? He had no money or prospect of ever having any as far as she knew. His past was littered with incidents too dreadful to confide, apparently, and he was still in the throes of an unresolved conflict and conversation with the God he had repudiated on the battlefield.

He was not a man you could boast about to your friends and family. Her more worldly friends, concerned and puzzled, had delicately suggested a reason for his reticence. 'Er, had you thought, my dear, that he may well be a man's man? They do exist, you know . . . the kind who only seek out male company . . . overgrown schoolboys, regimental types who never marry. They don't all have the self-knowledge of an Oscar Wilde and some go to the grave never even realizing . . .'

The hug had been close enough and long enough for Letty to establish that this was not one of Gunning's problems, and had given her hope.

'Aristidis gone off without you, then? Not like him! Why on earth didn't he wait for you? Would you like me to say something?'

'No, no! It could be because I told him to go ahead. I was waiting for you. But then I decided I liked my own company better and drifted over here. Thought I'd do a little moon-worship. Commune with the goddess Selene. I don't get much of a chance to be by myself these days, you know. There's always someone dancing attendance . . . watching . . . testing . . . being critical . . . it can get very annoying.'

'Yes, chaperonage does cramp your style. I had noticed. Sorry to intrude! I'll leave you to your thoughts.' He was getting to his feet.

'It's a perfect evening, isn't it?' She caught and held him with a question. 'So romantic! I stage-managed it well, don't you think? I calmed the sea to a murmur, I conjured up a full moon, I switched on the nightingale. And here I loiter, misty-eyed, lonely heroine, heart full of longing. And only one thing lacking . . .'

'I do know that,' he answered, with a touch of gentleness. 'I'm sorry, Letty – I'm not a total insensitive – I do realize how much you must miss him.'

'Miss him? Miss who?' Letty looked at him in puzzlement as he abandoned his pretence of leaving and settled down by her side again. And then, uncertainly: 'Oh! Daniel? My godfather, Daniel, you mean? Well . . . just occasionally, I suppose. But, William – it's been a year. I was fond of the old feller, as you know, but not so devoted I'd still be standing on a mountainside sorrowing.'

'Must you always wilfully misunderstand! It can be very

tedious! He's not far off – over there to the north. Across the Cretan Sea. You were looking and sighing in just the right direction just now ... Why don't you telegraph? He could be at your side in two days.'

Letty turned a horrified face to him, trying to read his expression. His eyes drained of their bright colour in the twilight, reflected the austere gleam of the moon. They chilled her.

'William, what on earth are you saying?'

'That the chap you're teetering on the edge of a cliff, yearning for, is in Athens and just awaiting your summons. Probably had his bag packed for weeks. Your lover! Andrew bloody Merriman!'

Letty was silent for a very long time.

'How do you know?' she finally asked him quietly.

Chapter Thirty

'Because your dashing friend Merriman told me himself. And he is not a man to be doubted. When the youngest professor of archaeology at a British university, a man fêted – notorious even – for his gallantry, good looks, and charming character, informs me that he has for some years enjoyed an intimate relationship with the girl I was being employed to keep on the straight and narrow ... well ... I'm astonished, but I believe him. Andrew was rather drunk at the time he made the confidence, but it's not the sort of thing you invent, even in your cups.'

He was trying to speak lightly but he could not disguise his hurt and anger. 'I'd just spent the summer squiring the young lady around France in accordance with her father's wishes, doing my best to keep her from harm and temptation. "To be returned virtue and fortune intact" – that was my brief from your doting father, who also, I noted, was thoroughly deceived.'

'And nearly getting yourself killed in the process, let's not forget,' she said. 'Well, since you seem to be making up a charge sheet –'

'And the notion came to me that I'd been wasting my time. Chasing after a wild goose? Barring the door of the stable from which the horse had already bolted? There must be a phrase to sum up my laughable gullibility. There's certainly a word: dupe.'

'And these revelations were made during your impromptu party at Fitzroy Gardens, last year, when we got back from Burgundy?' she said in a neutral voice.

'Accompanied by a matey dig in the ribs and a knowing chortle, no doubt. I don't wonder you disappeared in the night. But this is not right. It isn't like Andrew to betray a confidence to a man who was virtually a stranger. I don't understand.'

'It was probably something I said. We sat on together for a while after dinner. We got on well, as a matter of fact. Rather a surprising man, Andrew. Younger than me, twice as presentable, at ease with himself and the world. I liked him. He drew me out and I think I talked about you quite a lot over the brandy. Too much? Perhaps I gave a false impression of ... of ... our association. I think he over-interpreted the situation and, succumbing to male jealousy, warned me off, speaking of a long-standing affair. All delicately expressed, of course, but – man to man – I'd received a shot across my bows which I couldn't ignore.'

He hesitated for a moment and decided to add: 'I can't be unfair to the man – I'm certain that, had I been young, rich, and well-connected, he would have given me his blessing and kept his mouth shut. But, disreputable unknown that I was, he was doing no more than his duty in protecting you from me. He invited me to spend some time with him to check me out, I do believe. Just in case you were truly in danger.'

There was no warmth in his slow smile. 'Not sure what would have been my fate had he decided I really was a menace, but it would have been uncomfortable. He's a for-midable man. But he was taking no chances, and shipped me off to Crete in short order. I was actually grateful to him for the opportunity. And remain so – let me make that clear. Merriman's deeply fond of you, Letty. More than you realize or deserve. And, of course, I had at last an under-standing of why you'd insisted on hurrying back to London. Bad of you not to tell me he was to be there.'

'I didn't know he and father had arrived. And *we* weren't expected back for several weeks, if you remember.' There was little she could salvage from the situation, but she could at least insist on accuracy.

After a long silence, Gunning ventured: 'Are you going to tell me that Andrew was merely expressing a brandy-fuelled fantasy? That you haven't been indulging in a clandestine affair of an amorous nature for years?'

'Oh, Good Lord, William! Sleeping with him, you mean? It's none of your business, but – yes, we have been lovers on and off for a long time now.' She had nothing more to hide, nothing more to lose. The truth came as a relief. And, following on the relief, a surge of recklessness. He had no right to question or criticize her. He wasn't her confessor, not even her friend.

'I had thought better of you, William. But I see you are ready, like most other men I've met, to judge a woman by her past experience, though the same standards are never applied to your own sex, it seems. None of your fault, Son of the Rectory that you are . . .' Even in her grim mood, she noticed his shudder at her reference to his past. 'And I have to allow that you stepped out of the world ten years ago – again, certainly not your fault. You are to blame for many things, I think, William, but the Great War is not one of them, and you may not yet be aware that the world has gone on spinning. People are no longer what they were. I can only speak for girls of my own background, of course, and yes, I know you despise me for my advantages, but I can tell you – I acknowledge them, I celebrate them, I intend always to make fullest use of them. My friends and I read, we talk, we fight to get ourselves educated, and we claim for ourselves some of the freedoms men have until now kept for themselves. Perhaps you'll allow me to put a suitable reading list in your hand? Marie Stopes, perhaps? Yes, you should start there.'

'Ah! *Married Love?* Or has the lady then written a sequel to her first work?' he asked, bitterly. 'Un*married Love*?'

'It started, predictably, in a room over the Café Royal,' she went on, lightening her tone, intending to shock. The gloves were off and she wanted nothing more than to give him a bloody nose. 'As these things do. Not very original but an exciting experiment for me. He's an attractive,

290

experienced, amusing, and thoroughly nice man. If he'd been free, I'd have married him. I love him. Many women do. My father never caught on, as far as I know. Fathers are always, I suppose, the last to suspect what their daughters are getting up to. You don't ask but I'll tell you – we were together for purposes of mutual carnal enjoyment – as you would no doubt put it before rinsing your mouth with carbolic – for the last time three weeks before I ran into you in Cambridge.'

Letty started to get to her feet. 'Now, unless you're intending to bend my ear with a reciprocal confession of sin, to which I would listen with some sympathy – we sinners must stick together – I'll be off. This stone we're sitting on is suddenly quite chilly.'

He made no attempt to rise with her but sat on, glumly looking out to sea. She stood, silent, trying to calm her anger and her heartsickness, deep in thought. A chill wind suddenly swept up from the precipice, waking wreaths of mist from the land, and she shivered. On an impulse she turned around, bent, and kissed his lips. Her first kiss and her last, judging by his cold response. She took him by the arm and hauled him to his feet. 'Come on, Mr Misery! We've only got one flashlight and we've a mile to walk in each other's company. It's too dark to play "I Spy" so you're just going to have to keep up polite conversation all the way down.'

She passed him the torch and tucked an arm companionably through his. 'Now – have you heard the latest gossip to come out of the British School at Rome?' Her tone was intimate and involving. Frivolous flapper-talk. Calculated to annoy. 'No? Then prepare yourself for a sensation! Lalage Boyd-Brewster, one of the lady directors – you've heard of her? Fading beauty . . . did a lot of good work in Mesopotamia? . . . that Lalage? – has set tongues wagging the breadth of Europe! She's just taken a new lover. And not a female this time . . . No, no – this latest one is a young Italian man, thirty years her junior! . . . What do you think of that! . . . But you take such an interest in prurient gossip, William, I was sure you'd be fascinated . . .'

On the point of leaving the headland, she dropped his arm and turned away from him. She stood for a moment, offering wet cheeks to the sky and casting an aggrieved glance at the impassive moon.

Chapter Thirty-One

'There's a rider on the road!'

Demetrios's sharp eyes were for a moment distracted from the dig they were about to embark on.

'Twenty minutes away. Big black horse. Who's this?'

Aristidis shaded his eyes and stared. 'It's the boss. It's Russell,' he said.

'Coming at quite a lick. Make that ten minutes if he puts the poor beast to the slope,' said Gunning.

'Theodore? Oh, no! But why would he be coming?' Letty could not suppress her irritation. 'He was sent a message yesterday. What did you say, William?'

'Just what you told me to say. Aristidis's eldest took it down late yesterday afternoon when it became clear we weren't going to finish. I said we were staying on to work through Saturday, returning on Sunday, and staying over at the Europa for the funeral on Monday. I didn't go further and extend an invitation. Wouldn't have thought he'd have the time with so much on his plate at the moment.'

'Not more bad news? He surely can't be bringing more bad news,' said Letty anxiously. 'Didn't you tell me George was doing well?'

'He's curious. And you can hardly blame him for being intrigued,' said Aristidis. 'Let's not forget that the man is first and foremost an archaeologist. The report you sent would have fetched him back from the brink of hell – or heaven. I think, out of courtesy,' he said, looking around at the diggers, 'we should hold off for a few minutes. Let him enjoy the moment – or share in the disappointment – shall we?'

Letty scowled. Gunning shrugged. The men grounded their spades and each lit another cigarette.

Theodore came on site, leading his sweating horse, and handed the reins to one of the crew. 'Miss Talbot! Laetitia! Top of the morning to you! And William, there you are! Greetings! . . . Aristidis . . .' He nodded briefly. 'Wonderful! How good it is to be here for what may well be the find of the decade. Thank you for letting me know, William.'

'If you're in a thanking mood, Theo,' drawled Gunning, 'you should direct your thanks to Aristidis. We all should. For letting us dig up his land.'

'Of course, of course,' said Theodore. 'Care to show me around, Aristidis?'

He had already started on a circuit of the tholos tomb. Aristidis let him complete it by himself.

'Not much to look at, is it? No wonder it's been ignored for so long. Saw it myself the other week and never thought anything of it. Well spotted, Laetitia! And I see you've exposed a temple or some such? Will you do the honours, William?'

He inspected the diggings, listening to Gunning's commentary, exclaiming and questioning, intrigued by all he saw.

Finally, he came back to the group. 'Now, you'll all be wanting news of George? With all the excitement up here, I don't expect he's been much on your mind?' he said blandly. He was looking at Gunning when he spoke. The accusation of careless lack of interest was plain.

It was Aristidis who replied. 'William has said a prayer for your son every morning and evening in Ayios Pavlos. I have knelt at his side. And my son Nikolas, who returned at dawn this morning, brought back the news he had requested from Dr Stoddart.'

'Ah. Indeed. Then your information is as fresh as my own. The lad's out of the woods and will recover. Many bones broken and it's all going to take some time, but at least he's conscious and talking. I'm to be allowed to fetch him home tomorrow.'

'We look forward to seeing George on our return,' said Letty warmly. 'This is truly good news. And if we all stop gossiping, roll up our sleeves, and get busy, we may well have something worth reporting to him. Let's dedicate the day's digging to George!' She handed Theodore a pick. 'Here you are, Mr Russell, you can take the first swing. Aristidis will show you where to aim it.'

Archaeological zeal overwhelmed his desire for any further social skirmishing. He went off by himself to the spot his sharp eyes and experience had already identified as the place to make the first incision. They trooped after him. He paused before he swung the pick to smile mischievously at Letty.

'Well, it seems we're about to wake the King of the Gods! Got your kisses ready, Laetitia?' he said, reminding her of Stewart's taunt.

'Honed to perfection. I've been practising all week,' she replied, easily.

One by one, the limestone blocks were prised off. As soon as the hole was big enough to admit the broad shoulders of Aristidis, he checked the depth of the void and lowered himself down into it. They caught the glimmer of his flashlight as he moved about, along with an occasional low whistle and muttered oath. After what seemed an interminable time, he returned, looking up at them, his excitement only just held in check.

'It's a burial chamber,' he announced. 'Untouched, I'd say, since the last lamp went out thousands of years ago. Problem is going to be access. It's carved out of the rock – possibly a natural cave that's been extended. We could get in through what you might call the front door – through the wall of the tholos . . .'

'No! You can't do that,' said Gunning anxiously. 'The whole structure would collapse.'

'I thought you'd say that. Nothing for it, then, but to strip off the roof covering. Might be possible. Come down and take a look.'

Aristidis moved aside to make room for Gunning, and five minutes later two grinning faces appeared again.

'Well, man? Come on! Let's have your evaluation!' said Theodore.

'It's not just a grave shaft. More in the nature of a miniature temple! Sturdily built, and they've left carved stone columns in place as supports. Traces of wooden beams, rotted away, but the stone slabs they've covered it over with have settled into an accommodation with the hillside and they've done their work perfectly. There's no sign of masonry collapse that I can see. If we can get the slabs off without causing havoc, we won't have much clearance to do at all. It's going to take some muscle power, though. You may find yourself lending a hand, Theo!'

The remaining blocks were taken up, carted off, and stacked to one side. Men heaved on levers and pulled on ropes. Theodore rolled up his shirtsleeves and cracked his mighty muscles, giving a hand whenever the gang appeared to flag. Letty watched as the void below the surface was, foot by foot, exposed.

No one spoke. The silence was broken only by the grunts of the diggers and their occasional sharp instructions and exhortations to each other.

The morning's steady work had revealed the side chamber Gunning had predicted. It lay at their feet, untouched since the day the body had been sealed inside and the wall of the tholos built up above it. The last rites had been to sacrifice the horse and the bull whose bones lay sanctifying and guarding the entrance. Perhaps grave goods had been set out on the floor of the beehive, but these had long ago been found and taken away by tomb robbers. But no robber had intruded here and Letty gazed, at a loss for words, as the significance of what she was seeing silenced her.

On quiet instructions from Aristidis, two men let themselves down on to the floor of the tomb and carefully swept up the clods of earth and lumps of masonry dislodged during the excavation, placing them into baskets. They looked around them, satisfying themselves that the ground was clear and uncontaminated, and climbed back out again, waiting.

Theodore spoke. 'So! First impressions of the side chamber. Hewn from the rock and the blocks used to build up the tholos alongside. Seven foot deep, ten foot square. Built for single occupancy. And there's the single occupant. In the centre, lying east to west. Bearing bodily ornaments. Surrounded by grave goods of various kinds. A rich burial. From a first look at the important (and intact) pot I see at the corpse's elbow, I'd hazard: Neopalatial period. Between 1700 and 1450 BC.'

Letty gazed down at 'the occupant'. No god, this. The body had been stretched out on limestone blocks on the floor and over the centuries the flesh and sinews had melted away. What little remained had hardened and calcified until it was one with the same colourless rock. She could just make out the shadowy form of the limbs and the defenceless round shape of the skull, all that was left of a head that had lain turned on to its left cheek. The grey eggshell was still pitifully encircled by a diadem of glinting gold pieces; the threads that had held it together were long gone, but the lozenges themselves were annealed in place, defying decay, announcing to the world that here lay a person of vast importance.

The urn by its side was spilling over with jewellery. The gold still gleamed, gemstones still winked in the sunshine, lapis, glass, paste, rock crystal. Other metal, blackened by age, might have been silver. The body was overlaid by other jewels that would give clues to the identity of the body. Certainly the bronze rings she saw where the fingers had once curled would tell their tale. Her eye was caught by a trail of small glinting ornaments from where the waist would have been and on down to the ankles, and Letty was puzzled.

She looked again at the head with its curious turn to the left. She saw the dull oval object a few inches to the side of the face in line with the eye sockets and stared in surprise. Had anyone else noticed? Over the void, Aristidis exclaimed as he reached the same startling conclusion.

Avoiding Theodore's obstructing hand and deaf to Gunning's warning shout, Letty grasped her skirts about the knee in one hand and, putting the other on the lip of the tomb, she jumped down into it. She tiptoed, mesmerized, around the body and knelt at its side. Taking her digging knife from her belt, she slid it gently underneath the oval shape. It came free at once. She lifted it and held it to her own face and stared into the looking glass, her lips moving as she spoke words she was unconscious of speaking. She saw in the dusty bronze depths a ghost of an outline, a large-eyed, lovely, and questioning face.

One voice from above broke through her spell. Aristidis. 'Do you see her, Miss Laetitia?'

She shook her head. 'No, only myself. I missed her. By about three and a half thousand years.'

'Good Lord! What are you saying, Letty?' Gunning said urgently. 'That this is a woman? We're looking at a *female* burial?'

'Yes, I'd say so, wouldn't you? I'm quite sure Cretan males, cockerels all – and vain – might have cast the odd admiring glance at themselves in a polished bronze mirror, but I doubt they would have been buried with one alongside. And this lady would have been worth looking at! Do you see these necklaces still on her bosom? Amethysts? Could that be amber? Gold of the most exquisite workmanship! This one's been beaten into whisper-thin flower petals . . .' The rush of words ceased as, peering closely, she absorbed the significance of a second gold ornament. A broad pendant, intricately worked, this one showed, framed by arching palm branches, a goddess with arms spread out in a wide gesture. A dove settled on each wrist, and at her feet sprawled protectively two wild creatures that Letty took to be lions.

Letty looked up at her audience, ready at last to speak. 'I think we've found a deity. A Nature Goddess. The Mistress of the Animals? Or her priestess – this could be a Royal Priestess . . . the Ariadne of her day? And look here – have you noticed these?' She pointed to the rows of gold beads trailing below the waist. 'Back home, on the ball-room dancing floor, we'd call these sequins. They were sewn on to a garment. And if you count the rows –'

'Already have,' came Theo's dry voice. 'Seven! All that's left of a flounced skirt. Outlining each tier. Care to give us another sewing lesson, miss?'

He could restrain himself no longer. 'Get the girl out of there!' he said firmly to no one in particular. 'Camera, William? We must record this before the scene gets trampled by any more boots. I especially want a striking shot of that clay larnax over there in the corner. Had you seen? It bears a picture of a bull, tied by the heels and being sacrificed on an altar. Fresh as the day it was painted! There will be a huge amount of information on that! I may find myself having to rewrite chapter eleven . . . what do you say, William? Aristidis – remove the men from the scene now, will you? I'd like to have the place to myself for a bit. Surely you've got something to occupy them over at the temple? I thought I saw a row of underground cists they could well be taking a stab at.'

Aristidis put out a brawny arm and hauled Letty out of the tomb. As he steadied her on her feet by him she could feel his tension. If ever the man did lose his iron control, she decided she would not want to be standing next to him. The six diggers had taken a step back, beginning to mutter to each other, looking to their Kapitan for a lead. Poised, she thought, to down tools and stalk off. They'd done it once before; she sensed they would take grim pleasure in doing it again.

It was Gunning who defused the gathering bad feeling. He lowered himself into the pit Letty had just vacated and, holding up his hands and turning around with the confidence of a showman or a priest, gathered everyone's attention. Then, shielding his eyes with his right hand from the glare of the sun, knuckles to his forehead, he advanced on the regal remains.

He stood at the calcified feet and made up a prayer:

'*Hail, Goddess! Lady Mother,*
Mistress of Animals, Eldest of Beings!
Sister and wife of loud-thundering Zeus,
You are blessed and revered in these hills.
Happy is the man it pleases you to honour,
For he will have all good things in abundance:
Wine, honey, flocks, and fair women.'

He moved forward to kneel where Letty had knelt, looking tenderly at the bony skull. He leaned over and solemnly kissed the vestige of face where the lips might once have been. Then he stood, saluted again, and scrambled, with the help of many offered hands, out of the tomb.

The men had fallen silent, but were smiling and nodding approval at Gunning. Proper respect had been shown. This was not their deity, but it was the goddess of their ancestors, a priestess or a princess, and due reverence was to be expected. Some were crossing themselves and peering, fascinated, at the remains below. Demetrios, defiantly smiling, essayed a Minoan salute in imitation of Gunning. Aristidis seemed to have calmed himself.

The newfound peace was disturbed by a slow hand-clapping from Theodore. 'Good gracious, man! Whatever do you do for an encore? The fairy song from *Iolanthe*?'

The men looked at each other, hands clenching, not understanding the words but hearing the unmistakable sneer. Letty threw caution and convention to the winds. She stalked over to Russell, took up a stand an uncomfortable hand-span away from him, and looked him in the eye. What he saw there made him take a step back.

'The lady has slept in solitary state for too long. Perhaps we should offer up a companion? Like the royal burials at

Ur of the Chaldees. How do you measure up, Theodore? Are you volunteering to lie alongside or shall we chuck you in?'

Not pausing for a reply, she seized Gunning by the arm and walked off to the goat sheds to help him collect his tripod and photographic gear, still fuming. She suddenly realized that the arm she held so tightly was quivering. He was stifling a laugh.

'Not a bad idea, Letty! But why contaminate such a good site? Let's stuff him in one of those cists when we've got them opened up. Nobody's ever going to find him there.'

They stood together in the sudden dark of the goat shed workroom, gathering clipboards, notebooks, rolls of film, and photographic plates into a pile on the workbench, each understanding the other's working methods, not needing to comment or question.

'Are you ready?'

'Ready. Oh, no. Hang on a minute! Just move into the light, will you, William?' She took hold of his chin and turned his head, peering into his face. 'Oh, good! For a minute I thought you were growing a moustache again. But I see it's just goddess dust. A fine film of it on your top lip. Here, let me see to it.'

She took his handkerchief from his pocket and as he turned a smiling and obliging face to her, she suddenly regretted her intimate gesture. 'The life you lead, William, it's a wonder to me that you manage to keep your hankies so crisp,' she said nervously. She rubbed and dusted until satisfied, surprised that he was suffering her ministrations without resistance.

'There. You'll do. That's a nice mouth. It looks firm and honest. The goddess is probably counting herself fortunate indeed that there was such a handsome chap on hand to greet her. That grating noise we heard – it was the sound of her bony toes curling in ecstasy.' She was talking non-sense into the silence, hardly aware of what she was saying, confused by his closeness. For the first time, no mask of indifference or scorn was being raised in defence, his eyes were showing humour and ... and ... well, *affection* was as far as she was prepared to go. Until he kissed her.

'There. That's the second goddess I've kissed in ten minutes. I must say I prefer the warm, willing lips. I love you, Letty. Always have. And I think you've always known it.'

'No. You're wrong. I held no such hopes last night. You were quite ready to push me over the cliff.'

'It was a storm we had to weather. And we're not through it yet. There are squalls ahead still, I'm afraid. I'm not quite sure I'm standing here, holding you ... I didn't understand until a few moments ago that you might really care for me. When you rounded on Theo ... you didn't say much but you did something to shake him. I've never seen him give an inch before to anyone, certainly not recoil from a woman.'

'I looked a curse at him! It's very primitive, the urge to protect someone you love.'

'Someone you love,' he repeated softly, taking in her meaning. 'Are you sure I'm worth a declaration of war, Letty? Because that's how Theo will interpret your challenge – all the more demeaning to him for being delivered in front of the men.'

'Let him! He knows now that if he harms you in any way, he'll have me to reckon with.' She pushed her arms inside his jacket, sighing upwards into another kiss.

'The diggers, William? They'll be waiting for us. We've been here uninterrupted for ten minutes. I've been expecting the sound of clumping boots every second. They're not even whistling in a marked manner.'

'Ah. That's because I notice Aristidis is standing guard on the path. He won't let anyone approach.'

'What!' Letty looked about anxiously. 'You mean he knows?'

'Seems to have guessed. In fact he's offered to kidnap you.'

'Kidnap? Me? What on earth are you saying?'

'That's what they do here in Crete. If a girl is willing, her young man arranges with his friend – his best man, if you wish – to snatch her, like Persephone, away from her friends and family and deliver her, sobbing and distraught, to the church. Quite a few Europeans, witnessing such scenes, have been taken in by the high standard of performance by the principal actors and have intervened on the girl's behalf. Skulls have been cracked, backs belaboured with walking canes, only for the girl in the case to have turned on her would-be saviours for spoiling her fun.'

'I'm sorry, William. If this is a proposal you're making, it's a very odd one and I shall have to decline. Weeping and wailing and being dragged along, you say?' She shook her head. 'I would stride happily down the aisle with a nauseating grin of triumph on my face!'

'Well, if ever we get that far, there's just one small thing I must insist on. That your wedding get-up doesn't include a digging knife.'

He broke away for a moment to slide the belt at her waist around a few inches, moving the knife to the small of her back. 'Ouf! Thank God for that! Didn't like to mention it earlier. Could have broken the spell.'

Chapter Thirty-Two

With Gunning's presence being demanded at the burial pit by Theodore, Letty went over to the temple site with Aristidis, dreamy, radiating good humour. She was even content to sit on a stone and watch while they set about their work. A parasol would have come into its own, she thought, at this moment, to hide her pink, self-satisfied, and totally betraying face.

Aristidis went straight to work, directing three men to reveal and tidy up the storage room to the west, a room lined with large *pithoi* that must have contained olive oil, wheat, honey, wine – all the gifts destined to honour what she now had to assume was the Mother Goddess, the same one worshipped in palaces all over the island. Was Theodore disappointed when his theory – that the all-conquering young god of the mainland Greeks had lived, died, and been buried on this windy mountainside – was shot to pieces by the presence in the burial pit of a woman?

She didn't hesitate to answer her own question. Yes! He would have made much of a King of the Gods figure resurfacing to the world's attention. With his own forceful features on the front page of all the newspapers, dark-eyed, bearded like a Mycenaean warrior, aggressively masculine, people would have been entranced. They would have seen the rightness of it. They would have flocked in their thousands to the site. And Arthur Evans's star would have been eclipsed.

An excited shout broke through her daydreams. She recognized the voice of Demetrios and sat up, instantly attentive. Every crew seems to have one – a lead hound who runs ahead of the others, a finder by luck or instinct. She had learned to pay attention whenever Demetrios gave tongue. He was busy in the central room of the temple, opening up the row of cists. Large, underground stone coffers, they sometimes still contained remnants of a shrine's treasures. The snake goddesses had been found in one such at Knossos. But, Letty was aware, more often than not they had been broken open and the contents removed. She was holding herself back from a fevered anticipation.

She called out: 'What can you see, Demetrios?'

'An eye, miss! Someone's looking up at me!'

'Careful!' she shouted, with dire memories of her underground snake. She shot to her feet and ran over to him.

Aristidis got there at the same time, passing him a torch. 'Here, before we take the lid off, shine this through the hole.' He squinted up at the sun whose rays, almost overhead, must have struck something and been reflected back. 'A snake? A lizard? Better check before we release it.'

'*Blue* eyes? Never seen a snake or lizard with blue eyes,' muttered Demetrios. 'Sorry I yelled – gave me quite a shock!'

'Go on with you! What did you have for breakfast – a bucket of raki?' Aristidis teased him gently, taking back the torch and shining it down the hole in the cracked cover. The stone box, coffin-shaped, was four feet long and eighteen inches wide. He moved the beam about for a bit, then drew in a deep breath. 'Come and look here, miss! He's right! It's an eye!'

Dubiously, Letty took the torch and peered, following the beam. In her effort to restrain a female squeal of surprise she almost choked. 'Heavens! Oh, I say! Yes, that's an eye all right.'

A small almond-shaped object, silver-blue, with a crystalline appearance and a centre as black as jet, looked back at her – she was relieved to see – unwinking. 'Never seen anything like it before. Has anyone?' Heads were shaken;

eyes fixed her, willing her to give the order. 'Right then – off with the top? Shall we?'

It took four men to lift the lid and lower it to the ground. They stood, six figures, grouped around the cist, heads bowed, staring down at the contents.

'You look as though you're all gathered at the graveside, waiting for the trumpet to sound the Last Post,' came Gunning's cheerful voice. 'What's up, Letty?'

'I think this may be just that, William,' said Letty. 'A grave – of sorts. Designed for single occupancy, you could say. Come and look and tell us: Who do you suppose this might be?'

Gunning looked. He caught one of the young diggers, standing by openmouthed, by the hand. 'Petros, fetch Kyrie Russell, will you? Quickly!'

He looked apologetically around at the others.

'Oh, let Russell have his moment,' said Aristidis, comfortably. 'He's waited long enough.'

Theo came barrelling up, sweating and dishevelled in his shirtsleeves and breeches, suspicion and anticipation warring on his face. The men took a step back to allow him to gaze into the cist by himself. Surprisingly, he was speechless. No recitation of dimensions and enumeration of artefacts came from him. He fell to his knees on the ground, making a palpable effort not to thrust eager hands into the stone container and draw out the precious contents.

Finally, and they had to lean closer to hear his whispered words: 'He's very delicate. If you so much as *attempt* to kiss him, Miss Talbot, I will smack your bottom!'

Then, mastering his thoughts and aware once more of his audience: 'It is he,' he intoned, claiming their attention. 'We are looking on the face of Zeus. The young Greek god Zeus. And this is his tomb.'

His eyes flicked sideways to Gunning's notebook.

With a sardonic smile, William recorded the moment. 'I

say, Theo, can you be so sure of that?' He put a gentle hand on his shoulder. 'I mean ... well ... it's perfectly lovely, we'd all agree, but it's just a statue. Half life-sized. Three feet tall, would you say? Unique to date, I think. It's made of ivory, if I'm not mistaken, and carved most wonderfully. Cretan workmanship? I wonder? Brilliant ... unusual ... even for the artists of Minos. Do you know – I can't keep the name "Daedalus" from popping into my mind.' He smiled apologetically for his flight of fancy and peered more closely into the stone box. 'But I'll tell you what – whoever and whatever this is – it's been very badly damaged.'

'It's a god,' said Letty, her certainty cancelling out his doubts. 'It *could* perhaps be the young god the Mycenaeans brought with them to depose the Mother Goddess. But an Olympian? Straight from the Top Table? I'm not so sure of that.'

'Are you about to upend him to check his bona fides?' Theodore could not resist the spiteful jibe.

'His provenance is not in question,' she said tartly, annoyed at the interruption. 'Do you see his hair? Whoever damaged him left his hair intact. It's spun gold. The most delicate fibres of gold thread. And his eyes are blue rock crystal. His face is lovely, pale and of the finest-grained ivory. He's a Spring God, twenty years old at the most. *I* would worship at his altar! His limbs ... so slender – look, do you see, they're jointed on to the body like those of a modern doll. Perhaps you can move them? And look at his hands! Every vein, every fingernail is perfectly carved.'

She fell silent, keeping her gaze and her comments above the waist, reluctant to describe the devastation below.

It was Gunning who echoed all their thoughts: 'He's been badly treated. Do you know, if this were a human body we'd dug up, I'd be sending for our friend Mariani. I'd say he'd been murdered. It's not as though he's been crushed in an earthquake or been cut to pieces in battle. His injuries are calculatedly inflicted. He's missing some of his parts,' he said delicately, with regard for his mixed audience. 'And his feet are gone because they've been burned away. Do you see the signs of charring? Just to the feet. He's been held sideways over a fire, quite deliberately. Tortured to death, you'd say.'

The respectful silence as they contemplated the young god's anguish was broken by Theodore's voice, officious and prosaic: 'Tell you what I'm minded to do, William, when we've completed our recording,' he said. 'I'm going to box him up again and take him in to Stoddart. For a postmortem examination. Sounds ridiculous, I know, but on this occasion, the doctor may have something interesting to tell the archaeologists.'

Work went on until the customary hour before sunset. Exhausted but elated, Letty joined Aristidis, putting the finishing touches to the dig. Tarpaulins were being stretched over the exposed sections, the remaining crates of potsherds being carted off to the sheds. The only figure not scrambling to tidy up was moodily standing on the edge of the precipice looking out to sea, legs splayed – at the helm, you would have said, Letty thought.

She shared the thought with Aristidis. 'Ah, yes! I never forget that he was a naval man! And he never lets anyone else forget it,' he said.

'I wonder if he's a bit unhappy that the god he's uncovered looks so unlike him? Well, I mean – he couldn't be more different, could he? Slender, youthful, blond with bright blue eyes? Not a bit like any of the representations of Zeus in the art of *any* age or culture! You know – heavy of muscle, shaggy of hair, thunderbolt at the ready? Poor Theo! Nothing seems ever to be what he expects. Shall we go over and congratulate him on the day's achievements? He ought to be thrilled – cracking open the champagne!'

'He is not happy,' Aristidis agreed. 'But please, Miss Laetitia, do not think of trying to improve his state of mind. I know the goodness of your heart tells you to seek the happiness of others, but sometimes all human effort is in vain.'

Letty was surprised at his assessment of her character, and disbelieving.

'He is as God made him.' Aristidis nodded lugubriously. 'An unhappy man and a dangerous one, for he feels bound to communicate his unhappiness. He can stir up thunder-clouds over everyone's head!'

'I wonder what he's contemplating at this moment?'

Aristidis stared, suddenly alert, at the still figure stand-ing far too close to the crumbling rim for safety.

Letty gave an evil grin to lighten the mood. 'To jump or not to jump? Is that his question? Perhaps we could do him a favour? Help him to answer it?' She mimed giving a gentle push.

Aristidis, for once, did not laugh with her. 'A perfectly awful thought! I cannot joke about it. This is my land! Here he is my guest, though he does not acknowledge it.' He considered for a moment. 'If I thought he were seriously contemplating killing himself I would, at this moment, be running over to stop him. And you, I believe, would be the first at my side to restrain him! But, see – he's buckled on his spurs. He's prepared to take the conventional route down to the valley.'

They stayed on watch, however, but to their mutual relief, Theodore didn't put them to the test. Just cutting a dramatic figure, Letty decided. Playing Poseidon. He turned and walked slowly away from the edge, calling for his horse to be brought to him.

Stoddart was so surprised he could hardly get his words together when they arrived on his doorstep at midday on the following day.

'A postmortem? On ancient body parts you're carrying in a finds box? Are you mad? I know you lose all track when you're out in the country but here, in town, it's a Sunday.'

Theodore was impatient. 'Just take a look, will you. One glimpse will be enough.'

He slid the lid open a few inches to show the head of the statue.

Stoddart opened the door at once and ushered them inside. 'Laetitia . . . William . . . Good morning. Look – take that thing, whatever it is, into my examination room and put it on the table, will you?' He glanced at his watch and looked over his shoulder. 'I can give you half an hour before Ollie calls me in to lunch.'

The enticing smell of roast lamb followed them along the corridor, and they all prayed that Olivia would remain busily basting the joint and directing operations in the back quarters until their consultation was over.

'Good Lord! I've only just sent one smashed-up blond young man back to you, Theo, and here you are bringing me another,' he said as they laid out the figure on the examination table. 'What have you done to poor George this time?'

He took a few moments to stare at the figure, joviality giving way to awe as he spoke again: 'Extraordinary! Exquisite!' He looked at them across the table, his face full of wonder, and spoke slowly. 'Do you know, I can't think when I've been more moved by a piece of sculpture? Degas's little dancer? A clumping frivolity compared with this! "The Charioteer"? A mere lump of marble! There's a perfect grace in every limb.'

He shook himself out of his state of adoration. 'I shall want to know sometime where on earth you came by him but,' he looked again at his watch, 'time is of the essence and all that! William – you'll find a sherry bottle in that cupboard and some glasses. Do the honours, will you? I think we'd all like one. Large dry one do you?

'Now!' He put on a pair of spectacles, took a bracing sip of his sherry, and looked long and carefully before speaking. 'Male. Young, say between eighteen and twenty-two. In perfect health before death. Good grief! I'm getting as barmy as you! The boy was never alive – hang on to that,

Stoddart! Fair hair, grey-blue eyes, of a northern European racial type. If George were here, he'd specify: dolichocephalic, I'm sure. No evidence of excessive, emphatic, or imbalanced musculature. By that I mean one arm is not more developed than the other, which might have given us a clue that he was an archer or a discus thrower. His waist – normal proportions. And that's a surprise. I note he's not wearing the tight corset-belt that we see in representations of Minoan men.

'His thighs are to be envied – rounded and well-muscled but not to the exaggerated extent we see in Greek sculptures or pictures of hoplites who walk for miles and exercise constantly. I don't think we're looking at a military man. You'd say he'd had an easy life until misfortune struck him. You'll find out more if you examine his dog tag. Yes, he's wearing an identity bracelet on his right wrist. Ah! You hadn't spotted it? You should put it under a magnifying glass. It's of silver and what could be iron, I suppose, and there are seal markings on it.

'Moving down – had you noticed, yes, of course you had – this strand of gold wire just below the knees – binding his legs together, you'd say. And . . .' he prodded gently at the thin trace of gold, 'this ligature was affixed after the burning of the lower limbs.

'Which brings us to: his death. If this were a human – and it's surprisingly hard not to think of him as such – I'd say his death was long, drawn-out, and thoroughly unpleasant. He's been emasculated – had his penis sliced off with a sharp blade. I say – it wasn't in the box, was it – you did look? Pity. Testicles too, they're gone. Someone was making a strong point. He's had his feet burned away inch by inch. Held him out over a fire, most probably. Charred up almost to the knees. No damage to the eyes. Someone wanted him to witness his own suffering? Or wanted him to be eternally identifiable? The features are untouched.

'The coup de grâce is here, you see.' He pointed with a scalpel. 'They put him out of his misery with a cut to the neck. Not just a slash across the throat. They've gone for the jugular. With a . . .' he peered closely at the wound, 'triangular-bladed, slender knife. The tip of a lance head? This is the cut administered to sacrificial victims. And exactly the type of weapon used. The victim, usually a bull of course, would be tied up on an altar – ah! tied up! – and would bleed into a bucket held under the wound by a priest, I understand. But you know all that, Theo. I'm sure it's from you I have my information! I say, how'm I doing? Is this any use?'

'Fascinating, Harry! Quite fascinating! Certainly gives us an insight.'

'Oh, good show! Are you going to tell me what this is all about?'

'Yes,' said Theodore. 'Let me introduce you to your patient. This is Zeus. Straight from his tomb. The stripling Zeus, come over from the mainland to teach the Minoans a thing or two. It's my belief this young fellow proves the truth of the Theseus myth. Achaean warriors – were they the Peoples of the Sea of such terrible repute? – arrived in force, following on a catastrophe on the island – volcano, earthquake, tidal wave – in the mid-fifteenth century BC. They took over and converted the indigenous population to the worship of their own male gods.

'This could well be the idol set up for worship up there on Juktas, a religion imposed by the invaders. How long did it go on for?' He shrugged. 'No idea. No way of knowing for certain, though clues – like this one – are emerging. But this chap bears the evidence on his mangled body of a turning of the tables. Someone – priests? the ordinary folk of the village? someone attached still to the Old Religion at any rate – revolted, got the upper hand again, and made an example of him. They tortured him, put him to a symbolic death, and then buried him, right there, underfoot in the temple in the very spot where he had lorded it over the local goddess.'

The doctor was standing, hardly listening, still mesmerized by the pathetic form lying with its extraordinary aura of humanity on the crisp white sheet covering the table. Letty watched as he took his time to make the sign of the cross over the body, his eyes gleaming with tears, his nostrils quivering, and she knew he was seeing, not a small, lifeless piece of ivory, but the tormented limbs of any one of the young warriors his skilled hands had failed to save.

He blew his nose and joined in the debate. 'Seen worse in war, Russell. I'm sure you have, too. We know what men are capable of. Couldn't it have been the work of a further wave of loutish invaders, not understanding, not appreciating, raiding and wrecking? Having a bit of drunken barbaric fun?' he suggested.

'I don't think so. The emasculation, the sacrificial aspect to what I have to think of as a calculated killing, are saying one thing very clearly to me,' said Theodore. 'And it makes me shudder! I think I can guess whose malignant hand was behind this butchery.'

Chapter Thirty-Three

'Obvious, if you think about it! Our hero's been done to death by a chorus of raging women. Priestesses, probably, of the Old Religion.' He quivered with disgust. 'God knows what they did to any male followers of Zeus they may have caught loitering up there!' He glowered at Letty. 'And they call them the gentle sex! Malevolent, murderous maenads – and quite as capable of violence and sexual abandon as the worst of us. Never trust one, William. There's good advice for you. Wouldn't you agree, Harry?'

Olivia's voice was heard calling at that moment, coo-eeing from the dining room. A gong sounded.

'Um . . . I'll reserve my judgement on that, if you don't mind, old man,' said Harry, with a sly smile. 'We'll speak of it later. Interesting theory. I shall give it my best atten-tion.' He strolled to the door and called back: 'Just coming, my dear. Would you like me to fetch up a bottle of wine?

'You can show yourselves out while I nip down to the cellar. Oh, and tell George when he wakes up that I'll visit again this evening.'

Olivia's voice came again and he shouted back: 'No, no, dearest! It's only Theodore come to pick up a few pills for George. He's dashing off as we're about to sit down to lunch. He sends his regards. Bye, Theo!'

Letty chuckled when they were safely outside in the street. 'Poor Harry! Can Ollie really be such a shrew?'

'He's obviously not allowed to have friends round to play on a Sunday,' suggested William. He, like Letty, was certain that Theodore had no knowledge that he had just been standing a few inches away from his dead wife's lover. But he was equally certain that Olivia had put two and two together and extracted a confession.

'She keeps him in line, I'd noticed,' offered Theodore. 'She'd have his feet over a fire in no time if he overstepped the mark.'

George was awake and delighted to see them. Reclining in striped pyjamas at home on a chaise longue in the drawing room, he looked pink and happy and – disregarding the plastered limbs – healthy.

'Letty! Will!' He held out his good arm in a wide greeting. 'I'm well. Be as good as new in a few weeks. There! That's all the medical chat you're going to get from me! Pa told me before you all trooped off together this morning that you have something to show me?' He eyed the box Theo and Gunning were setting down on the table at his side. 'Ah! You've brought me a dolly from Hamleys?'

'Don't let him play with it roughly, William! Things to attend to . . . I'll leave you young things to it,' said Theo. 'Lunch will be at one. Ah, here comes Eleni bearing another of your little messes, George.'

Eleni had entered quietly, carrying a tray laden with dishes and glasses.

'Mmm,' said Theodore, sniffing the air and miming distaste as the tray went by, 'more herb-scented porridge of some sort. Sure you wouldn't prefer a slice of roast beef, my boy? I'll carve you a slice if you like? No? Well, whatever she's feeding you, I have to say it seems to be working!' He nodded at Eleni and left.

'Thank you, Eleni,' was all George said, but the three words conveyed a wealth of meaning to Letty. She'd heard him say them before – automatic words spoken from master to servant. But now she heard them – hardly able, in their simplicity, to bear the weight of affection and intimacy which suffused them. She looked a question at Gunning. Should they withdraw? Find an excuse to leave?

315

He shook his head. At once she understood that for Eleni's sake at least they should stay. There were things she would want to convey to them.

Eleni moved to the chaise longue, leaned over, and straightened the blanket draped about his legs. 'Roast beef would be a good idea, George,' she murmured, 'if you feel like it. I'm sure Miss Talbot and Mr Gunning would agree?'

They both hurried to agree.

And then, at last, the touch. Tender, proprietorial. She briefly cupped his cheek in her hand as she passed. 'I know what I'll do! I'll cut off the top slice for you. The brown, crisp bit you like best, shall I?'

Letty smiled, intrigued to think that for years George had been the recipient of such little clandestine treats. He thanked her again and, with a last long look, Eleni left.

Letty had a vision of the two, no more than children, twelve years ago, half-orphans both, thrown together in this depressing house. Each looking out for the other. Eleni must have become everything for George – nurse, mother, sister, and eventually, lover. And soon to be mistress of the house?

'You're both aware of my changed circumstances?' George asked quietly when Eleni closed the door.

William went at once to his side and clasped his good hand in both his. 'We are, and, believe me, old man, we couldn't be more happy for you both!'

'We've seen Andreos and Teodoro,' said Letty. 'Wonderful boys! You're very blessed to have them.'

'I'm fetching them both home when the plaster comes off and I can get about a bit,' said George. 'Though I don't expect they'll be happy here, away from their grandmother and their friends. They can be wherever they're comfortable. I shall be a shockingly indulgent papa, I'm afraid!'

'Quite right, too!' said Letty. 'I have one such myself. I heartily recommend paternal indulgence. But now it's time for your treat, George. Prepare to be amazed! Open the box, William.'

They enjoyed George's chortle of surprise and wonder.

'Ouch! Poor chap! Know just how he feels! But this man's problems were caused by malice aforethought, are we saying? This was no chariot accident.'

'Yes. We've just been present at his autopsy. Stoddart would agree – a case of murder. But tell me – what does an anthropologist make of him?'

'I'm sure you've seen it. He's not Cretan. He's a foreigner, like me! In fact he could be my brother! Quite a shock – seeing him like this . . .' He laughed. '*Greenery-yallery, Grosvenor Gallery, Foot-in-the-fire young man.* Give him a floppy-brimmed hat and a Charvet scarf and set him down in Bloomsbury and no one will bat an eyelid! He has northern European ancestry. Looks more like anyone's idea of Apollo, I'd say – all that sun-gold hair! Lyre player rather than javelin hurler. Definitely the arty type! He'd have appealed to the womenfolk, wouldn't you agree, Letty?'

'Oh, yes! And how! I have my own theory about who this boy is but, I wondered, George, if his bracelet might give us a clue? Do you see it? It appears undamaged.'

Gunning passed him a magnifying glass and George peered at the incised top layer of the bracelet. 'Odd mixture of metals . . . clasped and welded together. We're in the Bronze Age but this black layer is iron, wouldn't you say? Probably viewed as rare and imbued with magical powers in those days. The top layer is silver, and when you've cleaned it up, I think you'll find it's engraved with . . .' He paused and peered, turned the box around for a better view, and said: 'It shows a scene of epiphany. Here's a young god revealing himself in human form . . . long wind-blown hair . . . ascending to heaven. He's rising up in front of what looks like a shrine and a sacred tree . . . olive probably. And there's something in his right hand. A spray of wheat or barley.' He passed the glass to Gunning.

'Ah! When he first came to light, I wondered if he might be a spring god,' said Letty, encouraged. 'You know – an Adonis, a Tammuz, Osiris . . . reigning cosseted in luxury for a year before he's destined to die. And his death

317

ensures that the crops continue to grow, children continue to fill the cradles . . .'

'Aphrodite's young lover, Adonis? Letty – what a perfectly capital notion! Why, yes . . . it makes splendid sense. *Adon* is a Semitic word. It means "lord". Connections between ancient Crete and the Semitic world are known to have existed . . . The agricultural peoples of the eastern Mediterranean believed the Corn Spirit, their lord, died to guarantee perpetual fertility. It's thought that living men died a violent death, representing the god. Their blood and their flesh fertilized, literally, the soil, and their spirits returned with the spring flowers and the sprouting wheat and barley.'

'Oh, good heavens!' said Letty, 'didn't Robert Burns have something sinister to say on the subject . . . John Barleycorn – ?'

'They wasted o'er a scorching flame/The marrow of his bones,' Gunning remembered. 'It makes grim reading!'

'And what do we see from up there in the place where he was buried?' George prompted.

'Yes, of course! At this moment of the year we see fields green with crops. Mile after mile of them – wheat, barley, vegetables, herbs, groves of olives and oranges. Stretching all the way back to Knossos. His domain. The Garden of Adonis.'

'I wonder how many young men have given up their lives in that place?' said George. And then, uneasily: 'Look, shall we agree not to tell Pa about Letty's mad theory? He wouldn't want to think Zeus had slipped through his fingers again. You should have heard him this morning! He's already planning his next publication! Lecture tour of Europe and lord knows what else! I've heard him rehearsing already – ranting on about the conflation of ideas in the primitive mind or some such . . . His thesis appears to be that the double discovery of temple and tomb on the same site indicates a confusion and blurring of image down the ages. The worship of the god and the burial of the priestess have been stirred together and have filtered down through folk story into written history as one intriguing Divine Burial. And, inevitably, Letty – and I must warn you to prepare yourself for this – he's planning that it shall go down in the annals as Theodore Russell's great discovery. And, of course, in his scenario, the King of the Gods is firmly restored to his Cretan throne.'

George paused, apologetic and embarrassed. 'Somehow, I don't think he'll be at all entertained by the notion that *his* Tomb of Zeus has, overnight, become *Letty's* Garden of Adonis.'

'Tin hats on?' suggested Gunning. And, suddenly earnest and with an uncharacteristic impatience: 'Look – *must* we endure more petty squabbling? Why can't everyone see what is so obvious? That it doesn't matter a jot whether the presumed Divine Being is wearing a skirt or a codpiece! Is the goddess or god brandishing an ear of wheat or a thunderbolt? Fascinating stuff, but it oughtn't to provoke a tap on the head with a fan, let alone an all-out battle for supremacy. These ancient people were sophisticated; they had a sense of humour and proportion. They would laugh and despair if they could see the dry bones of their civilization being snatched at and snarled over by the lapdogs of archaeology. They reached sublime heights of skill and invention. Their religious art expresses a joy, a power, and a freshness that must dazzle and humble all who see it, but more than this – it brings the Divinity down to earth.'

He glanced at the statue. 'This isn't an epiphany we're being privileged to see; it's not a god revealing himself. It's the opposite of that. This beautiful young boy is *descending*. He's here with us. Close to Man. He *is* Man.'

Chapter Thirty-Four

Letty wondered, as she crept down to the ground floor, how many crimes were committed in the hour of the siesta. She guiltily hoped that the one she was about to embark on wouldn't be discovered and go down in Mariani's records. It was a fortnight since Phoebe had died and Letty was no nearer to offering her Shade the solution she felt was demanded. She was conscious that the excitement of her discoveries at Kastelli had overshadowed the concerns of the Villa Europa, conscious also that this was welcomed and even engineered by Theodore. She was becoming increasingly a thorn in the man's side, an irritating and openly hostile presence who would not be tolerated for much longer.

There was one more thing she felt impelled to find out, something she had been promising herself she would do the moment the opportunity offered. And here it was at last. The Sunday lunch had been a traditionally heavy meal. Stifling a yawn, Theodore had retired to his room, as was his custom. Eleni had taken George off for a rest and Gunning had cheerfully allowed himself to be lured to the library by Dickie and Stewart, who were desperate to be filled in on the developments in Kastelli.

'Don't worry about me,' she'd said, settling down with a book in an armchair in the drawing room. 'I'm going to pretend to finish *War and Peace*.'

She reached the hall and stood for a moment listening to the sounds of the house, calculating where everyone would be and how long she had to carry out her search. She moved silently down the rear corridor, almost feeling the ball of thread in her hand as she crept towards Theodore's lair, as George had called his father's study. A draught caught the back of her neck in icy fingers, and continued on its way, trickling down her spine. She stopped and listened again. Had she heard a door open? Nothing more.

Reaching the door Gunning had told her belonged to Theo's room, she tapped discreetly twice and waited. Receiving no response, she turned the doorknob and pushed. Like all the other rooms in this house, the door did not have a lock. She slid inside. She knew exactly what she wanted to establish. Theodore Russell would not, according to Gunning, have had the knowledge of the text of *Hippolytus* to enable him – had he killed his wife – to select exactly the pages to act as her suicide note. And yet his skilful steering of Gunning through the implications had made Letty suspect otherwise.

Trembling at her presumption, she left the door slightly ajar, though the warning sound of boots ringing down the tiled corridor would be of little use to her. There was no other exit from this small room. A window looked out over the garden but offered no escape route. Vile old Dionysos, directly in line, caught her eye and scoffed. The sill was high and a large desk occupied the space below it.

The ordinariness of the room began to have a calming effect on her. There was nothing alarming here or even noteworthy. She sniffed the air. A not unpleasant smell of tobacco and a trace of something else . . . something chemical. She noticed a half-smoked pipe lying in an ashtray on the desk, whose surface was perfectly neat; inkwell, blotter, and pen tray were arranged with naval precision. Books lining two of the walls were in alphabetical order within their categories. A swift glance along the shelves told her what she wanted to know.

To the left of the desk, within easy reach, was a group of six textbooks. Their spines were familiar to her from her own schooldays: grammars, primers, dictionaries. She took out one she remembered: *An Approach to Ancient Greek*. It was well-thumbed with answers pencilled in over the questions at the end of each chapter. The name in the front was *Charles St George Russell*, but the writing in the body of the text was Theodore's. Encouraged, Letty looked further, finding on a low shelf a collection of Greek and Roman literature.

A self-taught classicist? A man too unconfident, too proud, to embark on a discussion with a scholar like Gunning who came with a glowing reputation from Professor Merriman? Russell would never engage in a struggle with a man he knew he could not outdo, she thought. Yes, he would keep quiet on this. Letty sighed. It seemed a petty and demeaning victory she had won over Theodore, and she started towards the door. Hand already on the doorknob, her attention was tugged back into the room by a feeling of unease. She glanced around again, trying to locate the source, and suddenly she had it – At the heart of this intimate space, this quiet retreat, was an *emptiness*. There were no photographs. None of wives, parents, not even one of George. There was one painting on the wall. She went closer, surprised to find an oil of the young Theodore himself in naval uniform.

The only other framed offering was more surprising. She crossed the room to examine it. It was, strangely, a half-page of yellowing print cut from a German newspaper. Letty could just make out that it carried the report of the sinking of a ferryboat attempting to cross the Rhine in June 1914. Thirty-five passengers, German and foreign, had lost their lives in the disaster. Someone had written at the bottom: *R.I.P. ILSE RUSSELL* and below that in a child's hand: *I love you, Mamma*.

In a room crowded with personal mementoes it would hardly have been remarkable but here it stood out, the last, perhaps the only, reminder of the death of a loved wife and mother in a far-off land. Bleak and touching, it was the one emotional note she could tune to. Letty felt tears start to scald her eyes, the unexpected tragedy calling to her over a waste of seas and time.

Turning to leave, she caught sight of an object tucked away to the side of the desk and she stopped in her tracks. A small Vuitton suitcase nestled there. Surely *her* suitcase? The luggage label was still attached to the handle so the question was easily answered. She picked up the case and put it down on the desk. Empty, as it should be, judging by its weight. And, yes, the label was hers, one of the shipping company's own, the blue and white of the Stella Maris line, giving her address at the Villa Europa on one side and, on the other, her return address c/o Professor Merriman in Athens. She had assumed it was safely stowed away in an attic somewhere with the rest of her luggage. What was it doing here in Theo's room? And when did he intend to return it to her?

She clicked the clasps and opened the case. The sight of the dark blue silk lining greeted her, but nothing else. Eleni had emptied it on her arrival and nothing so much as a hair grip remained. Letty felt inside the two ruched pockets in the lid. Nothing. She was about to close the case when she noticed the smell. Glue. There was quite a strong smell of glue trapped inside the small space. Full of suspicion, she began to slide her fingers along the lining until she found what she was looking for: a stiffness in the silk marked the place on the left side where the seam had been cut open and stuck down again. She poked at the area below and felt a flat but lumpy form. Reaching for the paper knife on the desk she slid it carefully along, reopening the incision. It put up a very poor resistance, damp as it still was with unset glue. The operation was obviously quite recent. As recent as this morning?

Letty reached inside and drew out a woman's stocking. Not one of hers. Phoebe's, perhaps? She shook the contents of the stocking out into the suitcase. Five small objects gleamed against the blue silk, making her catch her breath in astonishment. Mechanically, she made an inventory: a pair of gold earrings in the form of bulls' heads, a ring with a representation of the goddess in a boat, a chalcedony seal stone set in gold, and, most devastating, a broad gold

323

pendant showing the goddess with spreading arms, a dove settling on each wrist, lions curled at her feet. The delicately crafted jewel still bore, in its crevices, crumbs of earth from Juktas.

Letty stood staring, unable to move, sickened as the wickedness of Theodore's scheme became clear to her. He would plan to engineer her departure to suit himself and, as she made her way to the port with her things, a messenger would arrive with a discreet note. The customs official would have no difficulty in spotting her. He would, smiling, summon the police officer on duty to witness events when he asked the young English miss to open up her baggage.

And, even if she escaped arrest, at the very least the young English miss would, at a stroke, find her reputation in tatters, any thoughts of a career at an end. Even Andrew would find it difficult to support her in such circumstances, she guessed. The establishment would sympathize with Theodore, who would, more in sorrow than anger, make feeble attempts to account for her actions. 'Well, women and jewellery, you know . . . Too tempting . . . Young Miss fancied herself as Sophia Schliemann, no doubt.'

She was standing holding the betraying pendant in her hand when she heard a heavy tread along the corridor. An unmistakable tread. Letty flinched and, ridiculously, looked about her for a weapon. Not even a doorstop presented itself.

Chapter Thirty-Five

And then, a shout along the corridor. A peremptory call. 'Sir! Mr Russell! It's found! You left your pipe up in the drawing room. Miss Talbot found it under the chair. She's about the house somewhere, looking for you to return it.'

The footsteps had halted. Theodore turned, grumbling. 'Thank you, Eleni. I'll go in pursuit. Though I'll probably get my head bitten off. And be subjected to a lecture on the evils of tobacco.' He stomped off back towards the stairs.

Letty swiftly replaced the contraband and pressed the lining together as best she could. She put the case back where she'd found it. A time bomb is no danger if you know where and when it's likely to go off. She'd let him go on thinking he had the upper hand for a while longer.

Before she left the room, she paused to pick up his pipe and put it away in her pocket, breathing her own thanks to Eleni. The Spirit of the House, Gunning had called her fancifully. Not necessarily the compliment he had intended, Letty felt, now she knew the house better, but it was good to think that someone in this malevolent place was looking out for her.

Her examination of the room had thrown up as many questions as it had solved but, with renewed vigour and knowing at last exactly what she had to do, Letty made her plans for the rest of the day. Plans that included a trip to the offices of the Stella Maris line at the port and an audience at the embassy if she could arrange it at such short notice. Depending on what she found there, a consultation with Inspector Mariani would follow. She had, since

Phoebe's death, been haunted, been harried, been drained by a need to find out the truth, and she thought she was within a whisker of turning up the evidence she needed. There could be only pain ahead, and most of it for others, but she was contemplating a noxious and growing boil that needed to be lanced, and as skilfully as possible. Mariani could do it. He had the instruments to hand. All she had to do was place them in his capable fingers.

The urgent knocking came at the door at six-thirty. Gunning, passing through the hallway in search of an ashtray, remembered Eleni was busy putting George to bed and the rest of the household was already in the drawing room having cocktails with Phoebe's younger sister and her French husband. They had chosen to stay in a hotel nearby during their stay on the island, rather than under Theo's roof. Good move, Gunning thought. Alice clearly disliked and mistrusted Theodore, and Theo had, in an aside to Gunning, described the pair as the leeches who were making off with his money. A potentially awkward party. Letty, who, strangely, seemed determined to enjoy herself, had set him the task of oiling the social wheels, being the life and soul and a few other impossibilities. Young Alice and her husband had turned out to be a charming and entertaining couple and he found, to his surprise, that he was annoyed by the threat of an interruption. He actually wanted to return to the gathering. He didn't want to greet whoever was on the other side of the door.

He opened it anyway and in rushed Harry Stoddart.

'Oh, hello, Harry. Come to see George? You're a bit late – he's just going to bed.'

'No, no! It's not George I'm concerned for. I'm quite sure he's in good hands or I wouldn't have released him. I would have come earlier – should have come earlier – but . . . there's been a problem. I need Laetitia. Please, will you summon Laetitia at once?'

'Not sure I can spare her, old boy,' said Gunning doubtfully. 'Not sure she'd want to leave the party. She's all dolled up in her best oyster silk what d'ye call'ems? Evening pyjama suit? Would that be it? Pearls down to her bum, you know the sort of thing. And on to her third cocktail by now.'

Harry was getting increasingly agitated. 'I don't care if she's in a rabbit suit or her birthday suit – she's got to come to the jail with me. Right now! It's Ollie! Mariani called by the house half an hour ago with his henchmen and they took Ollie away with them. They've got her in the lockup! Ollie's been arrested!'

'Ollie's got herself arrested? On a Sunday evening in Herakleion?' Gunning was disposed to laugh. 'That takes a bit of doing! What on earth's the charge?'

Harry could hardly allow the words to pass his gritted teeth: '*Disturbing the peace,*' he admitted. 'And *affray* – whatever that is. Lucky, I suppose, that they stopped short of a wounding charge but they could see that was never going to stick – the man could still walk.'

'Harry?' said Gunning faintly.

'She went for one of the coppers. Had the sense to keep her hands off Mariani but his sergeant really annoyed her. She, er, well, you must have noticed the elephant's foot umbrella stand in the hall?'

'Used it many a time, old boy. It's an arresting object,' said Gunning, guessing the outcome.

Harry glowered. 'It's not a laughing matter. She picked it up – must weigh a ton – that's how angry she was, and she dropped it on the man's foot.'

'Ouch!' said Gunning, cringing.

'Well, damage not too bad, considering . . . police boots being what they are. But, listen, William – that's not the worst of it. No, not by a long chalk. The "affray" is a holding charge. Just an excuse to get her down there and grill her. They've got their sights on her for something much, much more sinister.'

'Grievous bodily harm?'

'No, no! Murder! To be precise: murdering Phoebe. I know . . . I know . . . Piece of ridiculous nonsense! But Mariani was very sure of himself, and quite determined to get her away from the house, and me, to frighten her into a confession. Huh! He doesn't know Olivia!' Stoddart said with an odd flash of pride. 'She'll give him what for! But the officious fool wouldn't allow me to accompany her. Must have thought I'd speak for her, prompt her or something. She's quite capable of speaking for herself. But it's not right, hauling a chap's wife off into the night like that without so much as a toothbrush. I threatened. I pleaded. I called his bridge club membership into question. I finally got through to him using a lever Ollie herself would not have approved of: impropriety.'

'You've lost me, Harry.'

'In this town, you can't have it known that you've interviewed a lady by herself in a prison cell. Just not done. When he calmed down – I must say Ollie was being rather vociferously uncooperative – enough to raise anybody's blood pressure – he saw the sense of this and agreed to a chaperone. Only one name would satisfy the inspector, however. Mariani insists on Laetitia! He will accept none other.'

Harry looked for a moment at Gunning with speculation. 'I say, William . . . not something going on there as shouldn't be, eh?'

Gunning put on a knowing expression. 'Let's hope there *is*, Harry. I must say – I had wondered myself . . . It could all work to our advantage, don't you think? Look, I'll fetch her out and you must mark her card. I shall insist on escorting her there – and back again. I'm damned if that young squirt is going to hold on to Letty as well.'

Letty decided the inspector was already regretting his use of shock tactics by the time she presented herself at the police lockup down by the harbour. He looked subdued and hunted. He was pacing about by himself in an office and Ollie was sitting quietly in the adjoining cell, staring through the bars, looking, Letty thought, like Queen Victoria who has just detected a blocked drain in the Palace.

Gunning waved a reassuring hand at her and she nodded in acknowledgement. He then, and largely for Olivia's reassurance, went into a very English speech, genial, disarmingly cooperative, setting out for Mariani his expectations and requirements. Mariani assured Gunning that his niece would be treated with the highest respect. To his credit, Gunning didn't twitch an eyebrow, let alone send a wounded look at Letty. It was acknowledged that her participation in the interview was deeply appreciated. Compliments were exchanged. One officer to another before they went over the top, Letty thought. They even checked their watches together. Satisfied that the ground rules were clear, he retreated with Harry to the Stoddart house to ply him with whisky.

Mariani was pleased to see her. He rolled his eyes in a conspiratorial dismissal of the preceding flummery and got down to business. 'Miss Talbot. So glad you could come and accompany your friend. Mrs Stoddart has, I assure you, come along willingly to help me with my further enquiries into the death of Mrs Russell.'

An irritated 'Pshaw!' from the cell cast some doubt on this.

'She has not been arrested. My injured officer will not be pressing charges. It is important that I have her evidence and her account of her activities on that afternoon with reference to no other person – forgive me – including yourself. May I ask you to remain silent until I address you?'

'Yes, of course,' Laetitia agreed, more puzzled by the minute. She sensed that Mariani was questioning his precipitate action but he must, she calculated, have had a good reason for it. If intimidating Ollie was part of his plan, it wasn't working and the inspector was going to have to salvage what he could.

He went to the door of the cell and asked politely, 'Would you mind letting us in, Mrs Stoddart? We're ready to begin.'

Olivia glared and pulled away the chair she'd wedged against the door.

The women settled down opposite Mariani around a small table. Letty attempted to squeeze Olivia's hand encouragingly, but Olivia snatched it away.

'Now, tedious, I know, but would you please go over the timing of your return from Knossos on the Sunday afternoon when Mrs Russell was taken ill? Miss Talbot was with you on that occasion and has given her evidence.'

'Ah!' thought Letty. 'He's using me to keep Ollie on the straight and narrow path of truth. But then – why would she want to stray from it?'

Olivia accounted for her movements until she had said goodbye to Laetitia on her doorstep. That would have been at about two o'clock and Letty would confirm this. Letty nodded. She then went to the kitchen to make a cup of tea and had a snooze in her armchair, as she usually did on a Sunday. Harry must have got back at some time, because the next thing she was conscious of was a messenger from the Russells shouting and banging on about an accident at the house and demanding his instant attention.

'Yes. I accept that you were on your doorstep at two o'clock – an estimated hour before Mrs Russell died. It was a lively Sunday – a festival under way and many people and traders up from the country especially to join in,' said Mariani. Letty nodded again in agreement.

'I and my officers joined the crowds at the same time today – a Sunday likewise – noting the traders and others who might have been there in the streets at the same time on the fateful day. So soon after the event, they had not forgotten what business they did, what clients they'd seen, strangers who'd passed. Miss Talbot was commented on and described by several. And so, Mrs Stoddart, were you.'

Olivia's cheeks, mottled red with indignation, began to lose their colour.

'It took you, Miss Talbot, half an hour to return home to the Villa Europa, wandering as you did, past the boutiques along the busy avenue. It took my officer six and a half minutes following alleyways away from the crowds. But along these less used streets the inhabitants of the houses take a keener interest in passers-by than the ones who live on a busy thoroughfare. They sit on their doorsteps and watch what little of the world goes by, go by. We traced your passage along several streets, all heading by the quickest and most secluded route to the Europa.'

He flourished sheets of paper. 'I have sworn statements if you care to see them. We start with Mr Pappandreiou, who runs the bakery . . .'

Olivia shrugged her indifference.

'You reached the Villa Europa at two-fifteen, give or take a minute either way. You were seen not to approach the front door but to slip into the coach house alongside. From there, access to the rear courtyard and the open door of the library is available to all who choose to try. Mrs Russell's bedroom is also accessible by means of an obliging wistaria, as has been ably demonstrated, I understand, by Miss Talbot's disabled uncle. We must assume therefore that any reasonably able-bodied and determined intruder could have taken the same route. I must ask you, Mrs Stoddart: Why did you set off at once for the Europa and, having got there, did you enter the house? Having gained access, did you murder your friend Phoebe?'

Letty broke her vow of silence. 'I'm sure you're not obliged to answer those questions, Olivia. Your answers could be very incriminating. I advise you to keep quiet until you can summon a lawyer in the morning.'

'Don't concern yourself, Laetitia! I don't need counsel. The truth will speak for itself.'

Olivia couldn't have cared less what the inspector's opinion of her was, but Letty noticed she directed a defiant gaze sideways at her and she was troubled by it.

'Pretty obvious, I'd have thought! Adultery not an entirely new concept on the island, Inspector? King Minos is reputed to have suffered similarly. I suspected that my husband was having an affair with Mrs Russell and was determined to catch them out. In flagrante delicto if at all possible. In circumstances leaving no room for denial or argument. And who knows? If only Miss Talbot, here, had been able to cycle faster, I might have managed it!' she finished with a savage glance at Letty.

Letty was aghast. The thought of Olivia leaping from the wisteria crying, 'Aha! Unhand my husband!' or whatever people shout in these circumstances, was horrifying.

'I felt the bonnet of the car. The engine had cooled. So – they hadn't, at least, stopped en route for a little hanky-panky, I calculated. They must be still up there in her room.' She paused, pleased with her insight and waiting for this to be acknowledged by the inspector. Mariani had the good grace to nod in understanding. 'I went into the courtyard and listened under Phoebe's window. I knew where it was, of course – she called herself my friend – she'd treated me to the tour of her vast wardrobe, even generously selected a few items she thought might suit me.'

The grating resentment in the older woman's voice was beginning to chill Letty.

'I tell you this because, with your ear for backstairs gossip, Inspector, you will have little difficulty in establishing that I was familiar with the first-floor rooms.

'There was no sound. I must say I felt very exposed there in the garden. Windows on all sides, it's hardly the place you'd choose to skulk unseen. Like being onstage. The tree was inviting and I would have given much to catch the treacherous harlot at her games, but I didn't. She betrayed me! I'm not sorry she's dead. But I didn't kill her. I went away the way I'd come.'

'Tell me, Mrs Stoddart, what brought about this change of heart?'

'Not what – *who*! I was accosted in the courtyard – staring up at the window, assessing my chances – by that ruffian who seems to have appointed himself family guard dog. The big Cretan who's so close to George and William Gunning.'

'Aristidis, you mean?' Letty broke her silence again.

'That's the one! Lout! He came swaggering through the coach house, bold as brass, whistling, plonked himself down on the statue of Dionysos – whom he much resembles – in the middle of the courtyard, and lit a cigarette. Waiting to see Gunning and Miss Talbot, he said, when I challenged him. Business to discuss. Been waiting all morning. Then, having given an account of himself, it occurred to him to wonder what I was doing there. He's not stupid. And, as I say, loyal to the family. He became uneasy with my presence and escorted me off the premises, practically growling. What cheek! So – if you want further and better particulars, Inspector, you must interview your disreputable compatriot. If he's in a mood not to lie to the forces of law and order, he will tell you I left the villa at two thirty-five – or five cigarettes after the noon bell of St Minas sounded.'

Mariani made the mistake of catching Letty's eye and was ambushed by his Cretan sense of the ridiculous. His shoulders began to shake. He pulled out a handkerchief and spluttered into it. He pretended to take notes. He was lost for words.

Letty sighed. 'If I weren't already up to my ears in love, this man would be in some danger,' she thought. She decided to step into the gap. 'Ollie! This is quite disgraceful behaviour! You should have confided in the inspector earlier. You have cost him a week's work. Really! You are much to blame. If I were you, I'd apologize to Inspector Mariani for wasting his time and injuring his officer, and then go straight home to Harry and beg his forgiveness.'

A clamour at the door was seized upon by Mariani as his release. The inspector shot to his feet and went to open up. Stoddart bustled in, come to collect his wife. 'Mr Gunning's on his way, Laetitia,' he informed her as Olivia swept in glacial silence from the cell. 'I say, would you like me to wait until he gets here?' he asked, casting a reproving look at the inspector.

Letty made a show of getting to her feet and collecting her things together, declining his offer. Kind but quite unnecessary.

As soon as the Stoddarts had left, Letty sat down again and began to speak urgently. 'I was trying to find you for most of the afternoon! I thought I wasn't going to be able to see you before tomorrow. Listen! I've found out a thing or two – bribery still works well, I discover, in the Levant! I'm just surprised you weren't called on to come and arrest me at the port this afternoon! One official got quite suspicious. Anyway – there are things that simply ought to be clarified. And I think you're the man who can do this. I've got as far as I can without a quantity of gold braid on my shoulder. You will have to take it further. Now . . .'

Gunning arrived to find them sitting in the cell, heads together, still deep in conversation. 'I trust my niece has behaved herself,' he drawled sarcastically.

'Impeccably as always.' Mariani was gracious. 'A fruitful interview . . . which exculpates Mrs Stoddart from any involvement and sets me on another trail.'

'Another trail?' said Gunning as they made their way back to the Europa. 'Now who's he got in his sights?'

'Aristidis! Ollie found him loitering – or rather *he* caught *her*, loitering with intent – in the courtyard at the crucial time. He may have seen something. Those eagle eyes of his don't miss much. He was quickly on to Ollie and saw her off the premises. But at least his word should cancel out any remaining suspicion of Olivia's involvement.'

'Thank God for that! Was she intending to do bodily harm to Phoebe and/or Harry or just scare them to death, I wonder?'

'Hard to say. She probably didn't even know herself. But she has a terrible temper. Remember the mess in Harry's surgery? And people do extraordinary things for love. She was in love with her, you know. In love with Phoebe.'

'I had guessed as much,' said Gunning quietly. 'Poor old Ollie!'

'Poor old Harry!'

Chapter Thirty-Six

'Do you know – I've never viewed the scene of the crime – if crime it was – from the courtyard,' said Letty as they approached the Europa. 'It's not quite dark yet and the rooms are ablaze with light. Shall we?'

'You're just determined to lure me off somewhere secluded.'

'Well, yes, I'm sure you're dying to get back to the party, but I thought I'd try for just a little longer by ourselves. Hold your hand. So often wanted to. Let's not go back inside, just yet?'

They made their way through the coach house, where nothing but a patch of oil marked the place where the Bugatti had gleamed. Theodore's modest Ford took up very little space at the far end. They tiptoed through the fusty darkness, steering by the moon showing through the fanlight over the side door, and let themselves out into the lemon-scented garden.

'Now, let's be Ollie and Aristidis. Odd pairing! I'll go and sigh and fume up at the window and you swagger in and sit down, there, on Dionysos.'

Letty sighed and Gunning swaggered. He lit a cigarette and then caught sight of Letty, who turned and advanced on him, mouthing a challenge.

Gunning laughed and moved over to join her. 'Well, yes. I can see why Aristidis would have been a little spooked. You do look as though you're lurking with some intent or other. And she would have held back from blasting him with her usual halloo. That would have puzzled him. He wouldn't be accustomed to the sight of Olivia about the place in the rear quarters in the daytime, anyway. She's definitely what you'd call front door calling company. What's more, knowing her and the state she was in, I expect she hissed something quite offensive to Aristidis. It's not like him to be brusque with women. Anyhow – Mariani will interview him now in greater depth and sort it all out, man to man, Cretan to Cretan.'

'Do you think we should warn Aristidis he's about to have the spotlight shone up his nose?'

'Oh, I don't think so. They'll probably have a good laugh at Olivia's expense. But Mariani will want to know – I imagine – who else Aristidis noticed coming or going or standing still around the same time. If we think about it – he could have been right here when poor Phoebe was dying up in her room. Did he leave after shooing Olivia away or did he return? Either way, he may have seen something significant and not even be aware of it. Time – it has an elasticity and an unregimented character for Cretans. He might not have realized there was something going on.'

Letty shivered and clutched her cashmere wrap more closely around her shoulders. She was responding not only to the sudden chill whisper of a breeze that set the leaves trembling but to the deeper atmosphere of the place. She caught the leering eye of the stone Dionysos, wide-mouthed, wild-haired, and malignant. Sympathetic to the drunken character of its subject, the slablike statue leaned slightly to one side. Gunning went to perch on it and Letty pulled him away, scarcely knowing why she did so.

'Had enough of this ghost of a garden?'

'Garden? I'd hardly call it a garden! All this coy statuary! It's more like my aunt Joan's pets' cemetery. Or a mausoleum. There's something so posed . . . so mad about it all. I can almost hear someone laughing to see us standing about. Is there some sort of message we ought to be picking up?'

She pointed to the marble Artemis, unseen apart from her left toe and her gilded arrowhead. 'The Virgin Huntress would appear to be about to shoot dead the Goddess of Love. She, silly creature, is mesmerized by her own image and is completely unaware of the ambush from behind the laurel. The whole tableau is a murder frozen in stone.'

'And who's having the last laugh?' Gunning joined in her speculation. 'Ghastly old Dionysos!' He gave the bristling stone head a friendly pat. 'Mad as a hatter? Under the influence of something stronger than the grape? Whatever his problem, you can see, he plainly hates both "wimmin", as old Theo might say.'

'Well, I'm not comfortable here.' Letty shivered again. 'Even Ollie was uneasy, but then, she had retribution on her mind at the time. I feel ... things? ... people? ... crowding round, tugging at me for my attention. "It's a blood-soaked soil," George told me. And, standing here, you can imagine the "dead, ten deep, clutching at our ankles". Only one thing to loosen their ancient grip – action! I'm going to climb that tree!' On impulse, she kicked off her shoes and handed her wrap to Gunning. She walked to the foot of the writhing wisteria and began to haul herself upwards.

'Letty! Come down at once! You'll ruin your folderols! You'll be found hanging by your pearls in the morning! They'll drag me off in irons!' He paced about, anxiously, arms extended to break her fall, talking nervous nonsense, expecting her to crash to the ground at any moment, but she jumped back down five minutes later, hardly out of breath. 'You were right, William. As trees go – that's the nursery slopes. It's been constantly trimmed back at the top. It's grown outwards and upwards into a cup shape so it frames the window prettily, but it also makes a stable place to sit while you're planning your next move. Ideal spot for a Peeping Tom.'

'No such thing on the island.'

'Or an assassin.'

338

'Ah. Not short of those. But who from the outside would want to kill Phoebe?'

'We've been thinking about this from the wrong angle. We ought to have asked first – *Who knew she was there?* Remember she came back unexpectedly early. We weren't due back until teatime or later.'

'Apart from the Stoddarts, Eleni knew. She let them in. The only member of the household who was at home was Theo himself.'

'Sleeping on the other side of the unlocked door,' said Letty.

'Ah, we've come full circle! You've always fancied Theo for this.'

'He had reason to kill her – profit, anger, and revenge (if he'd discovered what she was up to) and he has the brute strength and coldness of heart to carry it through. But . . .'

'Something's bothering you, Letty?'

'I was just wondering. If Aristidis came back and heard something – a quarrel, Phoebe screaming, Theo bellowing – he'd have confided in you, wouldn't he, William?'

Gunning was silent for a moment. 'I honestly think he would. But more than that – you know the man well by now. If he thought a woman was in danger – from a snake or her husband – he'd intervene. In fact, he'd relish the chance to knock Theo to the ground with justification. He was, like the rest of us, fond of Phoebe. He wouldn't have stood by and let her die.' He had caught Letty's anxiety and added, 'Look, we'll be seeing him again on Tuesday morning when we've got over all this funeral business. I doubt Mariani will have got to him by then, as he's turning up on parade at the funeral tomorrow. We'll ask Aristidis to come and see us at his mother's house before we start work, shall we? Clear the air? Now, come on back inside and help me to get through this ghastly evening, will you? But, first, let's give the jealous shades a reminder of what they're missing in the way of fleshly comfort up here in the world above.'

He pulled her into a close embrace from which she emerged some minutes later warm, breathless, and dishevelled. Even Dionysos, she thought, was looking slightly aghast.

'Coffee!' announced Maria comfortably. 'If we're all going to sit around the table having a serious discussion about Kyrie Russell, we'll need some more to fortify ourselves! I'll put the pot on again.'

Aristidis flung an indulgent glance at his mother as she slipped away to busy herself at the kitchen range. 'Do you mind if she stays?' he whispered. 'There are things only she knows about this affair and you will find what she has to say interesting.'

Puzzled, they both nodded.

'Now,' he went on, 'you're warning me that I am to be questioned by Mariani and his men? Well, that's fine by me,' he said cheerfully. 'The innocent need fear nothing, I'm sure. I have the greatest regard for the inspector's ability to get at the truth. He's well respected on the island. I shall endeavour to assist him.'

'If I were him, I'd start by wanting to know exactly why you were in the courtyard at the time in question, Aristidis,' said Gunning. 'Do you have any objection to telling us?'

'None at all! Though as my mother is intimately concerned with my motives and my movements on that day, I will leave an explanation until she arrives with our coffee. But while we're waiting, I will tell you, because I see you are both suffering the torments of curiosity, what I was doing in the courtyard. I was there under the window for one purpose only on that day. I had come to kill Theodore Russell.'

Gunning's voice was commendably matter-of-fact: 'Ah. Here comes a pot of the best Greek coffee! Maria, that smells delicious! We were just hearing your son admitting to a desire to eliminate his employer. I have to say – we've all been tempted.'

Maria poured with a steady hand and handed out the tiny cups. 'For once he is not joking, Kyrie William. But you must forgive him; it was not his choice. He was sent by someone else to wreak vengeance on this monster for a crime committed by him many years ago. *I* sent my son to kill him.'

She moved to the sideboard and selected the sepia photograph of her dead husband. 'I will place him here with us while we talk.'

The silver-framed photograph joined them, a fifth person at the table, smiling and handsome. Fez at a jaunty angle, bristling Cretan features fearless and challenging, the man's strong presence leapt the gap of thirty years.

'This is all about Ioannis. I told you, miss, that he died in the revolt of 1898. True. An unjust and violent death,' Maria began her story.

'We were trapped in the city in Candia, that hot August. And worse, trapped in the Greek quarter. We'd gone to a family funeral, in our country ignorance, with our country ways, not realizing just how quickly and violently a killing spree can be unleashed in a densely packed city. It took all of us by surprise, not least the Turkish cousins who found themselves trapped with us. The last place anyone would want to be. We Christians were outnumbered by ten to one. The violence started, the burnings, the killings, the rapes and pillage. Ioannis decided the only thing for it was for me and Aristidis to try to escape dressed as Muslims. Word came that Muslim women and their children were being allowed to run away into the country through the gates, unchallenged. Our cousins, anxious not to be caught harbouring Greeks, put their hands on some female robes and veils and, though he would have preferred to stay and fight alongside his father, we managed to persuade Aristidis, who was only ten at the time, to put on a little girl's garments and try for it.'

Aristidis took up the tale. 'The big gates were in sight and were standing open. I peered round the corner, huddled at my mother's side, clutching a fold of her robe, as I'd been told . . .' he remembered.

'. . . I know my mother saw him one more time but she has never spoken to me of it,' he finished with a tender and beseeching look for Maria. 'And I wonder if she is ready to tell me now?'

'Ioannis went off to speak up for his cousin. He was a lawyer, fluent in Greek, Turkish, and Italian. But none of these got him very far with the people he had to deal with: the British. They had come in and taken control of the city. Killing, except for their authorized executions, had ceased. But they had a crime to avenge. Seventeen of their soldiers had been massacred by a Turkish mob and they intended to round up the ringleaders and ceremonially execute them. The same number were to hang from the tree the Turks used. Sending a message.

'Suleiman was arrested. I don't even know if he was guilty. Ioannis arrived to plead for him and was shown into the presence of the British officer deputed to deal with the problem. Ioannis was wearing a fez. Many Christians did. Many Christians were actually converts to Mohammedanism – to evade the extortionate taxes – but they still prayed in church every Sunday. It was a confused time. And one cannot wonder too much that the British themselves were confused. But the young officer, taking Ioannis for a Muslim and an argumentative one at that, though he did not understand a word he said, ordered his immediate arrest. He had reached sixteen suspects in number and needed one more for the execution to take place. My husband became the seventeenth prisoner.

'I went at once to plead for my husband. I was met with indifference and annoyance by the officer. I was not allowed to see Ioannis. He ordered his men to throw me out.

'But yes, I did see my husband one more time. Dangling from the plane tree.' Maria's tale ground to a half. She turned to her son, her eyes pleading and apologetic.

'My mother fled the town and would never return until a month ago.' Aristidis snatched the tale from his mother, sensing that her courage was losing the struggle with grief. 'I persuaded her to go in to my cousin's wedding. The town was much changed. I thought she would have no bad memories after all this time. But she had the worst possible reminder. Outside the church, she saw and recognized the officer who had ordered my father's death. It was Theodore Russell, walking by with his wife. A respected member of society and – my employer. I had no idea. All these years I had worked for the man who killed my father.'

'It is a son's duty to avenge his father.' Maria's head went up, full of pride. 'It is expected. It is necessary, if he is to keep his honour and that of his family. If he continues to fail to do it, I shall complete the circle myself. I shall make this snake eat its tail.'

Letty believed her.

'I waited for a moment when I knew there would be no one in the house but Russell himself and Eleni doing her household chores in the pantry,' Aristidis said. 'I had the entrée to the house – no one ever challenged me. I came and went as I pleased. I talked to the servants . . . I knew where everyone was likely to be at any moment in the day and whether they kept their doors locked or unlocked. But I had no intention of being caught out. I walked, behaving as I normally would, into the courtyard.' He smiled. 'Slinking and concealment do not come naturally to me and would have drawn attention. I intended to climb the tree and get into his room and stab him with my father's dagger.'

Letty stared, fascinated, at the silver hilt gleaming in his cummerbund across the breakfast table, between the coffeepot and the bread basket. She'd last seen its blade slicing through the neck of a snake, she remembered. The same dagger was proudly worn by Ioannis in his photograph. It had done its lethal work on those hot August nights thirty years ago and remained charged with one more task.

'George's car was in the coach house but I thought nothing of that – I knew he'd gone with William on foot to the cave on the coast. But there was an interruption. The doctor's wife was hanging about and I had first to send her away. I couldn't imagine why she was loitering there but I suspected she was up to no good. I returned and climbed into the tree. When I got to the top, just below the level of the sill, I froze. There were voices speaking in the room. I decided to stay still. If I'd been found I would not have liked to explain myself to Russell. He is a man eaten up by jealousy and suspicion. He might well have turned on his own wife.

'But it was no more than the good doctor Stoddart. He prescribed a sleeping pill for her ... Eleni came in and brought some water, and I assumed Mrs Russell was dutifully taking the pill. After a while the doctor left. I decided to wait until the sleeping tablet had worked and then creep in and let myself into Russell's bedroom adjoining. I knew he took a siesta there every Sunday afternoon. I knew the door was kept unlocked. But then, as I was about to make my move, I heard Mrs Russell sigh. She got off the bed and began to pace about. I heard her walk to the door. She moved around, sighing and muttering the while, for a few more minutes. She was praying, I'm sure. And then she went over to her desk. The next thing I heard was the sound of a chair falling over. I didn't guess what she was doing and when I risked an eye over the sill, I didn't at first see her. Then I caught sight of her twitching limbs hanging at the far end of the room, right by her husband's door. No one else had entered the room. No one had left the room.'

'Oh, my God!' Letty whispered. 'She did do it herself! She committed suicide.' She put her head in her hands in distress. 'Oh, Phoebe, forgive me! Did I wilfully misunderstand? I don't know. William . . .' Letty struggled with her memory. Only the strictest accuracy would do now. 'Her very last words to me were: "Time to go." It was *after* she'd said, "I'll be sure to test you when you get back." I've been deceiving myself, as well as everyone else. She was just making social noises, telling me to be a good pupil, saying what she would normally say. Her real message, I chose to ignore. "You've had your fun . . . Time to go now." I think she knew all along that Stoddart wouldn't help her. There was no other way out. I didn't mention it because it didn't fit with my theory. I *wanted* Theodore to be guilty.'

Aristidis breathed deeply, waiting for her outburst to end, impatient at the interruption. 'Wait! You must judge yourself, Miss Laetitia, when I have finished. And you must prepare for a painful outcome. She was dangling from the beam but she wasn't dead. She made a sound – a sickening gurgling noise. Worse – her arms suddenly went up to the rope and she tried to pull herself upwards to release her neck. In agony? Regretting her action? Men have been known to thrash around in a noose for many minutes before death.'

He acknowledged the insensitivity of his remark by covering his mother's trembling hand with his own. 'But I was glad to see it – there was time for me to save her! I had one leg over the sill to leap into the room and cut her loose when the door burst open. And there he was. Theodore Russell. Not at all sleepy and confused. He'd been listening, I thought, as I had. He hurled himself towards her and I shrank back down with relief. He had eyes only for his wife in her agony – he hadn't seen me. No need now to reveal myself. Her husband would rescue her from her folly.'

Aristidis paused, finding it difficult to choose the words to continue. 'He put his hands up around her thighs and heaved. But not upwards. He swung his whole weight down on that slender woman and I heard her neck break.

Then he padded over to the desk and I heard the rustling of papers. A minute later he went back into his own room. He closed the door.'

The stunned silence was broken by Maria clucking with irritation. 'A wasted opportunity, don't you agree, William?'

Chapter Thirty-Seven

'Um ... not entirely sure I'm following you, Maria,' said Gunning, stunned and apologetic for his confusion.

'He should have proceeded! He could have killed Russell in such a way as to make it appear the man had hung his wife and then done away with himself. What could be more obvious? It's what I would have done.'

'I sometimes think I'm being a great disappointment to my mother,' said Aristidis with a smile full of affection for the stiff old lady.

Letty had got up in a whirl of mixed emotions and gone over to the window to hide her disgust, pity, fear, and hatred. She was remembering her own instinctive dash forward to lift, to save, to fight with Death for Phoebe's precious essence, and she tried to imagine what depth of hatred it could have taken to pull down instead, to listen for the snap of her neck. Hatred or self-interest? A deadly combination?

She heard Gunning's voice, measured, practical: 'And are you intending to communicate this evidence to Mariani when he appears, Aristidis?'

She didn't wait to hear his reply. 'Well, here's your chance,' she said, staring out down the street, 'because here he comes. At least I think it's him ... Alone, for once. No attendants. And he's not in uniform – he's wearing Cretan clothes. Dressed for the country, you might say.'

She continued to watch as the inspector trotted up the cobbled street on a tall chestnut. He was greeted at the door by Maria, who went herself to tether the horse behind the house. Aristidis's wide-armed gesture at once welcomed him and dispelled the tense atmosphere in the room. Gunning waved the coffeepot enticingly.

The inspector was pleased to see them; the inspector was jovial and hearty. He exchanged a warm glance with Letty and gave an imperceptible nod before flinging his cape over a chair back and sitting down at the table. He accepted gratefully the glass of water offered, the cup of black coffee, and a chunk of fresh bread from the basket. 'No, no!' he responded at once to Gunning's suggestion that he be left alone with Aristidis. 'I'm delighted to find you all together, plotting and planning, no doubt. I take it that you, Aristidis, my friend, have been put, as they say, in the picture, concerning certain allegations made against you by the doctor's wife . . .? Good, that saves my time. Off you go, then – start from there.'

He listened with few interruptions to Aristidis's account, the ground gone over rather faster than the first time, since no allowances or explanations had to be made for lack of local knowledge. They rattled away in Greek and Letty quickly became lost, though she sensed Gunning was managing to hold on to the thread.

Finally – 'I think I can help you,' said Mariani, reverting to English. 'Impossible, as all would agree, to charge Russell for the murder of his wife, Phoebe, since she herself initiated her own death and we have the coroner's verdict of suicide, which would be, in any case, difficult to overturn. Aristidis, I am assuming, would refuse to appear as witness, disappearing into the hills, no doubt, at a moment's notice.' He raised a quizzical eyebrow.

'Naturally,' said Maria firmly as she re-entered.

'Cretan that I am, you must excuse me for understanding, at least, the compulsion to rid the world of Mr Russell, though I hurry to say I do not condone it and will never support or conceal such an attempt.'

Letty wondered.

'But there are more ways than one of skinning a cat,' he

said thoughtfully. 'Aristidis! Maria! Your need for vengeance stems from a hanging? Would this ancient injustice be avenged, your grief be assuaged, by a *further* hanging? I think that is exactly what I may be in a position to offer. Retribution – but without a drop of blood on your own hands?'

He caught sight of Letty's anguished face and hurried to add: 'A perfectly lawful proceeding, Miss Talbot! Do not concern yourself! I am not planning a country lynching party! But a man like Russell, a violent, arrogant, and mischievous man – if he did indeed kill his wife, and it was always my strongest suspicion – he is likely to have committed earlier crimes in his lifetime. I had not known about his treatment of your father, Aristidis, or I would have added that to my list of his sins.'

'Your list?' Gunning questioned.

'I'm thorough in my investigations,' said Mariani blandly. 'If a person takes my interest, I investigate him.' He turned and looked at Gunning until he saw in his face the doubt and suspicion he had intended to sow, and went on, 'Many records of business activities, shipping lists, newspaper cuttings, police and military reports are available to me should I be *inspired* to consult them.' He smiled at Letty. 'Filing cabinets fly open at my request. I investigated Russell. And I found something disquieting in his past. His past here on the island – I cannot answer for his previous life. And my suspicious mind began to pull together facts and weave them into a story. A story grotesque and distressing. And, in the light of what you now tell me, Aristidis, about this man's conduct, I think it is high time Theodore Russell's past caught up with him. Time for his Nemesis to step forward.' He added quietly: 'Indeed, I think she may already have presented herself.'

He smiled around the table, involving them all in his triumph and excitement. 'Miss Talbot? Mr Gunning? Will you meet me at the Villa Europa on Saturday morning? I need a few days to pursue my researches but I think by

Saturday all will be in place. And I shall need to call on the services of you, Aristidis, and several of your men.'

He added with evident satisfaction: 'I think it only appropriate, don't you, that a man who has lived by the spade should die by the spade?'

Chapter Thirty-Eight

Mariani had done his stage-managing discreetly and well. With efficient staff-work by his recruited lieutenants, Talbot and Gunning, everyone was in place. William had balked at the idea of deceiving his employer, and it was Letty who had welcomed the inspector and his officers to the Europa on Saturday morning. Theodore had come from the breakfast room into the hall to greet them, and he listened to Mariani's apologetic request that he accompany his men to the station, where a further statement and his signature on several more documents were required. '. . . A great nuisance, of course, but it would not take long . . .' Laetitia knew that orders had been issued to hold him until word was sent to release him. Mariani needed a clear field of operations. He also needed the time to make repairs in case his theories should prove embarrassingly wrong.

Theodore stood, eyeing the inspector in silence as he slid through his prepared speech. Finally, and still without comment, he turned to Letty. 'My hat and gloves,' he said. She fetched them for him. 'Pipe?' he asked. 'You wouldn't know the whereabouts of – No? I thought you might.' At the door he turned to her. 'Oh, tell William, would you, Laetitia . . . It's just come back to me . . . The lines we were searching for last night at dinner. They're from Tennyson, of course:

'Old age hath yet his honour and his toil;
Death closes all: but something ere the end,
Some work of noble note, may yet be done,
Not unbecoming men that strove with Gods.'*

'From *Ulysses*. Ulysses – splendid sailor, and a man who knew how to take his chances. *To strive, to seek, to find and not to yield*. You've got to admire that! I hope he made it to the Happy Isles.'

He nodded good-bye and left, walking ahead of the officers.

They assembled in the courtyard when invited by the inspector. To Letty's surprise, Dr Stoddart made an appearance, looking bemused and anxious. Mariani hurried to reassure him, 'Morning, Stoddart! Glad you could come. I've invited you here in your capacity of physician. Hope you don't mind? We may well need to seek a medical opinion. Here are Miss Talbot and Mr Gunning to witness events, you see . . . And now,' he said, looking about him, 'we just lack the presence of Aristidis and his men.'

'Oh, they're here,' said Stoddart. 'I saw them a moment ago – they were gathering outside in the square. A squad of four. Armed with spades,' he added, mystified. 'Now what trick are you pulling, Kosta? And I don't see Theo. Shouldn't he be here? What have you done with Theo?'

'Ah . . . Mr Russell has been detained in town. He will be joining us later,' said Mariani vaguely. 'If all goes well.'

The men emerged from the coach house, stubbing out their cigarettes, and presented themselves, quiet and watchful.

'Gentlemen!' said Mariani, gesturing them to come forward. 'Accompany me, will you, to the centre of the courtyard. There's someone I wish you to meet.'

They all trooped over and the inspector waved a hand at the statue of Dionysos, looking no less sinister in the light of day. 'Remove him, will you? Shouldn't present a difficulty – he is not, I'd say, planted on a very secure base. And, having set him carefully on one side, I want you to continue to dig down underneath. To a depth of . . . possibly . . . six feet.'

At the sinister measurement, the men looked at each

other lugubriously and made the sign of the cross on their chests. They looked to Aristidis before attempting to carry out the order. Silently, he nodded and himself made the first move to seize Dionysos by his thick neck to test his firmness. By waggling the stone and digging around at the base, they soon had the carving on its side and pulled to the edge of the parterre.

The earth underneath was removed a spadeful at a time and placed on a tarpaulin Mariani had spread out beside the hole. At a depth of five feet below the surface, one of the men called out. He had struck something soft. At once, experience took over. The gravediggers were, at a stroke, transformed into an archaeological team. Without a word spoken, the two senior men produced trowels from their belts, sank to their hands and knees and, with skilful flicks of the sides of their tools, began to expose the object that lay beneath. A pattern began to emerge. Inch by inch, the underside of a Persian rug was revealed. With a glance at all around, subdued now and almost fearful, Mariani dismissed the men and jumped into the pit. Taking up an edge, he began to tug at the carpet, peering underneath.

'I'd like you to lift this rug by the corners – careful now! – and lay it down on the grass,' he said when he had satisfied himself as to the contents. 'Doctor! If you would oblige?'

They peeled the faded fabric back and stood silently staring at the pathetic rotted remains it had covered and held together. No longer a corpse: a browned skeleton, an impersonal horror.

'Who is this? Was this?' Letty whispered.

Harry Stoddart was already on his knees, studying the body. 'Female. Dead some years . . . impossible to say how many on the spot but decay is complete, as you see. I think we can say,' he went on, 'looking at the improvised shroud, that this is no ancient burial. That's a jolly good Persian rug. She was youngish, judging by the good state of the teeth. A tall woman,' he said thoughtfully. He flashed a

353

glance upwards at Letty, 'and – dolichocephalic, I have to say. Not much else I can tell you from this regarding identification . . . but I think I can tell you right away how she died.'

They all unconsciously took a step towards the body, peering down. 'Here,' said Harry, magnifying glass in hand, 'just a first impression and I guarantee nothing until this has been confirmed in a postmortem, but d'you see this little U-shaped bone? The hyoid bone, and it's broken. She's been strangled. That much at least is certain. There may be other things, of course . . .'

Letty had a feeling that he knew the answer to his own question when he asked, 'Anyone have a theory as to who this might be?'

'My mother. It's my mother.'

The voice came from behind the huddled group. All whirled in shock to see George, propping himself on Eleni's shoulder, taking a hobbling step towards them.

Stoddart was on his feet at once, putting himself between his patient and the remains of the dead woman. 'Eleni! What are you thinking of? Take George back inside at once! His leg! You'll undo all my good work! To say nothing of upsetting his psychological equilibrium! He ought not to be here witnessing this! Off you go! At once!'

Eleni flinched, but she never had any doubt as to which man she must obey. She stood her ground. 'If anyone has a right to be here, it is surely George!' she said, bristling with defiance. 'You heard him! This is his mother, Ilse!'

'I feared as much,' said Stoddart. 'But – oh, as long as you're here, my boy – tell us, what makes you so certain?'

Pale but determined, George said, 'The rug. It's the one she had in her study. I remember it well. I used to sit and play on it when I was a child, while she wrote her letters at her desk. The border, you see? I used to race my toy cars around it. There may still be an ink stain on the lower left-hand corner. I spilled a bottle of ink over it and got my bottom smacked ... It disappeared when she left for Europe. It didn't occur to me to wonder why. Look – I've understood for years that my mother lay dead, drowned, somewhere at the bottom of the Rhine. Her body was one of the number never recovered. My father showed me the newspaper report. Is someone going to tell me why I'm to think I'm looking at her now, lying there in the soil with her neck broken?'

'Shall we go into the drawing room? Gunning? Letty? Doctor?' suggested Mariani.

'No,' insisted George. 'We'll all stay right here. All of us. Until we've heard a few answers. We all want to know. We all deserve to know. And I won't leave her by herself again until it's all settled.'

Eleni helped him to lower himself on to the statue and put a supporting arm around him.

'Blame me – or thank me – you will please yourself when you have heard all,' said Mariani. 'It occurred to me that your father had lost two wives in tragic circumstances. His first wife, your mother, George, we are told, met her death in a continent where war was raging and terrible things were happening. Millions died in those years ... what was one more death? Unfortunate but hardly surprising. Nothing to trigger an enquiry. But I have a suspicious and mischievous muse who leads me down corridors others would avoid. I made certain checks. I looked at everything I could lay my hands on published at the time of your mother's leaving for Europe. I found the shipping records for the day she sailed. There was a first-class cabin booked in her name, but it was a double cabin and there were two occupants listed. Would it surprise you, George, to hear that the second name was *yours*? Were you aware of her plans?'

George shook his head numbly, and looked again at the bones, his eyes filling with tears, his face suddenly that of a stricken child. 'Mamma didn't tell me that. Father would never have let me go. He'd have punished her if he'd known she was thinking of taking me away.'

'Punished?' Mariani asked gently.

George nodded. 'He was . . . unkind sometimes. Before she left . . . I can't remember how long . . . a week or two . . . they had a quarrel. Not for the first time. I remember when I was quite small . . . I'd forgotten all about it until the other day . . . I was playing behind the sofa in the drawing room. Pa came in and shouted at Mamma. Usually she didn't shout back but this time she did. He slapped her face. When I crawled out, crying, she was just standing there, silent, as though nothing had happened. But there was blood running down her face and on to the front of her white blouse. He used to wear a ring with a seal stone in those days. It must have cut her. He just stared at me and walked away without a word.'

George glanced at Letty.

'The wine Phoebe spilled?' she asked.

'Yes. The colours. Blood-red flowing on white linen, and Father's outburst. It all came back to me.'

'So. It would seem that for personal and domestic reasons, Mrs Russell was secretly intending to take her son home to Germany with her,' said Mariani, bringing them back into his framework. 'I had thought so. I asked myself why. I asked myself whether she had been planning to return. I asked myself why these two first-class places had subsequently not been taken up. The purser's log is still a matter of record.'

The young man was looking more sickened by the minute. It was Eleni who spoke for him. She chose to speak in Greek. 'Inspector, if you are willing to hear evidence reported by a servant from the mouth of her drunken employer, then listen,' she announced. 'In the early days, before he realized how close I was to George, he would often, when he had drunk too much, become maudlin, whining, and wearisome. And he would always harp on the same theme. His wife, Ilse, had deceived him. She had been betrothed to a compatriot before Theodore came on the scene, and somehow he had persuaded her to drop her young man and marry him instead. But the man remained

356

here on the island and when George was born, so fair, so grey-eyed, Theodore began to suspect that Ilse had failed to break off her association with her old lover, that she had regretted her choice. He thought George was not his son, though he never voiced these suspicions when he was sober. Indeed, I believe he loves George – as far as he is capable of loving. But he never had more children. And his second wife had no children. He thought he might be sterile. The thought was corrosive for such a man. He chose to blame the women in his world.

'This all happened before I came to work here and I've only heard his maundering, wine-fuelled version, but if I'm allowed my own theories, Inspector?' She paused and waited for the inspector's encouraging nod. 'The man has a suspicious mind and has his ways of gathering information. I'd say when Ilse told him she was returning home at a turbulent time, and he discovered she was taking her son with her, he became convinced that she was planning not to return to him. Perhaps if you were to study your lading lists even more closely, you might find a certain German name among the passengers? A lover who made an unexpectedly solitary journey home?'

'Indeed so, miss,' Mariani murmured his agreement. He sighed and glanced at the overturned Dionysos. 'I have also the name of the stonemason who was asked to produce this . . . um . . . marker. And the date of delivery. He is ready to stand witness.' Mariani turned to the doctor. 'Stoddart, will all this medical evidence stand up in a court of law, do you think?' he wanted to know.

The query, with its implications for his father, was greeted with a howl of despair from George and, at a sign from Eleni, the men came forward and carried him back inside the house. Letty reached out for Gunning.

'Nothing we can do, Letty,' he whispered. 'It's out of our hands. It's in the lap of the gods, you might say.'

'And I think I can hear bloody old Tisiphone swooping in for the third victim,' she said, softly.

* * *

357

They found the third victim an hour later dangling from the plane tree in the square by the cathedral. Gunning made a formal identification of the body.

Summoned by a distraught sergeant arriving hell-for-leather at the Europa, voluble in his account and excuses, Mariani had run off, calling Gunning and Aristidis to accompany him. They had come to the square, now cleared and surrounded by a police cordon. A crowd, gesticulating and horrified, bombarded the officers with their testimonies. Everyone's eyes were drawn to the body of Theodore Russell as it turned slowly and grotesquely over the café tables. One of the tables lay, overturned, beneath his feet.

'Not – I take it – an organized lynching?' Gunning thought it prudent to establish.

'Not at all. Police carelessness perhaps a factor,' admitted Mariani, 'but not malevolence. A clever man. And more than a match for my officers. He used his air of authority to get under their guard before ever they got to the station and made off into the avenue. Headed straight for the tree and hung himself with his belt. Waiter who tried to stop him got a kick in the teeth for his pains. Had Russell worked out that it was all over for him? A last flamboyant way of making amends? Will we ever know? I don't suppose he's left us the satisfaction of an explanatory note!'

'Hardly necessary,' said Aristidis, hypnotized by the sight. 'When we are granted the satisfaction of his death.'

'"Suicide while the balance of his mind was disturbed." I think this time the coroner may well feel justified in using the phrase,' said Gunning. He shouldered his way through the cordon to stand and murmur a prayer at Theodore's feet.

'No time for an explanation?' Unconsciously, Letty echoed Mariani's thoughts. She had fled after church on Sunday morning with Gunning to the anonymity of the harbour-front hotel, the familiar decadence of the potted palms, the tinkling piano, and the calming cup of Earl Grey. An essential touch of normality after the bleak drama of the previous day. And an opportunity to be alone together, to question, to regret and despair.

'Grossly unfair of the man, even in extremis. He had the audacity to tinker with his wife's suicide note but leaves not a clue as to his own dying thoughts.'

'Not sure I'd want to hear them,' said Gunning.

'Did Mariani ever find Phoebe's original letter? No, of course not,' she answered her own question. 'He would never have left it about the place. But I can guess, can't you? What Phoebe was saying to George at the last moment?'

'Oh, Good Lord!' breathed Gunning. 'Of course! When Theodore opened the envelope, whatever else she said by way of good-bye and ever so sorry and all that, she must have referred to the changes in the terms of her will. "It's all yours now, George, I know you'll make good use of it. My love to the boys." Do you think?'

'I'm afraid so. And Theodore, with his wife's death rattle still sounding in his ears, learns that he is not to get his hands on the fortune he might have expected – but his son is. At least, the man he acknowledges as his son. Except when he's drunk! I can't begin to imagine his disbelief and fury. Why should George be so favoured? His suspicions and his rage must have choked him. He stole Phoebe's letter and substituted the pages he tore from the play. He did know more Greek than he was letting on, you know! *"Hippolytus, what have you to say?"* He was prompting us, leading us on. And we couldn't see it. We were so blinded by the strength of a familiar myth, we never questioned it.'

'He was perfectly prepared for George to take the blame if the authorities judged that there was blame to be assigned,' said Gunning, his voice heavy with sadness.

'And, in any case, it gave him just the opportunity he'd been hankering after – to tear into George, with all the pent-up resentment of years. And with the added bonus of apparent justification for his bad behaviour. He could play

the part of wronged husband and wronged father. Everyone who knew would pity, not blame him. We did ourselves! He wouldn't have minded a bit if George had died
driving over the cliff, would he? He'd have got his hands,
legally, on the money, and I think Eleni and her boys would
have had a thin time of it.'

'It's all right, Letty,' Gunning said gently, anxious to
break through her bleak vision. 'George is still with us and
he's mending well. He's having the boys brought over
tomorrow and I must say that's a good idea. Just what
that old house needs – a couple of noisy lads tearing
about the place. I said we'd stay and help – thought you
wouldn't mind.'

'Well, that should complete its restoration to normality,'
said Letty. 'You were away giving statements for most of
the day and I don't suppose you've noticed, but George
gave orders for Dionysos to be buried. The ugly brute is to
be broken up and used as filling for the hole and the area
is to be turfed over. The goddesses were put on a cart, still
quarrelling, and I'm not going to ask where they've fetched
up. Though the Artemis was really rather special ...
museum, do you think? Anyway, I approve! The changes
will go a long way to banishing the shadows.'

'Of course I'd noticed. Like pulling out a bad tooth! The
swelling and the pain begin straight away to fade.'

'Sometimes, you know, I've heard my aunts say, it's hard
to pin down the pain to the right tooth,' Letty said slowly,
feeling her way. 'I thought I was being pushed by Phoebe
into avenging her death but I'm not so sure. I had uneasy
feelings about that house from the moment I stepped
through the door. Do you think, William, I was responding
to an earlier horror ... quivering like a violin string after
the bow has passed on?'

Gunning, the rationalist, was uncomfortable with the
thought. 'Ilse, you mean?'

'Yes. When I read that news cutting in his study, I had a
strong feeling of grief and anger. How could any man,
William, kill his wife and then lie to her son about her

death? He must have got hold of the paper from the embassy, days . . . weeks later and made use of it. A child is likely to believe a dramatic story like that, and the dates fitted. And no list of the deceased to spoil his story, I noticed. But Mariani managed to get his hands on the information from the German embassy. Theodore sat by and watched as his little boy wrote *I love you, Mamma*, on the bottom of a sheet of evil deception.'

'A deeply unhappy man,' said Gunning, his eyes lifting over the city walls, seeking the jutting outline of the sacred mountain.

'Who communicated unhappiness.' Letty remembered Aristidis's judgement. 'If ever a man had the ability to stir up thunderclouds, it was Theodore. I hope he's at rest.'

Chapter Thirty-Nine

'William! You haven't ever mentioned it, but it must surely have occurred to you to wonder why Andrew didn't raise any objection to my coming out to Crete? In fact, he encouraged me. Prepared my way. I've had an awful thought! Could the old bastard be trying to get rid of me, do you suppose? Perhaps Maud finally rumbled him! Went for his knick-knacks with a paper knife! William?'

Letty shot upright, suddenly alarmed to find she'd been talking to herself. The grass at her side still bore the imprint of his body. Oh well, she'd put the question to him the moment he got back from his ramble.

Ten minutes later, she was beginning to be concerned that he hadn't returned. She looked around her at the grove of oak trees where they'd chosen to have their lunch. Cheese and fruit packed up for them by Maria to take with them on one of their rare days off, away from the dig. An April sun scorched down, its heat filtered through the lush spring foliage, and she realized she had no idea where she was, but, whatever this place, it was a long way from home in Kastelli. The horses twitched their tails in the shade, content to be taking time off from the adventurous attempt to circumnavigate the massif of Juktas their riders had embarked on.

No one else had offered to accompany them, refusing with complicit smiles and covert glances. Aristidis was increasingly absorbed by his work on the promontory, grasping the reins of authority, which Letty was gladly passing to him. It was George who had made the suggestion: Why not hand the whole thing to Aristidis? George was prepared, with his newly acquired funds, to set him up in the enterprise. Letty had agreed to contribute half the expenses and eventually handle the publication of results from London.

Fifteen minutes.

'William! Where are you? If you've done a disappearing act again, this time I shan't forgive you!'

A shower of stones down the cliff face behind her announced the arrival of Gunning, red in the face and breathless, at her side. He pulled out of his shirt-front a bruised bunch of herbs and thrust it at her. Instantly she understood.

'This is dittany? *Erotas?* And you got it from up there?' She raked the face of the precipice in amazement, spotting an outcrop of the herb at the very top. 'Oh, my God! William, not even a mad mountain goat with a stick of ginger up its rear end would attempt that climb!'

He nodded, pleased with himself, still panting with the effort.

'Come and sit by me and get your breath back. I was really quite worried. Here, have a hug. And this is the proof of love George was telling us about?' She considered the sorry bundle for a moment, pressing her nose into it appreciatively.

'. . . *a sure relief,*
To draw the pointed steel and ease the grief,' he gasped.

'Whatever did I do with my life before you came into it, sketching and rhyming?' she asked. 'And climbing cliffs. Well, I have to tell you – it works. I'm impressed. Outraged at the risks you take but – impressed.'

'Jolly good,' he said. 'In that case perhaps the effort will have proved to be worth it.'

'*Will have* proved? Whatever do you mean? Is that the future perfect you're using?'

'Certainly is. In an hour, perhaps longer, I'll think again and substitute a past perfect. If the dittany does its stuff.'

'William! Am I to interpret that as a proposition?'

'Well, I'm not Zeus to just leap on a girl without a by-your-leave.'

'Very well, in that case . . .'

She bent and began to tug at his boots.

'I say, Letty. Um, I can't say I've had much experience of being undone by a Dryad in an oak grove, and I'm sure you woodland spirits have your ways, but I'd say you were starting at the wrong end, surely?'

She looked back at him with innocent eyes. 'Just doing what I was told,' she said. 'Checking for cloven hooves.'

We want to hear your thoughts on *The Tomb of Zeus*

Visit www.constablerobinson.com and send us your review.
We look forward to hearing from you!

Also, for exclusives, special offers and the latest news on
other crime titles, sign up for the newsletter at
www.constablerobinson.com